LOOK AT ME NOW

SIMONE GOODMAN

First published in Great Britain in 2019 by Boldwood Books Ltd.

Cover Design: www.judgebymycovers.com

Cover Photography: Shutterstock and iStock

A CIP catalogue record for this book is available from the British Library.

Paperback ISBN 978-1-83889-298-2

Ebook ISBN 978-1-83889-296-8

Kindle ISBN 978-1-83889-297-5

Audio CD ISBN 978-1-83889-299-9

MP3 CD ISBN 978-1-83889-414-6

Digital audio download ISBN 978-1-83889-295-1

Boldwood Books Ltd
23 Bowerdean Street
London SW6 3TN
www.boldwoodbooks.com

Surround yourself with people who believe in you – beginning with yourself

For Cat Hedge Farm

1

'Oops!' Rushing into the television station where I work, escaping the demonic gale that's sweeping across London this morning, I slide delicately across the wet tiles inside the entrance.

I say delicately. But it's more hope that I look like an accomplished ice skater as I clumsily regain my balance. Being a healthy size 14 – I don't consider myself fat, I'm just not reed thin – there's a risk I've come off more like a comedian on a banana skin. Thankfully, no one other than Mitzi, our receptionist, is here to hold me accountable.

'Golly, Gracie, are you okay?' Mitzi calls from across the foyer, where she's sitting behind the front desk, most likely reading a script.

'I'm okay, Mitzi.' By all accounts, my near miss looked distinctly less than elegant. Laughing, I steady myself on the death-tiles. It could have been worse. I could have toppled right over my own feet.

It's only a short few hundred metres dash from Oxford Circus Tube station to my workplace, our studios located in a narrow but deceptively cavernous Georgian building on Soho Square. My umbrella blowing inside-out against the pelting rain and wind this morning, I covered the distance as quickly as possible. My dash best described as a nippy jog, it's the most exercise I've done in months. It's early January, the time for New Year resolutions. Possibly, it wouldn't be the worst idea for me to consider joining a gym?

'I've been warning someone will break their bones on those tiles,' Mitzi says.

'We could do with a non-slip mat here,' I agree.

'We could do with a lot of things around here,' Mitzi sighs.

She reminds me of Daisy Lowe, the model. Dark hair. Doe eyes. Cherry-red lips. Though her role is to welcome visitors, Mitzi looks the part for television. Like many people who work here, she yearns to be in front of the camera.

I have my own show. But it troubles me, more and more lately, that I don't look like I belong. This isn't to say I don't have my finer points. Pragmatically speaking, we all do. What can I tell you? My eyes are sometimes so blue as to appear violet. Almond-shaped, they're generously framed with oodles of long, thick lashes. My dark locks cascade to below my shoulders and, at thirty-three years of age, I've not got a single grey hair on my head. My complexion is creamy, free of lines and, generally, spots. But before you picture me as some uber-glamourous cross between a young Elizabeth Taylor and a brunette Katy Perry, bear in mind I'm the more robustly packaged (sometimes size 14 plus) version. Some days, I fear I'm veering more into the territory of a Dawn French and Melissa McCarthy lovechild – without their comedy vehicles for kicks. But surely no one likes a thin chef?

I host my own daily cookery show, *Gracie Porter's Gourmet Get-Together*.

The title is a bit of a misnomer. It's impossible to prepare gourmet meals, haute cuisine of several aesthetically balanced and rich courses of food, within a short thirty minutes allotment of air time. Notwithstanding that with preparation of the set, the ingredients and me, it takes almost a full day to pre-record every show that then airs across the whole of England, Scotland and Wales at 10.30 a.m. the following week. Also, there isn't much 'getting together' with my format. I like to think I'm always engaging with my audience as they tune in to connect with me from the comforts of their own homes, but the original concept had me hosting the occasional special guest: other chefs, celebrities and perhaps the more interesting politician. With none of us, including my producer, Robin, moving in celebrity circles, with Westminster MPs otherwise occupied with their scandals, solicitations and squabbling and me reasoning that any chef who wants to be on television would surely want their own show, we failed to deliver. When no one pushed us, we let it slide. We don't even have a live audience. It's pretty much me and the crew who chow down after a recording finishes. On this basis, my cookery show has aired daily for almost a year and a half.

Previously, I worked as a normal chef. I prepared mouth-watering meals in lovely places where people came to eat. When it comes to food, I'm a consummate professional. As far as television goes, I'm still cutting my teeth.

From the beginning, both investment and expectation of our little cookery show has been low. Being at the bottom end of a long list of hot shows and hotter stars left me below the radar – and this has suited me fine. Things changed late last year after Titan Media, the US entertainment giant, acquired a large chunk of our relatively tiny UK operations. This afternoon, at 3 p.m., I have a meeting with the American executives who now run things to discuss my 'future services to the company'. It hasn't escaped me that not everyone summoned to such meetings returned from their New Year breaks. People have been literally disappearing from the studios in droves. And I know my ratings aren't the best.

I don't disagree with Mitzi that things around here could be better. However, today is a day for putting the best, most confident and upbeat version of me forward.

'I'm sure things will settle down and everything will be fine again soon,' I assure her. I put my wet umbrella inside a cotton shopping bag.

Behind me, the front doors burst open. I turn to look. Shadowing the doorway, wearing her long, spectral black-hooded cape, stands Zelda the Magnificent, our resident daytime television psychic.

'Gracie,' Zelda declares on seeing me. 'Dahling.' Her voice is deep and melodic. Her accent is old Budapest enchantment. She's like a darker, earthier Zsa Zsa Gabor. 'Please, stop for Zelda,' she implores in her dulcet tones. 'I have, for you, a vision.'

Pushing the hood from her head, Zelda releases a mass of black curls to topple down and over her shoulders. The curls are part of a voluminous wig. Rumours abound that, underneath, Zelda is completely bald. Rumours also abound that Zelda isn't merely old but ancient, a hundred years and counting. Because these conjectures add to her mysticism, Zelda does little to quash such blather. Having once shared a dressing room, I know from my own eyes that her scalp is in fact covered with a short mop of white-grey ringlets and, by the birthday card she received last summer, that she isn't more than eighty years young.

Closing the few steps between us, Zelda clasps my frigidly cold hands within her un-seasonally hot fingers. She smells of sage, vanilla and cloves. I breathe in her aroma. My mind drifts to thoughts of crispy sage in a burnt butter sauce, drizzled through ribbons of pasta. Of vanilla pods in pots of clotted custard. Of melt-in-your-mouth hot salt beef, boiled with cloves and juniper berries and served thickly cut with mustard on rye. Shutting her eyes, Zelda's face wrinkles with whatever wizardry she's conjuring.

'Um, Zelda, I'd rather—' I begin to protest.

'My child, I see a gathering of dark clouds.' Ignoring my attempt to dissuade her, Zelda begins her psychic vision. 'I see a storm is brewing...'

I don't need divine intervention to inform me of this. There are the pressures at work. At home, things aren't much better. This morning, I endured another cold flannel wash at the bathroom basin after my boyfriend, Jordan, again used all of the hot water in our flat. During, I should add, another of his suspiciously long showers – by his indifference towards me lately, Jordan could better be described as my supposed boyfriend. To fill you in a little bit, we met the same night I won the contract for the show. After a whirlwind courtship of the best sex I'd ever had, eighteen months on, our physical connection has fallen by the wayside. All less of him no longer being my hunk-a-hunk-of-burning-love and more Jordan no longer seeing me as his mi amore. On top of which, although we live together, we barely talk. Whatever friendship we shared has flatlined alongside my boyfriend's libido. There's the excuse that Jordan works ridiculous hours as an advertising executive. But things are so distant between us, we haven't properly discussed what is – or, more to the point, isn't – going on in our relationship. Let alone my professional challenges.

'Ach... so much rain,' Zelda clucks her tongue and shakes her head sadly. Over her closed eyelids is a poorly applied, pale purple eyeshadow. I don't believe in clairvoyants, but I love a character – I adore Zelda. Whenever I cook anything like a Hungarian goulash or a sweet baklava pastry, Eastern European dishes that I know she'll enjoy, I set aside a plate for Zelda.

Outside, lightning flashes, followed by a thunderous crack. A gust of wind slams the front doors shut. Zelda's emerald eyes pop open.

I sigh my relief that we appear done. Holding up a bejewelled finger, Zelda begs of me a moment more.

She fumbles amongst the pockets of her cape and then inside her patchwork bag, her charm bracelets tinkling. Eventually, she withdraws her hands and slips a small, pink crystal into my open palm.

'To help you little bit,' she says. With a warm expression, Zelda shrugs.

I clasp the stone, smooth and surprisingly warm, inside my hand.

'Quieten the storm.' Zelda gently taps my chest with her bony finger. 'Quieten the storm inside,' she murmurs. 'Then, all will be well.'

And with that, Zelda the Magnificent, resplendent in her sweeping satin cape and semi-precious trinkets, sweeps across the reception and disappears into the labyrinth of recording studios and meeting rooms beyond.

'Can I see?' Mitzi begs, intrigued.

I walk over and show her the small, smooth crystal. Pale pink, with ribbons of milky-white.

'Gracie, this is a rose quartz,' Mitzi exclaims, seemingly knowledgeable about such things. 'It's to attract romance and unconditional love.'

'That wasn't quite how Zelda put it,' I admit.

A deluge of rain lashes the floor-to-ceiling windows. Aside from my scepticism, I don't wish to believe there's a karmic storm brewing over my personal fate. As far as I'm concerned, I've got enough challenges in the here and now.

Mitzi returns the stone to me. I drop it inside the pocket of my coat.

'Did you hear about Howard?' she whispers, changing the topic.

According to the station grapevine, Howard is the latest person to be axed on Titan's chopping block. A cantankerous, borderline alcoholic whose show, *Nature's Best*, had, admittedly, seen better days, Howard is nonetheless something of an industry legend, having once jived around a live-to-air set as a – thankfully – tamed carpet snake chased a lively white mouse up and down inside his corduroy trousers. All of it was filmed in front of an audience of delightedly squealing schoolchildren, and no less a VIP than the highly amused HRH Prince Philip, consort to our lovely Queen. Legend has it Howard overdid his habitual morning vodka before taking to his small stage filled with animals. The mouse escaped the cage, the snake escaped Howard's clutches, the ensuing chase became TV gold at the time. Today, Howard Gladstone is something of a YouTube sensation for generations too young to have seen it first pass. When I first got the job at SC6, he was the only person Jordan asked about me meeting.

'He's gone,' Mitzi confirms. 'Howard. Who'd been here for, like, ever.'

I glance around the foyer where, under fluorescent accent lighting, posters of our most popular stars jockey for position. In pride of place, on the magenta wall opposite the entrance, hangs a full-body shot of Sonya Sokolov, a Russian bombshell in silver spandex who hosts, of all things, our children's cartoon programme. There are multiple pictures of the pale-faced and bushy-eyebrowed youths who present our various music video shows. I'm grateful the promo for my show is positioned down in the basement, outside the studio where we film. One bonus of working at the less illustrious end of this business is that I don't have to see my face, ten times enlarged and beaming over a bowl of whipped cream, up here on display. In the picture, I'm sporting a stupendously high-peaked white chef's hat I've never once been forced to wear on camera. Not one to play the shrinking violet, here in reception, on the back wall in an ornately gilded frame, hangs a life-sized oil painting of Zelda. Painted as nude as the day she was born, she's wearing only her gold hoop earrings and a strategically draped plum-coloured silk sheet. In the far corner are black and white photographs of the news crew and of Suzi Sunshine, the latest in a long line of attractive weathergirls – I'm not making up the name, though Suzi might be. Beside Suzi is a patch of canary yellow paint that's conspicuously brighter than the rest of the wall: the place where Howard's promo hung for a great many years, until today.

'Howard may have been a crotchety old goat, but isn't that what television is all about – personalities?' Mitzi proposes.

It seems to me profound wisdom for someone reluctantly stuck sitting behind a front desk. 'I'll miss the old goat nicking my cooking sherry,' I say, pricked by an unexpected pang of nostalgia. I will miss chasing Howard out of my studio, him plonking the bottle of fortified wine wherever it lands and cursing me for denying him a drop as I mock-threaten him with my rolling-pin. I will miss it all.

Not to mention that the forced exit of an industry legend doesn't bode well for my inexperience on a flagging cookery show. A storm is brewing indeed.

'Drinks are from six tonight at The White Horse,' Mitzi says.

'I'll pop by,' I say.

'One last tipple for Howie.'

'Old trouser snake!' shouts a baby-faced production assistant, as he crosses the room.

2

From reception, I head directly to the first-floor dressing room. Here, Brendan and Brenda, who ordinarily work for the newsroom, also attend to my hair and make-up each morning – the end result being that I arrive on my cookery set looking like I too should be shoved into a suit, shunted behind a desk and forced to read autocues about breaking headlines.

As usual, Brendan begins with my tresses. Forgoing a dampening spritz of water – the rain took care of that this morning – he blow-dries my locks with an assortment of brushes. Flicking my long hair up and out, he sets it all with an abomination of holding spray, bouffant style. Meanwhile, I'm browsing recent reports from marketing, hoping to discover something that may cement my success in today's big meeting. So far, there's no silver bullet.

Next up is Brenda, who layers on primer, concealer and foundation to my face until I'm slightly tangerine in colour ('Bronzed, Gracie,' Brenda insists) and then more 'high-lighter' on my cheekbones, nose and forehead. Brenda is also favouring a pale-coral lipstick that blends in so well with my newly applied skin tone that my respectably plump lips are barely visible (I've been sneakily replacing it with a generous smear of my French Kiss pink lip stain before filming commences). On my mobile, I google what the proper celebrity chefs are up to lately. There's not much help to be gleaned from out there either. It's all restaurant chains and marriages going bust. Not for the first time, I wonder if being a commercially successful television chef isn't more about being in some sort of personal spotlight, the worse the better, and less about food than it ought to be.

After about an hour of such pampering, preparing me for the bright lights, I'm sent on my way to my studio in the basement.

Unlike the explosion of colour on me personally, the room where we record *Gracie Porter's Gourmet Get-Together* is painted dull grey and holds only the necessary equipment. There are two cameras and a boom microphone, a laptop and monitor on a table, some other equipment I'm still unfamiliar with, plus a few foldaway chairs. The floor is littered with lengths of looped-up wiring and cables and spotlights are anchored on the floor and dangle from the ceiling above. The kitchen set itself is dated cream laminate with pine panelling – resurrected after a long hiatus in cookery programmes when I joined. I inherited the electric oven, gas hob and a refrigerator prone to hissy-fitting. Only the microwave was purchased new for me. Here in the basement, there are no windows and, save for a ducted fan above the stove, precious little ventilation. The air becomes stifling once the big lights come on for filming.

Working in television is not as glamorous as I once envisioned. But our set is friendly. I very much want to keep my job.

I cross the floor towards my assistant, Poppy. Nobody else is here yet.

There are two things to notice immediately about Poppy. The first is that she looks like a fairy. Small, delicate frame. Disarmingly large hazel eyes. Wispy bleach-blonde locks – the only aberration being Poppy's naturally dark roots. (Poppy's mother is Thai, her father unknown but allegedly Korean; though Poppy insists her only parent is her mother's second husband, Darcy, an Englishman of independent means, who kindly extended parental care after her mother upped and left them both when Poppy was a tender fourteen years old.) Anyway, Poppy, sweetly dispositioned, and seemingly unscarred by such events, also has a penchant for dressing in frilly layers of clothing – and her love of glitter would shame a toddler. The second thing to notice about my assistant is that her vernacular has a tendency towards the same, shall we say, 'exuberance'.

'Morning, Miss Gracie,' Poppy chirrups, looking up from where she's wiping the bench clean, preparing for the shoot. 'Ooh. I see Brenda's using the coral on your lips again. Like you're a mermaid? I could call you Ariel!'

'Morning, Poppy. Please, don't call me Ariel.' I wipe my lips on the back of my hand.

Poppy's eyes twinkle mischievously.

I also inherited Poppy. She was working an internship when I joined. One hundred per cent reliable and thoroughly committed, fresh out of college, my assistant has a fine diploma in home economics to accompany her sparkly personality. That her stepfather would happily provide so that she'd never have to work at all makes her dedication all the more admirable. If ever Poppy's childish vigour annoys me – her silly garble and excess enthusiasm can wear thin some days – I remind myself I'm lucky to have her.

I dump my coat and bags onto a chair.

To protect my clothes before filming begins – a personal uniform of black trousers and white shirt – I don my white chef's apron. My outfit isn't flashy, but given no one at SC6 has ever offered to provide my clothes or advise me on what to wear otherwise, it removes the stress of me having to think about what I ought to be wearing for the camera on a daily basis.

I wash my hands thoroughly. Before I forget, I retrieve and apply the pink stain to my lips and that's when I remember – my new shoes.

From the bottom of my tote, I pull out a felt bag containing a brand-new pair of Jimmy Choo designer heels. Removing layers of tissue paper, I place the shoes lovingly on the floor in front of me. They are, without doubt, the finest things I've ever owned. Silver metallic nappa leather, one hundred millimetres high at the heel, closed back with elegant straps of silver-inlaid crystals that crisscross over the foot and across the toes: these shoes were a rare splurge of luxury, purchased by me at the end-of-year sale at Selfridges last weekend. I have them with me today because my plan is to have them gently worn in, stumble-free and blister-proof, before the big reveal on Valentine's Day. I'm hoping to lose a Christmas pound or two before I shop for a dress.

Removing my winter boots and black woolly socks, I slip my bare feet into ultimate designer luxury.

'Va-va-voom,' Poppy croons at my first, tentative steps.

'Why, thank you, Poppy,' I reply, practising my walk over

the concrete floor. The heels are thinner and higher than I've ever worn. 'That is the plan. A bit of va-va-voom.'

'For the show today?' Poppy appears confused, as well she might be.

'No, for Valentine's Day, for a do at Jordan's work,' I say. 'I thought it best to wear them in first.' My left ankle takes a small dive, but I recover neatly. 'It seems only sensible...'

On February 14, the advertising agency where Jordan works is hosting a Sweetheart's Valentine's Day Ball, sponsored by clients in the businesses of selling jewellery, chocolates, perfumes and the like: gifts that lovers like to exchange on the day. Although Jordan hasn't mentioned it – it is absurd how little we communicate these days – an invitation appeared on our kitchen table last Friday, prompting my shopping spree while he was working at his office on some big commercial shoot. I have exactly five weeks to perfect my shimmy in these heels. Presently, I'm walking like a drunk on stilts.

If Poppy finds it unromantic that I'll be spending Valentine's Day with my boyfriend's colleagues, she doesn't say.

'I need to tell you something that happened on set last night,' she says instead. 'Something bad...' Smiling awkwardly, Poppy reveals a diamanté stuck to her front tooth.

Today, she's wearing black overalls cut off into short shorts over white woollen tights, with a white top, a pink bolero jacket and Doc Marten boots imprinted with panda bear motifs. Her make-up is a hybrid of Dita von Teese and Tinker Bell: heavy eyeliner, rosy cheeks and sparkles galore. Her lips are cherubic with nothing but Vaseline smear.

There is a funny odour on set. I smelled it the moment I entered.

We begin filming in roughly an hour. The crew will arrive at any moment.

The stench is dank and salty, with a hint of bleach.

Poppy is still pulling her funny face.

'Poppy, has something happened to the seafood?'

For today's show, I'd sourced a special order of scallops and monkfish from the same supplier to legendary seafood restaurant J Sheekey. As we were wrapping up yesterday, Poppy and I resolved that the ice-packed delivery box ought to make better overnight storage than our clunky old refrigerator. The label guaranteed 'Ocean Fresh for 24 hours from Delivery'. Now that we're discussing it, I don't see the box.

'The ice melted,' Poppy informs me. 'Apparently, the cleaners did some sort of steam-cleaning last night. I don't really know what happened. But when I got in this morning, there was stinky, rotten fishy water everywhere.'

'Oh heck.'

'I've bleached the entire room.'

'Poppy, thank you.'

'I had to throw it all into the big bin out the back.'

'Right.' It's too late to order more seafood, and I'd rather not have to nip out to the Tesco on Dean Street in this weather. 'Time for Plan B.'

'What's plan B?' Poppy asks, with more excitement than it deserves.

'We cobble together whatever ingredients we have to hand, whatever that might be, and then we wing it.'

The challenge – and by the look on Poppy's face, she sees it too – is that our on-premise supplies are perilously low. We only came back to work from the holiday break last week. And recent cost-cutting has started to bite. Our purchase orders aren't always approved. I don't mind buying the odd bits here and there. But whoever heard of a cookery show without any ingredients?

That's how it's been since Titan landed on us late last year, with their no expense spent policy. On top of which, our diary has been cleared of all off-site filming commitments. Last year, we grilled sole with lemon and capers down in Hastings, cooked a lamb roast on a big spit in the Welsh countryside, trekked all the way to Scotland and made properly done haggis, mixed entrails and all. We barbequed organic free-range pork sausages and quinoa vegan burgers across London, everywhere from the Leyton Mills B&Q car park to Richmond Park. None of it was haute cuisine. But it was lovely to connect with people who were right there in front of me as I cooked, rather than having to picture them following me in a future time and a different space via whatever device they happen to be watching on. More often than not, our ratings improved slightly in the weeks we ventured out of our studio. When we returned on set last week, the first instruction we received was that all future out-of-house activities were suspended until further notice. Our marketing cupboard, once filled with nifty kitchen gadgets to give away, is empty and my inaugural recipe book is on hold.

However, when it comes to kitchen emergencies, I consider myself a pro. Catering a wedding banquet in Norfolk, I once stretched half of the smoked chicken appetisers into a main meal of poultry with julienne vegetables, after the rib of beef was snatched by the groom's ridiculously short-legged dachshund. In a food crisis, I can excel.

'What have we got to hand, Poppy?'

Poppy opens the freezer. 'We have frozen prawns.'

I peek into the brown paper bag that the boys from *Science Lab* judiciously left for us yesterday. Inside are genetically modified chillies that will no doubt blow our heads off if we dare to eat them. 'We have chillies.'

'They'll be far too hot to eat!' Poppy objects.

I remind her that we cook for TV. Nobody has to eat them. 'Poppy, tell me we have rice?'

Poppy ducks her head into the food cupboard.

'We have rice. And tomato sauce. Tapioca flour. A can of butter beans. Some crushed garlic, rice flour, preserved lemons, coconut milk.' I hear Poppy scraping tins and jars around.

I open the fridge. We still have the spinach, cream and sweet potatoes I had planned to serve with the medley of glazed scallops with chilli jam for starters and oven-baked monkfish for the main.

'Pass me the rice, the butter beans and the garlic, please, Poppy. And the tomato sauce.' That's what I've been left to work with: staples.

With my hand, I guide Poppy to get out of the cupboard without banging her head

I do another memory check of dishes I've tried, tested and mastered over the years.

'Okay. How about we form some vegan-scallopy-things out of these butter beans, and for the main, we'll coat the prawns in these chillies, tomato sauce and garlic for a dish I call Cheating Hot Sticky Prawns?'

Poppy looks aghast. 'Cheating, Miss Gracie?'

'Because it's easy, Poppy. Only we'll be wiser.'

'Well then, it sounds perfect.'

It's hardly perfect. The frozen prawns are i) frozen and ii) not of the size or plumpness I'd prefer. The dishes are especially not what I'd have chosen for what may yet be my swan-song on the small screen, depending how the day pans out.

But it will pass as a seafood-ish extravaganza, as I'd promised viewers on the closing of our last recorded episode – and anything vegan is more popular by the day. Given the time we have, it will do.

From down the corridor, I hear the crew making their way towards our studio.

'Let's go for it, Poppy.'

'The show must go on!'

Poppy flashes her diamanté smile.

I beam my pearly whites.

'Fake it 'til you make it,' I concede, I hope charmingly.

3

The moment we wrap the shoot, I throw up in front of everyone and over poor Poppy's feet. I blame the stress of the last-minute change in menu and the big meeting looming. In about an hour's time, there's every chance I could lose my job. The crew blame the lingering smell of rancid seafood. I've never seen the set clear so fast. Only Poppy, her panda-festooned boots splattered with my sick, stays put to help.

'Miss Gracie, you go on to the bathroom and sort yourself out,' she insists. Usually, we clear up together and spend the afternoon ordering ingredients, sketching out future shows or completing paperwork with Robin. Today there's nothing to prepare for. If I don't survive the meeting, our show is toast. I insist I really must clean up my own vomit.

'Go on, you need to sort yourself out before you meet with those execs,' Poppy counters, escorting me out of the studio door. 'You'd do it for me.' I would do the same for Poppy – even if I'd perhaps start retching myself. 'I'll come find you when I'm done.'

I make my way to the Ladies'.

In front of the mirror, I see why my assistant was so keen to send me on: I look like death warmed up. My skin is sickly green. My lips, the pink stain wiped off with some kitchen towel, are not far off the same shade. My mascara is so smudged, around my eyes looks like hollow pits of black – I'd wiped my brow after chopping up the mega hot chillies and barely held back burning tears during the recording. Inspecting my reflection closely, I discover my very first grey hair. Oh, when it rains, it pours! I pull it out sharply.

No one is in here to see me in such a decrepit state. But this could change at any moment. The door to the cleaner's cupboard ajar, it seems a better place for me to recover in private.

I poke my head through the opening. Inside, the shelves are lined with cleaning products. A broom and a mop inside a steel bucket are propped against one wall, a small stepladder in the centre. On every surface, the paint is peeling. I tug a cord and the light overhead flickers on. I do a quick check for spiders. All clear. Stepping in, I sit gingerly on the top rung of the little ladder. I pull the heavy fire-proof door shut.

It's very cramped in here.

The smell of disinfectant is overwhelming.

What on earth am I doing hiding inside a cupboard?

Taking my mobile from my handbag, I call Jordan.

His mobile rings out, unanswered.

'Jordan Piper,' he answers, after the first ring to his work line.

'Jordan, hi, it's me. Can you talk?'

I wait for my boyfriend to make the usual excuse of running late for a meeting or being just in the middle of something. Instead, I'm greeted with a cheery, 'Grace, hey, I'm here.'

Jordan calls me Grace, as do my parents. I find it endearing that he calls me by my proper name. To everyone else, I'm Gracie.

It's a welcome surprise that he seems happy to hear from me.

'Jordan, thank heavens,' I say, relieved.

It's all Jordan needs to take me completely the wrong way.

'What's up now?' Jordan's swift impatience is palpable, as if I only ever call him with problems, which isn't true. These days, I hardly dare call my boyfriend at all.

'Nothing's up, Jordan,' I reply, just as curt. Hurt, to be precise. 'But since you ask, my shoot today was a disaster. The seafood was off. I got chilli in my eyes, which stung like hell. Then, to top things off, I vomited all over Poppy, right in front of everyone, the moment we finished the recording.'

I don't know why I'm fine telling Jordan I vomited over someone, but I do not, under any circumstance, desire him to know my hair is turning grey.

'You mean, you ate off seafood?' Jordan says.

'No, Jordan, I did not,' I swipe back at him, swallowing an acrid taste of sickness in my mouth.

In the background, at his office, I hear banter. Our conversations are never helped by Jordan's office being rife with mostly young, attractive females, all of them partial to eavesdropping. Many of who – as bulimics – also often happen to smell like spew.

'Jordan, I have the meeting at work today with the new owners,' I remind him. 'I'm so nervous, I think I've made myself ill.'

For some time, there's no response.

Then laughing heartily, Jordan screams into my ear, 'BOOM!'

'Jordan?'

Jordan isn't listening to me. The background noise fades. The phone is covered over his end of the line.

I sit alone, on the little ladder inside the cupboard in the toilets at work. In the flickering light, the crystals on my new designer heels sparkle prettily. This Valentine's Day, I'd hoped a perfect outfit might make all the difference. In my heart, I'd imagined we might put the sparkle back into our relationship. Now, I'm less sure. Even when things were good between us, socialising with Jordan's colleagues was a challenge for me. I get on famously with his creative partner, Robert (a good thing, given the amount of time Robert spends in my basement at home, messing about with Jordan – and no, absolutely not in that way). And the other girlfriends who sometimes join the Baker & Staines gatherings are friendly enough. But the girls who work in Jordan's office – they're quite another experience. No matter how hard I've tried to fit in, they've made no effort to include me. Jordan insists he doesn't know what I mean by this, to which I'm unable to state exactly what I'd like them to do. Ask for my number and invite me to dinner? Of course not. But it's tricky, sometimes, with girls who spend more time with my boyfriend than I do. What I'd like is for them to make me feel welcome, rather than as if I'm stomping uninvited onto their territory.

At the last event, a cocktail evening in Shoreditch two months ago, I gave up trying. While Jordan was busy networking with people he sees every day at his office, I propped up the bar with Robert. I sipped deliciously minty mojitos; Robert drained a good too many dirty martinis. (It probably bears mentioning that Robert looks a lot like the boyishly handsome comedian Jack Whitehall, with all of the charisma. Also, that Robert is impeccably attentive – in a purely gentlemanly way – to me at such events. We get on fabulously.) Together, we got rollicking drunk. I maintained some level of decorum; Robert got so sloshed, he toppled right off the back of his stool, causing quite the commotion. As a swarm of scantily dressed media assistants swooned to his aid, he slurred in my ear he doesn't think much of the emaciated little twits himself. Stung by their rejection, I laughed too heartily. Under other circumstances, I would have loved to be whooping it up with the girls.

'Jordan, can you hear me?'

No reply.

When Jordan and I first got together, we were always talking. And when we weren't talking, things were even sweeter, if you know what I mean. Now, apart from us not getting on well, the spontaneous can't-get-enough-of-each-other shagging that defined the beginning of our relationship has disintegrated into carnal abstinence. My boyfriend and I no longer have sex.

We've been this way for months.

Jordan blew out the flame. He just... stopped making the moves on me.

Afraid of rejection, I followed his lead.

Neither of us has mentioned a word about it.

Which is why I'm really rather miffed that, last night, Jordan went to the trouble of wearing his underpants to bed, where usually he sleeps butt naked. Things are so uncomfortable between us, I had to sneak a surreptitious glance to check, but they were ugly green underpants at that – the tacky five-pairs-to-a-packet, elasticised style of *undies* I wasn't aware my boyfriend even owned. I was mortified to think Jordan might have worn them as a defensive shroud for his privates. As if by depriving me of sex and sleeping next to me without them, I might otherwise jump on top of his flaccid penis without a moment's notice. Last night, I lay next to him feeling insecure and, though I'd done nothing other than hope that he might desire me once more, foolish. Now, more than worrying why my boyfriend no longer fancies the pants off me, Jordan is starting to make me perpetually cross.

'Jordan, I'm in a cupboard,' I say. Against my ear, my mobile is getting hot.

'What?'

'I'm in a cupboard, Jordan, so we can talk.'

I raise my feet to the bottom rung of the ladder, suddenly fearful of what six- or eight-legged creatures might be lurking in the corners on the floor.

Right now, I need my boyfriend to assure me that no matter what happens with the future of my show today, he'll be there for me.

'Grace, I'm at work, I can't *talk*. I'm sorry you were sick. Are you feeling better?' Jordan is intent on wrapping things up.

'I'm worried sick about this meeting.'

'I'm sure you'll be fine.' The line is temporarily muffled before Jordan screams into my ear, 'SEX SELLS!' Presumably, not at me. Nonetheless...

'Jordan, I host a cookery show, I hardly think that adage applies.' And he can talk!

Jordan calls to someone in his office, 'Of course the hot one!'

'Jordan!'

In the background, a giggling female also calls out to my boyfriend.

I hang up.

* * *

Jordan and I met the same day I landed the job with SC6. For years, I'd been working long hours, in hot kitchens, for pitiful pay. My best friend, Faith, spotted the advertisement: 'Chef Wanted for Daily Television Cookery Programme. Media Skills Preferred.' I protested I'd not so much as stepped foot in front of a television camera. Faith reminded me I'd been 'The Face' of the British Good Food and Wine Festival a decade previously. She went on about me being a natural-born entertainer. I reminded her that during such entertainment, the consumption of alcohol often plays a pivotal role. Faith encouraged me to go for it anyway. So I did. I almost couldn't believe I landed the job – I'm sure it helped that the only qualified competition was a lard-obsessed LBC food critic and a Marco Pierre White apprentice with oily dreadlocks. Apparently, all other applicants that wanted to be on television had no culinary experience whatsoever. When the station signed me up, I was elated.

Faith and I celebrated madly. She arrived from her city job to the Notting Hill bistro where I worked around 9 p.m. We were closing last orders. Effortlessly glamorous – tall, thin, blonde and very pretty, with an electric personality – Faith whooshed in wearing a typically expensively tailored black trouser suit, her décolletage highlighted by the plunging neckline of her jacket. Greeting my colleagues with hugs and kisses, she insisted we celebrate my new success together with champagne, I'd only just handed in my notice. Such was Faith's energy that everyone, including my boss, downed tools for a short toast to my future success on television before she and I continued on into town.

By the time we hit the West End clubs, I was sufficiently inebriated to hit the dance floor like I was Kylie Minogue in those signature gold hot pants – wearing, I must point out, my dark denim jeans. Grinding myself against the delightfully toned and debaucherously topless hunks in the club on Old Compton street, it mattered not that my gorgeous fans were all fabulously not-my-way-inclined. To my booty-swinging Shakira moves, they were my Ricky Martin partners in crime. From the side, where she was watching our drinks and resting her feet, Faith laughed and cheered.

I first met Jordan during a small break from such frivolities. Spotting a surly – but incredibly sexy-looking – lad by the exit, I boorishly asked if he was too straight to move his booty. I was pleasantly taken aback when he answered most tersely, 'Actually, yes.'

Over several gin and tonics, Jordan told me he was in the advertising game, and in the club to entertain the editors of a men's fashion magazine, all of them out and proud homosexuals. I found it endearing when he waved awkwardly at his bare-chested clients as they gave it their all under the whirling glitter balls – if only I'd known Jordan's work obsession would become the bane of our future relationship. Wearing black jeans and a blue Paul Smith shirt, in the dim of the club especially, he was the epitome of tall, dark and handsome – and my, oh my, was he brooding.

Full of alcohol and bravado about my new career in television, I did the unthinkable. I made the first move.

I asked Jordan if he'd like to come and dance with me.

Throwing me his sexy scowl, Jordan declined. 'Not here.' I boldly suggested, 'Perhaps at my place?'

Jordan smiled. It was that easy.

Our sex that night was a solid 10. The best I'd ever had. Jordan may not have wanted to dance, but between the sheets, the man had moves. For what felt like hours, he directed all of his passion onto me. Then, confidently, he guided me as to exactly what he wanted for himself. I saw fireworks.

It had been so long since I'd been with anyone. I rarely fancied anyone; I almost never took the risk of checking if they fancied me back. Not once had I picked up someone I'd just met in a club and taken them home with me.

Afterwards, Jordan held me in his arms. I rested my head onto his chest. Conversation flowed. Our passion came in waves.

I was instantly smitten. If you'll pardon the pun, Jordan was very much into me, too. We spent the following day together. The next evening, after work, same again. Night after night, we repeated. Jordan never really left.

Within the month, he'd officially moved out of his Willesden house-share and into my Maida Vale flat, just the two of us. Filming commenced on my cookery show the following week.

I believed I'd made it. The job, the man, the life.

What a difference it all is today.

* * *

In the cupboard, the light overhead has stopped flickering. It's better for my nausea. But the crystals on my new shoes have lost their sparkly lustre.

I can't keep pretending nothing is wrong in my relationship. Pretending isn't making anything better. Somewhere in my silence, I'm losing more than just my voice.

I call Jordan back, on his mobile.

'Grace, did you hang up on me?'

'Sorry, I, er, you seemed busy, Jordan,' I say.

'I'm at work.'

Jordan sounds busy, but not cross. Or maybe I can't tell the difference any more?

'Of course, Jordan. I'll be quick.'

'Please. It's not a good time.'

It never is. Jordan gets in late from his office and, usually, he heads straight down into our basement, more often than not with Robert in tow. My offers of sausage rolls and other home-baked snacks are well received. But it's clear I'm not welcome to loiter. Most of the time they're not even working; they're playing an awful zombie apocalypse game that hurts my ears from wherever I am inside the flat. I'm curious to know when, exactly, is a good time for me to interrupt my boyfriend?

'Jordan, did you feel compelled to wear your underpants to bed last night?' I ask. 'Or did you just, you know, forget to undress properly?'

I swear to you, it slips out.

For some time, there's a silence that neither of us fills.

'Grace, I really haven't got time for this.'

'Jordan, I know...'

When Jordan hangs up, my tears are streaming. There isn't a mega-hot chilli in sight.

4

I stay put on the ladder for some time after the phone call with Jordan ends. I can't believe I phoned my boyfriend at his work to talk about his underwear. I hope Jordan has the decency not to mention the specifics to anyone – with some of the office gossip he's repeated to me, I can't be sure he won't.

However, now is not the time to be skulking in a cleaner's cupboard with remorse. I have a meeting to attend on which my job depends. The clock is ticking.

I'm back in front of the basins when Poppy floats in.

'There you are! You disappeared? I looked for you in here. I looked for you everywhere,' she says. 'Miss Gracie, are you okay?'

Barelegged in her cut-off overalls, Poppy must have disposed of her vomit-soiled tights, her boots wiped clean. I honestly don't know how she manages to be so nice to me.

'I'm okay, Poppy.'

Albeit, I look worse than before. In the mirror, I see my

complexion has reddened from deathly-pale to scarlet. Mascara streaks now run down my cheeks. My hair is plastered in sweaty patches against my scalp as if I'm suffering from an exotic tropical disease. I'd go home if I didn't have this bloody meeting.

'Obviously, I look a sight…'

'Are you well enough to make this meeting?' Poppy asks, concerned.

Poppy doesn't need to know I'm more emotionally upset than physically ill at this point. She's a sweet kid. But I don't share intimate details of my personal life with her. I don't need her to know about my problems with Jordan.

'I'll make the meeting, and I'll do my absolute best. I know this all very much affects you and the crew, too, Poppy.' A burden I'm carrying seriously.

'That's very sweet, Miss Gracie. But we'll be all right,' Poppy insists. 'We're worker bees. Lots of people are leaving voluntarily. Titan will move us to another show, if it comes to that, which it won't. Let's get this face sorted for you.' Poppy jiggles what appears to be a cosmetic bag she has in hand. 'My magic bag of tricks,' she says.

The bag is emblazoned with hologram images of Astro Boy rocketing through space. I assess the array of make-up on Poppy's face. It's a look she can get away with – sort of. I, most certainly, cannot. However, neither can I meet with those impeccably groomed Americans in my current dishevelled state.

Poppy's favourite DJ plays the late set at a Brixton club on Sunday evenings, beginning at the ridiculous time of around midnight. She's well regarded for appearing as fresh as a daisy every Monday regardless. Perhaps, in this instance, she is best placed? It's that or I take my chances back with Brenda, who certainly does my face no favours.

'A bit less of the "magic", Poppy, and I might be persuaded. The meeting starts at 3. You don't have long.'

Perhaps, I should have requested David Blaine levels of magic?

Poppy plonks me atop the rubbish bin as a makeshift seat, out of eyeline of any of the mirrors. 'You relax here.'

First, Poppy dabs my eyes dry with a piece of tissue. Then with a wet wipe that smells of cucumber she removes all remnants of Brenda's professionally applied make-up. With her face right up close to mine, I notice the eyeliner that Poppy's wearing extends dramatically almost to her temples.

'Possibly, no eyeliner, if you wouldn't mind?'

'I'll keep it all very subtle.' Poppy smiles wryly. 'I do know you!'

I agree to let her get on with her ministrations.

Dipping in and out of her little bag to retrieve tubes and palettes of shimmery creams and powders, Poppy blends, dabs, brushes and sets my face. She finishes applying a second coat of black mascara. 'Your eyes are especially lovely today,' she tells me.

'Are they, by any chance, violet?' I enquire, perking up a bit.

'Um...' Poppy inspects closely. 'No. Blue. Super-duper shiny blue.'

The upside of tears, presumably.

I sit quietly on the bin lid.

With her fingers, Poppy loosens my hair from the stronghold of Brendan's spray. When I ask her to check, I'm relieved she can't see any more grey strands.

Stepping back, Poppy gives me a good once-over before she proclaims boldly of her handiwork, 'You look stunning.' With remarkable vigour for a girl so slight, she heaves me up from the top of the bin and plonks me in front of the mirror. 'Look.'

By the glitter over Poppy's face, I'm afraid to look.

When I brave my reflection, it's a pleasant surprise.

My eyes are clear, bright and super shiny indeed. My skin is radiant, with just a hint of rosy gorgeousness – you'd never guess I'd spent the best part of ten minutes sobbing to myself inside a cupboard. I check again, scrupulously. Highlighted by silvery-blue shadows and mascara piled as thick as you like, my pupils are what I'd confidently describe as iridescently lilac. My lips are so glossily delicious, I almost want to snog myself. Most miraculously, Poppy has given me the appearance of jutting cheekbones

'Poppy, how did you do this?' I ogle my reflection, unabashed as Poppy watches me, grinning. 'Actually, don't tell me. It might spoil "the magic". Thank you. Thank you, thank you, thank you.'

I'm assailing Poppy with my linguistic zeal when she interrupts to remind me this isn't the time to be indulging her.

'Don't forget your meeting starts shortly,' she says, tapping a steady finger against her fuchsia-banded, glow-in-the-dark (I'm sure she explained to me once) wristwatch.

Despite my seriously hot new look, I shiver.

* * *

Moments later, I find Faith in the corridor, searching for me.

'Weren't we meeting at your studio?' She kisses me on both cheeks. 'Darling, you look amazing!'

It is amazing what a makeover can do for a woman.

'All thanks to Poppy.' When Faith appears surprised, I acknowledge, 'I know. But... voilà.' I flash a million-dollar smile.

'Stunning,' Faith confirms.

Faith and I have known each other since primary school, before her breasts – and my hips – swelled. Faith was quieter back then; I was the gregarious class clown. These days, it's more likely to be Faith kicking up her designer heels. (Faith has an expensive wardrobe and she doesn't keep it for special occasions.) Naturally slender, she grew into her perfect C-cups by the time we finished at Our Lady's School for Girls of Perpetual Mercy, in Surrey, where both our parents still live. My best friend has always worn her naturally blonde-streaked hair long and, these days, when it looks sexily tousled, it's with good reason: Faith hops from one passionate dalliance to another, from whichever barrister or barista has taken her fancy for the week. Her eyes, set widely apart, are a kaleidoscope of greens and golds. With the faintest spattering of freckles, Faith is exquisitely beautiful. She's practically feline.

Faith also has an MBA and works for a venture capital firm funding post-seed fintech start-ups. (I can't tell you how long it took for me to remember this verbatim, though I still don't know exactly what it means, aside from it's a clever job, that sucks up many of Faith's hours, finances her aforementioned designer wardrobe, plus some other lovely lifestyle perks to boot.) She's here today, with all her business smarts, moonlighting as my agent. The arrangement began as a ruse for us to slip Faith into television industry events. That it turned out such events are scarcely as frequent, or as interesting, as one might imagine for the industry, I'm nonetheless grateful for her help. I've no idea how to enlist a proper agent to represent me otherwise. Faith is sufficiently financially astute to handle my contractual interests. As she says, who better? What I love most about our friendship is Faith's ferocious loyalty. She tells me often that I still make her laugh. Sometimes, whether I mean to or not.

'Are they Jimmy Choo's?' Faith stares at my pretty heels that, in the commotion of the last-minute change in menu and me being sick, and then the fight with Jordan, I've forgotten to change out of. 'Gracie, they're gorgeous! New look for the show?'

Not an outfit of design, the shoes don't look too silly with my white shirt and black trousers. I'm walking better in these heels already, too

Faith is magnificent in a black pencil skirt that skims her flat tummy and finishes just below her knees, a red silk shirt with tapered chiffon sleeves, flawless sheer tights and sharp-heeled, black suede ankle boots. Her boots are remarkably unweathered, as if, in getting here, Faith floated miraculously over the wet and muck outside. Her winter coat, with a luxurious faux fur collar, is draped neatly over her arm, her treasured black Birkin handbag in hand.

'Faith, I'm going grey. Today, I found a grey hair.

'These aren't all blondes on my head,' Faith scoffs, unperturbed.

When my laugh is less convivial than it might have been, she asks me, 'Gracie, what's up?'

The way my best friend asks isn't at all how my boyfriend put it to me earlier.

'Nothing. Everything?'

'Tell me everything.'

'I'll tell you everything after this meeting, Faith. For now, what is our game plan? As my trusted agent, do you have anything up your sleeve? I have crappy ratings and a cancelled sponsorship.'

Faith has been working a deal at her proper, paying job around the clock this week. We haven't had much time to chat.

'I have a sort of plan,' Faith sort of assures me. We carry on walking up the stairs towards the top floor. 'I popped in to see Adrian. He told me your sponsor went bust, nothing to do with ratings, so let's not worry too much about that.' Adrian, a strapping twenty-five-year-old, sells advertising here at SC6. Faith and he had a hot fling that ended mutually amicably a few months ago. 'Gracie, what we need is an angle.'

'An angle?'

'What's your USP?'

'My US–what?'

'Your unique selling point.' Faith smiles at me sweetly. She can't cook and I don't understand most of the business stuff she does. We get to the top of the stairs. 'What's the hook that's uniquely you, darling?'

I figure it's like Heston Blumenthal and his molecular gastronomy, his odd combinations of bacon-and-egg ice cream and snail porridge dishes that taste scrumptious on account of the ingredients being 'molecularly compatible'. Gordon Ramsay has his expletives, Jamie Oliver his fifteen-minute meals. Nigella has butter-rich recipes and her hour-glass figure – she reminds me I don't need to be size 0 to be popular. Mary Berry had a big tent.

What's my unique selling point?

'I don't know what my hook is, Faith, but Jordan

suggested sex sells,' is the best I can come up with at short notice.

'Ha!'

We exit the landing. The top floor is desolate, the offices empty. Titan has cleaned out most of the incumbent executives, too.

'Yes, well. Ironically, I accused him of wearing green underpants to bed to avoid having sex with me,' I divulge, walking steadily on. Faith stops me sharp.

'Gracie, what did you say?' Fit for laughing, she composes herself promptly. 'Sounds like someone forgot to take his HRT?'

Hormone replacement therapy – I wish they made it for men.

I talk to Faith about most things. But I haven't before mentioned my sexual dry spell. In the face of how easily she drifts from one banging fling to another, it seems so... excruciating. Not that Faith is here to judge me.

'Gracie, my love, with that face – and those heels – Jordan won't resist you tonight,' she says.

I do feel remarkably good about myself right now, with this new look. Also, Zelda's stone is in my coat pocket on set. With a bit of luck, that'll be attracting unconditional romance my way. We'll see how this meeting goes. But maybe it's not a bad idea for me to throw myself at Jordan this evening, see if he doesn't resist?

'Faith, what would I do without you?'

'And I you?'

We arrive at the imposing oak doors of the meeting room.

Turning to me with one eyebrow arched – it's Faith's thing and it packs a punch – Faith says, 'You know, it's some angle... getting steamy in the kitchen. Sex sells. I like it.'

'Oh God, Faith, is that really all we have?'

'I have a few tricks up my sleeve. Gracie, we'll not see you fired.'

'I hope you're right,' I say.

And in we go.

5

Inside the meeting room, Faith and I are seated at a small table positioned about a dozen feet back from a rectangular table, behind which sits the executive team with my future on the small screen in their hands. Our CEO, Timothy Sykes – silver fox and ageing Lothario—is chair. He's flanked by two Titan executives I recognise but haven't met.

'Grace, Faith, thank you for your attendance,' Timothy begins, unnerving me with his formality. Ordinarily, our CEO greets the pair of us with something along the lines of 'Why, hello there, ladies.' He's in his usual attire of navy chinos, a perfectly pressed white shirt and expensive brown leather loafers. A tennis junkie with his own central London court – perhaps now cemented over after wife number 3 ran off with his tennis coach – the man is in terrific shape for any age, let alone pushing sixty. His flirtations too bumblingly British to cause a #MeToo objection, our CEO is, rather, quite the catch. Faith says she'd do him in a heartbeat. Personally, I'm more endeared that, as CEO, Timothy knows me to talk to. He's always so... nice. Which is presumably how he landed himself in such a mess with his divorces – this last one cost him the shares he sold off to Titan. On top of which, his ex cashed in with every gossip magazine that would interview her about their super-charged sex life. How she simply had to run away with Stefan, the Swedish tennis expert, because Timothy's children from his prior marriages never included her as 'family'. (A twenty-two-year-old Ukrainian dancer, younger by far than all of Timothy's four children, none of whom still live at home, Milenna is the sort of woman rich old men are supposed to have a fling with, not marry without a pre-nup.) Poor Timothy. Always smitten. Perhaps, one day, it'll be fourth time lucky?

'This is Brian Bunce, financial controller for Titan.' Timothy introduces the middle-aged and balding man seated on his left. 'Brian is here temporarily from LA for group budgeting purposes.'

Brian barely looks up from his iPad. He's dressed 'casually' for his finance job in media in a green hoodie, pale denim jeans and white trainers. Sparing us no further attention, he jabs the screen with his finger, sucking his lips in furiously. Brian is the finance guy who's cut our budget down to zero.

Clearing his throat, Timothy turns more enthusiastically to the woman on his right. 'And this is Joanna Minnow, our new global vice president of content. Joanna, remind me for how long you will be with us in London, will you?'

'I'll be here for as long as it takes, Timothy,' Joanna says, in a strong New Yorker accent.

Timothy gazes at her with his flinty grey eyes. Joanna checks him by smiling neatly. Her mouth stays closed as her burgundy lips curl. Her dark eyes crinkle at the edges.

Joanna is small, yet wiry. Even from back here at the small

table, her biceps are defined beneath her tailored black blazer. Her hair is dark, sleek and cut sharply at the nape. Her fringe is cropped Audrey Hepburn-short. I know from passing her in the corridor that her skin is completely unlined. Aged anywhere between a natural forty and a 'well-done' fifty, our new vice president is undeniably attractive. Albeit in a very sharp way.

Rising from her chair, Faith crosses the room to introduce herself. 'Hello, I'm Faith Williams, agent for Gracie,' she purrs, shaking hands. 'Lovely to meet you both. Timothy, always a pleasure.' Working her stuff at the top table, Faith steals glances at Brian's little screen. Pedigree looks and the wiles of an alley cat – I'm glad she's on my side.

By the time Faith returns to her seat, I haven't moved or said a word.

For some time, Joanna stares at me.

'So, you're Gracie from *Gracie Porter's Gourmet Get-Together*.' Joanna sizes me up with her dark-as-black eyes. I'm betting her USP is: I always get what I want.

I need her to like me.

I need her to like me so much that she lets me keep my job – and, with a bit more luck, teaches me how to nail this business of being on television.

'I'm her. I mean, she... I'm Gracie,' is what pops out of my mouth.

I sense Faith looking at me sideways.

'Okay then, Gracie.' Joanna seems faintly amused, which wasn't my plan. 'Shall we proceed?'

'Indeed,' Timothy agrees cheerily.

Without further ado, the floor is handed to Brian, who proceeds to reel through a long list of statistics from his iPad.

'Blah, blah, blah negative.' 'Blah, blah, blah consistently poor.' 'Blah, blah, blah falling sharply.' Tapping his screen, he carries on without interruption for such a long time, I lose track of precisely which part of my performance he's tearing into – I'm pleased Faith is here for me to rely on. At various points, she sends him into a scramble about his calculations and corrects him sharply on what the total addressable market size of media spend in television is in the UK today. Joanna appears, at the very least, bored by it all, which could work in my favour. Timothy is still glancing at her, unchecked by any discouragement. Brian drones on. After a litany of numbers numbers numbers numbers, I actually jump in my seat when the conversation turns.

'Brian, you may stop now.' Without raising her voice, Joanna interjects. 'And turn that thing off.'

'But—'

'I'd like to talk business, Brian. Not bar charts that no one but you can see. Thank you.'

Like a petulant, albeit balding, child, Brian casts his device aside. He begins to pick at his fingernails. Joanna turns her attention on us.

'Ladies, let's distil the points raised so far. Television is a hit-driven business. If you don't have a hit, you don't have any business in television. You understand this, of course?'

I nod my head, perhaps too vigorously.

'So what is interesting to me is that cookery shows are, for now, very much a hit. You Brits set up your big-top and carry on about "soggy bottoms" and "icing-horns" and everyone tunes in.' Joanna sniffs a little laugh. 'It's all ever so politely tongue-in-cheek. What's not to love?'

'*Bake Off* was a wonderful show,' I enthuse, trying to bond.

Joanna narrows her gaze towards our table. 'Indeed. So tell me: what can you deliver to give me my culinary hit?' Joanna fixes her dark eyes on me. 'I must be clear, I find your current format – I'm sorry to say – rather stale...'

Joanna looks far from sorry as she forms another neat smile. Timothy is leering at her chest. But this slight curling of her burgundy lips is for me. I'm pretty sure I'm losing my job here.

There is a long pause that Timothy fills. 'Some studies suggest cookery shows, in general, may have had their day,' he says, I suspect to soften the blow. 'Channel 4 might well agree,' he chortles, but not unkindly.

I turn to Faith, my colour draining.

Faith rises. In her stunning outfit of silk and chiffon, she strides towards the top table. 'Excellent,' she announces, parading boldly up the front. 'In which case, we'll dispense with our argument that cookery programmes, in general, don't appeal any more. Stale? Absolutely.' Faith beams back at me. I force a smile. 'So what's fresh? What's fun? What do people want to watch?' Pushing a stray lock of blonde hair from her face, she continues in her I'm-here-to-do-business voice. 'We believe, something like a late-night edition of Jamie's *Naked Chef*.' Faith laughs heartily. 'Or a really naughty Nigella.'

I'm not sure where she's going with this. But Faith isn't looking to me for approval. Joanna's eyes narrow, I think pleasantly.

'Go on,' she says. 'I'm listening.'

I sink into my chair.

'Why not a cookery show that's a little more steamy, that whets all sorts of hungry. Shall I be bold and say, something more cock and bush than croquembouche?' my best friend, as my agent, suggests. For all intents and purposes, on my behalf.

My mouth drops.

Timothy's mouth drops.

Brian looks up from where he's been ripping at his nailbeds.

Joanna's eyes twinkle.

There's no stopping Faith now.

'Picture Gracie turning her hand to deliciously moist dishes, served with spicy banter on the side...' Her voice is like dripping honey.

When Faith turns to me, her cat-eyes, which run the spectrum from gold to green, are luminous amber.

'You mean food porn?' Timothy is first to query, not entirely awkwardly, but having first cleared his throat.

'I'm not suggesting Gracie serving up meatballs wearing nothing but her best silk panties,' Faith bats back, clearly enjoying herself. 'But PG-rated food porn? Sure. Let's go with that.'

Speechless in my defence, I gulp at the air I'm trying to breathe.

For starters, I don't own any silk panties – not that my underwear is all Bridget Jonesy big pants.

Timothy shuffles in his seat.

Joanna gives him a knowing pat on the arm, unperturbed.

Faith turns and winks at me.

When we get out of here, I'm going to throttle her.

'You could be on to something,' Joanna says. 'Maybe... I'm not sure.' She checks me out from top to bottom. 'You look... different. Not like on your show.'

'Oh, um...' I'm unsure how to respond. Is this a compliment? Joanna rests a steely gaze on my Jimmy Choo-heeled feet. The shoes are grand. What does she think of the rest of me?

'I tell you what I'll do, ladies,' she says. 'Show me what you mean by steamy. Make me... *hungry*... and we may have ourselves a deal.' She rolls her eyes to the ceiling. 'We're running out of fresh ideas around here otherwise. And never let it be said I don't love a challenge,' she adds, looking coolly – but not, I think, coldly – at me.

I'm wondering how to respond to this ludicrous proposal, and still keep my job, when Brian protests vehemently, 'Now, hang on a minute, Joanna...' At the top table, a fierce debate erupts regarding the correct process for contract renewals and who is authorised to do what. Under the cover of Brian's petition, Faith returns to our table.

'Faith, what are you playing at?' I hiss as she sits down. Everyone up the front is speaking over the other. 'I didn't know you were being serious earlier. Now look what you've done.'

'Gracie, this is good. I think Joanna's on board.' Faith is so pleased with herself. 'She was about to axe you on the spot. What did you want me to do?'

I tell Faith I would have preferred she hadn't mentioned the words 'steamy' and especially not 'moist' in the same sentence with regards to me doing anything recorded for television.

'The sexy angle was your idea,' Faith reminds me, unhelpfully.

'Jordan's, actually,' I remind her.

At the top table Brian is thrusting his iPad towards Joanna and she is sliding it back to him, refusing to look.

Timothy is piggy in the middle between them. It's almost comical – except that it's my livelihood hanging in the balance.

'It's the sort of cookery show I'd love to watch,' Faith carries on. 'And, let's face it, I could do with the lessons.'

Faith's domestic disabilities are diabolical. She once set her kitchen cabinets alight burning cheese on toast, then copped off with the fire engine driver who arrived swiftly on the scene. For weeks, I heckled her about sliding down his fireman's pole.

'I mean, just this morning, my house guest donated a little carton of eggs, with a note that said "Eat Me". Only, I haven't a clue how to cook eggs! What I served up for him instead is quite another story...'

Faith says this quietly, and under cover of the arguing at the front.

'Name?' I whisper.

This is our standard Q&A dissection of Faith's hook-ups.

'Toby Ellison.'

'Occupation?'

'He's a colleague.'

'Is that what you're calling them these days?'

'He's visiting from our New York office. You'll love this, Gracie. His assistant accidentally booked him to stay in a place called The Puss in Boots, which turned out to be not as "quintessentially English" as she believed. She sent him to spend the night at a massage parlour on Golden Square, with all the trimmings.'

I snicker appropriately.

'When Toby returned to the office, amused, but not wishing to play along, I did the only charitable thing.'

'You offered him a happy ending at your place?'

'I offered him my spare room. And, well, one thing led to another...'

Usually, I enjoy hearing about Faith's sexual conquests in detail. But this is neither the time nor the place.

I check the front and catch Joanna glancing our way even as she is rolling her eyes at Brian's incessant carping. Timothy's arm has manoeuvred its way around the back of her chair. Our silver fox.

'Anyway, I'm like the joke, right?' Faith continues. 'I can't even boil an egg.'

'I can teach you to boil an egg, Faith.'

'Would you, darling?' Faith leans in closer. She smells, like her signature perfume, Carnal Flower, of lusty tuberose and creamy sweetness. 'All I could think to do this morning was stick the Post-it onto Toby's naked torso.' Faith shrugs suggestively. 'Eat me...'

'Oh God.'

'Mmm. I wouldn't mind keeping this one.'

'You'll have new man candy to practice your egg boiling skills on by next week, Faith,' I beg to differ.

'You'll teach me some culinary tricks?'

'As Jerry Hall said, to keep a man, be a cook in the kitchen—'

'And a whore in the bedroom.'

Faith and I giggle in whispers.

Only, when we calm ourselves, it's apparent we didn't finish our private repartee in the hushed intonations in which we started. That we must have carried on our confab after the ruckus at the big table had finished. The room is pin-drop silent, all eyes on us.

'Gentlemen, what did I tell you?' Joanna exclaims, sweeping her hand triumphantly towards us. 'Food porn with a capital P! Ladies, that was wonderful!' She glares at Brian. 'The idea of man candy, a different guest each week, what a hook!'

She and Timothy launch into talking about multi-camera production for a weekly show, probably airing on a Monday or Tuesday evening, most likely after the 9 p.m. watershed.

Nothing comes out of my mouth.

Faith looks like the cat who got the cream.

Joanna beams very much like a woman who has just got what she wanted. 'I just love the name,' she gushes. 'Eat Me...'

Oh, no. No, no, no, no, no.

Before I can protest, to clarify the gross misunderstanding that's just occurred, Brian is instructed to work through numbers and get an offer to us as early as tomorrow. Evidently, he lost their spat. Timothy offers to put us in touch with a professional agent, if we prefer.

Does he imagine this is a show Faith and I will host together?

'That would be great, thank you, Timothy,' Faith replies.

Is she possibly thinking she wants to be on such a show with me?

Either way, I'm not sure I'll need an agent any more. They're all talking food porn – not the drooling over a perfectly melting-in-the-middle chocolate soufflé sort of food porn, but food porn with a capital P. That may, or may not, require somebody – certainly not me – sticking sexually loaded Post-it notes onto a new man's candy every week. That's close enough to what I think Joanna believes we just pitched. And I really, really don't think so.

I may not know my USP. But, given I can barely woo my own boyfriend, I know it isn't this. Absolutely not.

With a charm offensive, Joanna smiles at me warmly. 'I'm looking forward to working with you closely, Gracie, now I know you better.'

I can't believe I manage to spit out, 'Absolutely, Joanna. Me too.'

6

'Faith, I'm not doing it.'

'Gracie, are you home yet?'

I stumble out of the cab, tipsy. It's well past midnight. I attended Howard's farewell, which also turned into something of a wrap party for *Gracie Porter's Gourmet Get-Together* and, ostensibly, a celebration of whatever this next show may be.

After the big meeting, Faith had to rush back to her office. She breezily mentioned something about taking a three-month sabbatical so she could do *Eat Me* with me, that it sounded like it might be a hoot, though after the meeting ended abruptly when the executives called time, neither of us are entirely sure what she may have landed us into. We have to wait until Timothy's professional agent gets in touch with the new contract. In any event, I was less inclined to kick up my heels and celebrate. Wine, copious amounts of wine, seemed the solution.

We started at the pub, about thirty of us from work.

Tuesday night – I didn't plan on staying out. What happened was I didn't want to come home.

Steadying my feet on the pavement in my Jimmy Choo shoes – so much for not kicking up my heels – I wave the driver on.

I put my mobile back to my ear. 'Faith, I fell out of the cab.'

'You're home?'

'Almost!'

At the stairs leading up to my front door, I grip the handrail for stability.

One step, two steps... a small trip and a few more staggers and I'm onto the landing. Now, keys? Keys? Where are you, keys?

Tucking my phone beneath my chin, I search inside my bag. My mobile crashes to the tiles. Shhhhhiiiit. Picking it up, I'm relieved it's intact. Faith is still on the line.

'Gracie, you okay?'

I'm acutely aware it's only a very best friend who would put up with me being this annoyingly intoxicated, this late at night, this early in the week. Having wrapped the deal at her work, Faith was sleeping soundly when I called and woke her up to chat. For my entire cab ride home from Soho to Maida Vale, she listened patiently as I repeated myself down the line.

I find my keys and enter the building and then my flat.

'Gracie, are you home?'

'Sort of. Yes. I'm in.'

Tripping through the doorway, I hope I don't wake Jordan.

'Faith, you love me no matter what, don't you?' I say.

'Evidently, I do.'

Inside my head, words are beginning to slur before they make it to my mouth. I'm struggling to speak.

'I don't think Jordan does. Not any more. He wouldn't talk to me in the cupboard. Too busy to talk.'

Because Faith had to rush off, we didn't discuss my problems with Jordan after the meeting. But that wasn't because Faith doesn't love me.

In the darkness, I bang into the handle of the coat closet. I stop to rub my hip – this will hurt me tomorrow! I flick on the hallway light.

My eyes blink against the sudden brightness. Reaching out to steady myself, I slide my body down the wall, dropping safely on the floor.

'Faith, do you think Jordan doesn't love me any more?'

'Gracie, shh. Listen, I want you to drink some water and get some sleep. Okay? I'll phone you in the morning.'

The room spins. I will sit here until it stops. Oh God, please make the room stop spinning.

'Okay. But, Faith, I don't want to do the new show. Eat Me. Pffffft. It's so contrived. And it's sexy. It probably isn't even a cookery show. And it's... it's... what do we think it is again?'

'We think it's time for bed, darling. Goodnight.'

* * *

The next morning, too little sleep, too much booze the night before, the landline rings. From bed, I clutch the landline receiver from the side table.

'Hello?' My voice is a barely-there rasp. I remember smoking cigarettes last night. I only ever smoke when I'm exceedingly sloshed.

'Grace, dear?' It's my mother. 'What's wrong with your voice? Are you unwell?'

'Of sorts.' I splutter into the mouthpiece, burning with the shame only a doting parent can inflict on a fully independent thirty-three-year-old. 'I'm hung-over.'

My mother was forty-seven when I was conceived. Before I came along, my parents had long ago given up hoping for a child. For the first five months of her geriatric pregnancy, my mother assumed I was the menopause. Now, my parents are old. My mother is eighty. My father is eighty-six. Luckily, they're both in rude physical health, walking eight miles daily between them, and have a social life I sometimes envy. There isn't pressure for me to look after them yet, which is a relief. That said, my mother is prone to fussing. And my father, I suspect, is becoming senile – my mother insists it's selective memory that suits him just fine and I'm not to worry a dot.

'You were out on a Tuesday evening, dear? On a school night?'

My mother was an English teacher before I was born, my father an air-conditioner engineer with the NHS until he retired. Now, she volunteers at a charity shop and he reads the papers and does the crosswords.

'It was a work thing, Mummy. Please don't make it worse. Believe me, I feel wretched.'

Wretched – a word I'd only use with my mother. A bit like how I still call my parents 'Mummy' and 'Daddy', like I'm five years old, or posh enough to have grown up with horses and nannies, which isn't true. My parents are just old. My mother reads the classics. It's the way I was raised to speak with them.

I blow my nose into a tissue and the snot that comes out is rippled with black. London pollution is, if you believe the news, worse than Beijing.

'All these showbiz parties, I don't know,' my mother tut-tuts down the line.

'It wasn't a party, Mummy.'

I don't point out that I rarely go to parties these days, showbiz or otherwise – or that last night was a leaving do for someone fired by the station, let alone what's going on with my contract. My mother already worries about the stability of me working in television. Of course, she's pleased to say I have my own show – that's something she lauds cheerily on about whenever serving customers at the charity shop, or having tea after church (my parents aren't particularly religious; my mother goes alone for the social connection) and to all her friends at every conceivable opportunity. But I'm not sure my parents regard me being on the telly as having a real job. Sometimes, my mother asks when I'm going back to the bistro. As if I'm on some sort of extended field trip at SC6. She may have a point.

I check my watch. 9 a.m. It feels hideously earlier.

I don't remember him leaving, but Jordan must have headed off to his office in Farringdon some time ago.

I don't have to go in to work today. Whatever comes next, *Gracie Porter's Gourmet Get-Together* is finished, no more episodes to record. A fact I took into consideration before I obliterated my liver last night because, despite my mother's lofty aspersions, I'm not so rock 'n' roll as to recklessly go out boozing on a school night otherwise.

My mother starts on about how the council is making it difficult for the charity shop to host so much as a simple bake sale. Letting her ramble, my head slips back onto the pillow. I recall the events last night that led me to this sorry state.

At the pub, Howard was in more of a mind to celebrate his payoff than to commiserate the demise of *Nature's Best*. His farewell was a jovial event, unlike the depressing exits of last year. For the entire evening, he slugged at the bottle of sherry I'd gifted him. But from the moment we arrived at The White Horse, I wanted to go home. Apart from anything else, I wanted to sort things out with Jordan. To check my boyfriend wasn't ready to hang up on me permanently. For the longest time, Jordan didn't answer his phones. I left several messages on his mobile, including an apology, and a joke about the cleaning fumes in the cupboard perhaps getting to my head before I'd thought to ask about his choice of wearing underpants to bed. I'd hoped Jordan would call me back and we'd laugh it off – everything that had been falling apart between us lately. Time passed, the crowd thinned, and I didn't hear a peep. When someone suggested we move on after last orders at the pub, I was first in. Let Jordan sweat about where I might be, I'd thought. Let him miss me, I'd hoped. That might show him.

I downed several shots in a dingy bar before I realised my team weren't with me, Howard had slunk off home and I barely knew the people I was with. Uber rates surged, but there were no rides anyway. It took me some time mooching along Shaftsbury Avenue to find a black cab to take me home. Tottering outside in the winter cold in my fancy heels, I looked like one of those girls who might shortly empty her stomach in the back seat. I remember Faith being nice to me as I collapsed in the hallway at home. I don't remember anything about making it into bed.

I roll over to one side. Jesus, Mary and mother of God, my hip is on fire! I return carefully to the flat of my back.

Having finished regaling me with the latest village gossip, my mother says, 'your father will want a quick hello. I'll just go get him.' Clunking the phone down, she calls out, 'Derek, Grace is on the phone. Come say hello. She's not feeling well.'

I picture my father getting up from in his wing-chair in the front room, where he was inevitably happily absorbed with the papers, and dragging his slippers down the hallway to the kitchen. After lunch, my parents will pull on their wellies and amble for several hours across the local fields, hail or shine.

My father clears his throat into the mouthpiece.

'Morning, Grace.'

'Morning, Daddy.'

'How are you, dear? Your mother says not well?'

'Oh no, I'm fine, really.'

'Good-oh. How's the weather in London? We're getting a lot of rain down here.'

My parents still live in the small, semi-detached house in Surrey where I grew up. Under an hour by train from London Bridge station, they get pretty much the same weather as I do.

'Same here, Daddy. It's been very wet.'

Next, my father will ask about my work. Then he will finish our conversation briskly.

'And how's work?'

'Work is fine, thank you.'

'Jolly good. I'll put you back to your mother. You take care now.'

My father doesn't wait for me to say goodbye and I don't take offence. I love him enormously, but we can both do without the phone chats my mother cajoles us into. This morning, in particular, I appreciate the brevity. The phone passes between my parents.

My head throbs. My bladder is fit to burst. If I mention I don't have to go into work today, my mother will natter at me for hours.

'I must say, Grace, aren't you a bit old to be waking up with a hangover?' she jumps straight into. 'Isn't it time you settled down?'

'You mean get married, move to Redhill and have babies?'

'Why not? I could help you more if you lived closer.'

For starters, Jordan and I haven't come close to a conversation about marriage, let alone babies. My mother's vision of settling down isn't an offer that's available to me, even if I wanted it, and I don't want it. The thought of motherhood doesn't fill me with the joys of spring. My ovaries aren't tick-tocking like Big Ben beside my uterus. Babies aren't yet on my agenda. Apart from being terrified about what they'll do to my body, stretching and tearing me in places I don't wish to imagine, there are practicalities to consider. For instance, I'm still renting. And my rented flat has only one bedroom, so there isn't room for a nursery. I also don't have a lot of savings for all the things that babies require, including day care. I'm only thirty-three. If forties are the new thirties, why, I'd be practically a teen mum if I had babies now, which doesn't appeal. Faith is steadfastly single, so there's no peer pressure. And let's not forget, at the moment, I'm not even having sex.

'I'm not having children until my forties, Mummy. Like you,' is all I say.

'I could be dead by then,' she warns me.

'Well then, you won't be much help.'

We both laugh. My mother is not without a cracking sense of humour.

'Mummy, I must go. I'm not yet out of bed.'

'I won't go on, dear. One thing quickly. Beryl is hosting another of her famous murder-mystery dinner parties. Your father is refusing to come with me. He says he doesn't like to dress up, which is nonsense as he never bothers anyway. He also called Beryl an awful gossip and grumbled that life is too short to spend it not enjoying himself.'

'Beryl is a bit poisonous, Mummy,' I point out gently. 'You've said as much yourself.'

'She's also someone I've known a long time, dear. I worry about her since Gerald passed. These dinners might be the thing that keeps her going…' Beryl's long-suffering husband, Gerald, died of a coronary last New Year's Eve. He dropped dead in front of everyone at the party they were hosting. Because of Beryl's famous murder-mystery dinners, there was, apparently, a moment where everyone assumed Gerald's clasping of his chest and falling to the floor was part of an elaborate script. My mother told me it took several moments, and Beryl fainting to the floor, before anyone rushed to help. Sadly, to no avail. Why on earth Beryl insists on throwing such dinner parties still is anyone's guess. My mother trails off somewhere. 'Would you come with me, dear? It's a few weeks away, the first Saturday in February. You could stop the night, if you like?

I don't need to check if I have anything on. Ignoring last night, I don't go out often any more. I could easily tap Faith up for a night out if I desired, but, these days, I'm such a homebody. Aside from giving her grandchildren before she passes, my mother rarely asks me for anything. Of course I'll go with her.

'Okay.'

'Okay you'll come?' My mother's voice is tinged with delight.

'If you let me get off the phone right now, Mother dearest, yes, okay I'll come.'

'Oh, we'll have such a laugh. Oh, I am looking forward to it. Now, will Jordan stop with your father at home?' she prattles on gaily. 'I can make up the sofa bed for him. It's not a problem. I'll make a roast on Sunday, and perhaps you can both join us on our walk?'

Between my mother's unbeatable roast dinner and the opportunity for fresh air, most Londoners would jump at the chance. But Jordan has met my parents only twice in the year that he and I have been living together. Once, at their wedding anniversary party, last summer, when Jordan was set up on the sofa bed but sneaked into my bedroom while my parents slept (and we didn't). And again on Boxing Day just gone when he collected me in his rented Audi A3 after we spent Christmas separately with our own families. Jordan had been all the way down in Cornwall with his three brothers and a myriad of cousins – an awkward situation when, throughout the whole of Christmas Day, he didn't call to wish me Merry Christmas. I'd sent him a text immediately on waking. When Jordan hadn't replied by dinnertime, I'd been too nervous to call him. Until my boyfriend breezed in the next day and brushed the issue off as mobile coverage problems, I'd no clue how to allay my mother's concerns that something dreadful may have happened to him.

'Let's assume it's just me, Mummy.' There's zero chance Jordan will say yes, and I won't be asking anyway. Not to mention my father won't appreciate the inconvenience of them babysitting each other on a Saturday evening. His life is, as he warned my mother, now far too short. 'Mummy, I really must get off the phone.'

'For the murder mystery, you'll be Satine Featherbag,' my mother presses on obliviously, her hearing akin to the selective memory she accuses my father of. 'Satine is the secret lover of Billy Bragalot, who is the owner of the shoe factory where the murder occurs. You could wear—'

'Hanging up right now.'

'All right, dear. We'll talk soon. I love you.'

'I love you, too.'

'Goodbye.'

Putting the phone down, I brace myself to throw back the covers. The central heating switched off an hour ago. The air is icy. I'm still wearing the white shirt and bra I came home in last night. My black trousers – and knickers – are strewn over the dresser. Too drunk to undress properly, I suppose. I hope I didn't say anything of the sort to Jordan. I honestly can't remember.

I go to the bathroom, and take two Nurofen with water from the tap. I slink back into bed.

I'm lying very still, trying to recover, when the landline rings again.

'Mummy, please.' No one but my mother, and occasionally Faith, calls my landline. My mother because she believes mobile phones cause brain cancer and Faith because, sometimes, my mobile doesn't work inside my flat.

I've agreed to go to Beryl's murder mystery dinner, dressed up as the slightly slutty-sounding Satine Featherbag. What more can my mother want of me this morning?

A high-pitched voice, most likely male, certainly not my mother, responds, 'Oooh.' Then in a deeper voice, 'I've had Daddy before, but Mummy? That's a newy.'

'Who is this?' I gasp, sitting bolt upright and pulling the covers right up over my naked bottom-half. My black cotton knickers on the dresser aren't quite the lacy underwear Faith so brazenly discussed when pitching me as a food porn presenter. But still. It's quite the scene. What if this voice belongs to some kind of pervert, on the loose in Maida Vale? I hope Jordan locked the door behind him when he left this morning. He doesn't always.

'Sorry. I forget. We haven't yet met. But what an opening you gave me.'

'Who is this, please?' I repeat, burrowing deeper underneath the duvet – a better use of energy would be for me to get up and lock my bedroom door.

'Gracie Porter, this is Harrison Hipgrave, Agent to the Stars. Call me Harry, if you prefer?'

I breathe a sigh of relief. It's only Timothy's professional agent. By his opening, I picture Harry wearing a burgundy cravat and black velvet smoking jacket. Having greasy hair and girly hands, to match his high-pitched squeal.

'Gracie, you still there?' To be fair, his voice is now respectably normal. Quite gravelly, in fact.

'What can I do for you, Harry?' I say, my voice, shockingly, sounding equally manly-like. I'm never smoking again.

'Ah! Well, really, this is about what I can do for you, sweetheart,' is Harrison Hipgrave's smooth-as-smooth reply.

'Enough with the sweetheart, Harry.' With my husky throat, this sounds inadvertently sexy. 'As you say, we haven't yet met.' Good Lord. Am I still drunk?

Harry chuckles.

'Timmy sent me your new contract. Gracie, we need to meet.'

I'm too unwell to deal with this right now. I tell Harry I already have an agent, hoping Faith will deal with him later.

Harry insists, 'And that you do!'

'No, Harry, not you. I mean—'

'You mean Faith Williams?'

'Um. Yes.'

'We've spoken.'

'You've spoken with Faith?'

'I have contracts for you both. Apparently, you two made rather an impression at the station yesterday...'

After the mix-up during the meeting, it's hardly surprising Faith is confirmed as part of whatever this new show might be.

Also, whatever Timothy told Harry about our 'performance' yesterday might go a long way to explaining Harry's initial gambit on this call.

If Faith has already heard from Harry, why hasn't she called me to say?

'Is there a problem, Gracie? Timmy said you were expecting to hear from me. I hope it's in order I've called?'

My brain is whirring. If Joanna wants Faith, she may not want me without her. Despite Faith's throw-away line about joining me 'for the hoot', Faith probably won't leave her lucrative job in venture capital to work on a sexed-up cookery show for SC6 – this isn't the BBC on offer. Such thoughts begin to bother me profusely, regardless of whether I want to do the blasted thing or not.

Why the devil hasn't Faith called me?

'There's no problem, Harry.'

'Splendid. Can you meet sharpish? Faith is good for noon today, at my office on Piccadilly.'

'Noon is fine,' I say.

I'm meeting Liz Martin, journalist, later today in Mayfair. Liz writes for the weekend home and garden pull-out of the *Daily* that includes recipes from episodes of *Gracie Porter's Gourmet Get-Together*. Gosh knows what I'll say to her today, given the state of play with my work. A problem to solve later. Let's get these painkillers kicking in first.

'I'm at 24 Haymarket,' Harry says.

'I know the street.'

'Marvellous! Looking forward to meeting you, Gracie.'

'I'll be there with bells on,' I say, unplugging the landline.

7

After the Nurofen kicks in, I take a hot shower and get dressed into my favourite dark denim jeans and blue sweater. Discovering my Jimmy Choo heels scattered down the hallway – not in pristine condition, but not damaged – I brush them off, put them back in their felt bag and into my wardrobe. It takes me longer to find my mobile phone, slid right under the sofa. My drunken stupor last night.

I check my mobile. No messages.

I still can't remember how I got into bed?

In the kitchen, Jordan has left his usual mess. Toast crumbs, strawberry jam and a block of butter on the bench. An abandoned bowl of cereal on the table. A load of his wet washing in the machine. I don't take care of my boyfriend's dirty clothes. But if I don't hang his wet washing out or put it in the dryer for him, he'll leave it for days, until it smells like a swamp. Popping softener into the drawer, I run a quick rinse cycle to refresh the load.

Not for the first time, I contemplate that picking up after

my boyfriend like I'm his mother can't be great for our romantic life – it certainly doesn't do much for my libido.

Outside my kitchen window, the bare branches of the big oak trees sway with the gale that's blowing again out there today. I'm over these Arctic cold winds. But it sure is picturesque, in a wintery stark way, out there. I love where I live. Located just off Warwick Avenue, in the affluent suburb of Maida Vale, northwest London, my flat is fashionably close to the cafes and canals of Little Venice and an easy run into the West End for work. The bedroom is quiet, cosy and overlooks the pretty back gardens of the mansion blocks that line the street. The front-facing reception is spacious and light-filled. The ceilings are high, and a fire escape runs off the old but well-appointed kitchen. Being on the raised ground floor, I have a basement that's well-proportioned and, though unrenovated, dry. It leads onto a private, grassy patch outside. In summer, I enjoy pottering about planting geraniums, sweet peas and impatiens in pots and filling herb boxes with the gorgeous greenery and aromas of coriander, parsley, rosemary and the like. Sometimes, I fall asleep in the sun reading books. When it's warm and Faith is visiting, we have been known to get tipsy drinking wine on blankets on the grass.

Best of all, the rent is low. Even on my pittance of a chef's salary when I first moved to London, I could afford such luxury. The property belonged to Miriam Whitbury, who died at the remarkable age of one hundred and one, leaving it to her daughter June Whitbury, a close friend of my parents. June lets the property to me cheaply while she brings herself around to the idea of selling. She's eighty-two years old and I've lived here for almost a decade. Throughout the years, I've been a model tenant accordingly.

My phone on charge at the bench, I send Jordan a text.

Morning, sorry about last night. Hope I didn't wake you? Stayed out to celebrate new show! Will tell you more later after meeting with new agent. Not working today. Can cook us a nice dinner later? Gx P.S. sorted your washing

Jordan texts me back immediately.

Are you at home now?

Before I have the chance to text back, he calls my mobile.

'Hey.'

'Hey, are you at home?' he asks me.

'Yeah. I don't have to go into work today. Jordan, I think I've landed a whole new show.' I don't want Jordan to know I'm anything less than enthusiastic at this point. I want him to be proud of me. 'I'm meeting Faith, and a professional agent, Harry Hipgrave, in a bit to find out more. Why? Where are you?'

'I'm with a client. When will you be back?'

'Um, not sure? Later this afternoon? Jordan, I didn't lose my job. Did you get my messages?'

'Sorry, yes. I was exhausted from work and fell asleep early. Congratulations. By the way, you did wake me when you came in. I tried to help you to bed. You were really drunk.'

Jordan's tone is nonchalant. But I suspect I embarrassed myself more than being very inebriated last night.

'I probably don't want to know the details, Jordan. I'll cook us a nice dinner tonight to make it up to you? And... can we maybe talk, later? Or will you have to work?'

Jordan sucks his breath in. 'Not sure how my day will pan

out. Dinner sounds good. What time are you leaving and what time will you be home today?'

'Leaving shortly and I can be home by early afternoon. Do you need me to do anything, Jordan?'

'No. No, just wondering.'

'Okay.'

'I have to run.'

'Okay. Have a great day and see you tonight, babe.'

'See ya.' Jordan rings off.

My head isn't quite working the way it should, but that was a bit of a funny conversation. Not unpleasant. Indeed, it was nice of Jordan to call me. But it seemed to me... short? Odd? Pointless? Perhaps because it's been months since Jordan and I have called each other for short, pointless conversations about nothing? Surely, I shouldn't worry. I mean, we didn't fight. Jordan sounded happy about dinner and, subject to work, open to talking later.

I was worried sick about work, but I didn't lose my job – I can't say I'm thrilled with what I may be signing up to, but I didn't get fired. Maybe, the tide is turning for Jordan and me, too?

I decide to carry on positively. Even if my body feels like it's been to war.

To accelerate my recovery, I make myself a fresh fruit smoothie with banana, frozen raspberries, yoghurt and a handful of spinach. Not wanting to linger now that I'm up and at it, I ping an email to Liz Martin to see if she can meet earlier than our usual 3 p.m. She confirms she's free from 11. To squeeze in our catch-up before I meet with Harry at noon, and have the afternoon to myself, I'll have to get a move on.

Gulping my smoothie, I accidentally miss my mouth – I'm kidding myself to think I'm not still monstrously hung-over, possibly still intoxicated – and pureed fruit and yoghurt splashes all over my pretty top and favourite jeans. Gagggggghhh.

I clear up the mess also over the kitchen floor. Running late, I throw on some clean clothes and get myself out of the flat.

* * *

The cafe where I regularly meet Liz Martin is near Green Park Tube station. I rush in dripping water everywhere. Outside, it's raining again.

'Hi, Liz. Golly, this umbrella is soaked. Ugh, let me put it under the table. Oh gosh, sorry, that's your foot.'

'Gracie, it's fine. Sit down,' Liz instructs. 'I've ordered us tea.'

Liz used to be a sharp-nosed political reporter before her semi-retirement to write lifestyle articles for the glossies – there's no way she hasn't noticed I'm not firing on all cylinders. These days, alongside my recipes, she writes up my advice about the seasonality of produce or the importance of high-quality kitchen tools. The way Liz writes, she makes me read as infinitely more interesting than the verbal ramblings I offer her over cups of tea. I wouldn't describe myself as media-savvy. In this instance, as indeed all instances, Liz has been good to me.

'I've ordered you Earl Grey.'

My usual – but I'd sooner a Berocca. 'Thank you, Liz.'

The waitress promptly brings our tea.

'Apologies about the late change to the recipes yesterday,' I begin. Before we headed to the pub, but after we'd had champagne toasts on set with the crew following the big meeting, Poppy had helped me to quickly write up the last-minute changes for the vegan scallops and Cheating Hot Sticky Prawns and email them to Liz.

Liz adjusts her thick black reading glasses and tucks her short, greying red hair behind her ears. 'It's no problem. I understand there's a lot going on at SC6. Can we talk about that?'

Lukewarm tea dribbles onto my cream shirt.

Personally, I'd love to talk through the changes going on at the station with Liz Martin. Over this past year that we've been meeting, I like to think we've developed some sort of professional friendship. Liz has shared with me tales about her time as an investigative journalist – she's interviewed everyone from Oscar-winning celebrities to despotic heads of African countries. I could do worse than be guided by her opinion on matters going on at work.

Professionally, I know it's not for me to confirm to anyone from the press that people at SC6 have been losing their jobs.

At the very least, our press department might have instructed me on what to say regarding the cancellation of my old show. And whatever can I say about the proposed new format?

'Indeed, there have been a few... changes at SC6 recently.'

'What sort of changes?' Liz presses me.

'Well, we're taking a small break to work through the details, but I think it's probably okay for me to mention, off the record, that *Gracie Porter's Gourmet Get-Together* might be rebranded,' I reveal.

'That's better news than some things I've heard. Rebranded to what?'

'Still off the record?'

Liz puts her pen respectfully aside, indicating this part of our discussion won't make it anywhere near her column.

'Would you believe to *Eat Me*?'

Liz barely contains her expression to a small smile.

We get on very well, Liz and me.

'Sounds interesting.'

'Quite.'

'Will it be the same format?'

Not quite, I imagine. But who knows?

'It's probably best I don't discuss the details yet,' I comment delicately. 'New contracts and all, you know how it is.'

'I look forward to hearing more once you're free to talk,' Liz says. 'It sounds intriguing.'

We order cream cheese and cucumber sandwiches. I agree to contact Liz when production resumes. With nothing signed yet, I should have agreed *if*.

8

Leaving Liz to traipse through the incessant rain, tourists and touts around Piccadilly Circus, I arrive at Harry Hipgrave's doorway visibly frazzled. Faith is tucked neatly inside the entrance, dry as toast and immaculate.

'Well, you look awful.' Faith huddles me inside with a brief peck on my cheek. 'Did you get any sleep?'

I admire Faith's pea-green coat. The colour plays perfectly with the flicker of olive in her eyes.

'Faith, why didn't you call me when you heard from Harry?'

She takes my umbrella and gives it a good shake.

'Darling, I tried calling you all morning. Your mobile was dead. Your landline was busy, then it rang out, over and over. Although, I'd given Harry your number, and he said he'd spoken with you. So… here I am.'

After the conversations with my mother and Harry, I'd unplugged the landline at the wall to get some peace. I don't understand why my mobile reception is so erratic in my flat. Jordan reached me just fine this morning.

'I'm sorry, darling. I'm so hung-over. My head hurts horribly. You look amazing, by the way. As always. Did you get back to sleep last night? I was ridiculously drunk...'

'You were, it was funny, I'm not surprised your head hurts!'

'Funny or annoying?' I ask, concerned I know the answer.

'A bit of both. But, yes, I got back to sleep. I'm only sorry I couldn't join you. Sounds like you had a fun night?'

Faith and I were inseparable before I took up with Jordan. Out together all the time, having fun. We still speak daily on the phone. Some days, more than once. But we don't see each other face-to-face as often any more. Not that Faith isn't fully socially occupied without me. And then some. But any absence between us rests squarely on me.

'Darling, I miss you,' I blurt out, clasping my best friend in a big bear hug.

'Don't get soppy because you're feeling sorry for yourself.' Faith pushes me off her with affection. 'Now, Gracie Louise Porter, what's with this coat you've got on today?'

'It's from the charity shop, where Mummy volunteers,' I say of the woolly-grey coat that's two sizes too large for me, brassy-buttoned and pilling all over. My mother bought it for me eons ago, second-hand, when I passed through a chunky – but not that chunky – phase. I've never had the heart to throw it away or the desire to wear it. I chucked it on in my rush to leave the flat this morning. I couldn't find my regular black coat, which I have a horrible feeling I left inside the cab last night.

'Take it off,' Faith says. I take off the coat. 'Is your shirt also from the charity shop?'

I check the cream brocade shirt – tea-stained since my meeting with Liz – worn over a stretchy black skirt, both of which also shouldn't be seen outside of the house. 'Faith, no. It's just old. I spilled my smoothie. I'm unwell. Go easy.'

'Understood. And underneath all of that?'

'Underneath all of this is my underwear,' I reply, buttoning myself back into my coat like a grey, woolly mammoth, relieved to know I am, unequivocally, wearing knickers.

'Good to know,' Faith says. 'Come on, let's sort out the rest of it.'

Faith leads me up the stairwell and into a small washroom, wherein she locks the door and forces me out of my shirt and into a little black top she's just purchased for herself from Massimo Dutti. The material is stretchy, like my skirt, but the top is too tight on me: my breasts are squeezed in and pushed up, my nipples perilously close to a popping-out incident. I have what is best referred to as 'a bosom'. The sort of chest ladies past a certain age attempt to tuck into their reinforced, one-piece swimming costumes before performing breaststroke in such places as Hampstead Heath ponds. I squeal in protest and Faith removes the silver scarf she's wearing around her neck and manoeuvres it to hang in loose folds over my cleavage.

'That's better,' she says.

I check myself in the mirror. 'I look ridiculous!' I look like *The Mummy Returns*. Mind you, I could do with a nap in a lovely old sarcophagus. 'Faith, please don't make me wear this.'

I'm painfully aware how the top would hang loosely on her long, lithe torso.

'It works,' Faith replies, ripping off the tags. 'In fact, it's quite sexy on you. You can keep them both to wear with your new shoes. Now, come on. We're already late – you hate that. Let's go.'

* * *

Harrison Hipgrave opens his own door. It appears he has no staff. Certainly, no filing clerk. His office is messy. Papers piled high on every conceivable surface. Empty cans of soft drink. The furniture is tatty, albeit Harry is not. In real life, as opposed to in my vivid imagination, he isn't so ridiculous as to be wearing a burgundy cravat and smoking jacket. He's dressed in dark jeans and a khaki shirt. Tall, about six foot, his hair is lovely: thick, blonde and floppy. He's a bit Harrison Ford, Indian Jones-ish – give him the accoutrements of fedora hat and cracking bullwhip, I can imagine him easily swinging over a pit of snakes, narrowly escaping a thundering boulder, in a booby-trapped temple of doom.

I give it two weeks before he and Faith are screwing each other senseless.

'Come in,' Harry says. In person, his voice is nowhere near as shrill as he sounded on the phone this morning. 'Welcome to my world.'

He motions us through with an odd, circling arm swing. His hands are huge.

Inside, the walls are plastered with pictures of mostly attractive women, many in various stages of undress. It's disappointing to note none are familiar to warrant the claim 'Agent to the Stars'.

'Not everyone gets up there,' Harry says, noticing me staring – grimacing, I'm sure – at a particularly buxom blonde.

Some of them could be theatre stars. A few more are

soapy-looking. Could be there are a few reality stars up there – I don't watch enough television to know.

I smile sweetly.

Harry smiles warmly back at me. His skin is tanned. Sunbeds, judging from the crinkles around his eyes. Lovely eyes, though. Dark brown, bounded by bushy eyebrows and heavenly lashes.

He brushes past and his smell is intoxicating. As a chef, my olfactory senses are finely tuned. But I can't, exactly, place Harry's scent. Is it cedarwood? Smoky vanilla? Leather? Harry is wearing chunky leather boots. Whatever it is, it's divine.

Nervous I might smell of sweaty old wine seeping through my pores, I shuffle slightly away, just in case.

'Ladies, please, take a seat.'

Faith and I plop ourselves into a pair of squeaky green vinyl armchairs. In front of us is a big, old mahogany desk, on which sits a laptop and the messy piles of papers.

'First, a confession.' Harry stands across from us on the opposite side of the desk. 'I'm a fan of your old show, Gracie.' Harry is smiling broadly, and I'm not buying it. My typical viewer is female, over thirty and, generally, a retiree or a stay-at-home mum who's parked their brood at school for the day. Harry may be smooth, but he'll have to do better than this. 'Absolutely loved what you did with those little pork medallions at the beginning of the series.'

'The pork with thyme and rosemary marinade?'

'Served with hasselback potatoes.' I can't help a small smile. I conclude he prepared for this meeting by viewing an old recording of my cancelled show. 'Unfortunately, I can't cook myself. I rarely have any food in my flat.'

I'm keen to steer the conversation along and be in and out

of here. I need to pick up a few things and I'd like to get home in time to have a nap before I prepare dinner for Jordan and me. 'So, these contracts, Harry?'

'Indeed!'

Taking his seat in the swivel chair on his side of the desk with abandon, the whole ensemble – Harry included, arms flailing – topples backwards. At the last second, Harry hooks his boots under the desk and narrowly saves himself from ploughing head-first into the wall of boobs and blondes behind him.

'Whoa, easy does it, tiger!' he roars.

Faith bursts out giggling.

Harry chuckles.

My head *aches*.

'Must be that fetching outfit of yours getting the better of me, Gracie,' Harry then has the gumption to suggest.

I sit up straighter, with what I hope is a suitable look of umbrage – though to be fair, Harry was looking straight into my eyes, and nowhere else, as he said this. Nonetheless, I adjust the silver scarf more protectively across my packed-in bosom. In the process, the scarf slips completely off one shoulder. To not make things worse, I leave the whole thing as it is.

Harry's shirt is unbuttoned to halfway down his chest.

It appears he waxes.

Noticing me noticing, he raises an eyebrow.

It occurs to me that if Faith was a man, she'd be Harry Hipgrave, my potential new agent.

I avert my eyes

'Let's say, I'm not surprised the station is keen to have you back in this saucy new format.' Harry flashes another smile, a gorgeously lopsided grin.

I remind myself I'm here for business purposes – and so is Harry. I mustn't feel so flattered by his, frankly, outrageous flirting that I forget his carry-on is likely a well-honed play to earn himself a fat commission. By Faith's admission, I look awful today. From the shabby state of Harry's office, he can do with the work.

'So, the new show...' He picks up a wad of papers with the SC6 letterhead on top.

'Let's hear it,' says Faith.

And off he goes.

A little while later, Harry breaks away to buy coffees, leaving Faith and me alone in his office.

'Faith, tell me you're not considering being the single chick with the date?'

To say I'm appalled by Harry's explanation of the new format is a gross understatement. In short, Harry explained the premise of this new show as Faith inviting a man onto the set and me guiding her to cook him a three-course meal. Which sounds innocuous enough. Except, after selecting some ingredients, Faith's date then goes off camera to 'have a looksy through an *FHM* mag, or whatever floats his boat' – is exactly how Harry put it to us moments ago – and while we're cooking, Faith and I are supposed to discuss on camera the 'dramas' of being single (her) and in a relationship (me). To again quote Harry directly, such dramas as 'receiving a very respectable dick pic' via Tinder (Faith) and 'perhaps circum-navigating the sometimes chore-like romance that creeps into a "proper relationship"' (presumably, me). Faith will have a different date each week, making her look like the town bike on national television. Whether she's bothered by this or not – and no matter how she lives her life in private – I think it's outrageous.

I cannot fathom how Joanna, or anyone in that meeting, got from a note on a carton of eggs to this.

Harry put it all to us just so, without flinching.

'I don't know, it might be fun,' Faith says.

Harry had the gall to remark, 'Gracie, I'm not suggesting your relationship is at the point where sex has become a chore.' He couldn't have known, but Harry hit a nerve with that one. I almost choked. I definitely blushed.

'Harry is too familiar for my liking.'

'I think he's funny.'

'His wall of fame is more wall of shame – look at all those boobs! Who are these women?'

'No idea. He's very handsome.'

'Does that matter?'

'It doesn't hurt.' Faith smiles. 'Gracie, he was joking.'

'About which bit?'

If Harry was never a fan of my old cookery show, I can live with it. As for the rest of it, joking or not, I'm more than rather mortified.

'I don't ever want to hear the words "dick pic", Faith.'

Faith bursts out laughing. I can tell, at me. 'Oh, sweetie...'

At this point, I'd rather be back in the bistro – back to the long hours and crappy pay, where no one cares what I look like or wants me to talk dirty to them.

'It's vulgar. And creepy. In any event, I'm not interested in hosting a dating show.'

At that moment, Harry returns. At least, I hope he wasn't in the room when I called him creepy.

'It's not a dating show,' he insists, abandoning the

theatrics of earlier. Taking the SC6 contract in one hand, Harry perches on the thick arm of my squeaky chair. Leaning in, he reads aloud. 'The show will be crafted as a revolutionary fusion of our appetite for food... and our hunger for passion.'

Why is he is sitting so close to me?

Thankfully, I checked with Faith when he was out of the room and she confirmed I smell only of Elizabeth Arden Green Tea Scent. 'Refreshing', it said on the label, so I'd sprayed it liberally before I left the flat.

'Harry, that's great. Only, I'm not up for a revolution, thanks all the same.' Annoyingly, I like that this makes him laugh. 'I'm a chef,' I go on, softer. 'I'm not whatever this... *Eat Me* requires me to be.'

'I don't know, I heard your performance the other day was thoroughly entertaining,' Harry encourages. 'Witty. Irreverent. Seductive. Shall I go on?'

Hmm.

'There wasn't a performance, Harry. There was a conversation between Faith and me that got taken out of context. And now here we are.'

'Here we are,' Harry says.

'We always talk to each other like that,' Faith confirms.

Harry gazes into my baby blues with his dark-as-chocolate eyes.

'So, the show is banter between two besties.' Harry's dropped the overly saucy bravado of earlier, which, now he's talking like a normal person, was sort of funny. 'Throw in a bit of cooking. Some man candy for good measure. What could possibly go wrong?' He flicks through the contract on his lap. 'Also, your pay has been tripled, and I've insisted on better residuals.'

'My managing partner agreed I can take a three-month sabbatical, if I want it,' Faith announces.

'It's a ten-episode season and filming begins in two weeks,' Harry says.

'It's meant to be,' Faith says.

'But... your career in venture capital?' I ask.

'Will wait three months,' Faith insists. 'Gracie, we'll be paid to hang out together. What will you do otherwise? Go back to chefing in a pub? Come on. You can teach me to cook.'

Everything is happening so fast. I don't know what I think any more.

'You really want to do this, Faith?'

'Yes!'

If Faith is willing to do this, perhaps for the hoot, but probably also to help me not lose my job, how can I say no? As she says, it'll be the two of us getting paid to hang out together. Two besties.

'Can Poppy be on the show with us?' I ask. I owe her. And if I get roped into this, I'll need her around to do her magic with my make-up. Plus, with her bonkers look and bubbly manner in front of the camera, she'll be a great distraction. Between her and Faith, viewers will barely notice me slaving away at the hot stove – for this performance, that'll suit me just fine. 'Would you be her agent too, Harry?'

'Poppy?'

'My previous assistant. She'd be great on screen for this thing. She's absolutely mad. In a very sweet way.'

'I'd be delighted to propose it,' Harry says. 'I'll get in touch with Timothy and co right away. Subject to Poppy agreeing for me to represent her, of course. Speaking of which, my terms are a standard twenty per cent cut. If you're both happy with that, I'll take care of everything for all of you from here.'

Standing up, Harry plops the papers onto the desk.

My scarf slips all the way off into my lap. Faith raises an eyebrow and I shoot her a look I hope Harry doesn't notice.

For reasons that may or may not be related to my outfit, we all burst out laughing.

'This will be fun,' Harry promises.

Fun...

It sparks a thought, and the thought is running away with itself inside my head. I could do with some fun in my life, instead of rattling around my kitchen at home by myself, baking snacks and cleaning furiously. Being unwelcome in other areas of my home, and in other respects.

Harry winks at us both and Faith beams back at him.

Fun...

Not as much as I imagine these two will have at some point.

But I'm up for fun.

9

By the time we finish with Harry, Jordan has texted to say he can't make dinner at home tonight. He'll be staying late at his office. I'm unsurprised, but nonetheless dejected. However, moping over my relationship with Jordan isn't my idea of fun. Instead of rushing back to an empty flat, I accept Faith's invitation and we pop to our favourite restaurant, La Petite Place Française ('The Little French Place'), to celebrate our new contracts.

Located just around the corner from Faith's flat, in Covent Garden, the restaurant straddles three narrow floors. Decorated with Moulin Rouge posters, the tables are tiny – very Parisian – and the wooden chairs a little rickety. The food is rich. The wine is fine. The service is typically French, ergo a bit rude, and charmingly so. The maître d', Gaspard is wrinkly-old and inscrutable and quite in love with Faith. We are seated at the best available table, in a private corner, by the window.

'To new adventures,' Faith toasts, after our wine arrives dutifully. We clink glasses. 'Now, darling, tell me everything.'

'About the show?' I say. This wine is going down a treat. Hair of the dog or otherwise, my hangover has passed. 'Didn't Harry say we're discussing the details tomorrow, with Joanna?'

'I'm asking about you and Jordan,' Faith says.

'Oh. Yes, that.'

Though I've hardly taken two sips, Faith tops up my glass of the wonderfully crisp Sauvignon Blanc. Two servings of soupe à l'oignon, the best onion soup I've tasted, with garlicky croutons and melted cheese on top, and a cassoulet of white beans stewed with duck meat are on their way. I drain about a third of my drink. Then, to my best friend in the whole world, I pour my heart out about the relationship woes that have plagued me for months.

Wrapped up in a nutshell, it doesn't take me long.

Talking to Faith, I'm not as emotional as I thought I'd be. It's a relief to let it all out.

When I'm done talking, Faith sighs. 'Oh my, darling. You can't sweep this under the carpet. You'll wither on the vine. Better to rip off the Band-Aid, if it comes to that.'

'Do you think it will come to that?'

When Gaspard shuffles over with our starters, we pause our conversation.

'Personally, I don't see much point in having a partner you're not having sex with…' Faith carries on.

The soup looks delicious. And too hot to dive into just yet.

Jordan and I aren't married. There's no children to think of. The way things are between us, we barely qualify as friends. If we're not having sex, what is the point of us?

'However, the only people who know what's what in a relationship are the people in it. You and Jordan need to talk.'

'We do…'

'No matter what, I'm here for you, Gracie. Always.'

My phone rings. It's Poppy. She's heard from Harry – I'd given her the heads-up. True to his word, he bagged her a contract on the new show and she's signed him as her agent. Down the line, Poppy is over the moon she will continue working not just with me but also Faith. We invite her to join us at our favourite little French place and after Poppy arrives, late lunch turns into cheese and crusty bread for early supper. By the time we settle the bill, I've sat here for over four hours and, between three of us, we've polished off four bottles of wine.

Not half as inebriated as last night, I'm still more than tipsy by the time I get into a cab and head home, wearing my big, old and hideous charity-shop grey coat, that I don't lose on the way – I must hunt down my best black coat. I will have to check at work, the pub, the bar and then, if no luck, figure out how to track down a random Black cab tomorrow. Home safe, before I get into bed, I shower and put on flannel pyjamas. Jordan isn't home. He texted to say it'll be a late one at his office. Another big campaign.

Setting my alarm for 6.45 a.m., I resolve to get up early and talk to him in the morning.

I turn off the lights.

By morning, I'll have had nine hours' sleep. That'll clear the wine.

By morning, I tell myself, as I drift off to sleep, all will be well.

* * *

The next morning, I snooze through my alarm and I don't get up early. The afternoon and all of Friday, I'm at the station working next steps with Faith, Poppy, Harry and Joanna. Jordan is at his work, then out entertaining a client, then at a rugby day with Robert that ends well into Saturday evening. What with one thing and another, it's Sunday morning before we're together in the flat, awake and available to talk.

'Jordan, are you ready?' I call in the direction of the basement, where he's already working. It's 10 a.m.

'One minute,' Jordan shouts, his third time in as many minutes.

I pull the pan off the gas.

When he heard me out of bed and making myself a cup of tea, Jordan asked if I could make him one of my mouth-watering big breakfasts. Now, my boyfriend is behaving like I'm pestering him to eat.

If he carries on, breakfast will be ruined.

The eggs will poach to rubber.

The tomatoes will stew in their own juices.

I watch the sizzle cool out of the bacon.

On the kitchen table, in a cut-glass vase, is a glorious bouquet of soft-pink roses with sprigs of berries and dusty miller. The arrangement arrived yesterday, sent by Harry. Faith received the same bunch, as did Poppy.

I must say, it's nice having a proper agent.

Jordan makes his way up into the kitchen.

'Mmm, smells good.' He picks a piece of bacon from the pan. I shoo him off. 'Sorry, I'm starving.'

At the table, Jordan assembles a pile of weekend newspapers. He picks up the card by the vase. 'Who's Harry?'

'My new agent.'

'Ah.'

He flicks open the *Mail on Sunday*. I don't know why, because there isn't anything to it, but it bothers me Jordan isn't more interested at another man sending me a beautiful big bunch of flowers. He's sizing up a full-page advertisement of a grey cat leaping at a feather toy. Where my father reads the news, my boyfriend reads the ads.

'Here's the account I'm trying to close.' I scoop the poached eggs out of the boiling water. '"Pussy Paws, when only the best will do",' Jordan parrots from the sheet. 'Lame. But good for us the incumbent agency is rubbish!'

His toast pops.

'Can you believe the pet market is worth over eight billion dollars in the UK?' he goes on. 'Eight billion. For pets!'

Unless it's to eat them, Jordan isn't partial to animals. We had a cocker spaniel, Tilly, until I was twelve. I love dogs.

'Faith spends thousands on her cat Benny,' I say.

Benny is Faith's enormously sized and gorgeously fluffy tabby-brown Maine Coon, who lives with her on her second-floor flat in the middle of the West End. Something of a man about town, Benny wanders down Floral Street and as far as into the Covent Garden Piazza, by himself. Heading out when Faith leaves for work each morning, he later meows at the communal door until a neighbour opens it, then he's through the cat flap of the flat, home safe. Attended on by the local traders and tourists with pats and titbits of food, he's quite the attraction, if not what you'd call trim. An extraordinary personality, Benny's primordial pouch – his big belly of loose skin – swings side to side as he struts the cobbled streets of his turf. Six years and counting, he is, without doubt, the love of Faith's life.

'This Pussy Paws account is worth hundreds of thousands. When we win it, which we will, I'll have to make director. Robert and I are killing ourselves on this pitch.'

'Is Robert here now?' I ask, surprised, and not best pleased if he is.

I like Robert. I'm more than okay that he's often with Jordan in our basement on weeknights – I reason it's preferable to me wondering where Jordan might otherwise be of an evening. But if he's in my home first thing on a Sunday morning, I'll be annoyed – with Jordan.

Jordan studies me wearily. Or is that warily? 'Don't you think Robert has better things to do on a Sunday morning?'

I set a plate of food in front of him. Bacon, eggs, tomato, mushrooms, beans and toast.

'Thank you.' He stuffs another rasher into his mouth. 'Oh my God, that's good.' Won over by my salty bacon, chops full, he carries on, 'I mean, knowing Robert – as we do – he's probably muddling over the name of whichever dolly he's waking up to. Bumbling his way out of trouble....'

Usually, we share a laugh when it comes to Robert's romantic misadventures. Tales of mixed-up names, misplaced panties and women coming and going, not always in an orderly fashion, run rife. Robert is so popular with the ladies, he needn't bother behaving with any one girl in particular. He's so affable, he gets away with his behaviour. (Robert maintains some women chase the thrill. With Faith as my best friend, I've never thought to judge him.) This morning, though, I'm taking Jordan's comment personally.

'And you don't, Jordan?'

Looking across the room at me, Jordan stops chewing. 'I don't what?'

I wanted us to talk properly. It wasn't the best start, but surely a civilised conversation isn't too much for us to carry on with? By the look on his face, I believe Jordan worries I'm hinting for something more. As for anything amorous, believe me, I've given up.

The last time we had sex was over two months ago. Not that I'm counting, but it was my birthday. The sex was so horrible, it may not even count as copulation. I'd booked us dinner at our local Spanish restaurant, Del Marche, Jordan's favourite, where our meal was delicious and we shared a lovely bottle of Rioja. But a casual observer might have remarked, aptly, the intimacy was sorely lacking. Jordan checked his phone obsessively throughout our meal; I filled the empty space chatting with the waiter and, later, with the older couple sitting nearby. I'm not sure Jordan would have noticed if I'd upped and moved to their table, and at least the conversation would have been better. Although, the look on both of their faces when I mentioned Jordan had bought me a blender for my special day... Home earlier than expected, we nonetheless got ourselves naked and into bed, whereon Jordan proceeded to make love to me in a most perfunctory manner. To borrow Harry's remark, as if it were a chore. You want the gory details? There was no foreplay. Precious little kissing. Jordan basically dipped a finger and then proceeded to thrust inside me with his erection for several excruciatingly long, awkward minutes. About five, to be precise. That was it. Jordan didn't come. Of course, neither did I, but that isn't the point. Unless a man is so plied with alcohol as to be practically comatose or is hitting the age where erectile dysfunction is a medical diagnosis, men always come. On my thirty-third birthday, I had sex with my mostly sober, thirty-two-year-old boyfriend and he didn't even ejaculate. I sobbed silently in the dark. Jordan pretended to fall asleep. We never discussed it. Not then and not since. It's what Jordan and I do with our problems. We leave them to fester.

It had been many weeks prior since Jordan and I had last been intimate. We haven't been anywhere close since.

My toast pops.

'It's nothing, Jordan. I just meant that you're working and it's Sunday. Maybe you could take a break later? We could walk along the canal if the rain clears?'

As things are, it's not as if I'm not gagging for Jordan to wipe the table clear with my naked buttocks and take me unto him.

I think of Faith's comment....

What is the point of a relationship if there's no sex?

At our age?

When there's little else?

Because living with Jordan is more like having a flatmate than a partner – a crappy flatmate at that, given he's a lazy oik around the house and doesn't pay rent. (As agreed, he reimburses me the bills.)

And still I'm not ready to rip off the Band-Aid.

Right now, I need my energy for other things.

'Jordan, can I tell you about my new show?'

'Did you mention Faith's involved?'

Tuesday, I'd left several messages on Jordan's voicemail, including when I was out drunk with Howard and the others. In this instance, I'm relieved he doesn't get into the details.

'Yes, she'll be on camera with me. She instigated the whole set-up, I might add.'

'Dare I ask what this involves?'

As Jordan does about Robert, I often relay some, but not all, details of Faith's dalliances. Jordan may be unsurprised to learn that Faith has managed to spin off a sexed-up cookery show from the ashes of my old routine.

'We begin filming in just over a week and it's called *Eat Me*,' I begin.

'That sounds... racy.' Jordan looks up from his papers.

'The innuendo is deliberate.' I take a breath. 'As you said yourself, sex sells.'

Jordan nods with a puzzled expression, that could be condescension.

'So, what exactly is this show about?' he asks.

'It's a titillating cookery show, if you can imagine?' I've practiced this spiel inside my head a few times. 'It's basically Faith inviting a different date on to set each week and me teaching her to cook. We'll be our usual chatty selves and, to your point, it will be a bit racy... Obviously, I'm in a relationship, so I won't be talking about sex or anything,' I quickly add.

I'm only warning Jordan that this new show – the show we'll begin filming imminently and that will televise publicly shortly after – may include some spicy discussions that might reflect on him personally. Of course, the main banter will be about Faith and her man of the week. I'm there primarily to cook. And Jordan isn't expected to make an appearance – we're keeping his identity a mystery. (Faith suggested we could refer to him as 'Master J', which I protested was too *Fifty Shades of Grey* for my comfort – albeit that couldn't be further from what things are like between us currently; I understand Joanna is waiting for me to come around.) I've no intention of letting anything too personal about us become public fodder. I'll just be more comfortable if Jordan is fully informed.

From the look on his face, Jordan thinks I'm having a go at him about our non-existent love life.

In the right light, Jordan can look like a seductive cross

between a dark and stormy Tom Hardy and the sexily brooding Justin Theroux. This morning, the light must not be right. Frigid across the table, his tawny eyes seem soulless. Wishy-washy. His lips, pursed, reptilian. It's the dead of winter, but Jordan's complexion is otherworldly pale, like a ghost. Like someone who isn't really here – though I have been spending much time with the unnaturally tanned Harrison Hipgrave.

Meanwhile, I'm in my dressing gown and I haven't brushed my teeth.

'What I mean, Jordan, is that we'll leave the raunchy discourse to Faith, because she's the one with the date. And because she's Faith.'

Jordan pushes aside his half-eaten plate of food. 'I'm sure Faith will have a lot to talk about.'

Is he angry that we don't have sex or that I have broached it, however tenuously, as a subject?

Looking at me – and not his breakfast – Jordan adds, 'Sorry, I'm not that hungry.' He tucks the newspapers under his arm. 'I'm going downstairs to work.'

And off he trots.

10

Preparation for the new show rolls at record speed. Joanna is a force of nature, exacting in her requirements. Builders transform the set. Walls to an adjacent storage room are knocked through to create a dedicated dressing area in the expanded space, with plenty of room for our new SC6 sponsored outfits. The old laminate and pine kitchen is ripped out, replaced with elegant stone tops, white cupboards and a pastel-grey station tiles splashback. The clunky appliances are updated with Miele's best in class and all the pots, pans, crockery and utensils are brand new from John Lewis. Poppy, contractually appointed as on-screen kitchen assistant and unofficially as our personal stylist, takes Faith and I shopping along Regent Street for our inaugural outfits: classic for me, sultry for Faith, bordering on the ridiculous for herself. On set, it's all going on, even if I do have a few wobbly fits about the concept of this new format. Every time, Harry is on hand to smooth my nerves and keep me on track. On Friday, I invite my mother to London to visit the studio. Harry happens to be popping through at the same time. Easy-going and attentive to us all– it's honestly wonderful having someone dedicated to ensuring we are taken care of and primed for success – he flirts up a storm with my eighty-year-old mother, who laps it up.

At work, all things considered, it's going swimmingly. At home, I've hardly seen Jordan and there's been no change to our situation, emotional or physical.

Two weeks after our accidental pitch, we're on set preparing to record the first episode.

My doubts about the format have been tempered by all the fuss and care that everyone has been throwing at us – but not extinguished by the pressure. This time, there won't be blithe indifference for what we achieve. This show will need to be a recipe for success from the get-go.

Nervously pottering about the set, wearing a flattering, turquoise shirt with turned-back cuffs teamed with ultra-slimming Nicole Farhi black trousers, I remind myself: I've got this. And I've got Faith here if I flounder. Between us, we've definitely got this, is my current mantra. With her bag of tricks, Poppy has again worked her magic on my face. My blue eyes shimmer, enhanced by powdery creams and silvers over the lids. The blusher over my cheeks smells heavenly of raspberry. My lips smack of matte cherry stain. As he fiddles with his technical equipment, our cameraman, Jacques, looks up and comments, 'Tu es tres jolie.' 'You are very pretty,' he repeats in English, in front of everyone.

The glass shelving on the back wall of the kitchen has bottles of wine and boxes of cereal on display. While I appreciate this isn't a formal cookery show any more, I hope I'm not expected to be up here slurping on warm Chardonnay and serving bowls of Rice Krispies? I'm still unsure, exactly, what is going to happen. We're organised, but this show is unscripted. Of course, so was *Gracie Porter's Gourmet Get-Together*, but that was different. I know how to talk about food. But relationships? And sexy stuff? On television, no less? I'm distinctly less sure. The old shelves once held scales and some potted parsley. Although, I could do with a sip of something strong to calm the nerves, we're otherwise stocked full of ingredients. Whatever the penny-pinching Brian Bunce thinks of it, there's no skimping on budget for this programme.

I open the doors to our noiseless and glacial American-style refrigerator. Inside, front and centre, is a carton of eggs with a note 'You got this'. It's signed 'H', for Harry.

'Was it the eggs that got us into this?' asks a smooth voice from behind me, another American accent.

I whirl around and come face to chest with a handsome black man. He looks at me out of the greenest of green eyes. Seriously, they're the colour of jade.

'Toby Ellison.' He smiles warmly. 'Faith's – um – colleague. Friend? Date?'

I close the refrigerator doors. Of course, Faith talked Toby into flying in from New York to see her for a few hours on set, to be her first date on our fledgling production.

'Gracie Porter,' I hold out my hand. 'Faith's best friend.' Toby shakes my hand firmly and warmly. A good handshake. 'I believe you're known officially around here as her man-candy, Toby,' I inform him, trying not to giggle.

'What's she roped me into?' he laughs openly.

'A good question. Welcome to the set.'

Toby surveys the studio. An overstuffed red velvet sofa sits against the side wall, six professional-looking deckchairs face the kitchen set, and there is at least twice the amount of technical equipment – cameras, microphones, lighting and the like – than previously. 'This is pretty cool,' he says.

His gemstone eyes are unreal.

'Faith is just getting her make-up finished. She won't be long.'

Toby flashes me a smile. Also, the whitest teeth.

'I hope you don't mind me saying, Toby, but your eyes are incredibly striking.'

'Gorgeously green,' he replies, right off pat. Of course, it's me, the self-deprecating Brit, who seems bashful. 'They're called "Gorgeously Green",' he goes on. 'They're contacts, see?'

On closer inspection, Toby's pupils seem unnaturally sharp around the rims. Does everything look green to him? 'So they are. Are they strange to look out of?'

'Not at all.'

When Faith was telling me about the humungous size of Toby's manhood one afternoon, she hadn't thought to mention his fake green eyes.

'Do you wear them regularly?'

'Hell no.' Toby laughs heartily. 'They're just for the show today, so no one recognises me.' I smile weakly. It's a poor disguise. 'I know, but, hey, they do look good!'

Faith promised I'd be fond of him and I am.

'Are yours "Brilliantly Blue"?' he goes on, falling easily into the friendly banter of new lover buttering up oldest best friend. I let loose a small snort of appreciation. 'No, I'm au naturel.'

Harry materialises. 'Her eyes are stunning,' he says. 'Harrison Hipgrave, Agent to the Stars.' He extends a hand to Toby.

'Toby Ellison. Ordinarily, Mergers and Acquisitions. Today, I believe the term is, man-candy.'

Harry laughs loudly. 'Good to see you have a sense of humour. You're going to need it with these girls,' he warns jovially.

Toby laughs raucously.

To me, Harry whispers, 'Having fun yet?'

I'm having more fun than I thought I would.

No offence to Faith, but if I'd known it would make me this much more relaxed, I'd have got myself a proper agent sooner. Albeit I'm coming over in a bit of a hot flush now. Nerves. God, we're about to do this.

Harry brushes past me to go and chat with Joanna. His essence lingers. I've been trying, but I still can't place his scent. Definitely more woody than spicy. And not at all citrusy.

Before I have a chance to narrow it down, Faith emerges from the dressing room in a slinky black dress that skims her bottom and reveals her dimple-free thighs. High black boots hug her slender calves. It's apparent Poppy has also attended to her grooming. Faith's long blonde mane, often frizzy at the ends, is shiny-sleek. Her body is moisturised with bronzer, the small spots on her chin skilfully concealed. Her eyes, outlined with kohl, look exactly like a cat's – though the overall effect is full-blown minx.

Faith is first to bestow a compliment. 'Gracie, you look incredible.'

'And you, my darling, are an absolute vision. I'd kill for those legs.'

'You've warned me before.'

Toby kisses her hello, smack on the lips.

Faith brushes his cheek.

'Are we ready to do this, bestie?' She reverts quickly to me.
'I'm ready!'

All the old crew are on board. There's Jacques on camera, Lola on sound, Tom on lighting, James and Joyce on go-for. Other technical and prop people come and go. The new cameraman, Pugsy, looks exactly as you may imagine. Robin is back at the helm, though we all know it's Joanna, as executive producer, who's running the show.

Poppy crosses the studio. Her angelic face is overdone with colour and sparkles, her wispy blonde-dyed hair in pigtails. She's mismatched a rainbow woollen poncho with a lacy pink tutu, sparkly silver tights and ballerina pumps.

We're all here, ready to go...

Except I'm not. I may look fabulous. And yes, I signed up to this (almost) entirely of my own free will. We've brainstormed and prepared for over a week. But I'm not ready.

Seated next to Harry, in one of the professional-looking deckchairs, Joanna calls out, 'This is it, team. *Eat Me.*'

Someone yells, 'Ready on ten.'

Harry winks at me.

'I'm so excited, Gracie,' Faith says. 'Thank you!'

Robin begins the countdown. 'Ten. Nine. Eight.' Do I have the skills to pull off unscripted, on-action steamy? Time to give it my best shot. 'Three. Two,' so help me, here we go, 'Action!'

I'm standing behind the stone bench. Faith sits atop it, her long legs crossed. I'm nervous as hell. Faith epitomises calm, yet is brightly animated as we introduce ourselves to our future audience. A natural, she's already mastered the art of pretending the cameras don't exist and simultaneously playing up to them. As we'd practised – loosely, because the show is unscripted – we recount Faith's previous kitchen catastrophes. We let them know I'm on board as her culinary mentor. 'I'll be sharing some hot tips of my own,' Faith promises.

Poppy pirouettes into shot in her rainbow poncho and tutu, carrying a clapper board, her cheeks flushed soft pink. Faith slides off the bench and helps her steady it to camera. The board informs the following facts about our first guest.

Name: Toby Ellison

Profession: Banker (a nice one)

Age: 39

Height: 6'3"

Likes: Orderly English queues and sassy British blondes...

On a ding-dong noise of a doorbell, Poppy opens the false door at the side of the kitchen set. Toby enters.

'This is nicer than the Puss in Boots.' He launches a lively rehash of his near miss with the Golden Square brothel with Faith. They're taking to recording for television like ducks to water. I send them to the refrigerator to select ingredients.

After toying on-camera with the double entendres of 'tossed salad' and 'bangers and mash', we opt for a less salacious-sounding dish of pumpkin gnocchi (from a packet) and a fresh garlic and rocket cream sauce.

Faith and I don our aprons: a black lacy number for her while mine is a white cotton pinafore. Poppy escorts Toby out the false door. Plonked on to the red velvet sofa and cocooned in headphones, he's right there beside us, but he won't hear a word we're saying. A selection of men's magazines fan over an end table. Toby flicks open an *FHM* and when his eyes widen, Pugsy zooms in. Toby grins cheekily to camera. I know from experience it'll take us over an hour to produce content that the editors will trim to twenty-two minutes of showtime in post-production.

Over here in the kitchen, we begin to prepare the meal. Under guidance, Faith skins the pumpkin, cuts it into small cubes of orange flesh and puts it on to steam. Softening the gnocchi in a separate pot of boiling water, she and Poppy have fun scooping it out the moment it floats to the top. Without causing her eyes to water, but with knife skills that strike fear in me she'll lose a finger, Faith finely dices the onion and garlic. In a little oil, she sautés them until they are clear. On my instruction, she pours in the cream.

The sauce thickening, I take over. Poppy redirects Faith to a handful of wild rocket and a sharp, curved herb cutter.

'Careful,' I warn.

'I'm always careful.' Faith looks dreamily over at Toby, currently air-drumming to whatever music he's listening to, his green eyes closed. 'Rumours are true...'

Poppy giggles softly.

'You're alluding to rumours about handsomely endowed black men?' I finish.

Unexpectedly, Faith heads to the refrigerator. She returns to the bench wielding an exceptionally elongated purple aubergine that looks distinctly like what (I imagine) a black man's very ample penis might look like, if it were a vegetable.

'Good Lord!' I say.

'More like thank the Lord.' Faith passes me her phallic vegetable, which I drop immediately onto the bench.

Faith glides back over and returns with a medium-sized

courgette, a spindly-looking carrot and an uncooked, pork chipolata sausage. She lays them beside the aubergine – all we need here is a bendy banana. 'What tickles your fancy?' Faith looks like she's about to eat me. All for show. Such a pro. Meanwhile, I'm standing here like the stupefied new recruit.

Poppy clamps her hand over her open mouth.

I smile through gritted teeth. 'Faith, please remove these vegetables from my bench at once.'

As requested, she scoops up every last vegetable from the bench top, leaving the tiny sausage in front of me.

'Men, you may sleep easy,' she purrs sexily.

Pugsy pans in with his camera from me to the sausage and then back on me, up close. I blink. Frozen. The cream bubbles in the pan. Pugsy zooms in on the bubbling and back on me.

Behind the monitor, Robin looks as awkward as I feel. Joanna can barely stay seated. She motions for me to get on with things. Robin also gestures, but nobody says stop. Joanna almost flips in her seat!

It's Harry who thaws me. Leaning forward in his foldaway chair, his warm eyes encourage me – Come on Gracie, you got this.

Trying to appear, I don't know, sexily coy, but inwardly cringing, I announce, 'Faith, you do realise the metabolic advantage of meat over vegetables? You may be surprised,' I look scornfully at her oversized purple aubergine, 'but sustenance isn't all about size. It's about density.'

I pierce the chipolata with my fork and brandish it in front of Pugsy's camera lens.

'Gracie on fire!' Faith yelps.

'Sizzlingy. Like a good pork banger.' I drop the baby

sausage into the hot pan. 'Pass me the pasta. This sauce is getting sticky. Let's keep cooking!'^p

Joanna's grin stretches from ear to ear.

Faith slips in a few more racy innuendos. We finish plating the meal and Poppy leads Toby through to the kitchen, where the four of us banter over morsels of what turns out to be a strange but delicious concoction of pumpkin gnocchi with a creamy garlic and chipolata sausage sauce.

Harry winks.

Finally, I hear it.

'Cut!'

11

Joanna throws a party for cast and crew at Soho House after we wrap. It's my first visit to the iconic celebrity haunt. Harry, sitting next to me, is chuckling at my star-studded excitement.

Let me be clear: Soho House rules hold members' privacy sacred, and I'm not so audacious to ask for an autograph or take a picture anyway. But I'm keen to catch a glimpse of someone really famous – by all accounts, Prince Harry and Meghan had their first date here. By his interaction so far, Harry Hipgrave is acquainted with half the people in here, most of them bookers, agents and media people: the power players behind the famous fames. When he points out a hot young stud from *Love Island* and some prima donnas from *TOWIE*, I haven't a clue who any of them are. The celebrity-watching a wash, the banter a hit, it's an excellent night out. Champagne goes down a treat, and I don't overindulge. Poppy is bubbly, as ever, and Faith is on fire when she perches herself at the bar, all be she shoots down the advances of the *Love Island* hottie. If I didn't know better, I'd say she was wishing Toby hadn't had to catch a flight directly after the show.

The next morning, Harry texts me a picture of the Spice Girls, minus Victoria, papped arriving minutes after we'd left.

Damn, I recognise them!

I text back.

I'll take you to Groucho next time. You may even win Guess Who?

Harry replies.

At work later, and the following day, I'm preoccupied with the animation team, who are sketching us for the opening credits. With the first episode under our belt, *Eat Me* goes to air in just over two weeks!

More than usual, Jordan is conspicuous by his absence. Not only have we not spoken, but he's pulled a few all-nighters at his office. When I get in around 6 p.m. on Friday night, he's home, haggard on the sofa, the television blaring. By the time I've been to the loo and popped back into the front room, he's fast asleep. I shut down the television, place a blanket over his body and leave him to it. Saturday morning, I wake to an empty flat and a note saying he's on site all day somewhere south of Tooting for a client ad shoot.

And so the weekend whizzes in. Tonight, it's time for Beryl's murder mystery dinner party with my mother. I pack a small overnight bag and, after scrubbing the bathroom and vacuuming the floors of the flat, I head off to my parents.

I leave home just before 1 p.m. My travel plans will see me catch the Bakerloo Line from Warwick Avenue Tube station, change to the Jubilee Line at Baker Street, alight at London

Bridge, then board a Southern Rail train that shuttles me to Redhill. According to the online journey planner that I check dutifully for unexpected diversions, the entire trip should take me the usual one hour and twelve minutes. Instead, I cop electrical delays at Baker Street and Southern cancels two trains in a row until 'unplanned engineering work' forces us onto a replacement bus service.

Three hours of stop-start travel under my belt, I arrive at the little house I grew up in. My mother opens the front door.

'I was about to send your father to look for you.'

It amazes me, her steadfast refusal to call my mobile phone. Apparently, even under circumstances in which she'd send my father out on a search party. However, I'm in no mood to spark a lecture about all the possible causes of brain cancer.

'Come in, it's freezing out here.' The door closes behind us.

'Sorry, Mummy, I should have called. I've had a nightmare journey. I need a cup of tea.'

'I'll put the kettle on.' She rushes off into the kitchen.

I find Daddy dozing in his wing-chair. He startles when I kiss his cheek.

'Hello, Daddy.' He blinks his eyes several times and, half-asleep, places his hands on the arms of his chair, preparing to move. 'Don't rush. I'll drop my bags and be back in a tick.'

Upstairs, in my bedroom, is the same single bed with the same lumpy mattress I slept in since I turned ten. The painted white dressing table still holds the precious ceramic animals – miniature porcelain dogs, horses and cats I collected as a child. The bookshelf under the window is stacked with the classics from my youth, E.B. White to Lewis Carroll, *Charlotte's Web* to *Alice's Adventures in Wonderland*. My favourite teddy, Freddie the bear, reclines against my pillow. A lot of happy memories of my childhood are in this room. Though I don't do it as often as my mother would like, I love coming home.

I dump my overnight bag on the bed and cross the landing to the bathroom. I scrub my hands clean of travel grime, relieve my bladder and wash my hands again. The room smells of lavender. My mother places bowls of potpourri all over the house.

As I descend down the stairs, the aroma of boiled ham replaces the floral perfume. In the cosy kitchen at the back of the house, my mother prepares my father's early supper.

'Derek, are you sure I can't cook you any vegetables?' she says, as Daddy shuffles into the kitchen after me. 'I can boil some peas in a jiff. They'll be lovely with this parsley sauce.'

'You can cook them, Mavis. But I won't eat them.' For as long as I can remember, my mother has battled to feed my father greens, my father resisting her every effort. 'Tell your mother I'm happy with ham and potatoes, will you, love?' he grumbles good-naturedly.

I kiss his cheek again. His skin is soft, sun-spotted and crinkly. He smells of Imperial Leather soap and Old Spice cologne.

'Are you sure you won't eat with me, Grace? Not sure if you remember, but Beryl isn't the best of cooks. Not like your mother.' Daddy winks at me.

'Oh, go on, flattery will get you everywhere. You can have your ham and potatoes. Honestly, Derek, you don't set a good example for our only child.'

My mother fusses with a table setting for one and, after the kettle boils, bustles about making my cup of tea. She doesn't allow me to do anything in her kitchen, though she taught me everything she knew when I was younger. My mother is the reason I pursued a culinary career. When I come home now, it's nice to be looked after.

'Mummy, I eat my vegetables,' I laugh. 'Look at me, I eat everything.'

'You're a beautiful girl, Grace,' my father says. 'Just like your granny, God rest her soul.' I inherited my womanly curves from my paternal genes. Eighty years in, my mother retains her willowy thin figure. 'How's work?'

'Work's great, Daddy. The new show is... a lot of fun.' Now we've shot the first episode, I'm nervous how my parents will react. A matter for consideration in a few weeks' time, once it hits the telly.

'I told your father the new set is something else. They must have spent a fortune.' When she was on set, I'd mentioned the basic premise of the show to my mother, who I'm sure relayed it to my father. But, at that point, I wasn't to know I'd be asked by Faith, on camera, what sort of stonking big vegetable or little sausage winky I fancied for myself.

'Yes, it's all quite extravagant, for a bit of fun. What I mean is, the show itself is nothing to take too seriously. Apart, of course, from the money they've invested.'

My mother says, 'That's television for you.'

'Yes, Mummy. Spot on.'

'And how's the flat?' my father asks. 'How are things with Harry?'

'Harry?'

'Your fella.'

'Daddy, Harry is my agent.'

Confused, my father turns to my mother.

'He means Jordan.'

'Jordan...' my father repeats. They've only met twice. I understand the oversight. 'Well, who's Harry?'

'Harry is the lovely gentleman I met at the studio,' my mother says. My father both shakes and nods his head, not seeming much the wiser, not looking bothered either way. 'You are aware he's not married, Grace.'

'Who, Harry?'

'Yes, dear.'

'Mummy, what do you mean, "Harry's not married"? Did you ask him?' I've figured, given he hasn't mentioned anyone special, and by the way he openly flirts with everyone from the waitress to my mother – he does remind me of Faith – that Harry is single. But oh my God: what is my mother doing asking if he's married? Harry will presume she's trying to set me up with him. Which wouldn't be the first time my mother has, lovingly, and with the best of intentions, tried to help my love life. Which always makes me look desperate. Oh heck. 'Mummy, what have you done?'

'I haven't done anything. I'm just saying... that dapper young man, who seems quite intent on watching out for you, dear, isn't attached.'

'I'm not letting you near him again,' I say. For good measure, and because I'm embarrassed that I've enjoyed Harry's attentiveness, and I maybe have flirted with him a bit, now that I contemplate it, I add, 'Anyway, I have a boyfriend.'

'Yes, dear. How is Jordan? We never see him.'

'He's fine. Just busy with work.'

My father gives me a glance, a shrug, a smile. My mother continues pottering around the kitchen, with a beatific grin on her face. 'What outfit have you bought for me to wear tonight?' I'm served a properly drawn, overly sweet and utterly delicious cup of tea. I don't usually take sugar, so the sweetness is a treat. My mother makes my tea exactly as she did when, aged five, I'd race in from school to a milky, two-lumps-of-sugar cup of Earl Grey and a generous wedge of the most delicious home-made cake on earth. My mother's tea is so comforting, I've never thought to inform her of my adult habits.

Vis-à-vis my outfit for this evening, she reminds me I'm going as Satine Featherbag, seductress of the local shoe factory owner, Billy Bragalot. I shudder to consider what get-up is in store for me. My saving grace will be that the other attendees are all octogenarians. The worst I'll contend with is the endless questions about why a lovely, talented girl like me still isn't hitched.

'Come with me,' my mother says. 'Derek, here's your dinner. I'll fix your pudding in a bit. I'll just sort Grace with her new clothes.'

I follow her to the box room at the top of the stairs, where she keeps her sewing machine, winter coats, piles of her old school papers and dressing-up clothes for murder mystery parties. Plucked from the portable rail, my mother passes me a burgundy satin bridesmaid's dress, in a size 18, a fox-fur stole, with a real fox's head, real claws and plastic brown eyes, and a tangled pearl necklace and some clip-on glass earrings. 'I got it all from the charity shop,' my mother beams.

I get out of my jeans and sweater and into the bridesmaid dress. Several sizes too large for me, my mother pads it out with a flannel sheet underneath and pins it together with a new seam down the back. I refuse to wear the fox stole. My mother, playing the role of Lady Emily Whitstable, great aunt of Satine Featherbag, is wearing it instead, teamed with a frayed, golden threaded 1920's flapper-dress. I put on the jewellery.

'Ooh, I almost forgot!' Mother hands me a black feather boa and a matching clutch purse. 'Satine Featherbag!' she cries.

'We won't be staying late, will we Mummy,' I ask.

After my father is served his treacle pudding, we take a taxi to Beryl's, leaving him to the gas fire and his wing-chair.

Ten minutes out of town, Beryl's house is a big old pile of Edwardian red brick, with double sash windows and grandiose front doors. It boasts no less than six bedrooms, if only one bathroom and a downstairs lavatory, formal reception rooms and a proper library. Her husband, Gerald, had been a top lawyer in the City, from a long lineage of top lawyers. They never had children. I don't know whether because they couldn't or because Beryl isn't the sort to strike as particularly maternal. It's not really the thing to ask. The dining room features an open fireplace, a chandelier, centuries-old family portraits on the walls and a table seating for twelve. Everything in Beryl's home is opulent – all of it, past its prime. We settle in the dining room on cracked leather chairs at the table marked with the dents and watermarks from decades of good cheer. Outside, under garden lights, the pond is filled with leaves. My mother is forever worrying about the air quality inside Beryl's mouldy old conservatory, positioned directly off the kitchen, with its toxic fumes.

Tonight, six places are set at the table for twelve and everyone here is female. I see why my father made his excuses to stay home. In my memories, the hearth in this room was always roaring with flames. Tonight, it isn't lit. I suppose it was Gerald's job, to chop the wood and prepare the kindling and stoke the fire. Instead, a small electric fan heater is plugged in at the wall. The room, spacious and draughty at the windows and between the floorboards, is cold. Leaving my parent's house, I felt fat and absurd, swathed in a size 18 dress my mother padded out with a flannel sheet underneath. Now, I'm grateful for the layers of warmth.

Standing across the room is Miss Cochran – Sally, as she insists I call her these days – my mother's best friend and my old primary school teacher. It's apparent she's playing the part of Billy Bragalot, the footwear entrepreneur with whom I'm having an affair for the purpose of party proceedings. Sally is dressed in a gentleman's morning suit and a stick-on black moustache. I give her a warm hug hello.

Our host, Beryl, clad in a short, and somewhat raunchy, maid's outfit, is playing the part of Betsy the house servant. 'The maid with a perpetually sunny disposition,' Beryl says, without a hint of irony as she pours us each half a glass of white wine. 'Only one more bottle between us, so mustn't glug!' A tray of cocktail onions and bits of cheese and ham on toothpicks is on the table.

Sitting opposite me in an old wedding dress that's yellowed, Miss Haversham style, is June Whitbury, who owns the flat I live in. She's playing the long-suffering wife of my dear cheating Billy Bragalot.

Sweet old Angela Williams, a good few years older than the others, is wearing her usual attire of a white shirt and a plaid skirt, tarted up with the addition of a red carnation pinned to her chest and scarlet lipstick. 'I'm the sexy secretary,' she says, taking her seat next to June. 'This is a bit of fun!'

My mother was so concerned to be here to support her friends. As I look around the table, it dawns on me everyone else's husband is dead.

'Thank you for coming,' my mother whispers, as Beryl inserts a murder mystery dinner party game CD into the portable stereo set up on the table.

A man with a Vincent Price pitch and a dodgy French accent says, 'Good evening, Mesdames and Messieurs. My name is Inspector Jacques LeClue, and I must offer apologies for the late start of your little soiree. I regret to inform you there has been a murder on these premises.'

I gulp my wine.

12

‘How was your weekend? All good with your parents?’ Faith and I are sitting on the red velvet sofa in our studio, brainstorming the second episode of *Eat Me*.

‘They’re great. They send their love.’

‘I love your parents, Gracie,’ Faith says. ’I hope I look half as good as your mum at her age.’

It’s true. My mother has aged well. Slender, as mentioned. And it’s from her I get my striking blue eyes. She’s an old lady now, but when she was younger, she had an air of Grace Kelly about her, which inspired my name.

Faith’s mother is younger than mine, and also attractive, but in a different way. Faith won the genetic lottery. Her DNA is the pinnacle of her family lineage. Appearance-wise, it could easily have gone the other way. She possesses a myriad of other qualities that would’ve seen her through, had she not been blessed with beauty. But still. Lucky Faith.

‘And you survived Beryl’s party?’

‘Barely. I was dressed like a perennial bridesmaid. The wine ran dry during the first course. And at the end of the evening, sweet old Angela fell asleep at the table and wet her pants.'

'Oh my gosh.'

'We put her to bed in Beryl's spare room. It left me afraid of growing old, Faith.'

'Your parents are fit as a fiddle, Gracie. You'll be fine.'

After my mother cooked her unbeatable roast pork dinner for Sunday lunch, I'd struggled to keep up as we walked it off across Annie's field, my parents daily ramble.

'Daddy is a bit forgetful these days.' I pause and wonder why I hesitate. 'He got confused, forgot about Jordan and thought Harry was my boyfriend.'

'Ha!'

It pinches when Faith doesn't entertain the possibility of the notion. Not that Harry is my boyfriend. Obviously.

'How are things with Jordan?'

I'd arrived home to an empty flat, a pig sty, nothing like the way I'd left it. Dirty dishes in the sink. Cartons of mostly-eaten Thai takeaway in the front room. The place stank of prawn toast. Curtains drawn. The duvet was tangled on the bed and there was a pile of wet towels on the bathroom floor. I'd no clue where Jordan was – presumably, something to do with work. Exhausted from my journey – Sunday train timetables are no traveller's friend – I'd unpacked my overnight bag, tidied up, and hit the sack.

Jordan and I are like strangers passing in the night – except he's taken to routinely falling asleep on the sofa.

By day, I'm inclined to end things. And distinctly less afraid Jordan might leave me first. Alone, in bed at night, fear and doubts creep in.

I don't know what's happened to us?

'I got in last night, the flat was a tip, then Jordan rolled in half drunk and slept on the sofa,' I reply to Faith.

'Again?'

'Again.'

'What are you going to do, Gracie?'

'I don't know. But things can't go on like this.'

'No.' Faith reaches out and squeezes my hand.

Tears mist my eyes. 'I don't want to talk about this,' I say. I fuss about in my bag, looking for some lip balm and reapply it. 'Anyway... your date for the show this Wednesday, tell me, who is he?'

Faith cocks her head to one side and studies me before she carries on. 'Well. I was having my regular scale and polish, and my new dentist is pretty cute. Ben the dentist. Fit, blonde, great teeth.'

'He agreed to come on the show?'

'He asked me,' she says. 'Between spitting and swallowing, I'd told him about it. He seemed perfect. Now, I'm worried he may be a bit dull? Especially compared to Toby.' Faith's eyes light up, as they do at every mention of Toby. 'Even for a dentist, he's obsessive about the correct technique of brushing one's teeth. Gently applied. Not too much pressure. Two minutes to finish the job, every morning and every night. He banged on and on...'

It takes me a moment. I realise Faith's talking about cleaning her teeth.

'On and on? Every morning and every night? Does Ben the dentist recommend a circular or sonic vibration? Before or after your spitting and swallowing, Faith?'

'Um? Ohhhh.' She honks with laughter. 'Oh, Gracie, yes, we will have fun with this one!'

'You will, Faith. I'm just cooking,' I remind her, holier-than-thou and tongue firmly in cheek.

'Of course you are, sweetie.' She blows me a kiss.

* * *

Wednesday, Ben arrives on set in his dental lab coat. Faith is like an ingénue Bardot in an off-the-shoulder red number, her blonde hair piled high. My skinny blue jeans and crisp white shirt may not set any pulses racing, but they suit me just as well. Poppy's ensemble of blue leotard over purple tights is outlandish, even for her, but delightfully so. Harry is here to cheer us on. I hadn't expected an agent would come to each recording – but it's a comfort. (Do all professional agents spend this much time with their clients? Is Harry like this with all of the women on his wall? How would he find the time?) In any event, between the enthusiasm from everyone, and because I survived the first show with (most of) my dignity intact, I'm on top of the world before we begin our second recording. Timothy, our illustrious CEO, sits in the chair next to Joanna, a bee to honey.

Cameras rolling, Ben bounces through the false door and obliges with suggestive play aplenty. He waves his whirring, electric toothbrush about, none of us mentioning the word 'vibrator'. When choosing ingredients, he insists we slip him a sliver of the scientifically modified mega-hot chilli. Daring us to crank up the heat, he declares himself 'hot to handle'. After he chases Faith around the bench, I don't regret serving it up to him. Biting down bold as brass, within seconds, Ben's face inflames to plum. He runs around the set, his mouth on fire. I stop him with an offer of a drink of milk and he douses with a whole half-litre. We send him to lay down on the sofa to recover and Faith prepares to cook. At the end of the show, Ben, a total sport, rejoins us and we share a laugh over the incident and polish off delicious (non-spiked) Mexican chicken tortillas. Joanna hails it another steamy success.

Harry, Faith and I are loitering in the corridor when Zelda whooshes by and offers Faith a free reading. With a chuckle, Harry leaves us to it. You girls have fun,' he says, heading off to wherever he's needed next. Excited to hear her future fortune, Faith asks me to accompany her.

Zelda's studio is decorated like a gypsy's lair on a full-moon night. Darkened windows. Pitch-black painted walls, ceiling and floor. Above, soft-yellow lights – stars, planets and the moon – emit an eerie glow. Her stage is shrouded by heavy red curtains and is gaudily decorated like an old-fashioned caravan.

Zelda guides Faith up the steps to the platform. Faith drags me along. I drop into the brown leather wing-chair. Faith sits cross-legged on the rug in front of me. Zelda faces her from her three-legged stool. We're the only people in here.

Zelda reaches across her crystal ball that rests on a pedestal between them. She runs her bejewelled fingers over Faith's cheekbones. 'Such an interesting face.'

'Thank you,' Faith says.

'So, this new show is bit rude? You bring the men,' she looks at Faith, 'and there is cooking?' Zelda glances at me before turning back to face Faith. 'But is rude, no?'

'A little bit, Zelda.' Faith laughs. 'And yes, I'm the one with the dates.

'Please, tell Zelda all about this new eating show. Everybody talking. Big, big hit.'

I'm unsure whether our magnificent mystic, with her rich,

Hungarian accent, her jingly-jangly jewellery, her flowy satin cape and her untameable black wig is channelling the ambitions of SC6 or if it's part of her prophecy. I don't suppose it matters. I doubt Faith is regarding Zelda as a divinely gifted oracle either. A reading from her is all about the entertainment – and, boy, does Zelda, put on a show. Cabinets filled with tinctures and herbs surround us and a short table supports a Ouija board, tarot cards and what appears to be a book of spells. A camera hangs from the ceiling above, positioned to zoom in. Sage incense burns in a metal thurible on the floor.

Lettered in fluorescent ink on the studio walls are proverbs and sayings. *A broken watch is right two times a day. Do not mistake temptation for opportunity. Watch your thoughts, they become your destiny. No one is too old for fairy tales.* Throughout the studio, paintings of the occult – witches, angels and goaty-looking half-men – are faintly lit. I peer into the darkness. Rows of empty spectator chairs are just visible in the gloom. Zelda locked the soundproof doors behind us on our entrance. Paranormally sceptic, I'm a bit afraid I'll see a ghost.

Zelda rearranges the folds of her cape and kisses the amulet around her neck. It's deathly quiet. The lamp behind her casts grim shadows on the crevices of Zelda's face.

'Okay, so what happens, Zelda, is this,' Faith says, breaking the spooky spell. 'Each Wednesday, I bring a new man on set and Gracie teaches me to cook a meal for him. They're not really dates. It's all for show.'

'Ah, I know this,' Zelda says, with a wink. 'Tell me, who are these dates?'

'We had Toby the banker, a friend from work.' Faith omits saying she had him before the show. 'Today, we had Ben the dentist, my actual dentist.' Whose toothbrush ran audibly out of batteries as he was kissing Faith goodbye and she decided not to pursue it. 'Next week it's DJ Bassdog, a friend of Poppy's.' Who Faith is looking forward to meeting, having been told he has piercings placed all over him, for ultimate pleasure.

'What is bass dog?' Zelda shrieks with laughter. 'Is dog? Ah! Never mind. So, dates are not real. Okay, we begin.'

Closing her eyes, Zelda begins a rumbling chant. Ah-sha-ha-ba Sha-ba-sha-kala, she hums, over and over, raising her hands high above her head. AH-SHA-BA-KA-LA. At one point, she half-opens her eyelids and I observe her pupils have disappeared inside the back of her sockets. Faith looks at me nervously. She's lucky there's no mention of any storms of doom so far.

After a minute of such theatrics, Zelda announces in a booming voice, 'The spirits have spoken!'

'What did they say?' Faith whispers excitedly.

'My child, they speak of split hearts,' Zelda foretells. 'Jealousy. Guilt. Denial.'

'Oh my,' Faith mumbles.

'This is just a bit of fun, Faith,' I remind her, leaning closer.

Zelda is in full swing. She opens her eyes and rises from her stool to collect the metal ball of burning sage. Meandering around the caravan-stage, she swings it back and forth, chanting all the while.

When the air around us is thick with smoky incense, she sets aside her priestly contraption and takes to her stool.

'A damaged heart, it heals stronger.' Zelda glances at me. Her eyelids flutter as she takes Faith's hands in hers. 'I see good man. This man, I think, you know. Work man. Or, maybe, date.' Leaning in, Zelda bores into her crystal ball. But, apparently, the ball's not telling. 'Sometimes, the spirits don't talk too much.' She shrugs. 'But there is one man for you, not too long time. This, Zelda sees, for sure.'

Faith's face had lit up earlier when she described her first date on the show, with Toby. Zelda the Magnificent: darn good reader of people.

'I'm not sure I'm looking for just one man, Zelda,' Faith laughs. 'Can you check again?'

'She has a few more dates before we wrap ten episodes,' I add cheekily.

'Ah. Yes. And is few more men,' Zelda cackles. 'The future is clear. Few more men first.'

'Phew,' Faith says. 'That's okay then.'

'Okay. We finish now,' Zelda declares. She raises her closed palms to the theatrical night sky. 'We thank you, spirits, for your guidance. We wish you safe passage to the light.'

She flicks a switch and the room is bathed in brightness. The show is over.

'Thank you, Zelda. That was wonderful,' Faith says.

My eyes squint against the glare. When they focus, Zelda is staring at me solemnly.

'Eye is calm in middle of storm,' she says. 'You must yet pass through other side. You have the stone?'

The pink quartz Zelda gifted to help me through her foreseen spiritual downpour. It took a trip to the Taxi Lost Property office in Baker Street to retrieve the black coat I'd left in the cab after Howard's farewell. I haven't checked the pockets. I'm unsure if the stone is in there.

'It's stone of love,' Zelda says. 'Love isn't perfect, remember this, my dahling. But real love... you know it when you feel it.'

13

After the reading with Zelda, Faith and I go for coffee at a café around the corner. We rejoice how well our new show is shaping up and how great it is spending time together again. When I arrive home, on a high, the sight of Jordan pops my balloon.

'Jordan, you're home early?'

It's 6 p.m., so not early, as such. But early for him.

'Yeah, um, I worked from home a bit. How was your day?'

'Fun. We're getting the hang of the new show.' Wine glasses teeter in the drying rack. 'Have you been drinking wine?' Jordan will sometimes crack open a beer the moment he walks into the flat. But wine?

'Taste testing. We're pitching for a French vineyard.'

'Ah.' Two empty bottles sit by the bin. I'm guessing Robert's been here, and I presume he washed the glasses. 'Any good?'

'Not bad, actually.'

My apprehension dissolves. Jordan's merry.

'Jordan, while I've got you, I've been meaning to ask,

what's the deal for this ball?' I take the flyer from the refrigerator and scan the details, a reminder. The Sweetheart's Valentine's Day Ball, sponsored by Baker & Staines, is next week. The Jimmy Choo heels (and I) survived my drunken antics the other evening, but I haven't yet bought a new black dress. To be honest, I've been too busy to have thought about it much at all.

Jordan glances over. 'It's not really a ball.'

The flyer says otherwise.

'It's a work thing, a promotions event,' he goes on. 'No one is bringing their partner.'

'Oh. Right.'

In fairness, Jordan never invited me. I'd found the flyer on the kitchen table and assumed I'd be going. Not unreasonably, I might add, given it is to be held on Valentine's Day and we are, officially, a couple. I'd stuck the invitation under a magnet on the refrigerator. Jordan hasn't mentioned it.

'I know it's Valentine's Day,' he says, 'but we didn't go out last year.'

Again, technically correct. Last year, I'd cooked at home, filet mignon, and we had sex all over the flat. We definitely didn't go out.

I pass Jordan the flyer and he slips it inside his backpack. Out of sight, out of mind? He stands beside the table, eyeing the stairs.

'Jordan, we need to talk.'

'Grace, it's no big deal. I have to work, okay. I can't deal with this right now.'

Without giving me the chance to explain that Valentine's Day is the least of things we need to talk about, Jordan scuttles off to the basement. Our communication is awful. But this takes the biscuit. Upset – nay, angry – about his silly ball, his stupid underpants and that Jordan refuses to talk to me about anything important, I lock myself in the bedroom and call Faith to vent.

'Do you really think it's a work thing?' she asks me.

'I don't know, Faith.'

'And if it is, why can't you go? What sort of work makes their staff ditch their partner on Valentine's Day?'

I sigh into the mouthpiece, not as upset as I could be. Indeed, with Faith on the offensive, I feel, remarkably, defensive about Jordan's actions. Or about my decision to perpetually put up with them. At this point, with the demands of his job, I must assume the not-really-a-ball is a work event. And there is always the chance Jordan will surprise me with a romantic gesture when he gets in after.

'I never go out on Valentine's Day,' Faith adds. 'I was thinking the other day, I haven't had a boyfriend since university. Remember Carl?'

'Now married with three children Carl, whose heart you shattered when you refused his engagement ring.'

'Yes. I haven't dated anyone for longer than a few weeks since Carl. That was over ten years ago.'

'It's not for lack of offers, Faith.'

'Mmm. It's a bit for lack of good offers. Not everyone I want to sleep with is interesting. Or kind. Or wants to see me for more than a few weeks. Anyway, Valentine's Day. It's next Thursday, right? Want to sod it off and come to my place and order pizza?'

'Oh, darling, you're kind. We'll see. But thank you.'

'Well, ball or no ball, at least you bought new shoes.'

'There is that,' I agree.

After I hang up, I go to the hallways cupboard and check if Zelda's rose quartz is in my black coat pocket. It is

– again, so oddly warm to the touch. I hold it inside my palm.

I'm not as low as when Zelda gave it to me. I didn't lose my job and the new show is promising. Things could be better at home, but I'm having fun with Faith and, with Poppy's help, I look better than ever – if this is the eye of the storm, I'll take it. I don't believe in magic crystals, yet I clasp the stone to my chest, wishing it will all come true, and soon: I want to feel loved again. I want to push on through the other side.

When I go to bed, alone, because Jordan is still in the basement, I sleep with it under my pillow.

* * *

The following Wednesday, it's our third recording. Special guest for today: DJ Bassdog, real name Doug Walters. A DJ of Poppy's acquaintance, Bassdog isn't what I'd say is most women's type – his blue mohican hair-do, his studded neck collar and the piercings he has through his nose, eyebrows, tongue and, supposedly, his penis are quite a look. And yet... when he struts through the door to the beat of his own drum and bass music, there's no denying the man has the X-factor in spades. Requesting what could have been a rather mundane asparagus and parmesan risotto, much is made by us all about the tips of the vegetables, how the ridges on the end may work in the same manner as the piercings over B-dogs, a-hem, bits. It's all a lot of fun, and I don't force myself into it.

After the crew clears out, it's just Faith, Poppy, me, Harry and Joanna on set. Huddled around the kitchen bench, Joanna opens a copy of gossip rag *Chit Chat*. Several pages in from the cover is the official, studio supplied *Eat Me* promotional picture.

'How fabulous,' Faith purrs. 'Look at us!'

In the picture, taken on set, we're all dressed in black. Faith rocks a pantsuit, with a V-neck cut to her flat-as-a-tack tummy, no bra. Poppy is in a floaty little dress with silver sparkles and combat boots. I'm in Spanx – I'd never tried them before, but they are a miracle – under a slinky silk number, patent leather heels on my feet. There's no room for modesty. Each of us is at our most flattering, dazzling angle in this shot.

'Sensational,' Harry says.

He's standing closest to me, as he tends to do.

'You're all perfectly steamy,' Joanna says, delighted.

From the dressing room, I hear a succession of clicking sounds. The doors slide open and out steps a stranger, a well-built man wearing black jeans, a grey shirt and a scruffy grey leather jacket. A camera is looped around his neck and a satchel is slung across his shoulder. He's handsome, in that steely, chiselled-chin sort of way. Around forty, roughly Harry's age, at a guess.

Who is he and what's he been doing amongst our clothes and stuff?

And how did he get in there without me noticing?

'Alex, come and meet the team,' Joanna says.

Alex swaggers over, all hazel eyes, thick brown hair, cheekbones to rival Faith's. He's a good looking chap, no doubt about it. But when Alex grins hello, there's something sinister about it. Thin lips. His perfectly normally sized lips shrink when he smiles. You know the sort.

'Everyone, this is Alex Sutcliffe, the journalist behind this glowing article, and someone we'll be collaborating with for publicity,' Joanna says.

'Hello there, Harry,' he says. 'Ladies.' His eyes stop at Faith. Alex reeks of cigarettes. 'Harry Hipgrave, my old pal.'

Harry is first to precipitate a handshake. 'Alex Sutcliffe, it's been a while.'

'Still got your wall?'

'Indeed. I put the girls up there yesterday.'

Alex shows his teeth again and eyeballs Faith. 'I'll bet you did, old pal. I'll bet you did!'

I see fit to blurt out, 'You know Harry well then, Alex?'

'We were at university together.' Alex sizes me up. Grins again. 'For a bit.'

'I studied journalism for a while,' Harry says.

'He dropped out after the first year,' Alex adds, unnecessarily. Harry gives me a conspiring look. 'Word is you've built yourself an enviable agency. I must come and check out that wall of yours again some time.'

'Pop by anytime,' Harry says, but I sense a less than friendly vibe.

Joanna, also sensitive to the vibe, moves things along nicely. 'I'm pleased you two get along,' she says, and then turns to us. 'Alex will be pulling together some personal pieces to raise your profiles.'

'Usually, I take all my own pictures.' Alex pats his camera.

'What sort of personal pieces?' I ask, glancing at the copy of *Chit Chat*. Closed on the bench, the front cover is a collage of candid photographs of female movie stars – I won't mention who, as I find the whole thing distasteful – with pockets of visible cellulite on their behinds. The headline reads 'Celebrity Bum Notes'.

Liz is the sole journalist I've spoken with previously.

Though we chat about many things, she only ever writes about my opinions on seasonal produce, ovenware and the like.

Joanna observes my nervousness. 'Alex will play nicely or have me to answer to.'

'I'd very much like to continue my association with you, and with Titan in the US,' Alex responds, slickly.

'Good,' Joanna says. 'Ladies, I also have some invitations. Few big events coming up where the media will be snapping their lenses. It would good if you can pop in, get papped, and leave when you want. Or stay to mingle. Your call. But get yourself seen. We need to hype up your public personas pronto. Harry, I'll leave you in charge?'

'With pleasure.'

Joanna passes Harry a handful of envelopes. 'The Tricycle Club is opening this Thursday; you're all be VIP for that one. And I've pulled some strings to get you on the guest list with Drake this Saturday.' Joanna checks her watch.

'OMG, Drake! The Drake?' Poppy screams, over the moon to hear it's indeed an invitation to the famous Canadian rap star's London party. 'His lyrics are poetry, Miss Gracie.' She clutches the invitation Harry has passed over, a black envelope embossed with a flaming gold skull. 'Not, like, boring poetry,' she giggles.

'The press will be out in force for that one,' Joanna says. 'Don't miss it.'

She may have wangled us invites, but I don't think of myself as a VIP. Or, for that matter, a celebrity. And even if they are interested, the thought of the paparazzi snapping in my face with their cameras doesn't appeal. What if they want a full-body shot, and I'm not wearing Spanx? Worse, what if a gust of wind creates the perfect opportunity to capture my flashing underwear and I find myself on next week's Celebrity Bum Notes – then readers will discover what real cellulite is! I cover my stomach, my jelly belly, I'm sure is how the gossip mags would describe it, with my hand. With a hint of a smirk, Alex clocks me.

'Must fly,' Joanna says. 'Alex, let's keep in contact.' Out she goes.

'Pub?' Alex suggests, to all, but with his pretty, steely eyes landing on Faith.

'I can't tonight, I'm off to see a gig,' Poppy is first to answer. With a flurry of kisses, she dashes.

'I also have plans, Alex. Next time,' Faith promises.

Tonight, Faith's meeting Bassdog at his recording studio in Brixton, with plans to make some jungle beats of their own – she's promised me she'll report back on those piercings.

With Faith unavailable, Alex recalls a prior commitment and rescinds his invitation. 'Next time,' he says, slapping Harry on the back. 'Right, I'll touch base with you about the interview, Gracie. And see you again soon, Harry. We must catch up properly!'

When, with kisses for us all, Faith leaves, Alex is quick to rush and walk out with her.

It's just me and Harry left on set.

'I don't have any plans,' he says.

'Me neither.' Jordan is working late tonight.

'Groucho?'

'Oh, wow, Harry. Yes please.'

* * *

We go to dinner at the Groucho, where you couldn't swing a cat without hitting an A-list mover and shaker – Sienna

Miller, Grayson Perry and, though I don't recognise him by sight, when Harry mentions the name Damien Hirst, I know he's an artist. In a quiet voice, me leaning in close to listen, Harry regales me with funny stories collected over years in showbiz circles and, more personally, about growing up in Canterbury, until his mother died of cancer when he was twelve. How his father has remarried no less than three times since, and the collection of half- and step-siblings he's accumulated along the way as a result. He tells me his current stepmother is younger than him by a decade – Harry is bang on forty. About his 'second home', a flat down in Hastings, where he escapes London. How he jogs five miles along the Thames every morning and is also into clay pigeon shooting, when he finds the time. We talk about his brief foray into journalism. 'Watch out for Alex,' he says. 'He's got good connections, Joanna isn't silly. But he's a tabloid journalist. Be careful.'

I talk about my father – Harry jokes he's in love with my mother – about how Faith and I have known each other forever. I confess I'm still slightly scared of Joanna and how lucky I feel that everything is coming together with our show. I thank Harry for his contribution to this. It hits me that I don't have any hobbies or interests to share with him – no favourite bands, like Poppy, no succession of flings, or a cat, or Pilates and the occasional Thai-boxing, like Faith. What is it that fills me with joy, I suddenly find myself wondering, that's just for me? I make a mental note to at least enquire about joining the gym.

As we finish espressos, having shared a lovely bottle of Malbec over our dinner of chateaubriand with albufera sauce and truffle mashed potato, for two, Harry asks what I'm doing for Valentine's Day tomorrow.

Except to say he's busy working tonight, I haven't mentioned Jordan.

'Oh, well, my boyfriend has a work do, so not a lot, I expect. But it's fine,' I carry on, not wishing to elicit charity after such a wonderful evening, 'I'm not really into Valentine's Day.'

A lie I told myself every year that I was single. Last year, I loved Valentine's Day. This year, I'm trying to forget about it.

'Women deserve flowers every day?' Harry asks, cheeky grin.

It's a lovely thought. I laugh. And don't offer a response. Albeit, I want to ask Harry who he sends flowers to. I know from my mother he isn't married. He spends significant time with us on set, and he's been out with me of an evening now twice in as many weeks, so, probably, he doesn't have a significant other in his life right now.

'I best call an Uber,' I say, noticing the time is close to midnight.

'I'll book you a car,' Harry offers.

He settles the bill and we walk together out onto Dean Street. There'll be no mooching the streets looking for a ride home this evening. Minutes later, the gloved driver of a flashy Mercedes Benz sedan whisks me safely to my flat in Maida Vale, me marvelling at how my life became so glamorous so fast.

14

Monday evening, Jordan and Robert cloister themselves in the basement, working. They won the Pussy Paws account and are busy with a new campaign for cat food. I'm in the front room, about to view the first episode of *Eat Me* broadcast across the whole of the United Kingdom. Faith is on the landline with me.

'I'm so excited, Gracie.'

I pull a blanket over me. 'I'm worried.'

'Don't be silly, we'll be a hit.'

'A hit our parents, and all their friends, will see, Faith.'

This morning, my mother was on the phone confirming how she's told everyone from the charity shop and at church to tune in for the new show. I warned her, too, late, that the show is quite risqué. She just laughed and asked me how I thought I'd come to be here. With the thought of my parents having sex, I almost put down the phone on her!

'Your mother watched *Sex in the City*,' Faith says. 'Stop stressing. Pour yourself some wine.'

I hear Faith clunk down a bottle. Stupidly, I never thought to get any in.

'We're not like Sarah Jessica Parker, Faith. You do realise we're not acting.'

'We're dramatising,' she points out.

A fair point. I stow it carefully in mind.

'Is Jordan watching with you?'

'No.'

'Working?'

'Downstairs.'

'Shame...'

'Not necessarily...'

The first episode, airing any minute now, will include the incident with the chipolata – I can't tell you the amount of times I've wished I'd picked up the damn courgette.

'Too late now. It's starting.'

On the television, the opening credits in cartoon format, with catchy piano riff, roll. We had several sittings with the animators, but this is the first time we're seeing the finished product. Faith is drawn as toothpick-thin with masses of blonde hair, wearing a barely-there red skirt. She sits atop the bench, her long legs dangling. Poppy, delightfully pixie-sized by comparison, is in a prima ballerina outfit and has drawn-on rainbow wings, with which it appears she can fly around the set. The head on my caricature is sort of bulbous, but my blue eyes are spectacular. I'm at the bench, stirring a steaming pot with a big wooden spoon. My body is mostly obscured, however, my boobs appear much perter than in person. I can't complain.

'We're like the Simpsons, only cuter,' Faith gushes down the line.

On screen, Poppy flutters about on her pixie wings as our

names roll over the top of this sensational scene. At the sound of a doorbell, a handsomely drawn black man, with jade-green gemstone eyes, steps through the door.

'Toby,' Faith sighs, 'I miss him.'

Faith and he have texted since he visited for the first show – with Faith being on a sabbatical, not about venture capital stuff.

'Never mind, here's Ben the dentist and his electric hands,' I say.

In a nod to future episodes, in the promo, cartoon Ben is a pinhead with a ballooned white lab coat and spinning electrical toothbrushes as his hands. As he bounds at Faith – for reasons unknown, his feet are giant springs – my character pops an entire chilli in his mouth. Ben's cartoon head explodes.

Faith and I erupt into hysterics.

Poppy exits the animation with a flying, mid-air somersault and returns leading a… creature. Oh my gosh. A cartoon beast, with the head of a man, a Mohican hair-do and – oh my – a dog-like body. A tail, and EIGHT pierced nipples.

'DJ Bassdog, in da house,' I boom, sounding very much like a 300-pound MC from Detroit.

'Goodness me,' Faith mumbles.

'You had sex with that,' I remind her childishly. Faith had rung me on Valentine's Day after her visit to Bassdog's studio to confirm that yes he was indeed pierced everywhere. On screen, Bassdog sniffs at the hemline of Faith's short red skirt. 'Was it the big drooly tongue that won you over, darling?'

'The piercing on the big drooly tongue, if you must know,' Faith replies evenly. Faith had also confided that those piercings were very much for her pleasure. 'Not jealous, are we?'

I was asleep when Jordan got in after his ball, but he had

brought me home chocolates, perfume and flowers from the evening, and we'd laughed about him not actually buying them in the morning. No sex, obviously – though that wasn't a disappointment.

To be perfectly frank, I'm worried I may be losing my libido.

I hear Faith take another gulp.

'Faith, I don't have any wine.'

I'd had a quiet weekend in, while Jordan worked at the office almost round the clock, again. I started and finished a second-hand book my mother bought me, *The Rosie Project*. Saturday evening, thinking a glass of Malbec would go down well, I'd discovered the few bottles of red I'd stashed were gone. The white wine I was sure was in the refrigerator door was also absent.

'I'll have some for you,' Faith says. 'I'm getting quite trolleyed.'

I pop into the kitchen. With one ear strained on downstairs, I hear Jordan and Robert communicating about consumer surveys and market penetration. They show no signs or interest in coming up – and I deliberately haven't reminded Jordan tonight is the launch. If I can get away with him giving me his stock-standard level of interest, at least for this first episode, with the little sausage, I'll be happy with that. I check the kitchen cupboard for booze. Cream sherry and tawny port aren't appealing. I return to the front room, sans alcohol, and take my seat on the sofa. On the television, Faith appears in the flesh.

'You look like Giselle Bundchen,' I say. On screen, she's even more mesmerising than in real life. 'Faith, you look like a supermodel.'

The camera pans in and Faith smiles seductively into the camera.

'Oh no, my nose!' she howls into my ear. I hear a quick succession of swallows.

'What about it?'

'It's ginormous!'

It's not. It's the television angle – I had the same shock the first time I saw my backside on the small screen. Faith has a Princess Diana type of nose. She's beautiful, and so is her nose. Even magnified by the television.

'It's just the angle, Faith. Your nose is perfect.'

'Are you sure?'

'Darling, you are perfect.'

Faith says, very quietly, 'Gracie, thank you.'

We natter throughout the first block of advertisements. A promo for a furniture clearance sale, a jingle for a steam-cleaning vacuum, then an ad for another new dating app. When the show returns, I'm almost beginning to enjoy myself, sitting here watching our antics on the telly, as I giggle with Faith down the line. An awful grinding sound interrupts our call. Grrnnnnnnn.

I shall explain. When Jordan moved in, he insisted on setting up my landline to make free calls via the Wi-Fi. I've never once had cause to use it, but, guaranteed, whenever Jordan is downstairs on his computer working or playing a shoot-em-up multi-player game that sucks the bandwidth, it'll be my phone call with my mother or Faith that's scrambled.

'Jordan, are you on the internet?' I shout in the general direction of downstairs, without getting up.

With some indignation, Jordan shouts back, 'We're working.'

I heard the sound of machine guns killing zombies start up moments ago.

'I'm on the phone with Faith,' I call back. 'We're watching the first episode of our new show. Whatever you're doing, will you please clear the line!'

The line clears.

'Sorry about that,' I say to Faith.

'It's okay.'

I settle back against the comfy cushions on the sofa.

Jordan walks in front of the television, Robert in tow. Instantly, I grab the remote and mute the sound.

'Um, yes, boys? What do you want?' I try to sound casual, but my voice is clippity-clop. 'Your sausage rolls are cooking. I'll bring them down when they're ready. There's no need to mill around.'

'We're sorry,' Robert says, their faces sheepish. 'We didn't know.'

'I forgot,' Jordan admits. He seems sincere. Pity his timing is wrong.

'It's fine. Boring cooking stuff, really. I know how hard you're both working.' I glance at the television. 'Go on, the pair of you. I'll bring the food down in a bit.'

'Let them watch,' Faith says in my ear. She's tipsy.

The boys have turned to face the television, where Faith is licking a spoon of cream. Robert's jaw drops open.

'Who's that?'

'My best friend.'

He looks at Jordan. 'Cat lady?'

'Sorry?' I say.

'Didn't you say you'd ask Faith if we can borrow her cat?' Jordan reminds me.

He'd asked if he could borrow Faith's cat – something to do with the new account. I'd said I'd ask, but I forgot.

'We told the client Robert has a cat.' Jordan's posture tenses.

'I'd quite like a cat,' Robert says.

'We need to really get what it is to be a cat for this pitch,' Jordan explains. 'Would you ask Faith if we could borrow it tomorrow night?'

'Him,' I hiss, covering the phone. 'Benny, in fact. Not "it".'

I check the goings on on the television. Depending on how this has been edited, Faith is shortly to return from the refrigerator holding her stonking big aubergine. I probably have about one minute before I get going with my chipolata.

'Faith, remember I asked you about us cat-sitting Benny, so Jordan can get some cat-familiarity for a new account? Is that still okay?'

'Jordan hates cats. I didn't agree to anything of the sort.'

'Perhaps tomorrow?' I nod at Jordan. I need to wrap this up and get rid of them. In my ear, Faith warns I'm starting to get on her nerves. 'Yes, I'm sure,' I agree.

'Boys, it's all fine, cat-wise. Go on, scoot.'

They ignore me in favour of watching Faith comparing the length of the carrot to the chunkier courgette. Thank heavens I shut off the sound!

'What are you cooking?' Jordan asks.

'Gnocchi.' I think fast. 'But Faith's a terrible cook. The worst. She doesn't know a carrot from a courgette. I'm teaching her all sorts.'

'I wouldn't mind that she can't cook,' Robert grins.

Faith is clearing all the vegetables off the bench top as a smell of almost-burning pastry wafts into the front room – perfect timing.

'Boys. Faith and I are trying to watch this in peace and your sausage rolls smell like they're done. Grab them from the oven, Jordan, will you? Now. Before they burn.'

On the promise of food, Jordan and Robert retreat to the kitchen. Emptying the oven, they disappear to the basement in the nick of time.

'Faith, I'm so sorry, I couldn't get Jordan out of the room. He was watching. With Robert.'

'I want to meet this Robert one day. You always say he's my sort. Why have you never introduced us?'

'Because... I don't know, Faith. It just... hasn't happened.'

'What's this about my Benny Boo?' Faith carries on. She sounds faintly cross.

How did I get roped into this?

'Jordan needs a cat to impress his cat food client? I don't know. He asked me to ask you if he could cat-sit Benny. I forgot.'

'Is it for Royal Canin?'

I tell her the campaign is for Pussy Paws.

'Benny only eats Royal Canin, so there's no point.'

'Benny eats ham sandwiches from tourists,' I object.

'But when it comes to cat food, he's discerning. What can I say? He's a cat.'

'Can I please borrow him anyway? Or could Jordan and Robert perhaps visit at yours tomorrow? You just asked why you've never met charming Robert...'

'Tempting as that is, I'm out tomorrow. So I suppose, seeing as I'm your best friend, and I'd do anything for you, Benny may have to have a sleepover. Though I'm really not sure about any of this. Who borrows a cat?'

'Robert genuinely adores cats, and I promise I'll look after him. One night.' I lower my voice. 'Faith, I am sorry to have put you on the spot. You know I'm not in a great place with Jordan. I'm considering... other options. But, right now, I don't need a blow-up with him. I can collect Benny from you tomorrow after work and return him safe and sound the next day?'

'One night,' Faith concedes. 'And, Gracie, I'm holding you responsible.'

'Thank you so much, you truly are my best friend, and I'd do anything for you, too. You know this.'

The closing credits roll on the screen.

The first episode is done. Aired. We made it.

Faith chugs what must be the last of her wine.

'Gracie?'

'Hmm?'

'I think Jordan's been a terrible boyfriend lately. He takes you for granted and doesn't know a good thing when he sees it. Ending things may be for the best, I don't know. Only, I don't want you hanging your hopes on "other options". You see, darling?'

'Faith, what are you talking about?'

I know she's talking about Harry. I've not dared mention to her I may be developing a crush on our agent. But I know this is her point. When I'd asked the other day if Faith had noticed how nice Harry smells, she'd stared at me suspiciously and asked if it was perhaps his pheromones getting to my senses.

'Oh, I'm quite drunk...' Faith stalls.

We are cut off when Jordan returns to messing about with the internet.

15

I'm putting the kettle on to make my morning cup of tea when my mother calls. After I collect the receiver from my bedroom side table, she launches immediately into a bubbly review of the show. Full of a cold, my father had fallen asleep and couldn't be roused properly last night. But not to worry, she'd taped it on their VHS – I'd bought them a smart TV at Christmas, which my father has mastered and my mother, God love her, has not. They'd watched episode 1 together first thing today.

'It was quite a performance, Grace,' she finishes. 'It's not really a cookery show any more, is it, dear?'

'No, Mummy. I don't suppose it is.' I finish making my cuppa and sit at the table. Bracing myself, I take a small, steaming hot sip. 'What did Daddy think? Was he completely horrified?'

'Whatever do you mean, dear? Your father and I found it a hoot! Although, we didn't know you had it in you, Grace – this acting business.' If my parents choose to believe I'm an actress, I won't set them straight. They don't need to know our new show is more theatrical exposé. 'And isn't Faith daring. I say! What about her job at the bank?'

'Mummy, Faith hasn't worked at the bank for years. She's on sabbatical from her office job.' I don't want to get into a discussion about venture capitalism. I can't explain it properly, and I require caffeine before trying. 'However, I'm pleased to report the station is paying us quite well. More than I earned previously.'

'Oooh, that is good news. Derek, Grace has had a pay rise.' I hear my father mumble approval. 'A big one, dear?'

I tell her my wages have tripled. My parents would be aghast to learn how much I earn and how little I save. My mother cooks everything at home from scratch, shops second-hand for books and clothes and, aside from newspapers, they have few wants. The price of train tickets to London these days astounds my mother. She'd faint if she discovered how much I spend on lunch from Pret.

'Congratulations. And to Faith. Such a lovely girl.' In the background, my mother is scraping breakfast together as we talk. Most likely, bacon and eggs – my parents will walk it all off later. 'Before I forget, we're running a charity cake sale at the shop this Saturday morning. I'm baking a Victoria sponge. June is on for her famous apple turnover. Sally is bringing vegan beetroot cupcakes – not sure how well they'll sell. It's short notice, dear, but would you care to join us? Bit of an early start at 10 a.m. but there'll be champagne nonetheless, and I believe Angela's daughter, Janet, will pop by, so it won't be just us old ducks.'

After the relative success of Beryl's dinner party, my mother seems keen to loop me into her social calendar. She's not getting any younger. I want to enjoy my time with her.

'I don't mind you old ducks. What can I bring?'

'Just yourself. Will you stop the night?' She doesn't bother asking about Jordan. Twice in eighteen months. I guess she's given up.

'I have to be back in London for a work party on Saturday evening,' I say. 'But I'll stay for lunch.'

'Did I tell you Angela thinks Janet may be pregnant?'

'So, no champagne for Janet at 10 a.m.?'

'Ha! Well, that will be the tell... I won't go on.'

'I need to get to the studio, Mummy.'

'How is that lovely young man, Harry? Will he be on set today? He's still not married, presumably?'

'Mummy...'

'I'm just saying...'

'I know exactly what you're saying and I need you to stop please. And I have to go. Love you. And to Daddy.'

'Love you, dear. Congratulations on the new show. See you Saturday.'

When I hang up, I'm a bit annoyed at my mother for sparking the thought I might fancy Harry.

There is his general all-round-nice-guy behaviour. There is his, apparently, extra-special-attentiveness to me, in particular – my mother noticed it when she was on set weeks ago and, since then, I can't help but notice the way Harry stands close by me, telling me stories that make me laugh. There's also the lingering eye contact between us that's swept in, that I'm almost certain Faith has started to catch onto. Dinner at the Groucho.

After Faith's passing comment on the phone last night, I'm worried I've been errantly carried away by flights of fancy. That Harry is just being my agent, a fixer, and I think it's fair to say, a friend.

I don't need my mother encouraging me – and I don't like

that Faith is being discouraging. Though, with all the wine Faith consumed last night, it's crossed my mind she won't remember saying anything on the matter whatsoever.

I have some fruit and porridge, shower, dress and catch the Tube into town.

At the studio, it's only Faith and I in our dressing room, taking stock of our wardrobe before Poppy takes us out shopping to buy more clothes. Faith is first to revive our conversation.

'Darling, what's all this flirting with Harry?' she asks me directly. So much for her forgetting.

Today, she's wearing wide-legged russet trousers and a grey, woollen roll-neck sweater. Her hair is in a loose French braid, her face bare.

'I don't flirt with Harry.'

Faith raises an eyebrow. 'Okay. But you are encouraging him to flirt with you. Gracie, what's going on?'

'Does he?' I hadn't noticed,' I say, playing it cool.

'Gracie, he flirts incessantly, of course you've noticed.'

I rest awhile with the confirmation Harry flirts with me incessantly.

'It would make my mother happy if we ended up together.'

'Happy or jealous?'

We both giggle.

'Well, she's married. And, Faith, I have a boyfriend. Things may not be great between us, but I'm in a relationship. I'm not planning an affair. It's a bit of harmless flirting, that's all.'

Faith ponders this. 'I suppose so.'

I intended my demurral to alleviate her concerns, not launch a series of new ones in my head. Does Harry shower me with attention incessantly, because it's harmless – does he flirt with me the same way he flirts with my mother?

'You were far from enamoured when we first met him,' Faith carries on. 'You called him creepy. And said his Wall of Fame was more like the Wall of Shame!' She cackles at the recollection.

'Yes, well, we're up there too now,' I remind her.

'That we are.'

'Faith. I don't want to talk about this any more.'

'Okay. But don't forget Harry is our agent. Don't complicate things.'

But Faith can sleep with anyone she likes who happens to be on our show?

She changes the subject. 'Speaking of which, what on earth were you on about with Benny last night?'

Oh golly, the cat.

I attempt to explain about Jordan and Robert wanting to cat-sit. I don't really understand what they hope to achieve. Something about needing to understand the nuances of cats so they can sell cat food. Eventually, Faith agrees I can collect Benny from her place after we wrap and return him to her tomorrow evening. She insists he must stay inside the flat at all times – and if anything happens to him, she will kill me.

* * *

We shop. We shop until my feet ache and my arms are weighed down by bags of new clothes. When we are done, we take a cab to Faith's flat, where I hold the car until Faith bundles Benny into his carry cage and onto on my lap in the backseat. Beside me, she piles in all of his necessities: a litter tray, a bag of food, toys and, for good measure, his cat-nip-banana that gets him stoned.

It's only after we drive off, me gripping Benny's cage for dear life, that I realise I should have passed the bags of my new clothes to Poppy, who'd taken hers and Faith's back to the studio in another taxi. After all the traipsing about in the shops and trying things on, we were all worn-out to think. Poppy whizzed us through what felt like every boutique and chain store between Carnaby Street and Selfridges. I'd purchased slimming Seven denim jeans and an assortment of pretty dresses, skirts and tops from Ted Baker, with accessories to match. All of it on the company tab.

Home to Maida Vale, Benny and everything else transported in several missions back and forth from the kerb, I flop myself onto the sofa.

Jordan isn't in yet.

From the floor, there's a soft meow. I look down and Benny stares up at me through the slits in his carry cage with his gorgeous green eyes. I unhinge the latch and he steps tentatively out onto the rug. He lets loose a blood-curdling howl. I don't speak cat, but his message is clear. This is not my home and you are not my mummy. In a flurry, I offer him special lactose-free cat milk and some of his favoured Royal Canin pellets, all of which he refuses in favour of exploring.

He pokes about behind the curtains before crossing the front room to sniff my shoes and claw on my doormat. Scampering off into the bedroom, he inspects under the bed and inside the wardrobe. He prowls into the hallway. Relaxing into his surroundings, Benny performs a big cat-yoga stretch.

I race to the basement and check that the windows are closed. When I return upstairs, Benny is in the kitchen crunching his kibble. He curls around my legs and purrs. I set up his litter tray. When he goes straight in and does a wee, I relax.

Physically exhausted from the day of shopping, I flump myself flat on the sofa. Benny's footsteps tap on the stairs to the basement. I assume he's also finding a quiet spot to nap. Isn't that what cats do – sleep?

* * *

I doze off. I awaken when Jordan bursts through the front door. I'm managing a clumsy, half-asleep, 'Hey,' when Jordan shouts at me.

'I can't believe you've done this to me.' He's beside the sofa, shaking with rage.

I sit up. 'Jordan, what's happened?'

'What's happened?' he roars.

'Go on then,' I growl back. I'm awful when I'm woken. I'm like a bear.

'Let's start with what you said about me on the television last night, shall we?'

The show. I've been dreading this. During our shopping expedition, Faith suggested I ought to warn Jordan about what I'd stopped him seeing last night if I was worried about how he may react. If Jordan is to take offence, best he hears things from me. It's obviously a little late for that. One of those horrible eavesdroppers at Jordan's office must have got in first.

'Exactly,' Jordan says, at my look of horror. 'I've been the laughing-stock of the office all day!'

Of course, there is the teeny-weeny sausage play that could, understandably, be interpreted to reflect poorly on the perceived size of Jordan's manhood. And in the promo for the next episode, the editors had cut to me teasing Ben the dentist about how electrical products could add some excitement between the sheets, which also sounded more personal than I'd meant it to.

'Jordan, it's just a show, it's all dramatisation. And whatever we say, my boyfriend is a mystery.'

'I'm Master J.'

Coming from his mouth, it sounds worse than ever.

'Faith says that. I mean, on the show. I—'

'That bloody show.'

I tried to warn him. When we started, I'd tried.

'Jordan, please calm down. I told you this new format would be a bit racy. You were the one who said sex sells.'

'And now everyone believes we're not having any!'

I have to think about this a moment. Of all things, it's my off-hand, on-camera comment that my boyfriend is too busy at work to give me much attention that has him riled? And from this, everyone now believes we're not having sex? I can't think of anything else it could be. Huh. Of all the things I was worried about... I suppose the sausage was no bigger than a fat pinkie – too small to be taken seriously. Or maybe nobody at Jordan's work was brave enough to mention that bit? I'm at a loss what to say. What Jordan is most upset about is true. We aren't getting boogie-with -it any more.

'Jordan, it's true. We're not having sex,' I say.

Jordan storms off into the kitchen. I expect him to disappear into his work den swiftly. Instead, he returns to the living room.

'Jordan, what's happened to us?'

I'm calm.

'It's just been a while,' Jordan replies. Not shouting. Which is, perhaps, an indication that all is not lost between us. That in his mind, we're simply in a bit of a lull. But Jordan makes no move to get closer to me. To hold me in his arms. Or take my hand.

I sink back onto the sofa, wondering if he's referring to the bad birthday shag, our mutually non-orgasmic sufferance, when Jordan reflects on how much of a while it's been since we were romantically engaged.

'We can't go on like this. I don't want to,' I persist.

I've imagined this moment a thousand times over, crippled with dread. Now the words have slipped from my tongue, it's not as bad as I'd feared. My eyes don't well up. There's no cold sweat. I'm just numb.

There is a knock at the front door. 'That'll be Robert,' Jordan says. He answers and Robert steps through.

'Hello there, Gracie,' he says. Sensing tension, he looks sideways at Jordan. 'You're not still grumbling over the show, are you?' he says, a cheerful rebuke. 'I told you, everyone's impressed you're dating a celebrity.'

'Not everyone,' Jordan says.

'Yes, well, not everyone matters.' Robert's holding sticks with feathers attached on ribbons and a packet of plastic golf-sized balls with bells inside. 'Is this a cat box I see here?'

'It is indeed,' I say, running with the diversion. 'I believe Benny is somewhere that-a-way.' I nod towards the kitchen and basement area. 'I'm sure, eager to get you both cat-acquainted, whenever you're ready.'

I glance at Jordan, who doesn't respond.

'We're ready now,' Robert says. 'Thank you, famous Gracie Porter.' He heads towards the stairs. 'Come on, mate. We've work to do.'

Jordan follows him downstairs without a word.

I'm too physically worn out to ponder it now, but it's an

interesting thought, Jordan protesting we still have a sex life. How long must we be celibate until it's more than 'been a while'?

Is Harry flirting with me because it's harmless?

I hear Jordan asking Robert if he'll pick up the cat first and Robert is cooing sweetly to Benny, just as Faith does.

I close my eyes. Within minutes, I'm fast asleep again.

I wake in the middle of the night shivering on the sofa, despite that Jordan, presumably, has covered me with a blanket and Benny the cat is snuggled in the crooks of my knees. I've woken from a nightmare. In my dream, I broke up with Jordan and went boldly forth to declare my love for Harry, who promptly confessed his love for Faith. Faith! When in real life, I've never seen him give her as much as a single lingering glance.

I know dreams aren't real, but I feel it so intensely – the humiliation. I'm irrationally furious, at Harry and at myself, at the events that just played out inside my head.

I slide Benny gently off my legs onto the sofa.

I'll admit, my subconscious was carried away with my mother's fantasy about what it would be like to fall in love with someone who wants to take care of me. Who makes me laugh. Who coaxes out the best in me. Who kinda makes me swoon. But after my dream, everything is clear. Of course, Harry is kind to me – he's literally taken me by the hand and settled me into the new show, as he'd promised. As any good agent would. Ignoring the silly-heart nonsense, I'm sincerely grateful. As for anything else, we haven't had a single conversation pertaining to romance. It's all make-believe inside my head.

I pull the blanket up around me. Starting tomorrow, I need to sort myself out. No more foolish notions about anyone. And no matter what's not right at home, no more jokes on television about my boyfriend – Jordan is upset I've made a public spectacle of him and I don't blame him. It was fun and games in the studio, but what was I thinking? Perhaps, he isn't the only one who's selfish and career-obsessed?

The bad dream has shaken me. I decide, best to sleep out here on the sofa.

Benny curls against the back of my thighs and begins to purr.

16

In the morning, my neck has a crick from a restless night without a proper pillow or a comfy mattress. Dragging myself up from the sofa, I begin my day by banishing all thoughts of me running off with Harry – and Harry running off with Faith. I resolve to give it one last shot to recapture the magic I once had with Jordan. To summon the courage for an honest discussion, wherever that leads.

In the kitchen, the milk is out, lid off. Crumbs of Weetabix are over the table and a half-drunk cup of coffee is by the sink. It makes me rethink my last-shot plan. But no. Things weren't always like this. Or if they were, Jordan gave me so much more in return, I didn't mind.

Benny creeps out from the pantry. Having abandoned me at some point during the night, it seems he's been sleeping in my potato stacker. He welcomes me with a rumbling purr. I crouch down and tickle his chin. I drop a handful of Royal Canin pellets in his cat-bowl.

Jordan is downstairs, working from home today.

'You up, Grace?' he yells up, hearing me pottering. 'I can't find the cat!'

'He's right here eating!' I clear the table.

Jordan races up the stairs. 'What? Oh, no. I need him to try the Pussy Paws flavours, so I can choose the best one for the ad.'

Benny doesn't look up from his bowl. 'Let him have his breakfast, Jordan. Also, Faith warned me he probably won't eat anything but his special pellets.'

Jordan darts over to Benny and lifts him, gently, but awkwardly, away from his bowl. 'Come on, furball, you want to try some delicious Pussy Paws canned food?'

Benny squirms out of his grip and bolts into our bedroom.

'Jordan!' I hand him a stick with a clump of yellow feathers on the end. 'He'll be under the bed. Go and coax him out with this. And please don't do that again. Let him finish his food and try to tempt him later.' Two straggling tufts of yellow plumage dangle from the ribbon, the rest of the feathers scattered around the flat. Presumably, from Benny playing about last night.

Jordan sighs. 'I don't think Benny likes me. I'll wait 'til Robert gets here.

'Cats are fickle, Jordan. Perhaps you will win him over with the taste-testing.'

'Thanks for arranging this, Grace. I appreciate it. It will be helpful.'

I'm reminded of Jordan waving at his clients as they whirred, bare-chested, under the disco ball the night we first met. His dedication to his work was so endearing. Maybe, it still is?

'I'm sorry about what I said on the show. I should never have put you in such a position.'

'I remember, you tried to warn me.'

'Still. I'll be more careful from now on.'

Jordan clears his throat. 'It's not all bad. One of the partners asked if I can could get a cheap sponsorship deal with SC6. I'm on his radar.'

This morning in the kitchen, the light's just right.

'I'll see what I can do re a sponsorship of our show. Anything else to make it up to you?'

I don't say this suggestively, just brightly. I hope Jordan doesn't misinterpret. It's too soon for us to jump into bed. The magic will have to build first, this time.

'We cleared the freezer out of sausage rolls last night,' he grins. 'You could top them up again? They are the best.'

'I'll do some baking this evening. Sausage rolls, mini quiches, anything else?'

'Those prawn things in filo?'

'Deal.'

'Maybe those chocolate dipped nut things?'

'My home-made florentines? I think I have a tin of them stashed somewhere.' I check the pantry and pass the tin to Jordan.

'Amazing. Thank you'

'Pleasure.'

We exchange awkward smiles.

Jordan disappears downstairs. Where else?

* * *

After I clean the kitchen and set Benny up for the day with

sufficient water and clean litter, I head into work, determined not to make a mockery of Jordan, or our relationship, for our fourth recording. When we finish, I'm satisfied I managed not to mention my mystery boyfriend. Joanna, however, is not best pleased.

'What was that?' she barks at Faith, Poppy and me as we huddle on set after the episode has wrapped. Alex Sutcliffe is here. Harry is not. He had other business to attend to. I missed him today. But, given my terrible dream last night, it's probably good he didn't show. He'd sent me a text, *Remember, you've got this. H.* 'You have a hottie from *Love Island* as a special guest and – somehow – this episode lacks anything remotely steamy?' Joanna determines.

The hottie was the guy Faith met at Soho House. I've not seen *Love Island*, but Poppy told me the contestants have sex with each other right in front of the cameras – Faith didn't sleep with Jerry, nor was she planning to, but we all agreed he'd make an interesting on-screen date. Jerry was well up for it throughout the planning process, though Poppy had warned that many ex-Love Islanders require psychological counselling after they exit the show. Today, on *Eat Me*, this poor hunk froze. The chemistry fell flat. Alex hadn't helped by suggesting, right before we started, that comparisons could be made between his gonads and pieces of fruit in the bowl. 'Will it be the oranges, the plums or will these saucy ladies be popping your metaphorical cherries in a bit, mate?' he'd quipped. For food, we'd cooked spaghetti bolognaise.

'I'll see what can be done in post-production.' Joanna rolls her eyes to the ceiling. 'Perhaps the animators can sprinkle some thought balloons to cover those silent patch-es...' She packs up her things to leave. 'And you were supposed to be an observer. Nobody asked for your opinion,' she swipes at Alex.

'Completely my fault,' Alex grovels. 'Joanna, I'm so sorry. I will of course make it up to you. I'll do a special feature, some extra publicity, before the episode airs.'

'Yes, fine. Good. You can run ideas past me in the morning,' Joanna sighs. And out she marches.

Alex is the first to speak. 'Pub? Perhaps we can put our heads together for ideas over a drink?' I noticed he smelled of whiskey when he'd arrived on set early this morning. I'd thought fondly of Howard, and less so of Alex. Extra publicity or not, I'd trade this two-bit journalist Alex in for Howard nicking my cooking sherry any day of the week.

I'm meeting Liz Martin at 5 p.m. today. At some point, I have to go home, collect Benny and all of his accessories, and return him to Faith. After all that, I'd quite like to sort things out with Jordan, once and for all. If we have to brainstorm story ideas, I'd sooner do it here and now and get it over with.

'Pub,' Faith agrees. 'Come on, Gracie. I need a wine.'

* * *

We catch a cab for the short ride from Soho to the Lamb and Flag pub, located in Covent Garden, almost below Faith's flat.

Alex gets a round in. 'Well, cheers to that.' He raises his pint of beer.

'Cheers,' Faith says, more cheerily, clinking her glass of wine.

I oblige with my tumbler of cranberry juice. 'I'm afraid I don't have any publicity ideas,' I kick things off with.

'I do,' Faith says. 'I've been thinking, how about we run a

competition in *Chit Chat* to find my next date? Wouldn't that be a bit of fun. Would that work, do you think, Alex?'

Alex's lips pull back to reveal his bleached white teeth. His nostrils flare. It's interesting how someone so undeniably handsome can appear so utterly unattractive.

Faith flicks her long, tousled blonde hair. She's still made-up from filming. Eyes smouldering. Lips juicy red. Her outfit is a sexy rock-chick ensemble from All Saints. In this quaint little pub in the heart of Theatreland, her local, she stands out by a mile.

After we finished, I got changed into my own stretchy black trousers (that one might call leggings) and an oversized sweater. The outfit Poppy dressed me in for the show was a pretty blue dress, but it wasn't comfortable. My make-up had melted under the big lights and it was a relief to wipe it off before we left.

'That's a fabulous idea,' Alex says, having finished his Jack Nicholson, *The Shining*, impersonation. 'The public can't get enough of you, Faith, of course it will work. Look at you!' Instead, Alex glances slyly at me.

'Oh, stop. Only because Poppy keeps dressing me in these skimpy outfits,' Faith laughs.

'We could run a scoop on your mystery boyfriend. "The Unmasking of Master J".' Alex shoots me a cunning grin. 'What do you say, Gracie?'

'You want to interview Jordan?'

'Do you have another boyfriend?'

It annoys me when Faith bursts out laughing.

Seeing my scowl, she answers on my behalf. 'No. She doesn't.'

'You've let slip enough dirty sex secrets to make it interesting,' Alex carries on. 'We could do a saucy photo shoot of you both.'

Dirty sex secrets. The grubby git.

'Firstly, Alex, what we do and say on air is not real,' I state. 'Secondly, my boyfriend is supposed to be mysterious. Exposing Jordan won't win brownie points with Joanna. It's a terrible idea.'

'No photo of your fella, then.' Alex smirks.

'Jordan isn't obliged to expose his private life in some silly magazine,' I snap. 'Even if I am.'

Alex sizes me up. But he merely murmurs, breezily, 'There's no need to be scrappy.'

'Oh, but Gracie can be brilliantly scrappy,' Faith laughs. 'It's part of her charm.'

'I have to go,' I say, glaring at her. Faith's never referred to me as scrappy. What exactly does that mean?

'Darling, we're only teasing,'

Alex is clever enough to agree. 'Of course.'

I smile charitably at the pair of them. I wonder if, tonight, they'll go home together and shag?

'Scrappy or not, I have to go. I have to fetch Benny. After I drop him off, I'll rustle up more dirty sex secrets with my mystery boyfriend.' I put on my coat.

'Benny is stopping with you one more night,' Faith says.

'Sorry?'

'The boys called and convinced me to agree. I must say, Robert is rather charismatic. Is he as gorgeous as you've always said?' Faith asks.

It's stopped me in my tracks, learning that Robert, and Jordan, have spoken directly with Faith.

I remember she had included a note with her number and a copy of Benny's insurance with his things. Benny is her cat. This is Faith's business. But it pinches me, nonetheless, that I've been cut out of the loop.

On the set today, I'd noticed, again, with a small twinge of something not entirely pleasant, that lots of people pop by our studio to speak with Faith.

Am I jealous? This has never happened before. Not in all our years of friendship. My nightmare last night hadn't revealed how she'd responded to Harry's declaration of love, what Faith had done when I lost him to her charms. It's obviously making me act a bit mental today. I shake off all such thoughts from my mind.

'I also have an interview with Liz Martin. Sorry, but I do need to go. So, I'm returning Benny to you tomorrow, Faith. That's the revised plan?'

'Tomorrow morning. Give Benny a big cuddle from me will you please? I miss him so much.'

'Of course. So, we'll tell Joanna we're agreed on a dating competition tomorrow? Are we done?'

'Gracie, we're done,' Faith says. 'Go, darling. We have our plan.'

'Same again?' Alex asks, his hand around Faith's empty wine glass

'Yes please, same again,' she says. 'Bye, Gracie. Enjoy your evening!'

I recall Harry's warning that we should watch our backs around Alex.

In the corner, a trio of brass players assembles and strikes up the first notes. The tune is annoyingly familiar but it's only when I get outside that I realise what they were playing: There May Be Trouble Ahead.

* * *

I meet Liz without fuss, and am pleased to share the new programme recipes with her. Returning home, I'm barely through the front door when Jordan flies up from the basement. An unexpected greeting, I wonder if Jordan's taken our talk this morning on board.

'Thank God you're home,' he sighs. 'There's a problem with this cat.'

I gasp and hold my breath until Robert emerges up the stairs carrying a most contented-looking Benny.

'It's hardly a problem,' Robert counters cheerily.

'Robert, it's a disaster!' Jordan insists.

'Will one of you please tell me what's going on,' I say, dropping my bag onto the table. So much for Jordan simply being pleased to see me. 'I've had a long day, and I'm running on three hours of sleep.'

'This cat won't eat anything,' Jordan goes on. 'He won't try a single bite of the Pussy Paws samples. Not one.'

I'm with Robert on this. This isn't a state of emergency. Meanwhile, Jordan hops from one foot to the other in some sort of a traumatised shuffle.

'Jordan, I warned you twice that Faith insists Benny is partial to his own special pellets. I'm sure it's nothing to do with your client's food.'

Benny snuggles his head into Robert's armpit, not bothered in the least.

'Our entire campaign is premised on Pussy Paws being irresistible to all cats. It's a medicine, but it's delicious. That was our pitch.'

'Perhaps you need a professional advertising cat?' I suggest. 'Like, the Whiskas cat, the sweet silver tabby, with the golden eyes? Perhaps Harry could put you in touch?'

'We have people who can do that,' Jordan snaps at me.

'But those cats cost a lot of money. This isn't for the production. It's for ideation. And this cat is causing a problem because he's completely disproving our pitch.'

Robert and I exchange looks.

'Could you give Benny his own food and pretend he's eating Pussy Paws?' I venture to say.

At that moment, the hallway cupboard door flies open under the weight of the shopping I stored there yesterday. Bags of new clothes tumble out. I meant to take them into the studio with me this morning. I walk over and cram it all back inside. I close the door and everything falls straight back out. I set the bags neatly to one side.

Great idea, Gracie,' Robert says. 'We'll simply make it up. Won't we champ.' Robert rubs Benny's cheek. 'Tomorrow,' he confirms with Jordan. 'Must fly now. I have a date.' Robert kisses my cheek. 'Tomorrow, we'll work this out. Take the night off. Have fun, you two. Toodle-oo.'

Nuzzling his face into Benny's soft tummy before setting him down, without further ado, Robert leaves. Benny lolls on the rug in the hallway.

'Shall I help you to try and entice him, Jordan. I am, after all, a chef. I'm pretty good at getting people to eat.'

'I bet he'd go for your sausage rolls,' Jordan says, cheering up a bit. 'I'm sure it's the Sumptuous Medley of Tuna and Whitebait in Jelly that's the winner,' he goes on, inspired. 'Or the Turkey Chunks in Meat-Rich Gravy, hmm, Benny? Do us a favour, will you?'

Benny assumes flee position as Jordan approaches. However I'm surprised when, instead of scampering, he allows himself to be picked up. Stretched out over Jordan's arms – not exactly snuggled to his chest – Benny makes no effort to escape.

'Come on, puss, let's try this again.'

'I'll bring you down some food in a bit,' I say. 'Good luck, you two,' I add, as they disappear into the basement.

It's not what I had in mind when I thought about setting things straight with Jordan. But at least we're talking.

17

'Oh, my bloody God. That bloody cat. Grace, come quick. Shit.'

Jordan's hysterical screaming wakes me.

I fly out of bed in my pyjamas and into the front room. I'm met with carnage. Paper shopping bags are shredded all over the floor, my new clothes strewn everywhere. One curtain is hanging by a few hooks. How Jordan and I slept through the apocalypse, I'll never know. Streaks of what looks – and smells – like diarrhoea cover the cream-coloured sofa from one end to the other.

I check the kitchen and Benny's litter tray is tipped over the floorboards. 'Oh my God.'

'Where the hell is he?' Jordan thumps about. 'When I find him... Look at this place!'

'You can't find Benny?'

What if he's got out of the flat? What if he's been run over?

Faith will never forgive me.

'Beeenny,' I call, but there isn't a peep – or a meow – from anywhere. I dash into the basement, calling him the whole time. I'd overlooked how messy Jordan has made it down here – it's not far off the shambles upstairs. Piles of old newspapers everywhere. Not-quite-empty Coca-Cola cans dribbling beside his precious X-box. Harry's office was equally messy, but shabbily so. Down here, it's filthy.

Right now, all I can focus on is finding Benny.

In the midst of my panic, the old boiler sparks up. I can't believe it, but I hear the water. Jordan must have got into the shower. Benny is still missing, and when I pop upstairs to check, I hear Jordan whistling in the bloody shower.

I swear, if anything has happened to this cat, Faith will not get to Jordan. I will kill him myself first.

I scoot back into the basement and, for the second time, check that all the windows and the back door to the garden are closed, to reassure myself Benny can't have escaped. The whole flat stinks of poo. Down here, something else is... fishy.

A pile of empty sachets of Pussy Paws lie on Jordan's desk, my decorative icing piping bag beside them. It's smothered with something disgusting. On closer inspection, I discover my piping bag oozes with what appears to be a medley of tuna and whitebait in jelly.

A tiny murmur escapes from deep inside a filing cabinet. I slide the drawer out ever so slowly. Benny cowers inside. He meows at me. Help. He looks – and smells –awful. I burst into tears.

Wrapping him tenderly in a towel, I carry him upstairs for some much-needed water, a wipe-down and some love.

After I've done the dirty work, Benny chips in and begins to groom himself. He licks his front paw and wipes it across his sweet face – it appears he's regained bowel control. Soon, he's gobbling at his Royal Canin pellets.

I leave him to it and burst into the bathroom. Jordan is still under the shower, using up all the hot water.

'What did you do to the cat?'

'What did I do to the cat? Grace, did you fail to notice that cat has completely destroyed—'

'I found Benny. He's clearly been ill. He wasn't when I went to bed last night. What did you do to him?'

'I didn't do anything,' Jordan says, indignant behind his curtain of steam.

'Jordan, don't lie to me!'

'What the hell is wrong with you? Maybe the damn thing finally ate the Pussy Paws and it didn't agree with him? How should I know? He disappeared last night. Bloody thing hates me.'

I'm shaking. 'How, exactly, did Benny eat the Pussy Paws food? Did you inject it into his... into his tiny mouth, Jordan, with my bloody great piping bag?' I'm crying, quite uncontrollably. My boyfriend is a monster who would hurt a tiny animal. There is no talking that can get us out of this one. The best make-up sex in the world wouldn't cut it. Finally, there is no hope.

'Good God, of course not. I told you, he wouldn't eat it,' Jordan insists.

My lovely Maida Vale flat has dodgy plumbing, such that turning on the cold tap at the washbasin instantly renders the shower water scalding hot. I run the cold tap full force. Jordan leaps out from behind the glass screen.

'Seriously! What is wrong with you?' he screeches, his usually pasty skin scarlet all the way down his front.

'I hate you,' I hiss. 'You hear me, Jordan Piper? I hate you! Unless it's to help me clean up this bloody mess you've caused, I want you out of my flat. I'm done. I'm done with everything. I never want to see you again.'

Benny pokes his head into the bathroom to check on me. I follow him into the kitchen and drop into a chair. He jumps on my lap and kneads softly into my pyjamas with his claws. I'm still sitting there when Jordan flees, his rucksack and his sports bag slung over his shoulders, slamming the door behind him.

* * *

A few hours later, I drop Benny off at Faith's flat. I admit to her Benny suffered 'a touch of the runs' in case he still smells of poo. I don't mention anything else, because I don't know what else there is. Before he packed his bags and fled, Jordan had said he'd used the piping bag to serve up Pussy Paws in pellet-sized morsels for Benny, but he didn't force-feed anything. His parting shot accused me of being bat-shit crazy for thinking he could have done. For all I know, it's true. I hope it is – not the part about me being bat-shit crazy... Although, I've had my moments lately. It's possible Benny ate the food after Jordan went to bed and it didn't agree with him. It's pointless upsetting Faith based on my unsubstantiated suspicions.

Faith is a little cold – concerned about her beloved, is a fairer description. When she calls Dr Doolittle's Home Veterinary Service, and Benny is given the all-clear, she cheers up. That Dr Doolittle is in fact Dr Michael, hunky and kind to both animals and humans alike, doesn't hurt to lighten both of our moods. I insist on paying the bill. When Faith is satisfied Benny is settled in for the day, we head to the station together.

There isn't the appropriate time for me to tell Faith I'd kicked Jordan out of my flat and out of my life before we arrive at reception and Mitzi informs us Joanna is waiting for us in the animation department. By all accounts, pretty peeved.

On the second floor, where our animators work at their sitting-and-standing desk, with super-sized monitors and computers so powerful their fans sound like mini jet engines, Joanna is waiting at the far end.

'Ladies, nice of you to join us.' She checks her watch.

'Sorry, we had... *I* had cat trouble,' I say.

I get an eye-roll and a pinched look for my troubles.

'Well, thanks to these wonderful magicians, we've managed to save the episode with *Love Island* boy,' she says. 'Ivor, Pearle, I knew I could count on you both after the terrific job you did with the opening credits. This could be my favourite episode yet.' From where I'm standing, I can't see what's been done to save the episode, and I'm too nervous to enquire. 'As for you two, I've heard from Alex. I think the competition is an excellent idea. Faith, you're required for a photo shoot in the studio. Now. I recommend you change into something short – you have great legs.'

'Sure thing, boss,' Faith says, eliciting a small smile from our formidable global vice president of content.

'I hope that's not what Poppy has spent your wardrobe allowance on,' Joanna says to me.

I'm wearing the tea-stained ivory brocaded shirt. Yes, the same shirt I vowed I'd chuck after Faith whisked me out of it for our first meeting with Harry. It was in a bag in the kitchen, ready for the charity bin. After I showered and dressed, I tended to Benny one last time and my top got wet with water. Benny was in his cage ready to go. The shirt was the closest thing handy. It isn't even ironed.

'Which reminds me, I read a review in the *Daily*. I know it's a foodie section, but nonetheless, you came off as awfully dull,' she goes on. 'Do try and be more interesting. That will be all.'

* * *

Faith flounced her way through the photo shoot while Poppy and I assisted her in and out of various clothes. At 6 p.m., we're back in our dressing room, trying to sort me an outfit for tonight's opening of The Tricycle Club, my new clothes being strewn over the floor at home, potentially torn to pieces and almost certainly stinking of cat poop. (I scarcely had time to attend to Benny and then myself this morning, let alone the state of the flat.) Because the plan is for us to get photographed by the paparazzi, Joanna doesn't want us in anything we've already worn in any recordings – and she expects us to dazzle. Faith and Poppy have given up suggesting we take a cab to my flat and collect my new outfits, or even grab one of my trusty old dresses, even though I haven't provided a single good reason why we shouldn't do exactly that.

We've been trawling through the freebies sent by various designers. I don't fit into any of it. They're mostly too big for Poppy. It's all sized to fit Faith. On top of everything, it's putting me in a furiously bad mood.

Poppy tries to convince me her super stretchy, pink ruffled skirt paired with the slinky black top in Faith's stash looks remotely fine on me. The skirt fits well enough, but it's frilly pink. Faith's top is too tight – I have the nipples-almost-popping-out-bosom thing going on again, which I'm in no mood to monitor, or cover with a scarf in a club. They've also put me into Faith's high-heeled ankle boots – I barely have ankles.

From across our dressing room, Poppy says, 'Honestly, my angel, you look glorious.'

My cleavage pops up at the front.

'Glorious?!' I wail, attempting – and failing – to push my boobs back inside. I take off the top and pick up the paper by my side while Poppy and Faith comb through the clothes rails.

For the umpteenth time today, I skim bits and pieces in Liz Martin's article. In the entertainment – and not the foodie – section of the *Daily*, in her first review of the new show, Liz describes Poppy as being 'as effervescent as pop' and Faith as 'smoking hot, and just the right amount of humble, and not only about her terrible cooking skills, so that men love her and women want to be like her'. Whenever Liz mentions me, it's all about the food – 'Gracie confidently takes the lead on the slicing and dicing', etc. I didn't need Joanna to point out that I sound awfully dull – it jumps out from the page.

Liz, most likely because we get on well, respectfully steered clear of any raunchy association of me with the new format. Perhaps, when we'd met to discuss the new series, I'd overplayed my sensitivities? But with all the glittering praise heaped about elsewhere, I've been rather cast aside.

'Do you think I'm dull, Faith?' I throw her the slinky black top across the room. I'm sitting in the frilly pink skirt and my knickers and bra.

'Ha! Chance would be a fine thing.'

I look at her suspiciously.

'I mean, "dull" doesn't spring to mind.'

'You think I'm awful then? Because Joanna accused me of being awfully dull this morning. I'm wondering if it's true?'

Faith squeezes herself out of a micro dress and into a pair of skinny jeans. There isn't an ounce of fat on her. 'Gracie, she never said you were dull or awful.'

'Liz described you as "a saucy treat, hooking viewers with your never-ending legs and come-hither smile",' I read directly from the article. I cast the paper aside, too. Poppy makes to come over, probably to hug me. 'And you were magnetic and simply magical in your bloody tutu, Poppy. I'm strictly about the food.'

'Miss Gracie, what's wrong with you today?' Poppy flings herself at me.

'I'm sorry, Poppy. I didn't mean to be rude. But please get off me. Oh God, I am awful...'

Is my period due?

'I think you're beautiful,' Poppy says.

'She's stunning,' Faith agrees. 'But if she wants to be written about as a saucy treat, she needs to get back into that teensy top and start smiling come-hitherly. Even better, put this on.' Faith lobs me a lilac satin top from the not-yet-discarded pile.

The top is far too small for me – I'm not even going to try and get it on. And it's purple. Poppy has just finished going through the various 'vibrations' of colours and, apparently, purple is both for royalty, which is nice, and sexual frustration, which isn't.

'I'm not sexually frustrated.' I toss it aside.

Faith lobs it back at me. 'Are you sure about that?' I glare, but Faith is having none of it. She smiles. 'Come on, put it on. Let's see if your boobs fit.'

* * *

We arrive at the club on Wardour Street around 8 p.m. I'm not wearing the purple satin top. I couldn't get it over my shoulders. I'm dressed in the silly ankle boots/slinky black top/pink ruffled skirt get-up.

I don't want to be here.

I left the flat a tip this morning, the whole place smelling of poo. If anywhere, I want to be home with a bottle of bleach in my hand, sorting things out.

We have to be here.

I especially don't want to be here dressed like an oversized sugar plum fairy. Worse, I'm here, looking like this, in my newly single status: after the scene this morning, Jordan and I are over. In my mind, definitely. And I'd checked after he'd left with his big bag and Jordan had taken all of his best regular clothes with him. I guess he'll crash with Robert – he can't crash with his parents all the way down in Cornwall. Though I haven't phoned him and he hasn't phoned me, so I'm unsure where the heck he's staying. I didn't want to say anything in front of Poppy, but when she nipped to the bathroom before we headed to the club, I quickly told Faith I'd asked Jordan to move out. It wasn't optimal timing, but it was the last chance I'd had all day to mention something. Faith has gasped and looked worried. I told her I was doing okay and, before Poppy returned, we agreed we'd speak more about it later.

My God, I look ridiculous. The club will probably be packed full of sultry young stick insects dressed in black.

'We're VIPs,' Faith says. 'Should we go to the front?'

'I'll go and ask.' Poppy weaves her way to the front of the long line.

'You've pierced your belly button,' I say to Faith.

Between the many deliberate rips in her top, a distressed singlet with the word FRAGILE splashed across the front, I see a small, silver belly ring. I didn't know they were still fashionable. Mind you, anything looks good on Faith – if she started wearing leg warmers, I'm pretty sure it would be a hit. She's wearing skinny black jeans and a biker leather jacket – a fitting tribute for the opening of The Tricycle Club this evening.

'Oh? I got this a while ago.' Faith fiddles with the jewellery. Her stomach is so toned – Pilates every morning, now she's not working the long hours at her old job. I suck my tummy in then, realising the frills are handily concealing it, I let it all back out. 'A bit naff, hey? Did you really not know?'

'I don't think so. It's sweet, Faith.'

'I got it last summer.'

After a long winter snuggling with Jordan, last summer, I was up to the part of playing housemaid to my increasingly uninterested boyfriend. I was baking and cleaning and hovering around, waiting for Jordan to notice me. Faith was putting herself out there and getting on with piercings and who knows what.

'Are you okay? Gracie, we can talk about what happened with you and Jordan whenever you're ready. And we can leave here whenever you need to. All right?'

'Thanks, Faith. I'll be fine.'

Apart from my damn outfit, I am okay. I'm with my best friend, who's looking out for me. I'm a VIP at a swanky new club opening, because our new show is catching fire. And last, but not least, Harry will be here later – he texted me earlier to say he'd be late, but he'll be here. I'd warned him about my silly get-up and he'd texted straight back: *Who cares? You have those baby blues. You always look smashing. See you in a bit. H.*

Poppy waves for us to join her at the front doors. Her strappy dress looks like it's made of grass, fronds of green cotton twisted all over. We bump ourselves to the front of the queue, where a friendly bouncer ticks our names off a special list. Inside, we make our way down the stairs and into my first VIP-access-only area.

On the upside, the place isn't crammed with sultry stick insects. The downside is that it's completely empty. We're the only people in the selectively roped-off area.

We select the table with the best view over the rest of the club. Not a lot happening out there either.

Faith orders us a bottle of Veuve Clicquot.

18

We're on our second bottle of bubbly when Harry arrives at The Tricycle Club.

'Well, well, well,' he says, stopping behind my chair. Craning my neck, I check over my shoulder and catch his eye. Harry leans down and kisses my cheek. My tummy flips.

I'm tipsy – but it's something more. The feeling inside my tummy is the opposite to how I felt after the awful dream. Harry showers more attention over me, in particular. He motions for a waiter to bring us more champagne.

'Harry, you'll get us drunk,' Poppy giggles.

'It's good to relax every now and then,' he says. 'It's my night off.'

From my awkward angle, I see he's gelled his hair and his black shirt is unbuttoned, revealing a tight, white T-shirt underneath. I turn my head and face the table. Behind me, Harry whispers in my ear, 'You're working that outfit, don't worry.' I tell him something along the lines of 'having it' and 'flaunting it.' Harry laughs delightedly and stays put right where he is. Faith is watching us intently.

The club, both inside and outside the roped-off area, is filling up. The music is warming up too, but not too loud yet.

As he reaches forward for a glass of champagne, Harry grazes my shoulder with his chin. A flood of pheromones. My God, he smells amazing. For a fleeting moment, his breath is warm in my ear. Light-headed, and not just from the champagne, I take a deep breath in. When Harry's fingers brush lightly over mine, my eyes close momentarily. I'm giddy. Aflutter in my own world. Falling into my thoughts until, suddenly, I'm toppling off my chair – landing smack-bam on my ridiculously pink-ruffled behind, having experienced what can only be described as something close to a fully clothed orgasm. Thump.

'Gracie, are you okay?' Faith is the first over to pick me up and set me back down on my chair.

Coming around, I see Harry is no longer behind me – he's standing several feet away, flanked by two Barbie-doll blondes, both of them dressed identically in high white leather boots and silver mini-dresses. The girls stare wide-eyed at me. Harry appears startled. I'm startled. How did he get all the way over there, with them, while I was very much over here... with him?

'That's enough bubbly for you,' Faith laughs, now she's confirmed I'm not injured. Not physically, anyway. 'Think you can stay seated while we finish these introductions?'

'Sorry. Yes. I don't know quite what happened there.'

Harry gives me an intense look, of concern, if I had to guess. Confused by what's just happened, I avert my eyes.

The girls look familiar, I think from Harry's wall.

'I'm Bip,' says the taller of them.

'I'm Ban.'

'I'm, um, Gracie,' I say, so embarrassed. 'Hello.'

Faith returns to her seat.

I check my watch. It's just gone 10 p.m. I haven't eaten anything since lunch time. We didn't bother with dinner. I'm really rather drunk.

'You're the star of the new show Harry's working on,' Bip, I think she said her name is, says.

'We watched you on the television the other night.' And Ban?

I wonder if they were with Harry when they watched the show. And why, during our many conversations over the past few months, Harry has never mentioned them to me.

Now I pause to think, I still know so little about him. He knows so little about me.

'I don't know about star,' I reply.

'We wish we could do what you do.'

'You mean, you wish you could cook?'

'Ha.'

'Yes, that too.'

They giggle as one.

'The girls are also on my books,' Harry says. He's smiling at them protectively.

Where moments ago, I'd been aflutter, I'm smarting.

'Harry, you take such good care of us,' says one of them – I've already forgotten who is who.

'As I do all my special clients,' Harry says, looking at me.

What does he mean by this?

'It's lovely to meet you both,' I say, deliberately not answering him. I've had too much champagne to interpret his mixed messages – and maybe they're not mixed. Maybe Harry is simply a big fat flirt with everyone he meets, and I'm nobody special to him at all. My mother, me, these glamour girls in tiny dresses – perhaps Harry simply cannot help himself?

'Please, join us,' I say, most graciously.

The girls pile one on top of the other's lap on the only spare chair. Harry disappears swiftly under the pretext of finding another for himself. He is soon schmoozing several tables away with other people, where there are spare chairs aplenty.

'So, Bip?'

'No, I'm Ban.' Both girls giggle. 'She's Bip.'

The girl on the seat squeezes the waist of the girl on her lap. Their dresses are so mini, I'm sure if I squinted, I'd see panties. Assuming, that is, they're wearing any. Their boobs are enormous, and enormously upright. I bet they look awful without make-up.

'Don't worry, everyone confuses us.'

'We look so alike.'

'Are you twins?' I ask.

'Oh, no.'

'Sisters.'

'Half-sisters.'

'But the best of friends.'

'You look like Barbie twins,' I say.

Faith kicks me under the table. The girls giggle.

'That's cute.'

'I like it too.'

'I wish we were twins,' they carry on.

The back and forth is making me giddy again. Harry hasn't returned. I can't see him any longer. I decide to find out more.

'You know Harry well?' I ask. Faith raises an eyebrow.

'Well, we've never lived together.'

'But we've known him forever.'

'So I'd say we know him very well.'

'I'd say Harry knows us even better.'

'Oh yes.'

'Yes. For sure.'

The girls smile sweetly at me. I nearly bite my tongue off. Who are they? Is Harry dating the pair of them? One of them? Are they just friends? I almost don't want to know. I press on regardless.

'And Harry is also your agent. You're obviously... models?'

'Oh, yes, we are. Thank you.'

'And you spend a lot of time together, with Harry?'.

I refuse to catch her eye, but without looking, I feel Faith's eyes boring into me.

Poppy grins at us all. The girls start up again. 'Harry is very busy with his agency.'

'But we spend a lot of time at his place.'

'You should join us sometime, Gracie.'

My imagination runs wild!

'Well, um, yes, that would be lovely,' I say.

Beginning to feel nauseas, in need of fresh air, or at least a walk around, I politely excuse myself.

Standing up, I'm drunker than I thought I was. On top of which, Faith's ankle boots are less supportive than I'm used to walking in. One dainty step in front of the other, I navigate my way out of the VIP area and up the stairs to another bar. The music is quieter up here and people are chatting in cosy clusters. A photographer works her way around the room, camera at the ready.

A slender bald man grabs my waist. 'Having a good time?' he slurs.

'Ah, mm.' The photographer squeezes her way in front of

us. 'A lovely time, thank you,' I say. She steadies her lens. The man squeezes my waist and grins. I smile. The flash momentarily blinds me.

'Wonderful! Bye!' He wanders off to a group of young ladies.

I stand, grinning like a Billy-no-mates, for as long as I can bear it. But with nobody up here to talk to, feeling conspicuous, I escape quickly back down the stairs. The girls are still at our table. Harry is still nowhere to be seen. At the last second, I veer away from the VIP entry and towards the dance floor.

Approaching the lit-up platform, I spot the bouncer who checked us in earlier. I remember Poppy asking and he'd said his name is Duncan. As wide as he is tall, Duncan has pockmarked skin and a flat, shaved head. The music is so loud over here, I have to shout, and even then, Duncan lends me his ear. I ask how long he's worked here. He reminds me it's the opening night, which makes me laugh. I mosey on into the thick of the dance floor where I'm stopped by a good-looking girl, about my build.

'Oh my gosh, excuse me,' she says. 'Sorry to pester you – you must get this all the time. Are you Gracie, from the new show on SC6? You look so much like her!'

'That's me,' I say, a little cheesily. It feels weird, and a bit wonderful, being recognised. Apart from the occasional housewife in Sainsbury's, it never happened to me in the days of *Gracie Porter's Gourmet Get-Together*. 'What's your name? I love your dress!'

The girl tells me her name is Macy. Her dress is black, strappy and shows off her curvy figure. When I ask why she's here tonight, Macy says her friend is seeing one of the barmen and he put them on the guest list, but not as VIPs. I tell her it's better out here anyway. Macy introduces me to her friends, who seem as nice as she is. After we've all danced together for a little while, I'm invited to join the group for a drink at their table across the room.

I glance over at our VIP area. No change to the seating arrangement, and Faith and Poppy don't seem especially bothered I've not returned – Faith doesn't like to dance and she's used to me, when I'm drunk, wandering off to make new friends who do.

In any event, there's nobody over there looking about and worrying where I've got to.

'Macy, I'd be delighted,' I say.

Several cocktails later – called 'Dirty Biker', I've no idea what went in the drinks but they were potent and went down smoothly – I excuse myself to head back to my friends.

I'm more inebriated than when I left to sober myself up with a wander.

On the other side of the ropes, the area is crammed full – and if I'm not mistaken, with some properly famous people. Pretty sure I see Stormzy at the bar.

Whether it's the booze – or the attention my hefty cleavage attracted out there on the dance floor – I'm feeling bold enough to want to follow up with Harry about our earlier... whatever it was. At the very least, I'd like to know what the devil he was playing at. Striding towards our table – despite the wobbly ankle boots, I'm pretty sure I stride – it's a wasted effort. When I navigate my way through the crowd, only Faith and Poppy are sitting here.

'Where's Harry?' I ask. My words come out more slurry than they started inside my head.

'Gone,' Faith replies, not slurring at all.

I look around. 'What about Bin and Bap?'

'You mean Bip and Ban? I think they left too.'

'With Harry?'

Faith doesn't answer.

'Yes, my angel,' Poppy says. 'They left with Harry. Did you have fun dancing?'

My disappointment that Harry has left with Bin and Bap – Bin and Bip – Bip and whoever he was with – surely shows on my face. 'Um, yes. I met some nice girls.'

'Yes, Faith went and checked on you.'

'Darling, do you want some water?' Faith asks me.

I tell Faith I want a cigarette.

'You can't smoke in here.'

'I'm going to the bathroom.'

'You can't smoke in there either.'

Is Faith annoyed with me? 'I'm going to pee. Back in a bit.'

I head to the Ladies'. Inside, I'm surprised to see the girls are in here. As in the twins, but not really twins, are here in the loos, and not gone with Harry at all.

'Gracie,' they exclaim, inexplicably pleased to see me. 'We thought you'd left!'

'Me too,' I say, stumbling on these heeled boots. I only narrowly grab onto a washbasin to save myself from falling. 'I mean, I thought you'd left. And, er, Harry?'

'Only Harry left.' They smile gorgeously. 'We're still here.'

'Yes. I see.'

'He'll be back later,' says the shorter one.

'He had a call from a client, he had to get something from his office. He'll be back before midnight, he said.'

I reacquaint myself with the pedestal, my head spinning with thoughts and also the alcohol.

'Anyway, he wouldn't leave for the night without saying goodbye to you, Gracie.'

'Oh, no. Harry is always going on about you.'

Two pairs of heavily made-up eyes focus on me. I make a major effort to focus back.

'You mean, Harry is always talking about the show?' I ask, trying to sound casual.

At the washbasins, a girl who doesn't recognise me – or perhaps she does – rolls her eyes.

'That's right,' the girls agree eagerly.

'Because Harry is my agent,' I suggest.

'He doesn't go on about his other clients the way he does you.'

Harry hasn't mentioned the girls to me once.

'Oh yes, Harry talks about you all the time.'

'We think he's quite infatuated...'

'Yes!'

It dawns on me that it's scarcely their fault these girls are so porn-star-like attractive. They seem genuinely lovely.

'I'm so drunk,' I say.

'Oh, do you fancy, a little, you know...' Nodding towards an empty cubicle, the shorter girl pulls at her silver dress and slides her hand inside her bra. Her silicone breast bobs up and, for a split second, exposes a pink nipple. Before I embarrass myself and decline what I interpret as her offer of a quick fondle in the cubicles, she extracts a small paper wrap and whispers, 'You know... for a line.'

'Oh, a line,' I gasp, hoping she didn't notice me noticing her nipple. 'Um, a line of what, exactly?'

'Cocaine.'

'We don't do speed.'

'Speed is for peasants.'

'Yes, of course,' I agree, having never tried either.

The girls step inside the empty cubicle. One begins

racking up white powder on the top of the cistern as the other stands guard at the door.

'Do you want some, Gracie?'

The girls beckon me to join them.

I'm keen to hear more about Harry's apparent infatuation with me.

I'm very drunk, and rather intrigued.

I've heard cocaine is sobering.

'Girls, since you ask,' I say, 'I'd like to try.'

19

At first, nothing much happens. My nostrils tingle as I inhale. A chalky glob slips down the back of my throat. But that's it. Intoxicated and incredibly nervous about what will happen after my first ever line of cocaine, I refuse to leave the cubicle. I'm roosted on the toilet seat. Bip and Ban are squeezed in, standing in front of me. Already, it's like having double vision just looking at them. A few minutes later, it hits me: my inaugural line of cocaine. My body trembles. My brain, alert with all sorts of thoughts at once, feels like it's about to explode – I thought I'd be feeling fabulous.

The girls are being so kind. One of them holds my hand while the other strokes my hair.

'When will it stop?' I'm weepy. Tears aren't flowing, because my nervous system is too busy with all the other goings on, but my eyes are watery and when I wipe them, my finger is black with mascara. 'Look at me, I'm a mess.'

'I can fix this up.' Someone – I've no idea who is who and I'm not even trying right now – pats under my eyes with a bit of loo roll.

I fear I might drop dead of a coronary. They'll find my corpse in the toilet cubicle, covered in my vomit. That's how it happens. Drugs, vomit, death. What the hell was I thinking, snorting a Class A substance in a club with people I barely know? Who do I think I am?

And so we have spent the past five minutes or so, though it feels very much longer.

Eventually, my convulsions subside. I detect a faint jittering if I put my finger between my teeth – the girls tell me to do this, to distract me. Finally, intense elation rushes in. 'Oh my, I think it's working,' I say.

The girls smile. I'm embarrassed I ruined the experience for them – I'm guessing they usually pass straight to flying high without the check-in to paranoia.

Thankfully, the drug takes care of that niggling doubt post-haste.

'Okay, shall we get out of here?' I say.

'Let's tidy you up, Gracie.'

We exit the cubicle.

Other women have been coming in and out of the Ladies' during this respite, and a few of them knocked on our door to ask us to hurry out, but on the whole, nobody has paid us much attention. With the number of other people entering cubicles in pairs, it seems to me half of the clubbers in this place are bang on the charlie tonight – I'm pleased Faith or Poppy didn't spring us. Faith, in particular, won't approve of the state of me.

The girls take out some bits and bobs from their bags and attend to my face. Both of them having a go at once, I watch them closely, in the mirror. The final finish is more extreme than when Poppy attends to me – I have not one, but two sets of false eyelashes attached – but it's not tatty. I look pretty. I match my frilly pink skirt! Best of all, I'm feeling fly.

'Gracie, are you ready? Shall we go out and get a drink?'

'Um. Okay.' It sounds dubious to me – more alcohol on top of drugs.

'A drink will soften the blow.'

'All right. But I'm buying. For, you know... And these lashes.'

The girls wrap their arms around mine and, one either side of me, we exit the bathroom. Back out in the club, we find a spot in a dark nook at the back of the dance floor, outside of the VIP area. There's an extra little bar back here, and it isn't crowded. I order us another bottle of Veuve.

The girls are right: champagne goes down a treat. Within minutes, my physical rush calms, but I'm still feeling pretty damn great about... everything. The girls are feeling it too. I can tell.

They tell me they loved me the most when they were watching *Eat Me*. That I have the most luscious hair and bluest eyes. I confess to having noticed the girls, in particular, among the crowd on Harry's wall. They insist it's so cute that I keep mixing them up.

'Remember, Bip is shorter, with a small mole on her left cheek.'

'And Ban is taller, with shorter hair.'

Feeling an instant closeness to them, I tell them I ended things with my boyfriend this morning.

'You broke up with Master J?'

'Well, no. Sort of. I broke up with my boyfriend, Jordan.' I haven't stopped to consider what will happen with my mystery boyfriend for the purpose of the show now that I'm single in real life. I suppose, nothing. *Eat Me* is, after all, a dramatisation. Surely, there's no reason I can't keep my pretend boyfriend, if I must?

'Were you together long?'

'Over a year.'

'Was he horrible to you? Is that why you dumped him?'

The question takes me aback for a moment. I haven't yet discussed all of the details, all of my angst, with Faith.

'He wasn't horrible to me. He just... wasn't very warm.' It's surprising, how not-upset I am about us breaking up. I guess that's how it goes when your partner slowly dumps you first, surreptitiously, disappointment by disappointment, over many months. On the day you make the call, the hurt's been fully paid. 'More like a selfish twat than horrible,' I finish firmly.

The girls giggle. 'Aren't they all?'

'Most of them.'

They make me better, instantly. Like I'm not the only loser who can't be loved.

'Maybe there's someone else you're meant to be with,' Bin says.

'Mmm. Maybe, like, Harry?' Ban suggests.

'Oh, no, Harry is my agent.' I only half-object. 'I mean, he's lovely. But...

'But what? He's lovely. You're lovely.'

'You should go for it, Gracie.'

'And not hold back!'

'Definitely!'

I don't deny I won't.

With a little prompting, both girls confess to being 'not in a relationship' right now, then they each run through a short-list of men with whom they're engaging in some sort of sexual liaison. Harry doesn't rate a mention. I've poked about, but I still don't have a definitive steer on their relationship. The girls are twenty-one and twenty-two years old, work as part-time models, Harry as their agent, and live together in a one-bedroom flat in Elephant and Castle. They mention they often crash in Harry's spare room, in his amazing flat beside the Embankment. Yet they're keen to suggest a romantic involvement between Harry and me? They can't be lovers. Ex-lovers, maybe? I just don't know. And every time I get close to asking, our conversation curve balls. Albeit I'm happier than I think I've ever been.

I confess to having a fleeting thought the girls might have been propositioning me earlier in the toilets. In giggles, they're generous enough to insist that if they were so inclined, I'd be their number-one choice.

We can't stop talking!

A smooth voice behind me says, 'Well, well, well.'

I turn, aiming for... actually, I'm not sure what I was aiming for, but when I turn my head, my face is almost pressed against Harry's (seemingly well-kitted) crotch.

I bet you he's a decent cucumber, if not an aubergine.

'Well, well,' Harry repeats, making light as I correct my position. He's so adorable.

He takes the seat next to me. I inhale deeply, wanting to smell his scent. Nothing. The coke has numbed my senses?

Bip and Ban excuse themselves to the bathroom, I presume for another line. They mouth, not as discreetly as I'd like, 'Good luck,' before they totter off.

'I see you've been getting to know the girls,' Harry says.

I bat my insanely long lashes at him vampishly.

Harry brushes my cheek with his fingers and grins lopsidedly.

I catch him glancing, but not gawking, at my chest. 'Yes. We're having a lovely time, thank you.'

'And the others?' He looks over to the VIP area, where Faith and Poppy are surrounded by a pool of attractive men. They seem perfectly fine without me.

'It's too loud over there,' I say, mindful not to stare at Faith for too long, lest I draw her attention. 'The twins are looking after me.'

'The twins?' Harry chuckles. Sexy.

'Not really. But they like it. They think I'm cute.'

'You are cute,' he teases.

'And I, in turn, adore them.'

'They are adorable,' Harry says. 'Exhausting, at times. But adorable.'

I take the opportunity to make my final fact-check. 'Have you ever been particularly adoring of any one, or indeed both of them, at any point?' I ask. The cocaine is making me bold. Or I'm so comfortable with Harry? I do find it so easy to talk to him. Thus, on this matter, I have to know if Harry has any unresolved feelings. The girls, clearly not. But I want to know where Harry stands with them.

Harry stares into my eyes, into my yearning pools of bluey-violet for just that little bit too long. 'Are you okay?' he asks me. 'Gracie, can I get you some water?'

I'm not overly bothered that Harry skirted the question. I was, perhaps, being too comfortable. His history is none of my business. And it doesn't matter. All that matters is: what is Harry playing at with me? 'Never mind. But, I need to talk to you about something.' I bat my lashes, hoping he gets my point – I'm being seductive.

'I'm listening.'

'Jordan and I broke up today.'

'Oh.'

'We had to, really.'

'That sounds... ominous.'

I was rather hoping for more. Also, I think the cocaine is wearing off. I don't feel as euphoric. Actually, I feel a little panicked. Like it's fight or flight. And I don't want to flee right now. Not from Harry.

'There's a not-so-pleasant twist, but...' I also don't want to talk about Jordan. 'Bottom line is, we made each other miserable. I want to be happy.'

'You deserve to be happy,' Harry assures me, giving my waist a squeeze. Swooning at his touch, I sway in my seat, prompting him to repeat, 'I think you need some water.'

'I'd like to dance,' I say. I don't know where that came from. I wanted to sit here and list all the ways Harry makes me happy. Why I've fallen madly in crush with him. I'm unsure where the idea that we should cease our tete-de-tete and hit the dancefloor sprung from, frankly. Perhaps because it's how I got Jordan – a trusted icebreaker to move from talking to something more?

'I don't dance,' Harry laughs. 'The girls will love to.' He looks around the room for them.

'Dance with me, Harry,' I say, rising from my seat and pulling him by his hand.

In for a penny, in for a pound.

Harry stands, but he doesn't budge further.

I'm teetering precariously in Faith's boots. 'Come on, you know you want to.' I don't recognise the song, but the DJ is playing a banging tune. The room starts spinning.

Oh dear, those laser light beams aren't great in my eyes.

Harry reaches out and steadies me by my arms with his big, manly hands. 'Are you okay there?'

'Yes. No. Oh God, Harry...'

My head rushes and I don't know what happens because right there in the middle of the club I pass out.

20

I remember being helped into Faith's spare bed, where, fully dressed in last night's clothes, I'm currently unable to sleep. My eyelids twitch. My gaze darts hopelessly around the room. Repetitive snippets of events replay over and over in my head, cocaine coursing through my veins. A poo-smeared flat. Jordan. Poor, sweet Benny. Joanna calling me dull, and reminding me to dress appropriately. Liz's article describing Faith and Poppy as saucy and effervescent. Me, ensconced in the dark nook of The Tricycle Club with the girls. The Barbie twins. Me, informing Harry I'm single. Him not exactly biting his arm off to make the most of it. Dance with me, Harry.

Passing out, and bundled into bed, but no sleep. Just these endless thoughts that will not quit.

Benny. Jordan. Poo.

Joanna. Dull. Awful.

A ridiculously pink ruffled skirt, and popping out tits.

The Tricycle Club.

Duncan the bouncer.

Macy?

Faith.

Poppy.

I was rude to them. I know I was.

The twins.

The toilets.

The confessions.

And Harry...

Who cannot possibly be as infatuated with me as I was led to believe

... or as my mother would dearly love to be true.

It is torture.

I have only myself to blame.

* * *

Faith comes in to check on me as dawn breaks through the crack in her curtains. Visibly alarmed I'm still awake, she offers me tablets – sleeping pills presumably, though I daren't ask.

Last thing I remember, she's patting me off to sleep.

* * *

'Miss Gracie, wakey-wakey!'

I peel my eyes open. Poppy is sitting astride me on the bed, making what seems to be an attempt to mount me – a less worrying description might be she's performing the sort of bouncing-all-over-the-bed wake-up I did to my parents as a young child. (I was around five-years-old when my mother put a stop to such carry-ons.)

'Wake up!'

Uggghhh. Everything hurts.

I pretend I'm asleep.

I should have known it wouldn't dissuade Poppy. 'Miss Gracie, wake up. I want to show you something.'

I hit her with my pillow.

'Yay! You're awake.' From a more civilised position beside my feet, she opens a newspaper. 'Look.'

It's pitch-black outside.

'Poppy, what time is it?'

'It's just gone five o'clock.'

We were out Thursday night. Did I lose Friday? I hope that's all the days I've lost. My head feels split in half.

'Friday night?'

Checking me over carefully, as if I may be brain-damaged, Poppy confirms, 'Yes, Friday night. You've been sleeping since forever, my princess.'

'Oh yes, I'm a bona fide Sleeping Beauty,' I reply roughly, falling back onto the pillow. Albeit without the lithe figure and angelic vocals of your usual storybook heroine, nor the ladylike demeanour. Not to mention the Prince flipping Charming on horseback.

I was Cinderella last night. At the stroke of midnight, the spell was broken.

Faith enters the room and thrusts a cold bottle of orange-brown sludge at me. 'Here.' The label on the bottle reads '25% mango, 40% orange, 30% banana'. The liquid inside looks lumpy and vile. What's in the other five per cent? 'Drink it,' Faith says.

I drink.

She collects the empty bottle and marches out without further engagement.

'Look at this,' Poppy says, sliding the newspaper onto my

lap. In the entertainment pull-out, she points to a picture of me standing next to the wandering bald man from upstairs at The Tricycle Club last night. Apparently, he's a famous film producer. Also, the owner of the club. In the photo, I'm wearing the same slinky black top and pink ruffled skirt that's still on me. The producer, a stranger, had taken me so by surprise the camera caught me with a wide grin and my head tossed back. Only, instead of appearing alarmed, I look like his well-at-ease muse.

'Joanna is thrilled,' Poppy exclaims. 'She didn't even mind that we all missed coming into the station today. She said to tell you to rest up, her little star, and that she can't wait to see the coverage we get tomorrow at Drake's party.'

'Sorry, what party?'

'Remember, the invitations from Joanna? Drake. You know his songs. He did the duet with Rhianna. Ooh na na, what's my name? Ooh, na na, what's my name?'

'Poppy. Your name is Poppy.' I'm not that battered that I've forgotten her name, for heavens sakes.

'Oh, Miss Gracie. What a cutie you are. Okay, what about this one?' Using my legs as a drum, Poppy begins to rap. 'Trap, TrapMoneyBenny. This shit got me in my feelings. Gotta be real with it, yup. It's called "In My Feelings". By Drake. His party is tomorrow. I'm so excited!'

Is it a song about Benny? How odd. Not the point. 'Lovely. But there'll be no "real-ing it" at any party for me tomorrow, Poppy. I couldn't possibly.'

'Um, I don't think we have a choice, my angel. Joanna expects us to at least show our faces.' Sweet Poppy, who never gets exasperated, sighs audibly.

She checks my forehead with the back of her hand and

presses her palm against my chest. 'Oh my, I don't know whether you're hot or cold?'

Probably because I'm shivering, Poppy scuttles around the bed and tucks me tight under the covers. It's the end of February, so chilly outside. But Faith's boiler is cranked-up hot and toasty. Soon, I'll be sweating.

'I know you feel awful right now, but it'll be better by tomorrow,' she babbles on. 'I don't know what got into you last night, but I'm guessing you're on a comedown? Hmm... I probably have something that will help. Two secs. Let me check.'

As Poppy leaves the room, a frowning Faith appears at the doorway. 'Well? What happened last night? If I didn't know better, I'd suspect you were on drugs.'

I won't lie to Faith.

My silence is telling.

'Jesus. It explains the state of you. Do you remember getting home? You were a total mess. You'd fainted on Harry. His sisters were worried sick.'

'Whose sisters?'

'Harry's sisters. Half-sisters. The girls you spent most of the night with and who obviously fed you drugs.'

It's not the point Faith's trying to make, but I can't believe I missed the fact the girls are Harry's half-sisters. It all makes sense. They've known him forever – since they were born. They're practically inseparable, and Harry is clearly protective of them. Yet they were instigating a romantic relationship between him and me. How mortifying that I basically accused him of fancying them last night at The Tricycle Club! Harry must have mentioned their relationship when he introduced them, as it isn't news to Faith. I was obviously too busy fantasising about him, then falling off my chair, to have paid attention.

'The bouncers helped us get you out a side entrance and into a cab. Gracie, I found a set of false eyelashes between your boobs.'

For a moment last night, I'd imagined Harry mesmerised by my batting lashes and my heaving cleavage – not dumb-struck by the false lashes on my squished in boobs. Whatever the girls insisted he felt for me before, whatever must he think of me now?

Sober, Faith needn't remind me of the mess I was. I remember all too well – give me the blackout of a hangover over this total recall of a comedown any day.

'I'm sorry, Faith.'

'I almost called an ambulance. Please don't ever do that to yourself again.'

Faith leaves the room, mad as hell at me, and clearly upset, and I break down completely. Poppy returns and I sob, uncontrollably, into her lap.

'It's okay, Faith was up all night worrying about you, that's all. She's just tired.' Poppy wipes at my tears with her sleeve. 'We were all worried about you.'

'But you're not cross with me, Poppy. Or are you?'

I've never felt so sorry for myself in my life. I can't understand why anyone would become a regular drug-taker? From start to finish, my experience was less than pleasurable – the good bits were a big fake. I swear to God, I won't be touching anything like it again.

Poppy hugs me tighter. 'I'm not cross with you, Miss Gracie,' she says.

We've transcended being colleagues. Bless her, Poppy is my friend.

When I calm down, she props me up on the pillows. Fussing about in her handbag, she presses a few small pills into my hand.

'What are they?'

'Milk thistle to support your liver, St John's Wort to lift your mood and vitamin Bs for your nerves. They're drugs to help you feel better, poppet.'

I protest I don't want any more drugs and from somewhere in the kitchen I hear clanging.

Poppy insists the tablets are entirely herbal and perfectly legal. I agree to take them on the condition I can be left alone to wallow in private.

I swallow everything and Poppy leaves the room. Shortly after, I hear her leave the flat.

When Faith checks in on me about an hour later and I'm still restless, she returns with more sleeping pills – the strong ones. I know Faith has them purely for when she's had to take a red-eye flight from New York to London and head straight into her office after landing.

I take them without question.

'I'm going to fix my life,' I say.

'Shh. Gracie, it was just one night, a silly mistake.'

But it's not just one night. It's not just one silly mistake. My life isn't working for me. I'm sad, too much of the time. I'm lonely, even when I'm not alone. I'm becoming petty and jealous and I never used to be like this. I want to be the joyous, Gracie who everyone loved to laugh and have fun with. Mostly, I want to love myself again – because though I've never been the best or thinnest person in the room, I never used to compare. For as long as I can remember, until recently, I was always pretty good at doing me.

'No, it's not that. I don't like my life the way it is. I'm going to fix it. I'm going to fix me.'

'Okay, darling. But now shh. Go to sleep.'

I relent. I relax. Faith stays with me, silently, until I succumb.

21

When I venture out of Faith's spare room, she's stretched out on her living room floor, stroking a contented-looking Benny, both of them basking in a slither of sunshine. Faith embodies effortless chic in flannel pyjamas – words that don't usually go together, 'chic' and 'flannel pyjamas', but she pulls it off. I'm still in the Thursday night clothes. Cleavage-making black top. Pink ruffles to my knees.

'Afternoon.' Faith stretches her long limbs. On the carpet, Benny does likewise.

'Afternoon?'

'It's just gone noon.'

'No.'

'Yup. You've missed your mum's bake sale. She called me an hour ago when she couldn't get hold of you for two days straight. I turned your mobile off, by the way.'

Faith pours me a glass of water – and puts the kettle on. Her tousled hair has that just-got-out-of-bed sexiness they tout on shampoo commercials. Her cleansed, toned and moisturised skin is clear and dewy-looking. She smells like rosewater and jojoba.

My hair feels like an oil slick and my mouth tastes like the bottom of a birdcage.

'Oh dear...'

'She also passed on the message that June Whitbury wants to evict you. It's been a busy morning while you slept, darling. I was just about to wake you.'

I slump myself onto a kitchen stool.

In the cold light of day, I wrap my sober head around recent events. Jordan made Benny sick. Benny destroyed the flat. That pushed me to finally end things with my selfish twat of a boyfriend and I kicked him out. I attended the opening of a new club, in a ludicrous outfit, where I got drunk with Faith and Poppy and high with Harry's half-sisters, sort of hit on Harry and then passed out. I've lost a day and a half sleeping it all off in Faith's spare bedroom. This morning, I missed helping my mother with her bake sale at the charity shop. Now, June Whitbury is evicting me?

She must know about the carnage made in the flat she rents to me for a generously low sum, on the proviso I care for it as well as her dearly departed mother always had.

I imagine the state is far worse than when I left it Thursday morning. Putrid and festering, stinking of poo.

'Yup,' Faith repeats, as if reading my mind. 'You told me Benny had a touch of the runs? June believes her place is completely destroyed.'

'Why was June at my flat?'

June Whitbury doesn't drive and she won't take the trains, let alone the Tube. She hasn't left Redhill in decades.

'According to your mother, her solicitor attended to let in an electrician. Something about installing a fire alarm without delay for insurance purposes. You weren't answering your phone, so he popped by with the key.'

Benny jumps onto the bench and sidles affectionately close to Faith, rubbing his mouth against her hand.

'Apparently, he'll be back at the flat at 5 p.m. today to give you a stern talking-to and your notice. So, let's get dressed and get the place cleaned up before he arrives. Then we'll see what we can do about this eviction.'

I take a moment to take it all in.

'I can't ask you to help me clean, Faith. It wasn't Benny's fault.'

Jordan, on the other hand, can go and do one.

'You're not asking. Also, I should have known it was a stupid idea to send a cat for a sleepover.' Beside Faith, Benny is roly-polying on his tummy, being tickled. 'And I've promised your mum – I told her you've been sick with a tummy bug and I've been babysitting you through it, by the way. You're off the hook for missing the bake sale.'

'Thank you, Faith, for everything. About last night—'

'It was Thursday night, and I'm not sure I want to talk about it.'

'Okay. But, I am so sorry.'

'Will you go and get in the shower now please? I'll have a cuppa ready for when you get out. You can borrow my yoga top and pants. Come on. We'll leave in half an hour.'

* * *

Faith is wide-eyed at the stench – or the sight, they're equally grotesque – as we step inside my flat. She takes in the scene of ripped boxes, scattered clothes, de-railed curtains and faeces-streaked furniture.

'Benny did all this?'

'The shopping fell out of the cupboard on its own.'

'He's never so much as peed in my pot plants.'

I remind her Benny was in strange surroundings, without her, and most unwell.

'Just so you know, you're never borrowing him again.'

'Believe me, Faith, I'd never ask.'

She returns from the kitchen wearing rubber gloves and carrying an assortment of cleaning products. She sprays copious amounts of air-freshener and opens the windows in the front room. Removing her high-heeled boots, Faith rolls up her skinny jeans as far as they will go. She looks like a sexy cleaner who's about to leap into porn-star sex moves when the husband randomly comes home early while his wife is out.

Faith has a cleaner attend to her flat almost daily. In my stinky flat, with my champagne-cocaine abused body still on the mend, I have never been so grateful or felt so loved.

'Where shall we start?' she asks.

* * *

We clean. We spray, scrub and dispose. We get the place in order. I also call my mother to let her know I'm fit and well and to allay her fears about the situation with the flat. I assure her I'm confident everything can be smoothed over with June, after I meet the solicitor. She's relieved to hear Faith's with me, so she doesn't have to send my father, who also hasn't travelled out of Redhill in forever. She tells me she has a lemon poppyseed cake in the oven and will take it around to June's tomorrow as an apology.

'June's my friend.'

'Yes. I'm so sorry, Mummy. I promise, I'll sort it.'

'You'll let me know, dear?'

'Of course. Gotta go clean. Love you.'

Faith sifts through the boxes and clothes littered throughout my hallway. I sweat over the stains on the carpet and the sofa. As we go, I tell her everything. About the problems Jordan and I had been having for some time. How lonely I'd felt. How isolated I'd made myself. About the terrible birthday sex and his physical rejection of me ever since. That I didn't enjoy the cocaine and wouldn't ever do anything like it again. How I embarrassed myself in front of Harry. Throughout, Faith is patient and empathetic. My best friend doesn't make a big deal about how, after I collapsed in the club, she worried I'd had a heart attack or a stroke, or that someone had spiked my drink. But she does warn me off getting romantically involved with Harry. Again.

'Darling, we had this conversation. Harry's lovely. But he's our agent. It's for the best nothing happened. Though, by the sounds of it, you don't need to be embarrassed, you didn't exactly shove your tongue down his throat.'

In no time at all, the place is looking – if not yet smelling – decent when, lo and behold, Jordan waltzes in.

'Is it safe to come in?' He's hovering inside the front door. Faith's in the basement. He doesn't know she's here.

He's wearing his black Versace jeans, white T-shirt and black blazer. His 'going out' outfit. He has a three-day stubble on his face.

I'm startled to see him. I'd told him we're over. He'd packed his bags and fled. There wasn't a single message from him when I'd turned my mobile on – there were several from Harry.

You okay? H
Just checking in …
Spoke with Faith. Glad you're being looked after. Text me when you're up? H

Harry's texts were about an hour apart. In the cab, on the way to the flat, I'd texted back.

Most embarrassed, but up!
Don't be embarrassed. All handled discreetly. No harm done.
At least I didn't do a Britney and shave my head…
Be a Kate. Never complain, never explain.
Harry, I'm the new Queen of Cool?!
Ha! Leave it with me

I'd wanted Harry with me in person after he'd sent that. I'd wanted to look into his warm, darker-than-chocolate eyes as he turned my mortifying misadventure into a funny soundbite, including a reference to Kate Moss. Then, he texted me this:

Ps I've had words with my sisters. They're sorry and send their love x

The kiss was new. Unsure if it was from him or his sisters, I'd speculated if maybe my recollection of Thursday night was inaccurate. If, perhaps, right before I passed out, Harry intended to declare the infatuation with me his sisters had ballyhooed on about all night. If Harry were madly keen on me, beyond being my agent, surely Faith would support us giving things a shot?

Without delay, I'd texted back.

Not at all. They were wonderful, and looked out for me. Give them my love. Are you on set this week? x
Will try to make it, H

And that settled that.

None of it changes anything with Jordan, I remind myself confidently. We broke up. End of.

'You said not to come back unless it was to clean,' Jordan says.

What's he playing at?

'It doesn't change anything else I said, Jordan.'

'I know, Grace.' His voice is croaky. He looks exhausted. 'I've been working around the clock. We got a whole bunch of accounts in at once and—'

'I don't need to hear about your work.'

'Right. I was just explaining why I haven't been back to help with the mess'

The flat is nowhere near as bad as when he left it. Jordan's never given a toss about helping me with any of the housework. Though it's only been two nights, a lot has happened to me since Thursday morning.

'Hello, Jordan,' Faith says, coming up the stairs.

Nervously, Jordan kisses her hello on the cheeks. He's every reason to believe she knows every detail of what's gone on between us.

'I couldn't believe it,' Faith says. 'This place, usually so immaculate because Gracie is a domestic goddess, looked like a giant litter tray.'

Jordan sucks his breath in and nods.

He launches into a polished explanation about the mishap with Benny, giving a comedic slant to his attempt at making pellet-shaped morsels out of the Pussy Paws wet food with my piping bag. It's the first time Faith – or I – hear of the incident in detail. Jordan, in advertising executive mode, sells us a story that, despite the circumstances, has Faith finishing off with a laugh that she warned me to stick with his Royal Canin.

'Regardless, Benny was a trooper,' Jordan insists. 'Really helped us out. The team at Pussy Paws were most impressed, and believe I actually have a cat. How can I thank you properly?' Jordan glances nervously at me.

'You can help us clean this flat before the solicitor gets here,' Faith says. 'I won't beat around the bush and pretend I don't know what's going on with you two. But for your information, Gracie may well get kicked out of this beautiful flat that she's lived in and cared for since she moved to London. I, for one, am not keen to see that happen.'

'Crickey. Right.'

Faith explains the exact circumstances of my eminent eviction. Jordan offers to nip down to Tesco and hire a steam cleaner, which is good thinking – for someone who probably couldn't say where we keep our vacuum, not sure how he came up with it. And I'm still incredibly cross with Jordan. There are hard feelings. But I'm grateful he's going to help.

The three of us whizz around the place like Mrs Hinche and, by 5 p.m., the sofa is showroom fresh, if too wet to sit on, and the entire flat is sparkling clean. I light some scented Scandinavian candles. The place smells like a Nordic pine forest by the time Philip Maxwell of Maxwell & Maxwell solicitors arrives to enquire if I have any idea how 'very far off my interpretation of responsible tenancy is from the good and honourable Mrs Whitbury's?'

Intimidated by his stern demeanour, and unable to shake an image of a distraught June wearing the yellowed wedding dress I last saw her in at Beryl's dinner party, I rely on Faith to do her thing and step in. As only Faith can, she walks Philip calmly through 'the situation', as he keeps referring to it.

In her best business voice, Faith impresses there most certainly has never been an unauthorised pet residing permanently at the address and that the flat is usually kept in pristine condition. Philip acknowledges it's far more presentable than when he entered yesterday. Then he informs us that, while that might be well and good, events have nonetheless convinced June to sell. I'm to leave within the month regardless.

On such news, Faith leaps into negotiations that see me agreeing to purchase the property outright. I love living here, it's more than a silver lining result. The price set, though exorbitant, is reasonable. Faith assures me she knows a broker who will sort a mortgage. Within the hour, Philip leaves with a legally binding purchase arrangement – and a twinkle in his eye that I can only attribute to being well and truly won over by Faith.

When Jordan leaves to return the steam-cleaner, I ask him to come back with boxes so he can pack up his stuff in the basement.

Faith leaves to get ready for Drake's party. I can't believe I have to go out again tonight.

Jordan returns while I'm showering. Stepping out of the bathroom, I hear music wafting up from downstairs. I dry my hair and put on some slap. For a body suffering from champagne-cocaine abuse, I scrub up quite nicely. Getting dressed, I slip into an old dress, black and not too fancy, that feels refreshingly loose on account I've hardly eaten in three days. Jordan is still in the basement, packing his crap.

As I'm heating through a home-made chicken risotto from the freezer, he pops up.

'How's it going?' I ask.

'Getting there.'

'Do you want some food?'

'Um, yeah. Thanks. Only if there's enough.'

I sprinkle some sumac on the broccoli I steamed as a side.

'There's plenty.' I set out more cutlery and another plate and we sit at the table and eat.

Silence reigns. I'm on my laptop, a ten-year-old MacBook, sending flowers and an apology to June Whitbury. I also send a big bunch of lilies to my mother, which will make her whole house fragrant for days.

Jordan clears his throat. 'Grace, I think I can line up something next week, but I don't have anywhere to stay just yet. Do you mind if I take the sofa? Just until I can sort a place.'

I shut my computer. 'The sofa will be wet for days. You can't sleep there.'

'I can sleep on the rug, on the floor. I don't mind making do.'

How noble! I don't scream.

'Sure. You can have the extra duvet.' I'm not offering him half of my bed. Jordan wasn't sleeping in it when he could do. 'But I want you packed up and moved out within the week.'

If I didn't know better, I'd swear, by the look on his face, Jordan wishes things could be different. He looks... regretful. All at sea. I guess it's true what they say: you don't know what you've got until it's gone.

'I can keep myself scarce until then. I can work from the office. Where's your party this evening? You look nice, Grace.'

'Marylebone. Chiltern Firehouse. It's a party hosted by Drake. Poppy is beyond delirious.'

'Drake. Wow. You've hit the big time.'

Jordan is impressed. I'd sooner crawl into bed and skip the big time altogether. Aware of both my physical state and my sentiments, Faith suggested we could walk in, get our pictures taken and walk out again. I'd told her Poppy was so excited to see him, I'll stick to water and stay as long as possible. I was quite rude to them both at The Tricycle Club, abandoning them for Harry's sisters. I want to make amends.

'I can't believe you're buying the flat,' Jordan says.

'The circumstances could have been better, but it's a sensible thing to do. I'm happy about it. It's the right thing.'

Jordan nods. Again, sadly. I don't care. He had his chance. He blew it.

I drop my dirty dish in the sink and go to the bathroom to clean my teeth. I apply fresh lipstick. When I reappear in the kitchen, Jordan is doing the washing up.

'I'm off,' I say. What else to say to an ex-boyfriend who I'm still living with? Jordan doesn't need to know when I'll be in. Or if I'll be in (I will be).

It's odd, how we haven't talked in any depth about breaking up. Maybe not so odd for us – our inability to communicate contributed considerably to our split. But it strikes me, now I've put my foot down, how surprisingly easy it was. How despite the hound dog face, Jordan has accepted as a fait accompli that we are done. All that angst, for all those months, and here we are.

'Have a good night, Grace.'

'Thanks.'

And out I go.

22

At the party, Faith arrives in a sexy gold slip, channelling her inner J Lo. Poppy, in a tiny beige dress and a feather headband, resembles Pocahontas. I'm unassuming by comparison in my trusted black dress but it's much more me than all those frills and cleavage.

We're inside and seated at a table for four when Harry texts to say he can't get out of another engagement to join us. I'm still mortified at my behaviour – I hope I haven't scared him off. Whether he noticed or not, I laid my feelings for him bare and they weren't reciprocated. I'll get over it. Though he's my first professional agent, I can't imagine anyone better than Harry. I can't bear the thought of losing him altogether.

We've been here but half an hour when the second-to-last person I want to spend time with, behind Jordan, surfaces: Alex Sutcliffe. Looking dapper, and like the sheep in wolf's clothing that he is, Alex saunters over with a blonde waif dangling off his arm. Introducing her – Matilda seems as sweet as she is beautiful – he jabbers on about how they can't stay long as she's due on a catwalk in Milan tomorrow. When they slink off into the crowd, Faith tells me she turned him down flat the night I left them in the pub. Alex was apparently quite plain with her that, although he has a long-term girlfriend, he'd be happy to go home and screw.

'Cheating bastard,' Faith says. 'She's stunning.'

'Girl code,' Poppy says.

'I mean, be single and screw who you like,' Faith goes on. 'Why lie to someone you're pretending to care about?'

For a split second, I wonder if Jordan ever cheated on me. I understand the temptation. I'd grown fond of Harry before I was officially single – the circumstances were extenuating, and I didn't cheat and I hope I never would, but I didn't exactly put the brakes on my budding attraction. It's important to watch your thoughts, before they become actions, I remind myself. But it's action that defines character.

'Are we so surprised that Alex is an arse?' I suggest.

'A total arse. He hasn't stopped bombarding me with texts to meet for a drink,' Faith says. 'Not sure what that whole meet-my-model-girlfriend was about.' Unfussed, she shows us a picture Toby had messaged to her from New York Central Park. He's in a horse-drawn carriage with a bunch of banker-looking blokes. His message says he'd rather Faith was with him. 'He'll be here in a month. He's working on a big deal that will put him in London for weeks and weeks.' Faith's face lights up.

'Staying in your spare room?'

'Not permanently. I don't want to rush things. But I sincerely hope he'll be popping by often.' She smiles. 'And not, despite your best efforts, Gracie, for my cooking.'

'What are you going to do about your job?' Faith's sabbatical was only for three months. She's halfway.

'Maybe I won't go back. The show's going well. I'm having fun. I love working with you two.'

'I love it too,' Poppy chirrups.

'Me three,' I say.

The adventures so far on our funny little dating-cooking show have pushed me way beyond my old limits. There have been highs and lows to come of it. It's also been the most fun I've had in a long time.

'Let's make *Eat Me* such a hit that Joanna won't let us leave,' Faith declares.

We clink glasses. Water for me. Champagne, but not by the bottle, for the others.

Though it's early days, the show is going smashingly. I hope Joanna keeps us on. Unlike Faith, I don't have other options.

To Poppy's disappointment, she hasn't spotted Drake anywhere at his party this evening. Apparently, there's another area for the Very Very Important People, where the barman said he's hanging quietly with people he knows. Acknowledging it's a fair enough thing to do, how being so incredibly famous Drake must be exhausted by the stream of strangers seeking his company, Poppy suggests we leave him to it, no argument from me.

When I get home, Jordan isn't asleep on the rug on the floor. He isn't in the flat – though his sports bag of clothes is beside the wet sofa.

He returns late the following evening, Sunday, after I've gone to bed, having texted to say he was stuck in the office all day but would try not to disturb me later.

Now we're not together, Jordan hasn't once played his noisy shooting zombies' game on the X-box and he leaves the kitchen spick and span, every time. It doesn't make me want him back. It makes me wish we broke up months ago.

* * *

Back in the studio, we're in Joanna's good books. Though we'd only stayed at the Chiltern Firehouse a short while, and hadn't enjoyed the party particularly, we'd left holding hands and beaming beautifully for the press. I could get used to the attention, I'd thought for the first time, as the cameras flashed and Faith and Poppy giggled. Joanna shows us a gorgeous shot of us on The Celebrity Buzz site. 'I love your little black dress, Gracie,' she says. 'Who would have thought? My little star.'

Speaking of Joanna, rumours abound at SC6 of a blossoming romance between her and our CEO. Certainly, Timothy has refrained from fawning over Faith and I the way he used to. Instead, I clock him gazing into Joanna's eyes during what appears to be deeply meaningful conversations. On more than one occasion, they've rushed off together into his waiting, chauffeur-driven car. It's good to see him with someone closer to his age and who, presumably, doesn't need his money. And it's a relief that something, if not Timothy, has thawed Joanna's iciness. Whether we're in the press or not, she's much happier these days. Long may it last!

I watch episode two of *Eat Me*, with Ben the dentist, on the television with Faith at her place. Jordan planned to finish boxing up the basement but when I arrive home, he's not there and nothing's moved.

The week flies by.

Poppy and I help Faith select the winner of the competition: her date for episode number five. To avoid repetition, she rejects men who are bankers, dentists or covered in piercings. On personal preference, she also vetoes any man with visibly long fingernails, men who look like women, and women. After careful consideration, we agree on Kenny S, short for Kenneth Stoppard, a rental car manager from Luton. In his online submission, Kenny listed his passions as horseback riding and listening to country music. Faith was attracted by the whole cowboy vibe and, for the recording the next day, Kenny S doesn't disappoint. Affecting a slight Texan lilt whenever he talks about his favourite hillbilly ballads – Kenny grew up in Luton, it's claim to fame an airport and the site of the first Domino's Pizza branch – lookswise, Kenny is like a scrawnily-muscled, younger Brad Pitt. It's all very Thelma and Louise – and Faith is on fire for the cameras. Performing an impromptu pirouette across set, Poppy crashes onto Kenny's lap. I expected Kenny to go for a rack of ribs – and I made as much of that as I could get away with – but instead he goes for a more delicate minute steak with a Diane sauce and homemade French fries. By all accounts, the shoot is a success. No touch-ups from animation required, thank you very much.

Harry was on set to see it all. He'd rushed off afterwards, but though things were a bit awkward between us at first, he isn't avoiding me.

Inspired by my promise in Faith's bedroom to fix my life, I book an appointment and, after my free taster session with Nikolai the personal trainer, I join the gym on the spot. Nikolai has muscles on top of his muscles. 'Life begins at the end of your comfort zone,' he says, as he forces me to bench-press weights I fear will crush me to death. 'I'm not telling you it will be easy, but it will be worth it.' I pre-pay ten more sessions.

I meet with Liz Martin at our usual cafe. Dressed to kill in black denim jeans, low-heeled black boots and a leopard-print shirt, courtesy of Poppy's latest shopping expedition, I'm keen to impart all manner of juicy details of our upcoming performances on the show and some, but not all, insights from the parties we've attended.

When I get home early in the afternoon, and not a single item of Jordan's has moved, except the duvet which is now on the sofa and appears slept in, I decide enough is enough.

I call his mobile. It's switched off. I try his work line.

'Hello, Jordan Piper's phone, Rhiannon speaking.' Rhiannon, who's all of twenty and half my size, has a voice as husky as a burly Russian mobster.

'Hi, Rhiannon, it's Grace. Is Jordan there, please?'

'I'm sorry, who's this?'

'Grace.' There's a long pause. We've been introduced on at least three separate occasions. I don't know how to categorise myself. 'Jordan's ex-girlfriend' sounds stupid.

'Just a minute.' She covers the phone. Seconds later, she returns. 'I'm sorry, Jordan's in a meeting.' Sure he is. 'Can I take a message?'

'Just tell him I called, please.'

'That's it?'

'That's it, thank you, Rhiannon.'

She hangs up.

* * *

Joanna books us on the midday chat show hosted by Kiki and Patricia, who I've previously never spoken with, even though we've worked in the same building for well over a year. I attend another session at the gym. And then, when the weekend rolls in, I read in the *Daily* weekend pull-out Liz describing me as 'tantalising and tasty'. Relaxing at home – Jordan still hasn't moved out and we still haven't spoken, which isn't ideal – I read the article over and over and pin it to the refrigerator with a magnet. Inspired, I go for a run in the afternoon, which doesn't last as long as planned, and on Sunday, I book online and a masseuse called Nina comes to my flat with her own table and oils and rubs away my aches and pains.

On Monday night, I watch episode three, featuring DJ Bassdog, at home alone. Still no sight or word from Jordan – I may have to invite my mother down to do a charity sweep of all his things. Tuesday evening, I'm barely home myself when he rushes in. Apparently, to have a go at me.

'Grace, what the hell is this I'm hearing about some giant with piercings and a Mohican on your show accusing me of one having an affair with Robert and two that I have a teeny-weeny?' he snarls. 'And, what's more, did you agree with him about it?'

It's not, exactly, what happened. During the episode, Bassdog had said not many men could compete with the aubergine machine that was, allegedly, Toby's manhood. Then he'd jokingly reassured himself that I didn't seem to have a problem with teeny-weenies – a reference to the chipolata sausage. Fobbing him off, I'd joked my boyfriend was so often busy working downstairs with his colleague, I couldn't be sure I remembered.

'Jordan, it isn't true. That's not what happened. You need to watch the show. I—'

'Everyone at work is laughing at me. Every time I go in to the Gents, I hear laughter. Every time Robert and I are talking – and we sit opposite each other and you're bloody lucky he thinks it's all quite funny and isn't here with me to ball you out... Jesus Christ, Grace, what were you thinking?'

'Jordan, I'll fix it. Next shoot, I'll say—'

'According to you, we've broken up! Surely you won't say anything about me on that damn show?'

'We have broken up, Jordan, so surely you'll be moving yourself, and your stuff, out of my flat sharpish?' I snap back.

Jordan flinches.

'I have a photo shoot. But we need to talk, properly, about what we want this break-up to look like and where you're going to live. I don't want us to hate each other, Jordan. But this isn't working. I'll be back in a few hours.'

Jordan says nothing. Quelle surprise!

I slam the door behind me.

* * *

Down by the Little Venice canals near home, I pose for the shots for Alex Sutcliffe's upcoming article. The shoot has been arranged via SC6. I'm going along with it because I have to. Alex is going along with it because he's a brown-nose to Joanna. Alex is doing his own photography and is under the impression he's interviewing Jordan to gather some salacious snippets next – no pictures. I haven't yet told him this won't be possible.

'Look the other way,' he instructs.

On account of my mystery boyfriend, I'm supposed to look cloak and daggerish. The atmosphere is perfect. Pitch-black. Foggy. Overhead, dark clouds gather steam for what promises to be an almighty downpour. I'm kitted out in a long, beige trench coat, thick black-rimmed glasses and a trilby hat. I turn the other way and force another spy-like smirk. Flash, click. I'm more Inspector Gadget than glamorous spy – I'm certain these photographs will look terrible, and I'm equally convinced Alex arranged it by design. We've never hit it off. The feelings I have about him are clearly mutual.

'And now straight at me.' Flash, click. 'That's it.' Flash, click. Flash, click. 'Again, the other way.' Again?

'Are we done yet?' I ask, not looking the other way. 'Alex, I'm freezing. I want to go home.'

He drops his camera to hang safely by the strap around his neck. He checks his watch. 'Yes, okay. Time to interview the man of the hour.'

'I am sorry, Alex, and I know I ought to have mentioned earlier, but I'm afraid you can't interview Jordan. It's no longer possible.'

'What do you mean "no longer possible"?' Alex snipes. 'The interview with him was your idea.'

Before everything imploded, Jordan had agreed to do it, as a return favour for me facilitating the cat-sitting of Benny. After our argument at the flat just now, all bets are off. Alex doesn't need to know about this, or even that we're no longer a couple. I haven't told Joanna yet – last week on the show, talking country music with Kenny S, I'd joked about my brooding Keith Urban at home. Faith said it was fine. Dramatisation. Harry raised his eyebrows at the time but hadn't commented.

'I know, Alex. But Jordan is adamant I don't mention him any more, not even for the show. I am sorry, but there's nothing to be done of it.'

Alex huffs and puffs and stomps about.

'We can chat about anything else you like,' I offer, trying to make amends, and not wishing to face the wrath of Joanna if this article goes wrong. 'I can tell you about the time I won a singing contest at Butlin's.'

Alex ceases pacing. 'I'm sorry, did you just say a singing contest at Butlin's? Stop the press!'

'Fine, forget it. You can forget the entire interview with me, if you prefer.'

He packs away his lighting equipment.

'If anyone at your magazine asks, tell them Joanna changed her mind. That should cover you.'

I'm set to march home in my horribly oversized trench coat when Alex grabs at my arm with his grubby, philandering fingers.

'What do you mean, blame Joanna? I'm an independent journalist. I don't appreciate your implication.'

It begins to rain. I'm tempted to leave him to get soaked to his core – a good old downpour to wash Alex clean of his dirty-dog habits would do no harm to me or Matilda – but, no. That's best left for karma to deal with.

'You'd best come along with me, Alex. You can call a cab from mine.' I glance at the sky. 'Come on. It's about to bucket down.'

We leg it the short distance to my flat, before the rain hits. At my front door, I'm fumbling with the keys as Alex stands too closely behind me, reeking of cigarettes.

'I'm not sure this piece would have made it to print anyway,' he says, the first of us to speak since we left the canal.

'Hmm, yes,' I agree, not really listening.

'The editor might have tanked it.'

'Yes,' I repeat, still fumbling.

'I mean, Faith, with her looks, I'd get her on the cover any week.'

Why won't this bloody key turn?

'We get a tonne of interest for Poppy, too – she's developing a cult following. Have you checked out their Twitter and Instagram accounts? They have thousands of followers already.'

In the days of *Gracie Porter's Gourmet Get-Together*, I'd received the odd email and handwritten letter. I wasn't aware Faith and Poppy were doing these things. How do I go about posting tweets and finding followers? I'm a social media virgin. I'm not even on Facebook.

That Alex says such things to be hurtful doesn't make them hurt less. Faith is extraordinarily attractive and Poppy is as sweet as a button. I have my good points –although right now I'm struggling to think what they are. It's never been a popularity contest between us. Alex is being a savagely verbal brute.

'Alex, we may not get on, but let's agree to be grown-up. Let's drop the put-downs and snide remarks, both of us,' I counter, hoping this calls a quid pro quo to our little tiff.

As he says nothing further, I assume it has.

I finally turn the key and invite him into my flat. I show him through to the kitchen, where Jordan is sitting at the table, eating cat food. To be perfectly precise, Jordan is at our table eating Pussy Paws cat food out of the can, with a teaspoon.

Before I can ask Jordan exactly what he's doing and explain to Alex that this isn't what it looks like, a distinctive noise erupts behind me.

'Alex, don't!' I cry out. But it's too late.

Flash, click.

Flash, click.

Flash, click.

23

I chase Alex out of my flat and along Warwick Avenue, threatening to pierce him with the pointed end of my umbrella. For the pursuit, I'm still in my spy-like outfit, trilby hat and all. The rain is blinding and he escapes me – just. Darting into a side street, he hurls himself down a set of slippery stairs and disappears into the garden behind a mansion block.

When I return home, soaking wet and out of breath, Jordan has gathered all of his clothes in bin bags at the front door in preparation to flee. He tells me he's had enough and proceeds to list my misdemeanours.

After agreeing to keep him out of the spotlight, I invited a gossip magazine journalist into our home. My home, I counter. There is also the embarrassment of being caught eating pet food – I try to question how exactly I'm to blame for this and ask Jordan exactly why he was doing so, but Jordan is on a roll. What pushes him over the edge is that the sum of everything may have compromised his entire career. He shouts at me that Pussy Paws cat food contains a ground-breaking, flea-control ingredient and he signed a non-disclosure agreement not to divulge this top-secret innovation until the marketing launch next month. 'It's on the bloody label.' Jordan brandishes the can of Pussy Paws, then hurls it into his rucksack. 'If that picture goes anywhere near the papers, I'm done. No one will ever work with me again.'

'It's no bloody picnic for me,' I scream back, finally getting a word in. 'I'm a celebrity chef and you're sat in my kitchen eating cat food.'

Bin bags in hand, Jordan's parting shot is that nobody is supposed to know who he is anyway.

'Get out of my flat. And don't come back. I'm changing the locks,' I scream before the door slams shut.

Which is a decent plan. Except, when I check downstairs, boxes are still in the basement and I very much want them gone, too.

I call Faith straight after Jordan leaves. Her phone goes to voicemail. I remember she's at the theatre with her venture capital colleagues.

I could call my mother, but it would only be to vent. She won't know how to help me and it will only worry her, which I don't want to do. She'd taken the news of my relationship demise in her stride. I suspect my parents saw things going nowhere with Jordan long before I accepted the inevitability.

Harry will know what to do. And, as my agent, he has a vested interest. He'd warned me to watch my back with Alex. Only, the prospect of Harry cleaning up a mess I've created with Jordan is mortifying.

Instead, I call Alex directly. Once I know what the rotter

plans to do with the pictures, maybe I'll know what to do. He doesn't answer either.

Throwing Epsom salts and a few drops of lavender oil into the bath, I run the hot water – with just me in the flat, there's enough to fill the tub. Stripping off my wet clothes, it's cheering to see my stomach is tighter than it's been in years. That's one upside of tearing down the streets as if I'm Usain Bolt, Nikolai will be proud at my next check-in at the gym. I slip into the warm, scented water.

It doesn't soak my cares away, but it helps. At one point, I step out to check my phone. No replies. After I've soaked myself until my fingers are wrinkly and the water is getting too cool to be comfortable, with nothing more I can do this evening, I take a herbal sleeping pill and a St John's Wort tablet. I've been popping both daily since Poppy recommended them to me. The herbs help me sleep more soundly and the St John's Wort, a natural remedy for anxiety, has lifted my mood. I see no harm in doing whatever is necessary to get me over this hump.

I read a little, and sip on some Horlicks, to ensure I venture soundly to the Land of Nod. On my way to untroubled sleep, my mobile switched off, I tuck myself into bed, warm under the covers. My hand slips under my pillow. The rose quartz is still there, warm as ever. When the storm passes, I hope it finds me again: love.

The following morning, Alex hasn't returned my calls and isn't answering his phone. In our dressing room, I relay everything to Faith and Poppy. and they help me sift through newspapers and check the internet on our phones.

So far, there's not a single shot of Jordan at his feline banquet.

'Why was Jordan eating cat food?' Poppy asks, not for the first time.

'He's career-obsessed? Benny wouldn't choose the best flavour? Pussy Paws is supposed to be irresistible? I don't know, Poppy. I don't understand most of what Jordan does for his work. And he isn't talking to me, so I can't ask.'

I'd tried to call him this morning – to agree a mutual game plan for dealing with this, given the potential damage to both of our careers and to remind him, again, to shift the rest of his damn crap out of my basement. No answer.

I send Alex another text. Alex, this isn't funny. I need to talk to you about the photos. Please call me. I've already sent him three like it, all of them ignored.

Faith tries calling and Alex doesn't pick up for her either. 'Do we think it's time we brought in Harry? Or Joanna? Someone who can help?' she suggests.

I don't want to be back in Joanna's bad books.

I really don't want to bring Harry into this, but I agree I'll talk to him after the recording. This isn't just my career at risk, it's the entire show.

Faith and Poppy busy themselves rifling through a rack of complimentary clothes from a boutique in Notting Hill.

'Darling, look. This top matches your eyes perfectly.' Trying to boost my mood, Faith passes me a pretty, blue handkerchief with straps.

It doesn't work. 'And would maybe cover one of my nipples?' I pitch the top onto the expanding pile of not-big-enough-for-me garments.

Over her sufficiently ample chest, Faith tries on an even skimpier piece that fits her like a glove. Poppy discovers an enormous, orange kaftan with purple and blue tassels. It looks like some sort of beachwear garment and on top of being enormous, it's hideous.

'How about this then, Miss Gracie?' She grins cheekily.

'Poppy, I'm not in the mood,' I grumble.

Faith retrieves the handkerchief-top and tosses it back to me. 'Try it on. It may fit. And don't be in a mood. Alex may have no intention of doing anything with these alleged pictures – you don't know. Perhaps his phone is switched off because he's sleeping. Or waiting for you to calm down.'

'They're not alleged, Faith. I saw him take them.'

'You may have broken his camera while you were jabbing at him with your umbrella.' Faith chuckles. 'I can only imagine the scene!'

'Alex called the shots gold and it wasn't funny, Faith.'

Not at the time. And not now. Although one day, I'm sure I'll look back and laugh. Maybe.

'Gracie, Alex isn't so stupid as to bite the hand that feeds him. He won't risk crossing Joanna. And it's not like it was Jamie Oliver sprung eating pet food. We kind of all make fun of ourselves on our show. Right?'

I hadn't considered how I've become a joke chef for television – I don't think I mentioned it earlier, but we made spaghetti bolognaise with sauce out of a can for that *Love Island* hottie.

More importantly, I'd riled Alex with my crack about kowtowing to Joanna. If I get her involved, he might publish the pictures just to prove me wrong.

I scan another newspaper. Nothing. I check my mobile for any new texts, any threats from Alex. None. I google for anything online. Nada.

Wearing a beautiful new floral-print dress, Faith appraises herself in the mirror. Her mobile bleeps.

'Bugger,' she says. 'Christophe's pulled out. I don't have a date!'

* * *

It's three hours before we record our sixth episode. With no prior warning, Monsieur Christophe Laurent, a prominent Swiss architect, has fled the studio. Faith had met him through her circle and flirted with, but not dated him. A handsome man in his early forties, with a keen intellect and an acerbic wit, he seemed suitable. But the Swiss like to play it safe. From the safety of City airport, where he's about to board a plane back to Zurich, Christophe calls to say he isn't coming back. On seeing the set of *Eat Me* and getting a feel for what's involved, he's gravely concerned that an appearance on our show will leave his professional reputation in tatters. After what's happened to Jordan, a sensible consideration.

'What shall we do?' Faith cries, her usual composure noticeably absent. 'I've no one left in my little black book who's up for this. Who can we invite with such short notice?'

'What about this guy?' Poppy holds up a newspaper. 'Maximilian Modacious, Poseidon in the new blockbuster. American. Staying around the corner at The Met.'

In the picture, Maximilian has long, blonde, flowing hair – almost as long, blonde and flowing as Faith's – and his body is insanely ripped with muscles. A cloth girding his loins and a golden trident in hand, he's the temptation of the semi-naked mermaids at his feet. Clam shells cover their bosoms.

'Says here he's just split with one of the mermaids, so he's single,' Poppy adds.

In front of the mirror, Faith smooths her floral-print dress and sucks in her flat stomach. She looks like a glamorous throwback to the swinging sixties.

'It's a long shot. I'll see if the bookers can put me in touch. Fingers crossed.'

* * *

Maximilian isn't available. His agent confirmed he's busy with interviews all day. In desperation, Faith persuades young Adrian from our advertising sales department to step in. Harry, stuck in traffic somewhere, and Joanna, on a business trip to the States, are missing on set. But Robin and the crew are here and, given the circumstances, it's all nicely done. A brilliant save.

Faith jokes about her date ditching her at the last-minute. I comment mystery boyfriends aren't much more reliable – a cryptic reference to my non-existent relationship. And Adrian plays along nicely, enjoying his stint in front of the camera. It's clear he's going to be dining out on this tale for a long time to come. For food, we prepare a stir-fry beef with black-bean sauce and serve it with steamed rice and freshly made prawn crackers. I'd almost forgotten how much fun it is to cook prawn crackers from scratch, the way they puff up within seconds of hitting the hot oil.

But once the cameras stop rolling, and my worry over the pictures bubbles back to the top of my mind, I'm not inclined to celebrate surviving the close call. When the set clears and everyone else races to the pub, I tell Poppy and Faith I'll be along in a minute. Instead, I stay put in the dressing room, ruminating for some time what to do next. Building up the courage to rope Harry into my drama. First, I try to reach Jordan one more time.

'Good afternoon, Baker and Staines, Trudy speaking, how may I help?'

Trudy, bless her, is the only woman at Jordan's office who's ever been pleasant to me. 'Trudy, hi, it's Grace.'

'Grace, love, just a mo, I'll put you through, I'm sure he's in,' she says in her bubbly Northern accent.

I'm mulling over what I'll say when a familiar voice answers. 'Hello, Jordan Pipers phone.'

Husky voiced Rhiannon, who has worse manners than I imagine a Russian mobster employs.

I don't even bother – I put the phone down first.

I'm pottering around the set, organising the kitchen cupboards, trimming the fresh herbs growing in pots on the benchtop and then, in the dressing area, folding and hanging all of our clothes when Harry appears at the door.

'Am I interrupting?'

He looks gorgeous. Messy hair, a little longer than usual. Flushed cheeks, like he's rushed to get here. It's the first time we've been alone since the night I fainted on him at the club.

'In fact, I was about to call you, Harry.'

'How was the show?'

'Fine. Bit of drama to begin with. But, um, that's not it. Harry, I've got myself into a bit of a pickle. I could do with your help.'

Harry smiles. 'Faith told me what happened. It's why I'm here.'

Faith never mentioned calling Harry before she left with the others – probably for the best.

'You were right, Harry. Alex Sutcliffe is a snake.'

'We'll sort it. Don't worry.'

'I don't know what Jordan was thinking...'

'Have you eaten?'

'Shall we hit a bowl of Whiskas?'

'Ha! No, I was thinking I could take you somewhere nice for lunch,' Harry says.

'I'm afraid I've lost my appetite, Harry.' I respond. I've had a mouthful of rice with beef and black beans and one crispy prawn cracker. Too late, I realise, it would have been nice to go to lunch with Harry anyway. Then again, I'm trying to be professional, and not get my hopes up about anything personal with him.

It's been two weeks since events at The Tricycle Club. It's odd how, even as my agent, Harry hasn't enquired about my relationship ending with Jordan – maybe he thinks it hasn't ended, given I've been vague for the purposes of the show?

I certainly haven't the courage to bring it up with him explicitly. Not again!

'Nice shirt,' he says, about the sapphire-blue silk blouse I have in my hand.

'Probably, it won't fit me.' I laugh.

'If not, order another size.' Harry smiles his lopsided grin.

I smile, properly, for the first time all day.

'Sit tight, Gracie. Leave Alex with me. I'll be in touch.'

Harry departs, closing the door behind him.

I try on the shirt. It fits beautifully.

24

I'm in bed when Jordan calls. Not contrite. Not to apologise. He asks if I've heard from Alex. I tell him things are in hand. For the sake of our respective careers, we remain civil. I tell him what I know:

'Harry has apprised Joanna of the situation. She's contacted the chief editor at *Chit Chat* and is refusing to work with Alex henceforth. She's also threatened to blacklist the entire publishing group, and sue on whatever grounds her lawyers devise. She's contemplating Alex didn't have permission to be inside the flat. I believe her formidable reputation hit the spot.'

I then explain to Jordan the risk of Alex touting the pictures elsewhere. Harry thinks it'd be a hard sell, as I'm not a huge Hollywood star and it's not that big of a deal. When Jordan wails the label itself is an issue, I tell him Alex would have no idea that's anything to barter with.

'I don't care what he does with them after early April. At that point, it'll be free advertising.' Jordan is mollified. 'Bring it.'

I'd prefer the pictures never see the light of day.

'That's all I can tell you, Jordan.'

'Keep me posted?'

'Of course. When can you clear out the basement? And I'll need my keys back, please.'

Jordan does his usual sucking-his-breath-in, like he's inhaling the phone. 'I'm staying with Robert. There's no room for boxes.'

I admire the nails on my left hand during the prolonged silence. The peachy polish of my manicure is perfect.

Jordan clears his throat. 'I'll have to arrange a storage unit. Will you be in on Saturday?'

'I can be. What time?'

'Around lunchtime?'

'See you at noon.'

* * *

I hit the gym. I eat well, incorporating lots of healthy vegetable juices and protein shakes into my new regime. Thankfully, I don't have any promotional parties or engagements I have to attend this weekend. Friday after work, I shop at John Lewis. Not for clothes, because I have enough of that for the show. I go on a spending spree for my soon to be very own home – Faith will be over in the morning to help me with the final papers. I buy pretty mugs of fine bone china. Cut crystal ware glasses. Sparkly scatter cushions for the sofa. Girly linen for my bed.

When I arrive home and unpack, it occurs to me I do have a hobby – nesting. I find genuine joy keeping my home beautiful and full of comforts, so that every time I walk in, the mood is welcoming. I cook, bake and freeze delicious snacks and treats to share with the people I love, including myself. I am a domestic goddess – and I'm not ashamed to say, I revel in my pottering.

Stripping the bed back, I discover the pink quartz crystal has fallen between the mattress and the headboard. I tuck it inside my new mirrored jewellery box.

Zelda and her warning.

I haven't fixed everything in my life yet. But I'm on my way.

* * *

In the morning, Faith is at my place when Jordan calls to say he can't make it for the clear-out. Of course, he has more important things to do at his work. 'And there's a Baker & Staines cocktail evening tonight, at Sway,' he says. 'I'll be in no fit shape tomorrow. Could I perhaps come around one evening next week?'

No Jordan can't perhaps come round one evening next week – his perhaps will inevitably turn into another no-show – and I don't have to put up with his work nonsense any more. Surely, that's part of the deal of us breaking up. Furious, I tell him he has until noon tomorrow, or everything is going on the street outside.

When I put the phone down, Faith remarks he'll find another excuse tomorrow because she noticed when she was cleaning up the other day there's nothing worth keeping down there. Jordan took his X-box when he left the last time, after the scene with Alex. When I call him back to insist that he come today, as arranged, and he doesn't bother to answer, Faith offers to stay and help me chuck it all without delay.

We deconstruct every cheap piece of home office furniture that Jordan accumulated throughout our eighteen months of living together. It's cathartic, even if I do splinter my finger and nick my calf on some sticking-out screws. We cart everything to the back of my building, where our maintenance man, David, will dispose of it next week. We bin the old newspapers and empty soda cans. It takes a good few hours but, once the basement is clear, I feel free.

Excited by the prospect – I thought I'd be so terrified – I outline my plans to convert the space downstairs into a proper potting shed, ready for summer. Faith's excited to come round and sit outside on the grassy mound and drink white wine with me, like old times.

My flat exorcised of Jordan and my mortgage papers in order, Faith is preparing to leave when she asks me, 'Are you mad that I called Harry the other day?'

'No. You did the right thing, Faith. You always do'

'That's not true, but okay. I just wanted to make sure we're good. You haven't been yourself lately. I know you've had a lot going on.'

'I'm over Jordan. That's one thing off the list.'

'He doesn't know what he's lost.'

Faith collects her purse and puts on her cardigan. It's early spring. Intermittently wet, but warming up outside. Winter is over.

'I'm sure he's missing my sausage rolls.'

I'd served us a plate for lunch. So yummy. And after the labour in disposing the tacky pieces of plywood, well earned.

'And the mini frittatas are another favourite he's probably hankering for,' I add.

'Your delicious prawn dumplings.'

'And snack-sized beef wellingtons.'

'The cheeky cherry cheesecakes.'

'And lemon sherbet slices.'

'Ooh, those lemon sherbet slices. Will you please make those for me for summer?' Faith says. I agree I will. 'We can feast away while your ex-boyfriend literally starves to death without you. That will teach him!' She kisses my cheek. 'Call me if you change your mind about tonight.'

We all received another invite to the Tricycle Club, but it's not compulsory and, it's been a big day and I want to go to the gym again in the morning. That's another thing that's surprised me – how much I'm enjoying exercise. Nikolai has a lot to be proud of! 'We'll be there from about eight. Bye, darling.'

Faith leaves.

Without putting it off, I call Jordan to say his stuff has been disposed of, but I still need my keys back, he diverts the call to voicemail – I can tell by the number of rings. Bastard.

* * *

To soak my aches and pains from the DIY disposal and my gym sessions throughout the week, I take a long, hot soaking bath. Not bothering to get dressed or into pyjamas after, I crawl immediately in to bed, warm and cosy between my new rose-gold duvet cover and dusky-pink silk sheets. Ostensibly, to read. But before I open a page, my eyes are closed for a nap. Visualising a wonderful tomorrow – I may get up early and head to Clifton Gardens nursery for bulbs and seedlings, and I could paint the abandoned plant pots with a Farrow & Ball colour scheme, or I could pop to a market and spend the day baking, or all of the above – I doze off. When I stir, it's dark. Just on 9 p.m.

With my big plans for tomorrow still in mind, I decide to

get an early night and an excessively decent sleep. I get up to take my herbal pills, the happy and the sleepy one, and then I snuggle myself back in to bed.

Half an hour later, I'm still awake. I check the bottle of slumber-inducing hops, valerian and passion flower. Despite the warning on the label, I take a second capsule.

Another hour passes and I'm wide awake.

Saturday night. No reason I can't pop out for a little while and still stick to my plans for tomorrow. Deciding to join Faith and Poppy at The Tricycle Club, I call Faith to let her know I'm coming. Her mobile is out of signal and I can't reach her. Not to worry, Faith had mentioned she'd be at the club from 8. By the time I arrive, it'll be after 11. If I can't reach her, I'll find her inside.

In case the extra sleeping tablet kicks in later than expected, I gulp a strong cup of black coffee. And then another.

I get dressed to impress. Sleek black trousers, satin singlet, Stella McCartney blazer. Small concession on the low-heeled black boots. Overall, black is slimming. And my increasingly designer wardrobe is flatteringly tailored. By the time I've slapped on blusher, mascara, lipstick and boots, I'm fancying myself as pretty foxy. Even if I say so myself, my investment at the gym is working wonders on my buttocks, in particular. I look – and feel – like a billion-dollar babe. Fergi-licious is blaring from my phone. Old school bootilicious – moi? You bet.

And who knows? Getting myself out, I might well meet someone who's kind, funny, sexy, hopefully handsome, and who likes me back. I'm not looking back at Jordan – and I don't have to pin my hopes on Harry. Meeting my Prince

Charming could, in the realms of possibility, happen as early as this evening.

Letting go of my past failures and insecurities, I book an Uber.

As I set off into Soho in the back of 5* rated Nabil's Toyota Prius, I'm radiating positive energy.

Who knows what joyful surprise my future holds?

Whatever it is, I'm ready.

* * *

When I arrive at the club, it's just gone 11.30 p.m. The pubs have closed and the queue outside snakes around the corner. I haven't connected with Faith. If her phone is still out of range, it's because she'll be downstairs with Poppy, without reception. If she's left for home already, I'd be able to reach her. Harry is away in Brighton for a wedding. Tentatively, I make my way to the front doors, bypassing the line of people.

'Hello,' I say to the bouncer. He's short and stocky and his face is grumpy. Is this Duncan, from the door and dance floor on my last visit here?

'Name?' He barely glances at me.

'Gracie Porter.' He isn't as friendly as last time. But I'm not sure whether it's Duncan or not? I try to make eye contact. The Duncan-looking bouncer isn't looking up from his list. 'It might be under *Eat Me*,' I say, 'the television show. My friends – and colleagues – and I were VIP guests at your opening last month.' I don't mention I was the person who fainted inside the club at such opening. Poppy said it was attributed to the heat at the time. It doesn't warrant a mention now.

Checking his list, the bouncer replies, 'You're not on the

list tonight. General entry is back there.' He jabs a thick finger at the back of the long line.

'Oh. Um, how long?'

He shrugs. 'An hour. No guarantee you'll get in. Packed house tonight.'

'Really? That long, Duncan?' I venture.

'Duncan's not working tonight.'

'Of course, what I meant – sorry, what's your name?'

'My name's Gordon.'

'Right, Gordon. What I meant is, Duncan would certainly remember me. We had quite a chat, Duncan and I, on the night of the opening of this bar.'

'Lady, I've got to keep this line moving.'

'Of course, I'm so sorry to hold you up, Gordon. It's just that I was most definitely invited here this evening. I'm almost certain that my friends Faith and Poppy are downstairs right now. Perhaps you could check your list to see if they're checked in? And then, if you allow me to get to them, they can help to sort—'

'Lady, you're not on the list. You need to move to the back of the queue.'

'Gordon—'

'Line up.'

'But—'

'BACK OF THE QUEUE.'

I slink to the back, every face I pass smugly satisfied I've failed to push my way in at the front.

I walk a little way down Wardour Street and try again, now desperately, to get through to Faith. Again, her mobile rings out. Unbelievably, I don't have Poppy's number in my phone – I've never needed to call her. Poppy's always just been there for me.

Of course, it begins to rain.

I don't have an umbrella on me.

I check my app and there are no Ubers available.

I'm scouting the street for a black cab to take me home when a snivelling voice behind me says, 'Raining again, and here we are. Such serendipity.'

I turn and am shocked to see Alex Sutcliffe standing beside me.

'Leaving so soon?' he sneers.

'As it happens, yes.' Has he been watching me all this time?

'And how was it inside?'

'Alex, have you been spying on me?'

His lips curl in a malevolent grin.

'Alex, what do you intend to do with those photographs?' I persist, while I have the chance. Harry and Joanna may have taken care of things with *Chit Chat*, but, presumably, Alex still holds the shots. Nobody has spoken to him since they were taken.

'Oh, it turns out I have countless story opportunities now I'm unencumbered by the rules of some silly magazine. Or, as you generously pointed out, the whims of Joanna Minnow,' he says.

A black cab. Thank you, universe. I hail and it pulls up to the side of the road.

'Look, Alex, I genuinely regret how everything turned out. I never set out to—'

'Have me fired?' he hisses.

Recoiling from his breath, I step back from the kerb.

Alex laughs maniacally.

Then he jumps in my cab and disappears.

25

I can't find another cab. It's pouring with rain. I've no brolly. One after another, black cabs sail past me with the yellow light off. I'm a proverbial drowned rat when a car pulls up beside me.

'Gracie! Get in.' The rear passenger door swings open. Inside is Bip and Ban.

'Oh, girls.' I clamber in. 'Perfect timing!'

'What are you doing out here all by yourself?' asks Ban. Or Bip. Their cream-coloured outfits match and it's too dark for me to spot the mole that distinguishes their faces. Both are wearing heels, one in ankle boots and one in stilettos.

'They wouldn't let me into The Tricycle Club,' I say. 'I wasn't on the guest list.'

'Snooty place anyway,' Boots sighs, patting my cheeks dry with her scarf. 'They stopped serving us last time.'

'And when we got back from the bar, you'd passed out,' Stilettos chimes in.

'We were so worried.'

'It's so nice to see you, Gracie.'

They're talking so fast, I can barely keep up.

'We're going to Harry's.'

'Come with us?'

'Oh. Well. Um—'

'Harry won't be there. But come anyway.'

'Please will you?'

The driver calls out, 'Where to, ladies?'

'We've been dying to see you!'

'Has Harry not said?'

At that instant, the caffeine hits me. Or maybe the sleeping tablets wear off completely. Either way, though it's coming up to midnight, I'm in no mood to go home. 'Girls, I'd love to. Let's go.'

'Embankment, please.'

The driver pulls away.

Harry's pad is the penthouse flat of a purpose-built block right on the Embankment. A narrow balcony runs the length of his open-plan living room overlooking the Thames. The bathrooms – there are two – are floor-to-ceiling marble. The kitchen is granite and stainless steel, and looks as though it's never been used. In every room, the furniture is modern, tasteful and expensive. The place is immaculate. Despite his cruddy, unstaffed office, Harry's 'Agent to the Stars' business is, by all accounts, booming.

The girls settle us into the second bedroom, with champagne. The double bed is strewn with clothes, make-up and an assortment of accessories. It doesn't appear slept in – but neither did the master suite when they gave me the grand tour.

It feels a bit voyeuristic to be here, without Harry even knowing I am.

'Girls, why are you here without Harry?'

'We have our own keys.'

'We're often here on weekends.'

'Harry's always working.'

'He's at a wedding now, though?' I say.

'That's right.'

'He says it's safer for us to come and go from here than where we live,' Ban says – in the light of the apartment, and after a quick check-in with the girls, I can finally distinguish between them.

'He's always looking out for us,' Bip says.

'He is the best half-step-brother ever – and we have a few to choose from.'

'Do you agree he's the best agent, Gracie?' Bip asks but Ban sidles closer to me on the bed, expectantly awaiting my answer.

I pause to respond, prompting her to add, 'Sorry, we don't mean to upset you. We figured your chat with Harry didn't go quite to plan last time?' She pats my shoulder. 'We think it was just bad timing.'

'And bad circumstances.'

'I'm still sure he's got a soft spot for you.'

'But Harry was so cross with us about, you know, leading you astray, so we haven't dared asked,' Bip admits.

'It's fine,' I say. 'It was not the best of circumstances last time,' I concede. My stomach knots with the reminder of Harry rejecting me. 'The champagne, and other things, I think, got us all carried away that night.' I take a deep breath. 'But I assure you, all is well. Harry is my agent – indeed, the best agent, in my opinion – and, I hope, my friend. I'm glad I bumped into you tonight, girls.'

'Shall we blow-dry your wet hair,' Bip offers.

'And let's get you out of these wet clothes,' Ban suggests.

'Have you lost weight, Gracie?'

'Bip!'

'No, it's fine. I've toned up,' I say.

'You look amazing!'

'She always did.'

'Yes, but now she'll fit into our stuff.'

'Let's not get carried away,' I hasten to say.

I change out of my wet clothes and into a dressing gown. The girls blow-dry my hair as I drink champagne. At their urging, I try on garments from the piles on the bed. My resulting outfit is of Bip and Ban's design, a daring ensemble of a black leather skirt, strapless red top, rosebud headband, diamanté-studded belt and silver loop earrings. I ditch the belt immediately, feeling equally unsure about the rest. The top is designed to be worn without a bra – miraculously, it is holding me in quite well as in the chest department, at least, the girls are larger than me. However, I have to keep my tummy sucked right in otherwise the material rolls up and exposes my smaller-than-it-used-to-be muffin top. The skirt shows off more of my thighs than I'm comfortable with, and at my age, I'm not sure leather is appropriate.

I voice my concerns and the girls squeeze me into a pair of tan-coloured control-top tights. My belly shrinks to washboard flat. My thighs appear cellulite-free, like I have the legs of Beyoncé.

They tell me, repeatedly, how sexy I look.

Well and truly tipsy from the champagne they keep topping up, I'm open to believing them. We neck another bottle from Harry's fridge – apparently, Harry won't mind, the girls do it all the time. There's been no mention of cocaine, which is a relief. Like giggly teenagers at a sleep-over party, we dance around the room and jump across the bed. Little Mix is blaring out of the Sonos speaker via Spotify.

I've had a more languid snoop around Harry's flat. His refrigerator contains only apples, champagne and a bottle of vodka in the freezer. In his living room, his magazine rack is full of glossies, including a few of what must be the last bastions of printed porn. (Admittedly, the pages are dog-eared wherever there's a picture of a woman I vaguely recognise from his wall.) A game of Twister sits upon the sideboard.

'We saw DJ Bassdog on the show, on Monday.'

'He was so weird, and so hot. You pick the best guests.'

'Yes. Tell us, who's on next week?'

'Can you tell us?'

I make the girls promise not to tell another living soul – after out bonding in the toilets and how kind they've been to me tonight, they've earned my trust – I tell them about our upcoming guests. Jerry from *Love Island*, Kenny S from Luton, not Maximillian who plays Poseidon but super-cute Adrian from our advertising department. The girls clap their hands like baby seals.

'So, what are our plans for tonight?' I ask. When Ban suggested fun, I'd thought we might head out to a club and dance. Perhaps, meet some men and flirt. 'It's almost 1 a.m. and I'm older than you, so if we want to go out dancing, we probably should head off sharpish?

'We know loads of clubs that are open until 3 a.m.'

'And later.'

'I can't promise how long I'll last,' I point out, already

abandoning my plans to get up early. I decided to fix my life, but that includes finding joy. Having fun. I'm happy to be out, and being silly, with these two. And a spot of afternoon gardening is still on the table for tomorrow.

Little Mix are singing about getting an ex-boyfriend out of their hair – I'm dancing about, wearing rose-tinted clubbing glasses I won't be taking out of the flat – feeling so empowered by their girl-power lyrics that I suggest I wouldn't mind popping by Sway, to demand Jordan return my keys at once, on our way out.

I've already updated them on what's happened in my life since I've seen them. The girls venture my proposal might not be my best idea. The party may be over, they point out reasonably, and Jordan might not be there. Another glass of champagne and I convince them we should crash the stupid work event en route.

I know Faith, for sure, wouldn't let me go anywhere near.

* * *

We're pulling up outside Sway on Great Queen Street, in Holborn, before I realise what a whimsical, alcohol-induced and bad – very bad – idea it is. Now, it's too late to back out. Robert is out the front smoking a cigarette as the girls jump out of the cab before I can stop them. He rushes over as I tumble out after.

'Good heavens. Gracie, lovely to see you.' Robert greets me charmingly. 'And who are your stunning companions?' he adds, warming up to the girls.

Robert kisses my cheeks, always so kind, and I introduce him to Bip and Ban.

'Jordan doesn't know I'm here,' I say.

'No. What are you doing here?' Robert asks. He isn't being horrid.

'I've come to collect my keys. Jordan won't return my calls.'

'Right. Well, perhaps, let me go and get them for you?'

Too soon, Jordan appears at the top of the stairs outside the club, looking – I must say – exceptionally dapper in a tuxedo, wearing a furiously sexy scowl. Seeing us, he flies down the stairs to right in front of me.

'What are you doing here?' he spits.

I'm teetering on low-heeled black boots in the borrowed black leather skirt, strapless red top and rosebud headband. I don't even have a jacket—we went straight from the flat into a cab and, drunk, I barely noticed the cold. The girls are dressed in identical hot-pink micro-dresses with tiny, white fluffy cardigans.

'Jordan, you won't take my calls. I left you a message. I—'

'I don't care about my stuff and I don't want to speak to you,' he says. 'You shouldn't be here.'

'I know,' I say. 'Give me my keys and I'll go.'

'Fine, here.' Jordan fumbles to remove the key to my flat from his ring. 'Have your key. Now please, you shouldn't be here.'

There's a commotion at the entrance up the top of the stairs. Horrible Rhiannon, and her equally unpleasant work friends, saunter down.

'What's she doing here?' Rhiannon barks at Jordan. Wearing an elegant cocktail dress over her skeletal frames, she looks me and the girls up and down. Her friends snigger rudely at our outfits. I shoot them a stern mind-your-own-business glare.

'Who are they?' Bip asks me.

'They don't seem very nice,' Ban whispers.

'Girls, they're nobody,' I say.

'Actually, I'm his girlfriend,' Rhiannon says, looking at Jordan.

'Oh blimey,' Robert sighs, not knowing where to look.

I'm gobsmacked. Rhiannon. With the poker-straight brown hair, who weighs half of me. I attended drinks for her twenty-first birthday six months ago. It takes a few moments for it to sink in. Rhiannon is now Jordan's girlfriend.

'What's she doing here?' she repeats, glaring at Jordan.

'She wanted her key. I didn't invite her.'

'Jesus, Jordan,' is all that comes out of my mouth.

Jordan turns on me with his tawny eyes. 'Grace, we broke up.'

'Three weeks ago,' I scream at him.

'I'm not doing this.' He grabs Rhiannon by her arm and practically drags her back inside. She turns to glare at me before she recommences growling at him.

'That didn't go well,' Robert says.

'No, Robert, it didn't.'

I'm shaken, but not stirred. I'm upset. But I'm not crying. In shock, I presume.

'Gracie, I'm sorry, you didn't deserve that. That girl is an utter little cow,' he says. 'Let me get you a cab.'

A lone redhead in a decadent long dress offers me a kind smile. I smile forlornly back. Trudy, the lovely receptionist.

Robert escorts us safely away around the corner and, I don't know how, hails us a black cab within seconds.

The girls give directions to another club, an underground place south of the river, where, they assure me, their bouncer friends will let us all in, most likely for free. I tell them I'd really rather call it a night.

'Gracie, no.'

'That was too upsetting.'

'Stay with us.'

'We'll look after you.'

'I'm drunk and I want to go home,' I say. 'Oh no, I think I'm going to be sick.'

'Gracie, hang in there,' Ban takes my hand.

They whisper among themselves. Something about Harry saying they mustn't and not having anything anyway and, after I make a funny gurgling sound, they worry that I may well be about to vomit. Then right here in the back seat of the cab, Bip loads her fingernail with some white powder from a little plastic vial she's retrieved from her bag and she puts it under my nose. Without thinking, I breathe in.

'Oh no,' I repeat, too late.

26

I wake up with a hazy recollection of the night before. Last thing I remember, I was counting the traffic lights on the drive home from Brixton, where I'd been clubbing with Bip and Ban in a musty-smelling vault. A club with frenetic music – boof boof boof, whiiir, weep, boof – and overly familiar people. Everyone kept offering me sips of their water. I stayed only until I was certain I'd fall asleep the moment I got home to bed. The girls bundled me safely into a minicab in the wee small hours of the morning.

My head is beginning to wrap itself around the idea that we crashed Jordan's work party last night when someone knocks at my front door.

BANG, BANG, BANG, BANG, BANG.

'Gracie!' A voice calls through the slightly ajar reception window. It sounds like Faith. 'Gracie, this is serious. Let us in.'

I pull my dressing gown around my state of half-undress. The leather skirt is on the floor. My legs are still ensconced in the tan control-top tights. I'm braless under the strapless red top, and I've slept in the make-up I applied with the girls' help last night. I pause briefly at the mirror in the hallway. I look like a prostitute at the end of a long shift.

As I open the door, daylight blinds me. I rub my eyes and my hands retract covered in blue eyeliner. Faith is at my door, and she's here with someone else, and that someone is... Oh my Lord, Harry is here.

'Thank you,' Faith says, passing by me briskly and plonking herself down on the sofa. She's wearing low-slung velour tracksuit bottoms – the trendy sort – a sporty singlet and a hooded top. Her long, blonde mane is in a high pony-tail. Her face is devoid of make-up. Presumably, Faith was out last night at The Tricycle Club, but she looks like she's just returned from a health spa. 'You've really done it this time,' she says, slapping a large yellow envelope on my coffee table. 'Even for you, this is good.'

From the front door, Harry clears his throat. 'It's nothing we can't sort out, Gracie.' His appearance is as rumpled as I feel. He's wearing a wrinkled shirt and muddied jeans (it must have been some wedding). His eyes are bloodshot when he removes his sunglasses. He gives me one of his trademark grins. 'May I come in?'

Embarrassed to have left him standing – embarrassed that the tan control tights, with reinforced toes, are visible beneath my dressing gown – I stutter, 'Sorry, Harry, of course. Come through.'

He comes inside my flat and into my front room, where he takes a seat in the armchair opposite Faith.

I take immediate leave for the bathroom.

I've made some dubious fashion statements recently, but this morning takes the biscuit. My hair has a streak of green paint on one side, transferred from one of the ravers last night. Dried-up bits of azure mascara cake my eyes. A huge spot on my chin threatens imminent eruption. My tongue is brown – I was chain-smoking inside the club, and nobody batted an eyelid (or lost their eyelashes).

When I sit down and pee, it comes out dark yellow and burns. I finish up and quickly comb my hair, swirl some mouthwash and rub a damp flannel over my mucky eyes. It's a marginal improvement, until I mistakenly give the pimple a big squeeze, causing it to weep quite unstoppably.

'Hurry up,' Faith calls. 'We don't care what you look like. Trust me, it's a little late for that!'

The spot is an angry volcano. I dab on concealer in a futile attempt to cover it. My broken skin is too oozy for it to hold. Desperate, I slather on some talcum powder for absorption – needs must – then more concealer. It'll do.

By the time Faith calls again, it's one spray of deodorant and I'm done.

Suppressing the urge to run back to bed and pull the covers over my head until they leave, I force myself through to the front room.

I position myself strategically at the end of the sofa, spot side facing away from Harry. Faith gives my tights a cursory wince before her gaze moves to where the strapless red top peeks through a gap in my gown. I curse myself for not getting changed and avoid further eye contact. From what I could see out of them, my pupils are still dilated.

'So?' I say.

'So, Harry received this, first thing this morning.' Faith hands me the yellow envelope.

'Actually, the girls received it first thing,' Harry clarifies. I don't mention I was with the girls until very early this morning, and in his flat the night before. If Harry doesn't already know this, I'm not telling. 'They saw Alex Sutcliffe lurking about after it was pushed under my front door. They called me straight away.'

'These are the photographs of Jordan?' I unseal the envelope.

'See for yourself.' Faith says.

I slide out the photographs. The first is of Jordan spooning cat food into his mouth. The label on the can is legible: Pussy Paws – Packs a Punch Against Fleas. As Jordan feared, the big secret revealed.

'Oh dear.'

'Keep looking,' Faith says.

I bristle at her tone.

The images get worse. Jordan gagging on a mouthful of sardine heads in jelly. Cat food spraying out his mouth, eyes wide with shock as he clocked Alex. A sequence of me thundering down Warwick Avenue in my ridiculous detective outfit, threatening the slimy photographer.

'I would've speared him if I'd caught him,' I joke.

Harry and Faith are ominously silent. They don't laugh. I keep looking.

It's more of the same. I'm tearing after Alex in the rain – looking not what I'd call athletic, but the shots aren't as unflattering as I'd imagined. The next picture shows me outside The Tricycle Club, pleading with Gordon the bouncer to please, please, please let me in.

And then...

Me, slinking to the back of the long queue, desperately trying to reach Faith on her mobile.

Me, flailing my arms in uproar as Alex snatches my cab, the photo taken from inside the moving vehicle.

Me, wandering the streets of Soho alone and piss-wet through.

Me, entering Harry's apartment block – rendering me unable to meet his eyes now, sitting in my front room with his offer to help me.

Me, looking less like the glamour puss I'd supposed I was and more like a drag queen in a black leather skirt and racy red top, staggering drunkenly between two perfectly formed Barbiesque sisters, about to gate-crash the Baker & Staines cocktail party. Shots of me hovering on the footpath as Jordan storms away from me, Rhiannon's arm in his hand.

Me, unkempt among the tacky fluorescent backdrops and on-ecstasy revellers at the 456 Club in Brixton in the early hours of this morning. And slumped in a windscreen-chipped minicab, the Rastafarian driver toking a marijuana spliff, as I made my way home. Through the back window of the cab, the sun is rising.

There's one last picture from last night and it's mounted beside a station-approved promotional photograph of Faith, also dressed in black leather skirt and skimpy red top – the outfit she wore to promote the competition. The images are underscored with a handwritten caption: Gracie's Leap of Faith Flops. With both of us in almost identical clothes, the comparison is striking. Where Faith is all long legs, sleeked hair and sex-kitten pout, I'm control-top tights, hooped earrings and amphetamine grimace. The cocaine, though only a tiny amount off a finger nail – I didn't have any more voluntarily or make the same mistake twice – had made my jaw jittery again last night, for some time.

'I didn't mean to dress like you. Faith, I—'

'Never mind that,' she snaps. 'What were you doing in that club? What were you thinking crashing Jordan's work function? And were you on drugs? With those girls. Again?' Faith looks at Harry. 'Sorry, Harry.'

He throws his hands in the air to signify no offence taken.

'I know you've had a rough trot lately, Gracie, but it's too much,' Faith insists.

I look directly at her – it doesn't matter now if she notices my pupils – and when I see a hint of smug on her beautiful face, I'm consumed with rage. I hate her sitting in my living room in her ghetto-fabulous hipster bottoms and tiny singlet under a hooded top. I hate her pretending to understand what it feels like to be me, when she couldn't possibly have a clue.

Me, who struggled to keep my boyfriend sexually interested.

Me, who practically climaxed on my own in a public place and later passed out over a man who likes me well enough, sure, but doesn't fancy me.

Me, whose professional success is now so dependent on Faith, it may as well be hers.

I'm sitting here with talcum powder coagulating on a pimple on my chin. To be me... how can Faith possibly understand?

'If you'd answered your phone, Faith, none of this would have happened,' I growl.

'This is my fault?'

'It's not your fault, Faith. But do you honestly believe I planned to go and embarrass myself in front of Jordan?' I don't want to mention Rhiannon. I can't. Not in front of Harry. It makes me look so pitiful. I don't need this situation any worse than it is. 'I couldn't get in at The Tricycle Club. You didn't answer your phone. I didn't intend to dress up like a two-bit whore, but my clothes got soaked after that git Alex Sutcliffe stole my cab. I got caught in the rain and it was a godsend when Bip and Ban picked me up. Thank heaven someone was there for me.'

Faith's cold stare turns glacial. 'You think I dress like a two-bit whore?'

I hate she is playing it cool, making me the spectacle – albeit Harry is doing his damnedest to pretend he isn't listening to us fight.

'No, Faith. You looked fabulous. You always do. Which is obviously why you deem fit to preside over me, because you're so perfect.'

'I'm not perfect, Gracie. No one is.'

'Oh, but you've been judging me because I'm not. Bip and Ban don't do that. They like me just the way I am. Not like you.'

The saddest part is, I know this isn't all about how Faith is judging me now. It's about how I've started to see myself in her shadow. Ever since Faith became the main attraction on the show, a storm's been brewing.

'Then we agree on something, because I would have judged you last night and I wouldn't have let you humiliate yourself like this.' Faith waves an especially savage shot of me staggering after Jordan. A roll of my tummy fat spills between the strapless top and the leather skirt. 'Look at the state of you! High as a kite!'

I snatch the photograph from her. 'For your information, I wasn't on drugs at that point. I mean, maybe the sleeping tablets kicked in. And I'd had quite a lot of champagne. But the cocaine I took later on was by accident anyway. I didn't mean to do it.'

'Because you look so sleepy in these photographs,' Faith roars back at me. 'And how exactly does one accidentally take drugs? Pray tell.'

'Do you know why I don't tell you everything any more? Because of your sanctimonious bullshit,' I scream at her. Faith likes being the one to swoop in and save me. But I have to ask: does she want me to be successful off my own bat? She certainly didn't want me to end up happy with Harry. Oh no, she warned me off him. And that dream! Even asleep, I never dared imagine her reaction when Harry hit on her. 'Who do you think you are?'

'I thought I was your best friend,' Faith says. Sadly. So that it flummoxes me.

After everything we've said and everything that's happened, I didn't expect this. It throws me. However, I'm too upset to be reasonable – those photographs side by side, globs of fat on me and not an ounce on her.

'You have sex with multiple men you hardly know. You parade it all on camera for everyone to hear about and you're frantic because some trashy pictures might make a public spectacle of me? Get over yourself, Faith,' I hiss.

'Gracie, we're here to help.' It's the first Harry has spoken since we sat down. 'Faith suggested we—'

'Save it, Harry.' Faith rises sharply from the sofa. 'I've had enough of this. I'll keep my sanctimonious bullshit to myself from now on. Gracie, you're on your own.'

In her ghetto-fabulous skinny outfit, she flounces out of my flat.

I ask Harry to leave, too. Instead, he moves closer to me on the sofa. When I catch a whiff of his gorgeous scent, I'm tempted to let him stay. But the state of me this morning – I don't need further humiliation. When Harry touches my cheek to turn my face towards him, I'm so ashamed of myself, and my festering spot, I dash into my bedroom and slam the door behind me. 'Can't you all just leave me alone?' I wail, locking myself inside.

A long time passes before I hear the front door close.

When I creep back out to the living room, I'm alone.

Harry is gone.

Faith is gone.

Jordan is long gone.

I'm completely alone.

On top of the yellow envelope is a scrawled note.

It will be OK, Gracie. We'll fix everything. Call me. Love, Harry. PS. Sorry about my sisters, they mean well.

27

When you reach rock bottom, there's nowhere left to fall. It takes me a few days to realise this. Monday, I call in sick. Tuesday, I also stay home, where I have the epiphany that things can't get any worse. Rock bottom. Not such a bad place. The only way is up.

Throughout my hiatus, Harry and I have been texting:

Are you ill or hiding? Shall I bring you soup?

Hiding… I'm okay, Harry, thanks.

Don't hide too long. I'll miss you. Alex gone underground. Don't worry, I'm on it.

Since our argument at my flat, Faith and I haven't made contact at all.

* * *

Wednesday, I make it into the studio for our seventh recording. The station is abuzz with the news that Faith has invited a girl to be her date this week. Apparently, they've slipped off somewhere to chat. Is Faith avoiding me?

'What's she like?' I ask Poppy in our dressing area. It's just the two of us.

'Who?' Poppy twirls my hair and then lets it fall silky and bouncy down my back. I'm lucky I have good hair. I'm grateful.

'Faith's date, obviously. Poppy, is that dreadful spot covered?'

'Yes, my sweet. But promise me you'll stop picking it.'

Faith isn't gay. Bi-curious, maybe. She's likely on this girl-crush-exploration after my cutting remark about her being promiscuous with loads of different men. If I've hurt her feelings, this could be payback.

'What's her name?'

'Lucy. Look up. Not that you need mascara with your lashes.' Poppy applies lashings of it anyway.

'Poppy, please tell me, what's she like?' I repeat. The suspense is killing me.

Poppy applies a peppermint-flavoured gloss to my lips. It's tingly and, allegedly, will make my lips plumper. I surmise from Poppy's hesitation to talk that she's caught wind of my falling out with Faith. 'She's Australian,' she eventually divulges.

'Is she pretty?'

'Oh, very.' Poppy lets her guard drop. 'She has the most amazing green eyes. Do you know how rare it is for a Chinese person to have green eyes?'

'I thought you said she's Australian?'

'She sounds Australian.'

'They're not green contacts, are they? It's a bit cliché if we have another guest wearing coloured contacts. Surely?'

'I'm pretty sure Lucy's green eyes are real.'

She's not the only one.

'Miss Gracie, are you okay?'

I back off. 'Sorry, Poppy. I'm just a bit taken aback that Faith has sprung this on us without warning. I have a few days off...'

'Sprung what on us, my angel?'

'Never mind.'

I don't want to sound homophobic when I'm not. Countless nights on Soho dance floors to counter the very notion.

I look in the mirror. The mask of soft, feminine prettiness Poppy's given me hides my feelings of guilt, resentment and profound sadness.

'Poppy, I don't know how you do it, but I look the best I ever have.' I give her a quick hug, worry I might cry and cause her to have to start over. She'd do it without complaint, sweet Poppy. Who never lets me down. Who never gets cross, no matter what I do. 'Thank you, for everything you do for me, Poppy.' I have to leave before I do start blubbing and spoil her good work. 'I'll go get us a can of ginger beer. Stay here. Back in a jiff.'

On my way to the canteen, I catch Faith chatting in the hallway with Harry, both of them laughing. I don't know where Lucy is, but she isn't with them. Faith affects not to notice me. At the last minute, Harry turns and gives me a smile.

* * *

Lucy is gorgeous. Skin the colour of honey. Slight build. Long dark hair. Eyes that are, amazingly, vividly and all-naturally green. She and Faith suit each other perfectly – apart from the fact they both have vaginas and Faith has never, in the entire time I've known her, batted an eyelash at our fairer sex.

Although there's no script, and things are far from normal between any of us, we all slip easily into character for the recording. I tease Faith about her new-found fondness for lady-loving. Faith hams it up with Lucy accordingly, exchanging sizzling innuendo and smouldering glances.

Despite the banter, Faith and I avoid eye contact.

I'm plating up Lucy's requested chickpea and aubergine curry – Toby's phallic vegetable, curried for Faith's date with a chick – as Faith ogles Lucy from behind. Pugsy, capturing it all up close with his camera, verges on visible excitement at the prospect of some girl-on-girl action.

Wearing a figure-hugging, lace-up black dress and vegan leather boots, Lucy shimmies her tushy towards his lens. Laughing, Faith professes that if ever a bottom were to turn her, it would be her's.

Guffawing in response, I speculate it's more likely a good tongue cuts the mustard with 'the turning' Faith is referring to, prompting Lucy to lick her lips, juicily, at me.

Joanna beams like the Cheshire Cat at our sultry performances.

Poppy waves her hand over the small dishes of curry and rice in the manner of a seventies game show host.

From where he's standing, behind the cameras, Harry smiles at me, gorgeously, for the second time today. Albeit we haven't spoken since he was at my flat on Saturday, he's kept me informed via text. So far, there's been no word from Alex.

Harry's unyielding support is keeping me together – I'm grateful he isn't so petty to be holding anything against me, unlike my best friend. In my more cynical moments, I remind myself he is on commission. To some extent, I do pay Harry to be nice to me.

I'm in such deep deliberation that I don't notice how close Lucy has sidled beside me, behind the kitchen bench on set.

'I love a bit of spice,' she says. Dipping her finger into a bowl of cumin, she licks it clean. Then taking my curry-stained-from-cooking index into her hand, Lucy manoeuvres it into her mouth, whereon – with Pugsy's camera right in close on us –she sucks it as if it isn't a finger at all!

My blue eyes peel back.

Removing my finger from her orifice, I grit my teeth and smile.

'Cumin: a nutty flavour,' Lucy laughs, 'with somewhat bitter undertones,' Faith, for the first time during the shoot, looks directly at me. 'A penetrating aroma with hints of lemon, it does have an intensity to it. A most versatile spice. Great with vegetables – and meat – alike.' With a wink to camera, I dip my finger in the little bowl and lick myself clean.

Then, with a reminder to our viewers to log on to our website for recipe details and to follow us on our new Twitter account – to my great relief, we now have a team managing social media on our behalf – I wrap the episode.

Robin calls cut and the crew erupt in applause.

Harry saunters over and gives me a hug. It's so healing, I almost forget the trouble I've caused and the embarrassments he's witnessed. I could stay safely in his arms forever. Instead, I pry myself free.

Without sticking around to talk to anyone about anything, I flee for the gym and then to home.

* * *

When I get in, I call my mother. I can't tell her everything that's going on. But I need to talk to someone.

I update her with a PG version of events. There's much to share, even in the watered-down version.

When I tell her about Jordan having another girlfriend already and me ditching all his stuff to the rubbish, she says, 'I'm sorry to hear that Grace. But you dodged a bullet. Let him be her problem now.'

When I spill some of the story about Alex and how I almost impaled him, my mother bursts into a fit of giggles. For the first time since the incident, I see the funny side and laugh, too. She's in disbelief that Jordan was eating cat food. She reiterates I dodged a magazine spray of shrapnel that are Rhiannon's problems now.

I tell her how wonderful Harry has been, as my agent. My mother remarks how attentive Harry is, for an agent. I recount the night at The Tricycle Club – again, the filtered version. She says it doesn't sound like I romantically threw myself at him at all. 'You asked him to dance, dear. I'm quite sure the poor chap has no idea you meant anything more by it. And with all this business, he must be wondering what's really going on with you and Jordan. Talk to him, Grace. What have you got to lose?'

My dignity, for starters. What is it they say a woman should never do – oh yeah, chase a man. If Harry were to reject me when I make perfectly clear that I like him as more than my agent and friend, I'd be crushed. I'm not brave enough to try.

'Mummy, it'll be complicated even if it works, because we have to work together.'

'I don't know that I agree with that,' my mother says. 'But it sounds like you've got enough on your plate to deal with right now. So in any event, something to park for later.'

She is dismayed to learn Faith and I have fallen out.

'Is there a chance, dear, you feel Faith is stepping on your toes? From what you've told me, your nose could be a bit out of joint?'

The tinge of jealousy I'd felt. My mother is, of course, spot on.

'Mummy, it's Faith who says her nose is big.' My incredibly juvenile response, prompting my mother to sigh down the line. 'But, of course, she's perfectly beautiful.' She is. Faith is perfect and beautiful, in every sense. She's amazing. 'I don't want to take anything away from Faith, Mummy. I just... don't always want to be me. And now I don't know how to unwind how awful I've been. She's my best friend. I can't believe we're not even talking.'

'Oh, Grace. Dear. I'm going to tell you something I've not mentioned before. I almost left your father once, when you were a baby,' my mother says. 'I was an older mother, as you know, and you came as a complete surprise. I loved you to bits, but I wasn't coping. These days, they call it postnatal depression, but back then, it wasn't talked about. Everyone just got on with things. Beryl was the only person who even noticed.'

'Beryl?' I'm unable to hide my shock.

'Beryl being Beryl, she'd made me so mad over something I can't even remember, and before I could control myself, I'd blurted everything out to her, my torment and my guilt. She just stood there and took it all. Then she told me that life was tough but I was tougher. That this little baby that I didn't know what to do with would make me happy, but first, you'd make me strong. Beryl came to the house every day after your father left for work and cleaned the place and changed your nappies and bathed you. Most days, she also forced me into the tub to wash. She'd leave before your father got home. She did this for a few months until, one day, I told her she could stop coming. As if by magic, I felt okay again. Beryl never breathed a word to anyone. Not even, after all these years, with me.'

'Mummy, I never knew,' I say, overcome with emotion.

'Oh, dear, there was nothing for you to know. You're a blessing and a joy to me and your father. My point is, over all our years of friendship, Beryl has mostly been a crotchety old thorn in everyone's backside. But when I needed someone, she was there. That's what friendship is, dear. It's about who shows up. Since Beryl became a widow, I've tried to return the favour.'

'Mummy, that's lovely.'

'It's love.'

'With Beryl, tough love, nonetheless?' I laugh.

'Yes.' She laughs too.

'What if it's Faith who makes it hard, sometimes, to be me?'

'Jealousy is only poisoning yourself, Grace. The Faith I know has always been your biggest cheerleader. I'm sure there's no good reason to compare.'

I ruminate on this the rest of the evening.

Something I know I need to fix inside myself.

* * *

The next morning, I'm regaling Liz with the story of Lucy fellating my finger during the show. Liz is absolutely tickled.

'From the simple days of *Gracie Porter's Gourmet Get-*

Together,' she muses, finishing her tea. 'Goodness, it's got my juices flowing again. Such tales you tell me these days, Gracie. I look forward to writing this week's column.' As Liz chuckles, her face wrinkles most attractively. 'Shall we order wine?' she asks, apropos of nothing.

'Oh? I've, um, been trying to abstain.'

'Another Earl Grey then?'

'I said trying, Liz.' I smile. 'To be honest, I could do with a wine.'

'If I'm not poorly influencing you?'

I order us two glasses of Pinot Grigio without delay. When the waitress delivers them to our table up the back, Liz enquires, 'Any particular reason you're in need of a drink?'

'We're off the record?'

'Completely,' Liz assures me. 'Whatever you're comfortable sharing.'

I sip slowly. Liz has always been good to me. I trust her and I value her opinion.

'Where to start? Do you happen to know a journalist by the name of Alex Sutcliffe?'

'I know he was fired off a paper years ago.' Liz sips her wine. 'Barely a journalist.'

'Right. So, I'll jump straight to the bit where the little snot is blackmailing me. Or threatening it. I'm not sure what he wants, but he has some compromising photographs of me.'

'Naked photographs?' Liz, who has twice interviewed a prime minister, is pink-cheeked.

'Worse.'

'Worse than naked?'

'I think so, yes.'

I spare Liz no details. It takes a while, but I tell her all about Jordan, about Harry, Alex, Faith, Bip and Ban, about the drugs, the photographs – everything. In greater detail than I've shared with anyone, I unload on Liz.

When I'm done, she offers me a solemn, 'That is quite the tale – and I've heard some in my time.'

'I'm sure.' I swallow the last of my wine. 'As I say, every bit of it, regrettably, true.'

Liz frowns and pushes her smart black-rimmed glasses up her nose, thinking.

'I might have an idea that takes care of those photographs.' The corners of her flint-grey eyes crinkle. 'And, perhaps, some of your other conundrums to boot.'

I dare say Liz has heard it all in her time. If she says she has a plan, I want to hear it.

'Shall I get us more wine, Liz?'

'I think, given the circumstances, one more is still in moderation.'

I motion for the waitress to bring us another glass each.

'Right, here goes my thoughts on all of this…' Liz begins.

My turn to listen.

28

I leave Liz with a bold plan in mind regarding Alex and his terrible photographs. Strolling through to St James's park, I take the time to walk off the wine. The flower beds are in early bloom. The tulips, primroses, hyacinths and daffodils usher in their annual show. Though it's getting onto dusk, people wander, enjoying the surroundings. Couples. Parents with infants in pushchairs or toddlers feeding the ducks. Some, like me, are alone. I amble past the elegant little lakes, the thatched hut and the graceful pelicans perching on their rocks. My hand clasps around the pink quartz crystal Zelda gave me. I've been carrying it with me often lately, for luck. Love isn't ever perfect; I remember Zelda telling me.

Squeezing the stone inside my palm, I know what I have to do.

Cutting back through Mayfair to Covent Garden, I arrive at Faith's door.

I buzz her intercom.

'Hello?' She's in.

'Hello, it's me, Gracie. Can I come up?'

Across the street, a couple walking by stop and huddle. I've been spotted. It's happening more and more lately. I wave. They wave back and move on.

I buzz again. 'Faith?'

'I heard you the first time.'

I'm considering leaving when the door clicks ajar.

I take the stairs to the first floor. Faith is waiting for me on the landing outside her entrance.

'Hello.'

'Hey.' Faith doesn't smile. And she doesn't invite me in.

'Faith, I'm here to apologise, unreservedly, for everything.'

This evening, Faith's eyes gleam with flecks of golden amber. She looks at me for some time before she lunges forward. Holding me so close to her, she says, 'Oh Gracie, I'm so sorry.' Tears stream down her face.

Soon, mine too.

We break our embrace.

'I've been a nightmare,' I say, wiping my eyes.

'Crashing Jordan's work party, not your finest hour...' Faith laughs, wiping her own.

I laugh. 'No.'

'Attacking Alex with your umbrella.'

'He deserved worse.'

Faith cackles. 'Agreed.' Her expression sobers. 'Darling, you scared the life out of me. I wanted to snap you out of it. I never meant for you to think I didn't care.'

'I know.'

She was perfectly supportive, but I didn't want to hear it. 'I was jealous of you,' I confess hurriedly, lest I lose my courage. 'I haven't always been. But I have been lately.'

'I was sometimes full of sanctimonious bullshit and acting like a style gestapo and always thinking I know best...

and whatever else you accused me of.' Faith grins sheepishly. 'That was on me.'

'Love isn't ever perfect, Faith,' I say. 'But you're perfect for me. You're my best friend and I love you.'

'Well, you're still completely bonkers and you're perfect for me, too. You still make me laugh.' Faith bursts out cackling. 'Bloody hell, these past few months… we have to laugh, Gracie. Don't we?'

On the landing outside her flat, we giggle through our tears and hug each other until Faith says, 'Come inside. Darling, I've missed you.'

In her living room, Benny lounges under the big window watching the world go by below, outside. I plop on a stool at the kitchen bench. Faith produces a bottle of Riesling from her refrigerator. 'It's German. And very tasty.' Faith opens the wine. 'Oh Gracie, I kept replaying in my head how you accused me of being perfect, meanwhile we're shooting an entire series about my failure to find just one man, so how does that work? You know, I'll be thirty-four in two months.'

'I'm not long after you.'

'We're getting on, darling. I can't say I'd mind settling down with someone decent soonish.' Something I've never heard Faith contemplate. 'I've been reflecting on a lot of things.' She pours two glasses of the dry white and passes one to me. 'I know I can get a man to sleep with me, but I've never been brave enough to see if anyone wants to stick around. I've never stuck with anyone long enough to find out. Isn't that a little sad?'

I know what she means. Not the knowing I can get a man to sleep with me, obviously. But her words resonate. A man who wants to be with me. That's what I've been missing, too.

'I get it, Faith.'

'I envy how fearlessly you put yourself out there, Gracie.'

'I wouldn't say fearlessly,' I correct her swiftly. 'And I wouldn't say to any great success. More like a glutton for punishment. A bit bonkers, I believe you said.'

'I said completely bonkers. And you are brave. Like no one else I know.'

I'm set to fob Faith off with a self-loathing one-liner, but I stop myself. I stop myself from beating myself up. I haven't always made the wisest choices. But it's true: I've given things a go.

'Thank you,' I say.

Faith clinks her wine glass against mine.

'I will try with Toby,' she announces. 'I will be brave, I will be honest with him, and I will try.'

'I wish you well, Faith. He's gorgeous and lovely. I'm sure he'll be thrilled to know he won't be ditched in under a month. I really am so confident for you. Go for it!'

'Okay. I will. And you'll hold me accountable if I waiver?'

'Deal. By the way, I have some interesting news.'

'Go on.'

'I've just come from seeing Liz Martin and you won't believe it, but I think she has a plan that finally finishes off my problems with that snake Alex Sutcliffe.'

'Really? Tell me all.' Riesling in hand, Faith settles on the stool beside me.

I don't know how I missed it earlier, but there's a packaged Rabbit vibrator on her benchtop. The attached pink Post-it note reads, Enjoy! Love, Lucy xxx.

'Lucy is sending you sex toys?' I ask, side-tracking our conversation.

'Um, I suppose.'

'Are you guys...'

'You mean girls.'

'Faith, are you sleeping with Lucy?'

She raises her eyebrow and watches me squirm. 'We kissed – but that's it. But what a kiss! Kissing a woman... it's a whole other experience. You should try it at least once.'

'I had enough with her finger sucking, Faith. But good for you.'

'I was tempted to go further,' Faith carries on. 'There was a bit of groping and fondling. My goodness, Gracie, you're actually blushing!'

'I do have one question,' I say, glancing at the Rabbit – a big pink dildo with, according to the packaging, a gun-shaped clitoris-tickler on top.

'Truly, the best vibrator for pleasuring one's self. I've got one already,' she says. 'You can have this one.'

'I'm, um, good, thanks. Where did you meet Lucy?'

'You don't remember? She was one of the women who entered the competition. It was her and "Mitch the Bitch".'

I remember Mitch, Michelle Stevens, who'd christened herself with the bitch moniker, we didn't put that on her. Her close-shaven head resembled a fuzzy bowling ball atop shoulders wider than Duncan's.

'Shall we go out and get a bite?' Faith suggests. 'Mexican? You can tell me all about Liz's plan over a strawberry daiquiri.'

'Yes.'

We're preparing to leave when Faith's mobile rings. Her mouth agape, she flashes the caller ID at me: King Neptune. Maximilian Modacious, blockbuster superstar, is calling Faith. I can't believe she diverts the call to voicemail. Putting her phone on speaker, we listen to the message together.

'Faith, babe, Maxi Modacious. Sorry I couldn't make your

shoot. I've just seen your picture – you and me, woulda been bodacious…'

I burst out laughing.

'Gracie, shh.'

'I'm back in London next week, let's chill. I'll be at The Met. Call me. Muah!'

'Let's chill? Ewwww. And Muah? I've never met the guy. Faith puts her phone into her bag. 'Come on, Gracie. There's a tequila with our name on it.'

We're walking out of her flat when her phone rings again. I warn her it's King Maxi, still trying it on – that this is what happens now she's put it to the universe that she wants a man who wants to be with her for real.

'Okay, Gracie the Magnificent,' she laughs, grabbing her phone.

It's not Max. It's Toby.

Faith answers the call without delay.

From her side of the conversation, I gather Toby is returning to London sooner than expected and not just for work. Faith, laughing coyly, tells him of course he can take her spare room. She signals me to sit down and wait.

If Faith wants a man who sticks around, I know who it is she wants. I have no intention of this conversation ending on my account. Blowing her a quick kiss, I slip away.

I'm at her downstairs entrance when Faith, mobile pressed to her ear and giggling, shoves the Rabbit vibrator at me and pushes me out onto Floral street with it firmly in my hand.

* * *

Later that evening, I call Liz Martin to ensure I have the

details correct and then I talk to Faith and then Robert about The Plan. I'll get you the details later but suffice to say, Liz's ingenious scheme will require a) nerves of steel from me and b) participation from both Jordan and Faith, not to mention Pussy Paws.

I've just stepped into the shower at home when my landline rings. I rush out of the bathroom to answer it.

'Hello, Gracie.'

'Harry? Hi, um, hello. Oh, golly, I'm dripping wet here.'

'Is that right?' Harry chuckles suggestively and I feel myself blush even though he can't see me.

'I'm wet from the shower.'

'Shall I let you go?'

'No, it's okay.'

'Would you like to get dressed first?'

'I have a towel.'

'Now I'm distracted...'

'I presume you've called for something other than to talk dirty to me, Harry?'

We're getting on well again, and this rolls off my tongue. Importantly, I know, it doesn't mean anything – all this harmless flirting between us. We've become firm friends, Harry and me.

'Gracie, I've just finished an interesting conversation with Liz Martin. I'm up to speed on The Plan.'

I'd sent a text asking Harry to speak with Liz directly. Liz, bless her, had offered to do so.

'Will it work, Harry?' Liz's plan is brilliant. But it's bold.

'I've no doubt about it,' Harry says, to my great relief. 'Is Faith on board?'

'Faith's on board.'

'Have you spoken with Jordan?'

Things may be getting on a great new track with me and Harry, but I still feel uncomfortable talking about Jordan with him. I haven't spoken to Jordan since I crashed his cocktail party and discovered he's seeing Rhiannon.

'I've spoken with Robert, and he talked to Jordan, I understand they're waiting on the go-ahead from Pussy Paws. Robert believes we're on track.'

'Let me know if I can help? I'm here for you, Gracie. Not just with the show, but also for you. It's a package deal.'

'I know, Harry,' I say. 'You're wonderful. You know that?'

'I try. You're still wearing the towel?'

I look down. A nipple has strayed out over the top of my wrapped-around towel. 'Yes.' I cover my breasts properly.

'In which case, I have to go. The thought of you in a towel is too distracting.'

My towel falls to the floor. 'You're a tease, Harry. But fine, you toddle off.'

Harry is silent for just that little bit too long.

'I've never teased you. If I gave you that impression, it wasn't my intention. I think you're wonderful, too.'

What is Harry saying?

What does he mean?

Whatever hopes creep into my mind, I dash them promptly. Harry can lavish on me all the funny, smutty, complimentary lines as he likes, but I'm not letting myself get carried away on nothing but banter. Not again.

'You remind me that conversations with you can easily stray, Harry.'

Harry laughs heartily. 'A little birdie told me they saw you in the West End carrying a vibrator?'

'Oh my God, Harry. Faith gave me that. She got it from Lucy. Who is your little birdie?'

'No one who will cause you any trouble of it,' he assures me. 'By the way, speaking of vibrators, Oral B want to sponsor your show. Ben the dentist may be part of the deal.'

'And so it begins?' Saucy sponsorships. The gossip will spread like wildfire through my mother's church group if I have anything to do with a toothbrush commercial that's premised on anything to do with a sex-toy. 'On that note, I'm off to the shower.'

'To get wet again?'

'Your smutty mind,' I chastise him. 'Goodnight, Harry.'

'You can't imagine my mind right now,' he says. 'Goodnight, kitten. See you tomorrow.'

29

Actions for 'The Plan' gather momentum. I'd pitched the idea to Robert, who'd sold it to Jordan, who'd convinced Pussy Paws, the world's first cat food with flea-busting properties, to sign as an official advertising sponsor of *Eat Me*. Liz's genius connected the dots. The unlikely affiliation arose from an April Fool's Day tradition. Each year, British convention calls for newspapers to run amok with spoof: deliberately sham announcements and hoaxes, written tongue-in-cheek, of which advertisers sometimes get in on the act. Logitech once announced a wireless hamster, Burger King a Chocolate Whopper. One year, Guinness claimed the Royal Observatory had agreed to an official Guinness Mean Time. This year on April 1st, Pussy Paws will run a carefully curated campaign using images uncannily similar to Alex Sutcliffe's photographs.

Saturday, we're on set. Faith, Poppy, me. Harry. Robert, Jordan and the production company employed by Baker & Staines for the Pussy Paws campaign.

That the original pictures exist is on a need-to-know basis

and there's barely anyone on set today who needs to know – apart from everyone involved in planning, it's only Poppy who's been looped in. Jordan and I are coping remarkably well, having slipped into professional mode and talking only about the necessary. Which could also be described as having slipped into our old relationship mode. Either way, we're avoiding conflict and each other as much as possible, pretending nothing is wrong, whilst knowing darn well it isn't right. All very civilized, for the greater good of our respective careers.

Harry observes the proceedings from the back of the set. In case you were wondering, I haven't dwelled that he'd called me the often highly sexualised and romantically affectionate 'kitten' after picturing me naked last night. The me of old might have read something into it. The new and improved me doesn't imagine it.

For the Pussy Paws shoot today, Poppy took us shopping. It was belittling to have to refer to the terrible photographs, but with the girls' good humour, I got through it. We bought wigs. A long, dark one for Faith and a long, blonde one for me. Right now, Faith is wearing the blue silk shirt I wore for the episode with Lucy earlier this week. Fitted and gorgeous on me, it's like an unflattering art-smock on her. She's behind the bench, her long legs hidden, stirring an empty saucepan. Camera at the ready, I'm perched on top of the bench, facing the front, in a short black leather skirt, and tan-coloured tights, a tiny red top that gives me a heaving great cleavage and slutty black boots that come up over my knees. I'm sporting two sets of false eyelashes.

Over and over for the camera, I seductively feed a suit-clad executive spoonfuls of Pussy Paws cat food from a can. Flash, click. The man is a bit-part actor on Harry's books, pale-skinned and dark-haired, about Jordan's age and build. Flash, click. A bag of flour – the word cocaine isn't mentioned by anyone – is sprinkled around all over the set and all over each other, as if we're baking up a storm. Flash, click. Flash, click. Flash, click.

All in, we're on set almost all day, longer than it takes us to film an entire episode, for what will be only two photographs used in the final finishes. We all head off separately at the end of it.

Sunday, I make it to the gym and the garden centre and get in some baking for the freezer. For me – yes, just me – to enjoy at some later stage, I lovingly prepare cheesy-top lasagne cups, savoury muffins with freshly grated vegetables and chocolate protein balls jammed with healthy goodness. My beautiful flat sparkles and shines with cleanliness, and it's so easy to maintain these days because I tidy as I go. My life, I realise, is becoming the best of the new me and the best of the old.

Nigella, eat your heart out.

For our next episode, Maximillian is back in London and on set to play Faith's date number eight – which may not go down entirely well when he gets back to his hotel, given the papers this morning suggested he'd reconciled with his mermaid girlfriend, Esmerelda. Max is a fine specimen of masculinity and, surprisingly, given his cringy voicemail message, quite the charmer. Running with the 'King of the Sea' theme, we cook up an extraordinary platter of monkfish and scallops with creamed spinach and piped potatoes, an extravaganza for this series – a discrete nod to myself about how far I've come since the same feast flopped on the last episode of my old show. For kicks, Faith chatted about all the naughty things she and Maxi might get up to with his trident!

My mother, on set to watch, has enjoyed the fawning attention of both Maz and Harry. At the end of the recording, she makes it perfectly clear there's no competition when it comes to who she'd prefer as her future son-in-law.

'You must come out to Redhill, Harry. With Grace, one Sunday. I cook the best roast pork.'

'It's true,' I say. 'And her potatoes are to die for.'

'You can meet Derek, he's Grace's father. We can all go for a walk across Annie's fields. It's lovely this time of year. Be sure to arrange something, won't you, dear,' she says to me, with a wink she doesn't try to hide.

Harry takes it in his stride. I don't push on him firm plans for such a visit.

After I put my mother into a cab to go to Victoria station and home to Surrey on the train, I nip back on set to collect my gym kit. Harry waylays me in the corridor.

'Got a minute?'

'For you, Harry, always.'

'In here.' I follow him through to the deserted studio of children's programme *Squiggly Winks*. Decorated like a playground, with swings, slides and a sandpit, the green carpet simulates grass and the walls are painted with blue skies and white clouds, a yellow Mr Sun in a corner.

'I have to be at the gym for a PT session. I'm getting right into my fitness these days, Harry.'

'I can see.' Harry smiles.

'Can we make it quick?'

'A quickie?' he says, affecting a Dean Martin accent and giving me a wink. He twirls himself around a swing pole, like he's Gene Kelly on the lamp post in *Singing in the Rain*. What on earth has got into him? It's adorable, nonetheless.

'The plan worked.' Harry ceases him circumnavigation and grins. 'Alex has conceded his big scoop looks like a sneak peek at a pet food commercial. He won't be lurking around any more.'

It's a big relief. I hug Harry spontaneously. 'Thank you Harry. For sticking by me. No matter what.' I step back and regain my composure.

'I promised I'd look after you.' He leans against the pole, looking all ... oh golly, Harry is looking all sexy. In a slight departure from his usual style, he's wearing a black cashmere jumper over dark jeans and boots. He's wearing it well.

It's a hearts and flowers moment. I can't say I'm in control of my emotions as my mind wanders to picture a future where it could even be Harry and me in a playground with him pushing a swing with a little bundle of joy squealing, 'Daddy, higher,' me smiling at them proudly. I almost don't want to put the brakes on – I've never before envisioned what it would be like having a family. No wonder my mother has been gunning for me to be with this man, in particular, since the get-go.

Harry smiles his lopsided grin.

My stomach somersaults inside the pretty Ted Baker dress I'm still wearing from the shoot.

'You always smell so good Harry,' I say. 'Why is that?'

'Have you made plans for the TIARAs?' he says. An odd reply. I play along.

'The Television Innovation and Recording Awards?'

'Yes.'

'Usually, I watch with popcorn and wine from my sofa. Unless you're inviting me to the actual TIARAs, dear agent?'

'You're invited.'

I was playing obtuse. Now, I'm shocked.

'Goodness,' I gasp. 'You really must think a lot of me, Harry.'

'I've told you I do.'

'Oh, well, um.'

'We're all invited,' he goes on. 'Joanna said she'd distributed the official invitations?'

I take a gold embossed envelope from my handbag. It arrived at home by post yesterday. I'd presumed it was an invitation to another wedding of the son or daughter of some friend of my parents – an invitation I'd come up with an excuse to decline.

'The after-parties tend to be the most fun,' Harry says. 'It's plus one for the awards. I'm thinking I may ask your mother.'

'Ha! She'd love that!'

'If you can't think of anyone as yours, I'm happy to help.' Harry smiles.

No thank you, Harry,' I say. And I'm quick to do so. I don't need his help to find a date – although, maybe I do. But I don't want my romantic life part of his package deal to look after the show and me personally. Hearts and flowers! What a ninny I've been to imagine it. Thank heavens I didn't throw myself at Harry this time – the spontaneous hug was purely platonic. It was the feelings that followed that could have been troubling. But anyway, they've been nipped in the bud.

I realise I sounded rude, and Harry appears taken aback.

'I'm sure I can sort myself out, thank you for asking,' I add.

I've no immediate idea who I'll bring, but I refuse to have my personal life become a charity case. I tuck the envelope away in my purse.

Harry doesn't say anything further. He tilts his head to one side and oh, those darker than chocolate eyes. I can so easily get lost in those eyes.

'I'll admit I don't have the best track record when it comes to men...' I carry on lightly. 'But I'm reliably informed you've been inundated with callers asking after me recently. So...'

Harry chuckles. 'Are you referring to the perverts who want you in skimpier clothing on the show or are you thinking of dating another ad exec?'

'Harrison Hipgrave!' I say, in mock outrage.

Harry chuckles again and gives my cheek a quick peck. 'Quite. You know where I am if you change your mind.'

30

I stick to my gym routine. I potter around my home. With the mortgage sorted, Philip Maxwell finalises the settlement in record time. The flat in Maida Vale I've resided in so happily for over a decade is legally mine. I throw a dinner party to celebrate, inviting Poppy, Faith, and Toby, who's back for his UK work secondment – and back in Faith's bed, her still keen to give things with him a proper shot.

Today, we're shooting our penultimate show of the series. So far, we've been charmed by handsome banker Toby, amused by Ben the dentist and his electric Oral B, and ogled over Bassdog in all his studded glory. We've taken pity on *Love Island* boy Jerry and proudly paraded competition-winner Kenny S, Lutonian country music crooner and rental car manager. We've plonked sweet, young Adrian from accounts in front of the camera after Christophe the Swiss architect got cold feet. Faith had her fun with Lucy and, in a scoop, Joanna is sure will top the ratings when it airs in two weeks, we landed sea king Maximillian Modacious. We've cooked pumpkin gnocchi with a creamy chipolata sauce, blow your head off mega-hot tortillas, a delicious risotto and spaghetti bolognaise out of a can. My seafood banquet finally saw the light of day. We've gorged on steak Diane and beef with black-bean stir fry and I, for one, will always remember the finger-licking good vegetarian curry.

For eight weeks, over eight episodes, we've had a giggly, girly good time dishing up serving after serving of fun food and man-candy.

Publicly, I became properly single. Liz announced it in her weekend column – leaving audiences to ponder whether my mystery boyfriend ever existed at all, further distancing Jordan from our hijinks and my calamities. I have Joanna's permission to exorcise the ghost of Master J for the recording today and, for the season finale next week, I'll be the one with the date. At present, the only problem I have with this is that there's no one yet lined up. Since the big meeting and the first shoot, my trepidations have abated – I love being a part of *Eat Me*.

For this penultimate episode, by popular demand, Toby is back on set. Him and Faith will be smooching and making googly eyes at each other for the cameras, just as they're doing in real life.

Toby walks into the studio, looking even more handsome than I remember.

'Hi Toby, welcome back to where it all began,' I say.

Today, he isn't wearing his green contacts. His real eyes are warm brown with golden flecks. He's like a manly, sexy panther to Faith's hot, sultry minx.

'Hey Gracie, good to see you.' We kiss cheeks.

Faith saunters out of the dressing area in a fiercely fitted little cream dress, her hair twisted in a loose chignon, her eye make-up smoky.

Toby brushes her lips with a kiss and slides his hand around her waist.

Faith asks if I can teach her how to cook a proper breakfast on the show today – perfectly poached eggs and all.

Love… it's in the air and all around.

I smile at Faith and she beams at me.

Harry hasn't made the recording today. I haven't seen him all week. He's had other clients to attend to and our contracts to negotiate. He called yesterday to tell me SC6 agreed to a new series, with a substantial pay increase, and that Joanna had floated the idea of shooting the next season in LA. Faith is happy to do another season and convert her sabbatical from venture capitalism into a resignation, but she isn't keen on LA – for starters, she doesn't want to uproot Benny. Fat chance she'd leave him for even a few months. So it isn't something I need to consider. We're a team, on this show. We're a squad.

Harry hasn't mentioned the TIARAs again.

The one thing that has been playing on my mind is that I need to find a date for the blasted thing. I have but ten days' time to sort it.

* * *

After we wrap, Poppy and I venture to La Petite Place Française for wine and nibbles. Faith rushed off with Toby, something about his UK visa. She promised to join us next time. Unaccompanied by Faith, Gaspard seats us in a cosy corner downstairs, behind the cast-iron staircase. Poppy and I order an exquisite assortment of aged cheeses and fresh, crusty bread to accompany the delicious white wine. The Chardonnay has blissful notes of pineapple. The Brie de

Meaux is to die for, as is the triple-cream Billat-Savarin, though I'm trying not to be gluttonous – I don't want to undo my recent dedication to an exercise regime with a cheese-belly. Pouring our second glass of thirty-eight pounds a bottle vino – the fruity aftertaste makes it worth every penny – I ask Poppy her opinion of the shoot today.

'It was very romantic, wouldn't you say?'

'Oh, yes. Toby and Faith are perfect for each other. Do you think they're in love?'

'I think they're well on their way. And, yes, perfect for each other. I've never seen Faith so happy with any man and I've known her almost all of her life.' I break off another piece of bread, top it with a sliver of cheese and pop it in my mouth. 'How old are you, Poppy?' I can't believe I don't know. 'Twenty-one? Twenty-two.'

'I'm thirty-three next month.'

I almost choke on my pineapple tinged wine. 'You're not!'

'I know, I look young. It's because I'm small.'

'Thirty-three? Okay. And you don't have a boyfriend?'

'Not really.'

I probe Poppy as to what she means by this.

'Well, I'd love to be with someone in a committed relationship – I think, at some point, everyone does – but no one's fit the bill for me so far. So...'

'So?'

'So, while I pass the time, and hope it happens, one day, I have friends. Special friends.'

'What do you mean "special friends"?' I suspect I know what Poppy means.

'Miss Gracie, I have special friends that I have sex with,' Poppy confirms. 'I call them my shag buddies.'

Pineapple wine sprays out of my mouth. Poppy passes me a napkin and I dab my face clean.

'These friends are purely for booty-calls?'

'Pretty much. They're not friends I call to hang out with. I wouldn't invite them to a nice French restaurant to drink wine and eat cheese.' Poppy grins. 'They're just for sex, you see?'

Gaspard comes over to ask if we want another bottle. I decline, mostly to get rid of him without him returning, so we can continue our conversation in the utmost privacy. It's early, only 6 p.m., so we're alone in the downstairs section. Upstairs, I hear the restaurant filling up.

'Poppy, I get the whole Netflix and chill thing,' I go on. 'But you said shag buddies, as in plural. How many do you have?'

She lowers her voice to barely a whisper. 'A few. We all have lives. It's good to spread the load.'

'Ha!'

'Yes, so to speak.' Poppy giggles at her accidental joke. 'That's the beauty of it. No strings. And no inhibitions. Miss Gracie, the sex is the best I've ever had.'

'Goodness. I say, Poppy…'

'It stops me getting too lonely, while I wait for Mr Right, whoever he might be.' Poppy shrugs her slender shoulders with forced nonchalance. I want to hug her, but it's not really my style. I'm not one to make a fuss if it isn't warranted. But it's a comfort to know I'm not the only one who battles to stay positive. 'There's no attachment, but it's friendly, and there's mutual respect. Nobody gets hurt. Everyone needs sex, right?'

It's more than I was getting in my relationship – regular sex.

I finish my wine.

Sitting opposite, wearing a lilac smock dress with pink leggings and navy Mary Jane sandals, sweet, wide-eyed Poppy has told me sex is a basic need. A need she has no qualms in satisfying outside of a proper relationship. And no one gets hurt in the process.

'Poppy?'

'Yes, my angel?'

'If one was of a mind to find a shag buddy, how would they go about it?' I say. 'Asking for a friend, obviously. But I don't think I could do the whole internet thing.'

Her mouth forms a small grin.

I return her smile broadly.

'I know a place,' Poppy says, beaming. 'If you like, we could go now?'

31

We have a few drinks in the upstairs bar while things warm up inside and hit the downstairs dancefloor of the salsa club around 9 p.m. The place is hot, dark and heaving with people. From the moment Poppy and I enter, the odds are stacked in my favour: men outnumber women two to one. The men predominantly young, attractive Latinos, clad in white T-shirts and skin-tight black trousers. The women mostly English, older and dressed up to the nines. I'm still made-up from the shoot, slightly sloshed on wine and gin and tonic and feeling fruity.

We order sangria. As we're waiting at the bar, a strapping young man introduces himself as Carlos. Without further conversation, he asks me to dance.

We hit the floor. Carlos, wrapping his muscular, olive-skinned arms around my waist, guides me into an erotic, three-steps-to-a-four-beat rumba across the polished wood. Thankfully, this womanly, curvy body of mine can move: my parents being of an older generation, I've been dancing to waltzes, swing, rock and roll and all sorts at weddings, parties and celebrations with them since I could walk. I'm a natural with the salsa beat. I'm fit from all my gym workouts. I'm an instant fire-cracker on the dance floor in the arms of sexy Carlos – I've got this.

I glance back at Poppy and she gives me a congratulatory thumbs-up. I sway and turn with sizzling dexterity. My hips swivel. Carlos pulls and pushes me with his masterful manliness. My body moves in perfect time. My eyes are fierce. My endorphins flood.

After our second, madly passionate routine, Carlos tells me he has to dance with other people. Turns out, he works here. He promises he'll be back to move some more with me as soon as he can and, true to his word, he is. With assurances that I'm happy for her to do so, Poppy leaves me to it.

Carlos and I dance and dance and dance. We barely talk, but I discover some nuggets of info. Recently arrived from Venezuela, Carlos speaks only rudimentary English, so our attempts to communicate are sweet and funny, but not really what I'm here for anyway.

At midnight, as the evening ends, and Carlos helps me into my coat, we both know where we're heading.

Back at my place, in my bedroom, our last dance of the evening doesn't disappoint.

Over and over, my body aches with pleasure.

Again and again, Carlos is keen to oblige.

* * *

The following night, as arranged, after I exercise and shower and do my hair at the gym, I swing by the salsa club. Carlos greets me with a firm, sweaty embrace. His lean muscles bulge beneath his tight T-shirt.

'Crazie, you come again for Carlos.' He kisses me, lingeringly, on the lips.

'Carlos, not here,' I admonish, but I don't push him off. It feels so good to be so desired.

'Come, I finish work. We dance,' he answers boldly.

From what I gather, Carlos works at the club as a cleaner in the mornings – and as bartender/dance instructor in the evenings, attending English lessons in between. I suspect the job is illegal and the lessons are for his visa, but none of it concerns me. I'm not looking to invest. I'm looking to have fun.

Again, we heat up the dance floor and, after closing, I feel a swell of pride when Carlos scoops me into his arms, leaving the other women he'd danced with throughout the evening milling around at a loss, but also smiling at me conspiringly. 'Congratulations, sweetheart,' one well-put-together lady, early fifties, says as Carlos helps me into my jacket. He kisses me on my lips. My neck. My lips once more.

We head directly home to mine.

The week plays out in suit. Four nights in a row, I've spent hot and heavy between the sheets – and I don't have to go dancing first any more. Carlos and I quickly fell into an arrangement whereby I go to the gym and home to potter and, around midnight, he arrives at my door.

Saturday morning, Carlos heads off to his English school and I'm out shopping with Poppy and Faith, a regular event these days, except that this expedition is extra special. Today, we're shopping for our outfits for the TIARAs. Joyfully, I'm recounting the sexy encounters that mark the end of my many months of reluctant celibacy.

'He has moves that would make you blush, Faith – and I'm not talking fancy dance steps.'

'You're having fun, Miss Gracie,' Poppy giggles.

'Darling, he sounds divine,' Faith purrs. 'Why don't you invite him on the show next week?'

I'm half-naked in a changing room. Having discarded five dresses as unsuitable, I'm getting back into the tailored silvery-grey trouser suit Poppy first suggested. 'As my date, you mean?'

'Yes, as your date. You need to find someone. Perhaps I'll show off all I've learned and cook for you?'

Clapping her hands, Poppy squeals in excitement. 'Yes'

'He is incredibly good-looking,' I say, weighing things up. I'm not opposed to the ego boost I'd get from flaunting Carlos on television – a bit bitterly, I imagine Rhiannon and all her friends watching when it airs and realising that, in Jordan, she scooped the consolation prize. It would, among other things, provide indisputable proof that I've moved on from the romantic slips of my past – that someone so hot, physically way hotter than me and any man I've ever been with, can't keep his hands off me. 'I suppose I could. Do you think Joanna will go for it? His English isn't great.'

'My cooking isn't great,' Faith says.

'He is gorgeous, Miss Gracie.'

'Our women viewers will love him. In which case, so will Joanna.'

'Oh my, Gracie. That's the outfit! It's perfect on you.' Faith gasps as I button the jacket up. I step outside the changing room to inspect myself in natural light. I can't believe I'm contemplating wearing a trouser suit to the TIARAs – Faith will look old school glamorous in an off-the-shoulder Grecian dress and Poppy has chosen a girly, floaty little number. But of all the outfits I've tried on, in all the boutiques we've visited, I feel most comfortable in this suit. The silver flecks play beautifully with my eyes. It will go perfectly with my crystal Jimmy Choo high heels. And although a pantsuit, it's incredibly feminine. And sexy – the jacket clinches at the waist but it's otherwise slit open and worn with a matching bra that's meant to be seen. The trousers are slim over my legs, taper at the ankles and hug my bum in all the right places. This is not me attempting to go all Annie Hall, the suit is gorgeous.

However, the TIARAs are one of Britain's most prestigious television ceremonies. It's not the BAFTAs – it's more populist – but the press will be out in force. Men may wear kilts – but a woman in a suit?

I check my figure once more in the big mirror, from the front, the back and the side. I'm not convinced my thighs are thin enough for silver trousers. My tummy isn't half as flat as it could be for such a nipped-in-at-the-waist jacket.

'Poppy, I'm not a hundred per cent convinced. Are you sure?'

'I'm two hundred per cent sure.'

I do another whirl. The colour is divine on me. The matching silver-threaded, crystal-adorned bra underneath is stunning – and not too revealing. These past few weeks, I've done push-ups until my arms collapsed. My chest supports itself these days.

I step one foot forward in the manner of a red-carpet pose. It's not bad. I check the rear view – it really isn't bad.

A handsome and debonair man hovers outside the changing room, intermittently consulting with the attractive woman prancing about beside me – his wife, presumably. He's ogling my behind.

'You look scorching,' says Faith, dipping her head furtively at my admirer.

The man blushes, the woman scowls and my decision is made. The suit it is.

* * *

Sunday is Mother's Day. I catch the train to Redhill and, instead of my mother cooking, I take my parents to the local pub for a roast dinner. I insist Beryl joins us, given as she doesn't have any children of her own, and after what my mother confided in me, it's an honour and a privilege to treat her in a different light.

It's a lovely day out. Beryl doesn't grumble and moan half as much as she usually does and my father is happy because when we get to the pub, he knows a few people he can sit with at the bar, leaving us ducks to it. When my mother asks after Harry – thankfully, when Beryl nips to the toilet – I tell her he's fine, which he is, although he's been so busy with his other clients that we haven't spent much time together lately. I don't mention my pre-occupation with Carlos. I don't expect he'll be around long enough for my parents to have to know anything about him.

As I'm heading out the door and home to London on Sunday evening, my mother is caught in the kitchen cleaning up shattered ceramic where my father dropped his cup of tea. I'm rushing for the train.

'Mummy, I almost forgot, we've been invited to a special do next weekend'

The invitation is for a Sunday afternoon tea hosted at

Fortnum and Mason. The press office passed it along to me after my mother won them over on the set last week.

'I have to rush for the train, I'll leave the invite on the table. I hope you can make it. Call me! Love you!'

I reach into my bag and throw the envelope onto the bowl of potpourri that's on the hallway table.

She calls back, 'Sounds lovely, dear. I'll call you! Don't miss your train. Stay safe! Love you.'

* * *

The following morning is April 1st. Yup. Here we go.

Faith and I meet in Harry's office. Though we've spoken on the phone and texted, it's the first time I've seen him since the shoot with Maximillian, almost two weeks ago. The Pussy Paws April Fool's promotion in today's *Daily* is open on his desk. In the advertisement, Faith is behind the bench stirring a pot in the dark wig and my too-big-for-her silk blue shirt, one eyebrow raised. I'm resplendent sitting up on the bench in the long blonde artificial tresses and wearing the short black skirt, tan control-tights and racy red top ensemble. White flour is splattered all over us. I'm feeding the executive-looking actor from a can of cat food. The picture is captioned: *Eat Me...* Unscripted. Unsupervised. Who knows what these cheeky cats will get up to next? Catch the action Mondays, 9 pm. Only on SC6.

It's all there – everything Alex threatened me with.

From the other side of Harry's desk, Faith smiles at me reassuringly.

Harry wraps his arm around me. 'Alex's big scoop – outtakes of a cat food commercial.'

I scan the advertisement. I've toned up – not a roll of fat in sight. But an awful lot of my bare flesh is on show. I don't exactly scream thin enough to dress like a hooker. 'Or we carried his threat out for him?'

'No.' Harry squeezes my shoulder. 'This is you, Gracie. Fun, funny, wonderful you.'

'It's a little too much of me...'

'It's why your many fans adore you.'

'Because I'm not size zero?'

'Because you're real. I assure you, it's irresistibly attractive.'

I glance at the picture. I look down at my tummy. I'm not perfect, and I never will be, but the most miraculous thing happens: I like me, too.

'Joanna is thrilled. Also, she warned us not to pull anything like it again.' Harry grins.

'All's well that ends well,' Faith says.

Harry puts the clipping in a file labelled with my name. I'm relieved it ended with my friendship, my career and (most of) my dignity intact.

'I've sent thank-you flowers to Liz,' he says. 'Pink lilies, with a silk butterfly in the centre.'

'Harry, that's very thoughtful.' For her ear and her idea, I made a sizable donation to a charity of Liz's choice. 'They sound lovely.'

'Would you like me to send you some?' he asks.

'No, I didn't mean—'

'I don't mind,' Harry says, beaming cheesily. 'It could be thanks for the dirty talk the other night.'

When my towel was slipping and I was on the phone with Harry. It seems so long ago and yet...

I smack him playfully. He removes his arm from my shoulder.

Faith shakes her head. 'I don't want to know.'

'How are the girls?' I enquire.

I'm changing the topic, but there it is – that lopsided grin.

'The twins?'

'Your sisters.' I smile.

'They're good. Behaving themselves. They've asked after you.' Harry had started sorting his papers, but he stops to look at me. 'We should all catch up soon.'

'That'd be nice,' I say.

And I mean it.

But neither of us follow up as to when.

The day after, I'm up early to check out the second instalment of the Pussy Paws campaign. This time, in another full-page ad, the Jordan-lookalike actor is alone on the *Eat Me* set, wearing a Venetian-ball plaster-of-Paris cat-mask, feeding a professionally trained Russian Blue cat – Benny having put his advertising days firmly behind him – from a can of Pussy Paws. The tagline reads:

> Master J remains a mystery, but there's one secret we're happy to share. Pussy Paws now contains a secret ingredient that knocks fleas dead!

The label on the can is clearly visible: PACKS FLEAS A PUNCH.

Below the photograph is the disclaimer.

> * No advertising executives were harmed during the taste-testing of this delicious product.

I'm heading on to the gym when Harry calls my mobile to say a number of agencies have approached him wanting us for their marketing campaigns. With a chuckle, he informs me he's also fielded a few calls from heavy breathers happy I've taken it on board to get my booty into skimpier clothes and would I mind a bit more of it for our regular recordings, too.

I'm still amused by the thought when I hit the weights with Nikolai for another gruelling and most-excellent workout.

On the way out, between the endorphins from the exercise and that things are falling into place for me everywhere I turn, I'm walking on air.

I'm heading into the studio when I think to call Jordan.

He answers his work line on the first ring.

'Jordan Piper.'

'Hi, Jordan. It's me, Grace.'

'One minute.'

The last time Jordan and I spoke was during the photography session for Pussy Paws, where plenty of other people from SC6 and his agency floated about for distraction. I'm on hold a long time before he picks up the line.

'Sorry, I've popped into an office. It's, ah, hectic out there.'

His girlfriend is listening?

'I'm just calling to say thanks.' I jump straight into the purpose of my call. 'I presume you've seen the ads. I just want to say, they got me out of a very sticky situation. I imagine it wasn't easy to swing Pussy Paws on such short notice, but you did it. Thank you, Jordan. I hope they're pleased?'

'Oh, no problem. Yes, the ads are brilliant. The client's thrilled.' He pauses. 'I've been promoted to director.'

I congratulate Jordan on his news, insisting it's a well-earned promotion for his hard work and effort over many years. I'm delighted to say that, without a hint of resentment, I mean it.

'By the way, I liked your postscript, in the ad. "No advertising executives harmed by the taste-testing." Very funny.'

Jordan laughs heartily. 'I thought you might like it.'

A month ago, he was storming out over the cat food-eating incident and I was throwing his stuff to the rubbish. Today, it's a funny story we can laugh about.

'It's nice to talk to you, Grace.'

'You too. How's Rhiannon?'

After a short – but not uncomfortable – silence, Jordan says, 'I don't think we should discuss her.'

'No, you're right.'

'I best get back to my desk. Thanks for calling. Take care.'

'You too.'

Which is a pleasant enough finish to a pleasant enough conversation – things could have gone worse. Yet as I enter SC6, my feet aren't as light on the ground as they were earlier this morning.

After my conversation with Jordan, it's some time before the spring in my step returns.

32

On set to record our tenth and final episode of the first season, today I get to showcase sexy South American Carlos as my first ever on-air date.

Small hiccup is Carlos isn't here yet and he should be.

I'm increasingly concerned Carlos didn't understand my instructions regarding the shoot. It was probably also a mistake not to answer any of his numerous calls yesterday and last night – I've been cooling things off with our private arrangement, but my timing was perhaps ill-conceived. While the orgasms are incredible – I can't overstate the importance of restoring my self-esteem, my mojo, after Jordan flatlined it – the thing is, Carlos is starting to grate on my nerves. My appetite for him is, regrettably, waning.

It's the little things.

How he hums salsa tunes incessantly – even, sometimes, when we're in bed.

And leaves the toilet seat up after he pees.

And doesn't close the door on his other ablutions.

The sex-stained boxer shorts strewn across my pillow.

Used condoms in my bathroom sink.

Pubic hair in my soap.

Bless him, but Carlos's cheap aftershave plays havoc with my sinuses.

There's also the somewhat delicate matter that, sometimes, sex with Carlos is too uninhibited. I don't want his spunk over my face. Ever. Nor his attempts, on more than one occasion, to put things that don't belong inside me inside me. How he screams in ecstasy 'CRAZIE,' every time he comes, so loud I worry we'll wake the neighbours.

If all that wasn't enough, I'm increasingly concerned he's angling to move in with me. From his broken conversation, I've learned he shares a studio apartment on Leicester Square with three other grown men. He's already ceremoniously moved his toothbrush into the glass beside mine – I suspect it's only a couple of white T-shirts and a spare pair of black trousers to make it official.

I've only known him a week.

When I called Faith last night to dissect the good and the bad, she laughed voraciously. 'You're getting sex, darling. Orgasms, no less. What did you expect from someone you picked up at a dance club?' She told me it's the sort of nonsense she put up with for years. For all our in-depth conversations about her romantic life, for all my envy about her raunchy affairs, I never knew.

When I talked to Poppy this morning, she'd warned me I have only myself to blame. Apparently, it's my fault for seeing Carlos so regularly – thereby breaking the rules of the buddy system. I tell her I don't think I am cut out for casual sexing. In my heart, I know I'm girlfriend material. I need more than meaningless orgasms.

Whether I dump him as my sex partner now or later is

one thing. But if Carlos is a no-show on set, I may be forced to drag Pugsy, the man with the face of a pug, in front of camera as my inaugural love interest – scarcely the ego or ratings boost I or Joanna are after.

Then in he waltzes – bronzed, strong and looking sexy – Carlos.

'Ola, Crazie,' he shouts happily.

I disengage respectfully from Harry, who's had his arm casually around my waist. We've been like this recently. Warm, friendly, tactile.

'Carlos, I'm pleased you made it.' I narrowly avoid Carlos snogging me in front of everyone with a deft turn of my head. His lips land moistly on my cheek.

'Harry, this is Carlos. Carlos, this is my agent, Harry.'

'I pleased to meet you,' Carlos says, shaking his hand.

'Carlos, pleased to meet you,' Harry says. Harry knows only that we met at the salsa club and he is my date for today.

Carlos is several inches taller than Harry. He clasps his long, strong fingers around mine. He's wearing his white T-shirt and tight black trousers. Joanna, speaking with the crew, gapes her mouth behind his back. Carlos is a hit.

'You are Crazie's boss?'

'I'm her agent,' Harry says.

'Her servant?'

'Yes, I'm her servant.'

'Harry, behave,' I growl.

He grins mischievously.

'I meet Crazie at dancing,' Carlos carries on. 'She es great dancer. Very sexy. We dance together all the nights.'

'Do you now?' Harry looks at me, trying not to laugh. 'Well, that explains her joie de vivre of late.'

I'm trying not to laugh now, too. I'm not even sure what's funny. 'Stop, Harry.'

'Har-i,' Carlos repeats, practising.

Poppy rushes over.

'Carlos, sweetie,' she squeals, lavishing kisses on Carlos's chiselled cheeks. He drops my hand to lift Poppy's tiny frame off the ground. When she enquires if we are still dancing together, Carlos sweeps me into an impromptu shimmy across the studio.

I protest at once, stopping us dead immediately. 'No, Carlos. We're not at the club. Work, okay? No dancing.'

'We no dance on TV?' Carlos is bewildered.

'No, Carlos, cooking. We're here to cook, remember?'

I wanted to finish the series as the one with the date. Now that Carlos is here in all his attentive gorgeousness, I don't think I can cope with the spectacle.

Poppy offers to show him around set.

'Poppy, that would be most helpful,' I say, grateful for her intervention.

'Carlos, honey.' She links her tiny arm around his muscled bicep. 'Come with me, I'll explain how everything is going to work today.'

'Sí, I am working for Crazie.' Letting go of my hand, he tags along.

When they're out of earshot, Harry whispers, 'So, Crazy...'

'It beats him calling me Tolerancia.'

'Excuse me?'

'It means grace, in Spanish,' I explain, sighing.

'Tolly for short? I quite like it. Does he call you that in bed?' Harry doesn't bother to suppress his chuckle. His eyes cloud as he contemplates me. 'All that dancing, every night.'

'Let's just say Carlos and I were spending an inordinate

amount of time dancing, but then...' I can't bring myself to admit things aren't exactly working out with my sizzling piece of man-candy.

'You haven't tired of all that hot Latino loving already?' Harry says.

'Not that it's any of your business...'

'But?' Harry has a teasing smile.

'But I can do without it. From Carlos. To be honest.'

'I see,' Harry says, and we both fall silent.

'I'll tell you a secret,' I say, to lighten the mood. Harry leans in close. I breathe in the smell of him. Sandalwood. Vanilla. Leather. And ... Harry. 'Although the hot loving, as you put it, with Carlos has waned, it was, for a while, so hot, I actually called him my shag buddy. Harry, is that too awful?'

Looking unexpectedly aghast, Harry asks me, 'Not to his face, surely?'

'Of course not to his face. Just with Faith, and Poppy, and now you.'

'Dear me, Tolly,' Harry sighs. 'I'm pleased I'm not your rebound man.'

'It's not – what? No, it's not like that.'

'But you've no feelings for the man?'

'It's not about feelings, Harry. The whole concept of a shag buddy is nobody gets hurt.'

Harry glances over to where Poppy is showing Carlos around the kitchen. The crew is busy setting up the equipment. Noticing us looking, Carlos waves vigorously and blows me a flurry of little kisses.

'I think Carlos may have feelings for you.'

'I picked him up in a salsa bar. We can barely understand each other. I'm sure he's as happy with our arrangement as I am.'

'You've reduced him to a walking penis,' Harry suggests.

I burst out laughing. It's a crude thing to say. But I suppose I have.

When we first met, I'd thought if Harry was a girl, he'd be Faith. I wondered if they'd hook up. Instead, Harry's become another best friend for me.

At the kitchen set, Carlos knocks a metal bowl to the floor. There's a loud clang, clang, clang as it skims across the concrete. Carlos shrugs an apology and picks it up.

Harry and I try not to giggle.

He enquires about my plans for the TIARAs. 'I heard a rumour you haven't made arrangements for a date?'

With only three nights until the event, I haven't invited anyone. I thought, initially, Carlos. Then I got cold feet. As the clock ticks, it starting to strike me as a damn fine idea after all.

'I don't know what rumour you've heard—' Agent or not, why does Harry go so far out of his way regarding my personal business? Poppy still hasn't sorted who she's bringing. He isn't bothering her about it.

Carlos sidles up beside me and clasps my hand. His grip is strong. His looks are stunning. I could do a lot worse than to be photographed arriving with Carlos for these awards – I could arrive alone.

'Harry, I'm afraid you've been misinformed. Carlos is attending the TIARAs with me, aren't you, sweetie?' I give Carlos's hand a little squeeze. 'Hmm, we're going out this Saturday, sí?'

On cue, a beaming Carlos repeats daftly after me, 'Sí. I go with Crazie, all the day.'

33

Carlos leaves the station merrily, a print out of details for the TIARAs in his hand – I couldn't find my invitation, but the press office promise to assure my smooth entry on the day. I leave with a golf-ball-sized lump in my throat. Though he was fine on the show, with his broken English and high-energy actions, I regret asking Carlos to such a public occasion. Later, at home, it occurs to me it won't be at all funny if he rocks up to the TIARAs in his too-tight black trousers. In a state, I call Poppy to check if she wouldn't mind taking him shopping for a new suit, at my expense. Poppy isn't as keen as I'd hoped.

'Angel, why ever did you invite him?'

'I don't know.'

'He won't fit in.'

'He'll fit in even less wearing his salsa outfit. Please, Poppy, will you help?'

I flop onto my bed. I told Carlos not to come over tonight, as I need my sleep. It's nice having the flat to myself.

'All right,' Poppy says. 'But you're not coming with us. No

offence, but you're a grumpy shopper and you'll only be a nuisance.'

By noon the next day, I owe Poppy a small fortune, but it's worth every penny to hear her relay how the whole shop gasped as Carlos paraded his new Tom Ford tuxedo. He will, at least, look the part.

I thank her profusely.

Meanwhile, I've squeezed in a training session at the gym and a painful waxing session with an overzealous beautician named Gretchen. In the afternoon, I attend the hairdressers and have my first facial at a private medical clinic on Harley Street. When I'm done, my body is fighting fit and fuzz-free. My locks are perfectly trimmed, and a soft semi-permanent covers the niggling grey hairs that have been popping through. My complexion is like porcelain.

In the morning, I attend the final fitting for my trouser suit. I'm delighted to find it's in at the waist – the tummy crunches have paid off.

I'm running the last of my errands for the big do tomorrow – the lymphatic-draining, anti-cellulite massage isn't half as relaxing as I anticipated and the manicure and pedicure gobble more time than I planned to spare – when Joanna calls to say she's heard I've invited Carlos to the TIARAs and she thinks it's a terrible idea.

'He's your first date. I want you to film a whole other season with more. It'll look like you're a couple. Can it.'

I'm in a jewellery shop on New Bond Street, collecting a diamond necklace on loan to me via arrangements with SC6, when she puts the phone down on me. I'm standing there, wondering if Faith might possibly know anyone who can escort me as I'm certainly not going to embarrass myself by asking Harry for his help at this last minute, when my mother calls.

'Mummy, hi, is everything okay? Why are you calling my mobile?'

'I dread to think what it's doing to your brain, dear, all those radioactive waves, but I haven't been able to catch you at home all week. Grace, about your invite, I'm so excited! Thank you for choosing me. I can't believe it, dear.'

'It will be lovely, Mummy. I'm so pleased you can make it. And of course, who else would I bring? Daddy would hate it. It's definitely a mother daughter thing.'

'Oh, dear.' My mother's voice is soft. She's touched. I'm... busy.

'Mummy, I'm sorry I haven't called you to make arrangements, I've been ridiculously busy. These TIARAs take a lot of preparing for.'

'Yes, dear!' My mother says something to my father with her hand over the mouthpiece. 'Right, I don't want to talk too long on your mobile, but am I meeting you inside or at the station, Grace? Your father wants to be sure I won't get myself in a muddle.'

'Mummy, if you could meet me there, that'd be great. Get a cab directly from the station and I'll meet you inside.' The assistant behind the counter is pretending not to listen. We're alone in the shop. 'Mummy, I have to go. I'm in a shop about to sign my life away to borrow some very expensive diamonds,' I whisper.

'I've bought a new dress,' my mother exclaims. 'Second-hand new. But Grace, it's stunning.'

Rambling on to describe her frock in great detail, I don't have the heart to stop her. Full-length, navy satin, sequinned and with matching clutch, it sounds far too posh for a Sunday luncheon date, even if it is at Fortnum and Mason.

'Mummy, it sounds divine. I can't wait to see you in it. But I can't chat just now.'

'No, dear, you're collecting your diamonds!'

In the background, I'm alerted to another incoming call. Checking the screen, I see it's Carlos. Apart from a short call to put him in touch with Poppy, we haven't spoken. If Carlos is on his way to the salsa club, I won't be able to reach him until after midnight. I have to answer and let him know, delicately, because Carlos hasn't done anything wrong to deserve this, that my invitation for him to escort me tomorrow is cancelled.

'Mummy, bye. I can't wait to see you in your fancy frock. I love you.'

'I love you, dear. See you at the do! Bye.'

I pick up with Carlos.

'Ola, Crazie.'

'Hello Carlos.'

'Crazie, I have new suit, thanks to you so much.'

'You're very welcome, Carlos. I hear you look very handsome in it.'

'Es very good suit.'

'Poppy is quite the magician.'

'Es magic?'

'Carlos, never mind.'

'For flower, what colour your dress?'

'Actually, I'm also wearing a suit. A silver suit.'

'No black?'

When I turn to check, the shop attendant is still affecting disinterest in my conversation. I lower my voice anyway.

'No, Carlos, silver.'

He breathes heavily and breaks to speak to someone in Spanish, I presume for translation. He returns saying, 'Okay. Sil-ver.'

'Carlos, I need to talk with you about tomorrow.'

'Sí?'

'I need to walk the red carpet.'

'You no walk, Crazie.'

'Yes, I have to, for the cameras.'

'I book car,' Carlos insists excitedly. 'I have friend with Prius. You no walk.'

Carlos and I can barely converse in person. By phone, it's nigh on impossible.

'I bring car, no problem.'

'Carlos, that's very kind.' And it is. Carlos has been super. He's held up his end of our arrangement beautifully – I'm the one who's been flaky, on all counts. 'But no car. No Prius, Carlos.' Without further hesitation, I bite the bullet and un-invite him. 'I'm sorry, but I have to cancel.'

'No car.'

'That's right. I have to cancel with you, Carlos. Joanna is concerned because you were a date on the show, you see?'

A bell above the shop door tinkles at the entrance of another customer. Finally, the attending assistant gives me an impatient glance.

'Carlos, I have to go.'

'No problem. Si. Date on show. I know.'

'I'm so sorry. I'll call you.'

'No sorry. You call Carlos any time. Adios, bomboncita.'

Ringing off, I turn to the counter.

'Will madam be requiring the jewellery?'

'Yes, please. Where do I sign?'

'Just here, madam.'

I sign.

'And here.'

I'm signing my life away when my mobile rings again. Initialling clauses hurriedly, I let it go.

'And here. And here.'

Eventually, I'm handed a black velvet box containing a diamond necklace worth more than the deposit on my flat.

'Thank you kindly,' I say, and exit the premises.

My phone wails on and on. 'Hello?' I answer. I hate unrecognised numbers.

'Hello, Grace?'

As I step into the busy pedestrian traffic of New Bond Street, the wheels of a passing pushchair, driven by a meandering yummy mummy clad in designer activewear, clips the back of my feet.

'I'm so sorry,' she says, throwing her head of long, brown curls about as though she's shooting a shampoo ad.

My heels smarting, I assure her, 'Not at all, completely my fault.' Ugh.

I duck into an alley. Further in, a gang of hooded-topped teenage boys mill about on bicycles. They stare eagle-eyed at my velvet box. I hope I signed something for insurance.

'Hello?' I repeat, ready to hang up and ignore my phone completely.

'Grace, hello. It's Jordan.'

'Jordan? Oh. Right. You, er, have a new number?'

'I do. Is now a good time to chat?'

'Sure.' I'm relieved to see the BMX bandits ride off. 'Just picking up some expensive jewellery. On loan, I might add.'

'I presume for the big event tomorrow?' Jordan says. He sounds chipper. 'You made the list in a who's who for the TIARAs.'

I sit on a bench in the little alley in one of the nicest parts of London and narrowly avoid some pigeon poop. 'I didn't know there was a list.'

'In today's *Daily*. It's amazing, Grace. You must be so excited.'

'It is exciting,' I say.

Jordan and I fall into our usual silence.

'I've been thinking a lot about how I never supported your career,' he says.

'Oh, right...'

I did not expect this. I didn't expect Jordan to call. Let alone this.

'I was always so focused on mine,' he carries on. 'I figure, I owed it to you to say how genuinely proud I am of all you've achieved.' He laughs awkwardly. 'I hope we can be friends?'

'Jordan, you really helped me with the ad. We are friendly, as far as I'm concerned,' I reply, my head spinning.

Why is he calling me?

'In any event, the TIARAs! Enjoy yourself tomorrow. Maybe, ah, don't do anything you might regret.' Jordan chuckles most congenially. 'Although, if you do go mad, let me know. We might get another campaign out of it.'

I giggle.

Then Jordan and I break into nervous, raucous laughter that says, more than words, that whatever our past history, in this moment, all is forgiven.

'You can come with me,' I say, without overthinking whether I should.

'What?'

'You can come with me, to the TIARAS. If you want to.'

'Are you serious?'

I'm serious, but I'm not about to beg.

'Jordan, as of about two minutes ago, I have a spare ticket. We're friendly, and I'd sooner the seat next to me not be empty. Would you like to come or not?'

I swear you could knock me down with a feather when Jordan answers without reservation, 'Yes.'

34

Poppy fastens the diamond necklace delicately around my neck. She's used rollers to set my hair in cascading waves of ebony silk. My eye make-up smoulders. The silver trouser suit fits me like a glove. My spotless Jimmy Choo crystal heels pair with it perfectly.

'Miss Gracie, you're beautiful.'

I check myself in the full-length mirror Faith has set up in her living room. I could cry with happiness. 'Poppy, thank you.'

Poppy is wearing a strapless white gown over a pink tulle petticoat. Her shoes are slipper style and, though made of plastic, look like glass. Her wispy blonde hair is pinned into a high bun on top of her head, adorned with sparkles and a large ruby crystal. Her make-up is, surprisingly, sparse. Shimmery creams on her eyelids. Sweetly rosy cheeks. Soft-pink lip stain.

'I look like a giant macaroon.' Poppy laughs. 'Cherry on top and all!'

With her delicate features, she's angelic.

Faith passes us each a flute of champagne.

She's ethereal in white silk, with whispers of purple through the fabric. Her dress skims the ground and twists, toga-like, across one shoulder. Her long, blonde hair is down and loosely tousled.

'To the TIARAs,' she toasts.

'To that dress,' I say.

'To those diamonds,' Poppy chimes in.

We sip stylishly, until we explode in delight.

'I can't believe we're going to the TIARAs!'

'I'm so excited!'

'I'm a little nervous,' I admit. 'This is something more than smiling for the paparazzi on a night out. Right, girls?'

'Where is Jordan meeting you?' Faith asks. We haven't properly discussed the topic of me inviting him. 'Inside?'

'Yes.'

'Let the mystery of Master J live on?' Faith laughs, but her expression says it all.

I take another small sip of champagne.

'We're trying to be friendly, but don't worry Joanna canned Carlos, and it's not like I have a plethora of men to step in. Jordan gets professional kudos at his office in attending. It's really just another friendly business arrangement, like the Pussy Paws shoot. That's all.'

'Well, I'm sure it will give Jordan pause to think about what he's lost regardless – look at you now, Gracie,' Faith says. 'Tonight, the world is your oyster.'

There was a time it wasn't. I'm grateful for the experiences that shaped me. They made me stronger. They made me love myself and my life so fiercely that now I know how to show others how to do it. It reset the bar – never again will I allow anyone, including myself, to treat me with less than I deserve. Love. Care. Acceptance. That's the bar.

'Look at me now,' I say, beyond joy.

Faith beams.

'Miss Gracie, what about poor Carlos? Was he very upset at getting dumped?'

'I wouldn't say he was dumped, Poppy. But when we spoke, Carlos seemed to understand the circumstance. He left me a garbled message sometime in the middle of last night and he sounded fine.' In his message, Carlos was still anxious about me arriving without his escort, and might have mentioned something about his new suit, but what with his indecipherable English and my non-existent Spanish, it's difficult to know. He certainly didn't sound cross. 'Poppy, let's not forget, he scored an expensive Tom Ford suit on me for his trouble.'

'It is a very nice suit,' Poppy agrees, letting me off the hook.

Faith strokes Benny at the windowsill. 'I'll walk the red carpet with you,' she says. 'I'll meet Toby inside.'

'Can we do it together?' Poppy asks. 'Lucy could go in with Toby, if that's all right with you, Faith?'

Unable to discriminate between her many friends, family members and buddies – and spurred on by a publicity-savvy Joanna – Poppy invited Lucy the lesbian as her date for the TIARAs.

'Of course,' Faith says. 'How can we not do this together?'

* * *

A white limousine arrives to convey us the short distance from Covent Garden to Mayfair. Various roads are blocked for the occasion and the streets are lined with onlookers. We pull up near Grosvenor House.

On what has turned into a cool and blowy spring afternoon, it's perfect weather for a trouser suit. Within minutes, we're making our way down the red carpet. With me in the middle, we glide along the corridor of cameras and microphones as though we're old hands at this celebrity business.

Flash, click. 'Yes, we are the best of friends,' I say, in answer into a reporter's microphone. We walk on.

Flash, click. Shoulders back, tummy in and smiiiiiile. 'Thank you. Yes, it was a brave move, wearing a suit. I'm delighted you love it.'

Flash, click. Flash, click. I thought I'd be so nervous. Together with Faith and Poppy, I'm having the time of my life.

Flash, click. Flash, click. Flash, click.

We reach the stage, ready to be called for our official photo. The cameras shutters and flashes go crazy. Then, we're ushered indoors.

Inside is decadent. Chandeliers, shot silk, bow ties and Bellinis at every angle. The crowd is a sea of familiar faces, everyone from soap stars, actors and actresses, comedians and the odd smattering of reality-show people. The who's who of British television entertainment are gathered in one place – and so are we.

'Come on,' Faith says, taking my hand. 'I've spotted the others.'

On our way to find the SC6 team, we pass Thandie Newton and Stephen Fry. Through the crowd, I see Hugh Laurie to my left and the pretty girl who starred on *Downton Abbey* to my right. Actors from *The Crown* are ubiquitous. Poppy offers an impromptu curtsey to Matt Smith. Enchanted, he bows back.

Toby stands out in what Faith mentioned is black-tie Armani. Faith rushes to his side. Joanna and Timothy are here together, petting publicly. Lucy is deep in conversation – flirting, I would say – with Sonya Sokolov, Russian bombshell presenter of our children's cartoons, who appears to be rather enthralled in return. Poppy giggles to me, 'Oh, Miss Gracie, what have I done?' Zelda is here in all her magnificence, cloaked in a deep-purple satin and a lace gown and dripping in jewellery.

I don't see Harry and whoever he's invited. Given his inquisitiveness about my date, I can't believe I didn't think to ask.

I also don't see Jordan.

When Poppy wanders off to mingle, Faith re-joins me.

'You okay?'

'I can't see Jordan. Do you think he's had trouble getting in?'

'Toby and Lucy got through just fine,' Faith says, scanning the room.

We keep looking. Jordan isn't in sight.

'Maybe it's a good thing?' Faith says.

I'm glancing around the room. Faith waits for my attention.

'Go on.'

'Gracie, I promise I won't go on. But I do want to say, you're so happy. You're glowing. I don't want Jordan slipping back in and ruining it. Giving you less than you deserve, and you deserve it all.'

I don't want Jordan – and I don't want less. Next time, when it comes to love, I want it all.

'I can't see myself in a relationship with Jordan again, under any circumstance, Faith.' The room is packed, but he isn't here. 'But you can stop worrying, I think he's a no-show.'

'Shall we take a scoot around to check?'

'Will you wait here for me? I'll go.'

'Darling, I won't move an inch.'

* * *

I'm weaving my way steadily through the crowd when Harry finds me.

'Gracie Porter.'

'Harrison Hipgrave.'

'You look... just... wow.' Harry checks me out, top to bottom. He's looking sharp himself in a trim black suit, no tie. 'Are you wearing purple contact lenses?' Harry is right up close to check.

'My irises are sometimes violet,' I reply, flattered. 'Have you truly never noticed?'

'Of course I've noticed,' Harry tells me.

Unusually, we don't embrace.

'Did you enjoy the stroll?'

'The red carpet? I did. And I believe we wowed them, windy weather and all.' I bat my (real) lashes dramatically.

'Come here, you,' Harry says, pulling me inside his arms.

My face presses softly into his neck. Harry nuzzles his chin to mine. I'm wearing my new favourite perfume, Philosykos by Diptyque. Lusty notes of fig and white cedar. I feel Harry breathe in my scent.

Slowly, he breaks away.

'You're on your own?' he says.

'Not at the moment.'

He grins at me lopsidedly. 'Where is your date? Where is

your, ahem –' Harry lowers his voice and clears his throat '– shag buddy, wasn't it?'

Unbelievably, he mustn't know that I cancelled with Carlos. Or that I'm supposed to be here with Jordan. For reasons I don't wish to dwell on, I'm reluctant to tell him.

'Are you on your own, Harry?'

'No, my dates are powdering their noses – and not like that.'

'Dates? Plural, darling? Charming.'

'The twins, as you might say. I'm here with Bip and Ban.'

I was being chummy. Forcibly – it's lovely, but it's always forcibly that I put the brakes on with Harry. But he is here with his sisters. Half-step-sisters. Not dates. Not even one.

'Oh.'

Inside my tummy, a knot tugs. Or maybe this trouser suit is too tight after the champagne.

'They're looking forward to seeing you. We must all catch up later. I haven't forgotten, I promised you the best after-parties.'

'That sounds smashing.'

Why am I speaking like a Peaky Blinder?

'So, the girls, ah, stepped in,' Harry carries on. He looks nervous.

'Right…'

'After you so brutishly declined my offers to accompany me this evening,' he finishes.

I check for signs of mischief. There's nothing in his eyes to suggest it. I wait for him to laugh. Harry does no such thing.

'You invited me as your date, Harry?'

'I certainly tried. Didn't I?'

'No, I…'

I avert my gaze. I cannot look into those gorgeous, dark eyes without wanting everything with this man. Thoughts are racing through my head. My heart is skipping beats.

For months, to survive my humiliation, with a mortal fear of being rejected, I've numbed my feelings. Afraid to fail, I refused to dream. Now, a flood of hope sweeps over me.

'Gracie, I—'

Without warning, Jordan arrives at my side. Interrupted, the moment between Harry and I evaporates. I watch the colour drain from his face.

'What a bloody nightmare.' Jordan runs his hand through his hair. He kisses my cheek. 'Bloody security wouldn't let me in. Wouldn't go and get you to sort it out. Absolute nightmare.'

'Jordan, I'm sorry.'

'Never mind, I'm here now. Grace, you look... lovely,' Jordan says, as if he's seeing me for the first time.

'Jordan, you remember Harry?'

'Of course, we met at the shoot. Harry, good to see you. Thank you, again, for working through the deal with Pussy Paws, the special rates. I know it got you lot out of a bother, but it also got me a promotion.' Jordan pumps Harry's hand vigorously. 'If you have any further opportunities like that, please do get in touch.'

Slipping back in to agent mode, Harry says, 'As Agent to the Stars, I'm at your service. Right, so, I was highly concerned that a woman who looks this beautiful has more than diamonds to worry about being taken.' Harry's eyes meet mine for a second and it lasts a lifetime. 'Now that Gracie is safely in your company, I must dash. People to see. An agent's work is never done at these things. I'll see you later.'

'Catch you later, Harry,' Jordan says.

I can't speak.

Harry is gone.

'You do look beautiful, Grace.'

'Thank you, Jordan.'

Moments ago, I'd been aflutter. Now, nothing.

Jordan scans the crowd over my shoulder. 'Is that your mother?'

Obviously not, though I turn my head to check, tempted to suggest Jordan might not recognise her if it is.

'Over there.' He points. 'In the blue dress, talking with the old Dr Who.'

I look and it is my mother, talking with none other than David Tennant.

I watch as she extracts from her new second-hand sapphire blue clutch purse what I know is an old cookery school photograph of me. In it, I'm seventeen years old, chubby-cheeked with poorly applied liquid eyeliner, wearing my first white chef's hat. David nods politely and looks earnestly around the room, presumably for me.

'Jordan, it is my mother.'

'I thought so.'

'Golly. I – I'll go and get her.'

'Shall I get us all drinks?'

'Thanks. I'll meet you back here.'

I dash across the foyer on legs of jelly in my crystal embellished high heels. It was fun playing grown-up television star on the red carpet with the girls. Now, I feel like a little minnow in a very big pond.

'Grace!' my mother calls as I draw closer. 'I was just asking this lovely gentleman if he knows you. David, this is my daughter, Grace,' she says. 'Isn't she lovely?'

Nodding, David says to me, 'Your mother has been an absolute delight.'

'Thank you.'

'Lovely to meet you both, have a wonderful evening.' He scuttles away.

'Mummy, what are you doing here?'

'Well, I didn't know where we were meeting, dear. You said inside, but it's so crowded. I'm sorry I'm so late. The car had all sorts of trouble getting me here. The roads were blocked, and I'd promised your father I wouldn't walk around town by myself. Anyway, I'm here now and that's all that matters.'

And then I realise. I screwed up the invitations. The rush for the train – I'd pulled the wrong envelope from my purse. I'd left my mother the invitation to the TIARAs instead of to the luncheon at Fortnum and Mason.

Seeing her here, I can't imagine her anywhere else.

My mother's dress is full-length navy satin with a neck-line plunging to her cleavage. Tall and willowy, as elegant as any woman in the room who's half her age, she's wearing it well. Her silvery-white hair is coiffed into a neat chignon. Ravishing burgundy on her lips.

'How do I look?' she says.

'Mummy, you look beautiful. Grace Kelly would be envious.'

'That's what your father said. Grace, I wouldn't have missed this for the world.'

'I'm glad you're here. I must warn you, there might be a small mix-up with the seating to resolve...'

This isn't the Baker & Staines Annual Advertising Awards evening I'm crashing. It's the TIARAs. I've no idea how I'll wangle an extra seat – I don't wish to be rude and dump a second person with no notice, but with circumstances again mitigating, if I have to, I'll ask Jordan to leave. There's no way I'm letting my mother down now.

'Of course, dear. Is that Judi Dench over there?'

'You know, I think it is. Come on, let's find Faith and Jordan and the others.'

'Are you here with Jordan, dear?'

'Oh, Mummy. I have so much to catch you up on. Let's get our seats sorted first.' I take her hand in mine. 'Follow me.'

We're crossing the floor together when a thundering crash stuns the room, a commotion at one of the fire exit doors.

Unfortunately for me, the commotion was caused when Carlos burst through the fire doors chased by a swarm of burly security men.

Carlos hollers a ludicrous mix of Spanish and broken English, peppered with the word Crazie.

Clearly, he did not understand my communications – nor I his. His suit is not the black Tom Ford tuxedo Poppy bought for him with my money. It's shiny silver, and far too tight around his crotch. He spots me standing here, shrinking.

'Ola, Crazie! Crazie!'

'Dear, is that a mad fan calling for you?' My mother grips my hand.

'He's not a fan, Mummy. He's... Carlos. Oh my gosh. Mummy, can you stay right here a moment? Jordan will be back with drinks any minute. Everything's fine. I have to sort this.'

Skirting the edge of the room, not daring to clock how many guests observe me moving towards the disturbance, I make my way to him as quickly as possible.

'Crazie.' Carlos waves his piece of paper, the photocopy of

the TIARA invitation I'd given him at the studio. 'He say no good. Es good, sí? Carlos with Crazie. Sí?'

'Lady, is he with you?' asks an angry security guard who, like Gordon, bears a remarkable resemblance to Duncan.

'Well, it's a funny thing, really,' I begin to explain.

'Crazie give to me, Carlos. I am Carlos,' Carlos continues to rant.

'Yes, he's with me. I'm sorry for the trouble. I, um, lost the original invitation. And... oh, thank you kindly,' I say, as security steps aside. 'Thank you so much.'

A vision in silver, Carlos bounds up and clasps me to him. Fumbling, he attaches a pink carnation to my lapel. It comes complete with a tiny fondant of fern and smells like it's been sprayed with toilet freshener.

'Es nice?' Carlos asks, stepping back admiringly.

I don't have the heart to disappoint him.

I look over to where my mother is waiting, staring at us with some alarm.

Jordan is approaching her.

As for my conversation with Harry... I want to circle back on that.

They're all here – Harry, Jordan, Carlos and my mother. By my own hand, it's one almighty Freudian slip.

Now, what do I do?

35

Amid hushed whispers, Harry appears at my side. As the room returns to its own business, he escorts Carlos over to Poppy and consigns him to her care. With a grin as wide as an ocean, he asks me what the devil I've been up to now.

It's my chance to explain that I invited Jordan here as a friend, and as a last resort, having tried to cancel Carlos – and the subsequent miscommunications with both him and my mother. Harry dissolves in hysterics. Then, as usual, he sorts out everything for me.

Sending Bip and Ban happily off with a wad of cash, he creates a space for my mother, and Carlos, to join him at the SC6 table. To avoid a further scene, he arranges alternate seating for Jordan and me away from them all.

It's not what I'd like to be happening – and I hope I make this clear.

Given the options, it beats spending the evening wedged between two exes, in front of my mother and him, cameras rolling.

For a while, Harry is busy dashing back and forth

between us. For all his chivalry, he doesn't revisit our earlier conversation. By the time everyone is ushered inside to be seated for the awards, I haven't had the chance to raise it with him.

Jordan and I make our way to a table four back from the others, where none of the guests we're seated with are recognisable.

'Who have you managed to upset?' Jordan whispers to me, not as quietly as he should have.

'Jordan, shhh,' I say, smiling at our new companions. The fat lady beside me and the balding man beside her overhear. They scowl furiously at the pair of us. 'Jordan, there was a mix-up with some extra guests, as you probably saw. It isn't a problem.'

It hasn't gone unnoticed by me that where Jordan was all kisses and compliments earlier in the foyer among the who's who of showbiz, he's grown surly.

The lighting dims. An orchestra begins to play. To see proceedings at the front, Jordan turns his back to me. Mel and Sue appear on stage to a round of applause. For a good ten minutes, the room is entertained with excerpts of comedic television moments and banter that, to my absolute delight, centres around cooking.

Laughing heartily, Jordan turns briefly to me to say, 'They're really very good. They'd be perfect for a new canned fruit campaign I have in mind. Can you introduce us later?'

I tell Jordan I don't know them personally, so this might prove challenging. I see the fat lady and her bald companion exchange swift glances.

'Harry seems well connected,' he continues, unabashed. 'I wonder if he could help?'

I nod and sip my water. I miss my friends.

Jordan downs his champagne and waves a waiter to top him up. He's been knocking them back since he arrived.

Four tables away, my mother is chuckling intimately with Harry. Both Lucy and Carlos appear to be flirting with Sonya Sokolov. Poppy seems suitably amused. Faith is looking adoringly at Toby and Joanna is whispering in Timothy's ear. Zelda has her eyes closed and could even be chanting. On stage, the presentations commence.

We are several award categories in when Sonya is called up on stage. I'm clapping when Jordan turns to me. 'Is she the girl from the cartoons?'

'Yes. But this award is for a dramatic role she took on last summer.'

Jordan nods, deep in thought. 'We've been pitching to Mattel. She'd seal the deal.'

I suggest I can introduce them later.

His smile is electric.

I watch the entire SC6 table rise from their seats in applause at Sonya's speech. Too shy to stand on my own, I stay seated.

'Thank you for inviting me,' Jordan says.

'You're welcome.'

'You do look incredible.'

'Thank you.'

Then, out of the blue, because I'm not thinking about him or us or that skinny cow from his office Rhiannon, Jordan says, 'I miss you, Grace. I'm sleeping on a futon in Robert's studio. I'm barely eating. I'm not sleeping.' Jordan rambles on nervously. Quietly, because we're not supposed to be talking, although the whole room seems to be as people strut on and off the stage in between laughter and applause. 'Not that Robert is home much. I've practically got his place to myself.

He's been putting himself about left, right and centre, as only Robert can. I have a few tales to share...'

He laughs lightly. Instinctively, I do too. Robert's romantic misadventures.

Only, this isn't jovial. Jordan also had his own shot at putting himself about, how quickly he took up with Rhiannon. And why is he telling me this now if he's still with her?

'Jordan, missing me looking after you isn't the same as missing me. Why don't you move in with your new girlfriend?' I don't bother to hide my bitterness, because while my words may be scathing, my heart isn't holding a grudge for what Jordan put me through. My heart is free. And if I can find the courage to chase it down properly, ready to love again.

'She lives with her parents.' Of course she does. 'Also, we broke up. Rhiannon left Baker & Staines. I had to change my number. She wouldn't leave me alone.'

'That's what you get for dating a twenty-one-year-old,' I say.

Without warning, Jordan turns in his seat to face me. Dramatically putting down his glass on to the table first, he kisses me – I expected a rebuke for my sharp comment. Instead, right here at the table at the TIARAs, Jordan leans his face right up close to mine, parts my closed lips with his tongue, and kisses me.

Compared to the way Carlos seduced me, every time, it's devoid of passion.

Compared to the way Harry looks at me, always, it's without feeling.

I put my hand to Jordan's chest and push him off me.

Jordan studies me warily, the way he always has done.

'I don't want Rhiannon,' he says. 'She was a mistake.

Robert tried to warn me. Grace, I want you. I should have always only wanted you.'

I glance at the SC6 table and Harry is staring at us.

My world shrinks. Sounds muffle. My breath catches. Pennies fall.

I remember the late nights Jordan worked. The shirty phone calls when I rang his office. The wine glasses in my kitchen. The tangled bedsheets on our bed. Oh God, was he even with her at Christmas?

'Jordan, how long were you seeing her? Was she in our home? Did you sleep with her in our bed?'

The audience claps wildly after another announcement.

Jordan sends furtive glances around our table as though he does care what the nobodies here at the back might make of him after all.

'Jesus, Grace.'

Of course, Jordan turns this around on me. But the answer is in his face.

'Jordan, you need to leave now and I won't see you again. I haven't missed you.'

'Then why ask me to come to this?'

'Joanna forced it on me.'

'I've had enough of this.'

'Good. Me too. So go.'

Scowling furiously, and not at all sexily, Jordan gets up from his seat and storms off.

Two seats away, the kind bald man shoots him a parting death stare. The lady beside me passes me a napkin. I didn't realise I was teary. Smiling gratefully, I dab my wet eyes. I'm not crying for me. I've grown so strong. These tears are for the old me, who lay in bed, alone, countless nights, sobbing herself to sleep, unloved and undesired. I wasn't needy, but I needed someone. It was supposed to be Jordan, and I know now that it wasn't my fault he couldn't show up for me. The prick just doesn't have it in him.

Thank heavens for waterproof mascara, and that I'm at the back of the room out of sight of the cameras.

I check on Harry, but his head is down, and he doesn't look over at me again. Faith whispers in Toby's ear and gets up out of her seat.

'Oh pet,' says the lady who has the warmest smile I've seen. Irish. A lovely warm Irish smile. 'Don't mind that one. He's best off long gone. What's meant for you, won't pass you by.'

'Thank you,' I say, drying my cheeks. 'I'm sorry for the fuss. I'll leave you all in peace now. Please, enjoy your evening.'

I slip out discreetly and Faith joins me in the lobby.

'I saw Jordan leave,' she says, hugging me at once. 'Darling, are you okay?'

'I believe I'm in love with Harry.'

'Um, okay. Is that why Jordan left?'

'No. Jordan cheated on me.'

'Oh, my darling.'

'Faith, what should I do?'

'About Jordan? I know what I'd like to do to him...'

'About Harry. He told me earlier he'd invited me here as his date. And I'm not sure exactly what that means, because we were interrupted by Jordan, and then my mother, and the commotion with Carlos...'

Faith checks me over and decides I'm not devastated by the news my ex-boyfriend cheated on me.

I shrug, and half smile at her.

'Well, no one does drama quite like you, Gracie Louise

Porter.' Faith laughs. She looks at me lovingly and takes my hands in hers.

I laugh, too.

Faith squeezes my hands. 'Darling, Harry has left. He said the girls had texted to say they'd broken their key in his front door and he had to go.' Faith swallows hard. 'He didn't say he was coming back.'

'Do you think he saw Jordan kiss me?'

'Oh my gosh, I don't know – I didn't see that.'

'It wasn't anything to see, believe me,' I say.

'I have no clue what's going on with any of you any more.' Faith shakes her head. 'Lucy's been snogging Sonya. Carlos is telling Poppy you told him to ditch the Tom Ford suit for that ghastly silver pimp number.'

'Faith, I think I might have.'

Faith jolts a little and then carries on. 'Your mother and Joanna can't stop nattering. Timothy is thoroughly charming them both and Zelda is quite pickled and reading the waiter's palms.'

'It all sounds very entertaining,' I say.

'I'm pleased Toby is here. Gracie, I think I'm falling in love, too. Can you believe it?' Faith is radiant.

'Yes, darling, I believe it.'

'Why don't you join us? You can take Harry's seat.'

On reminder of Harry's departure, I squeeze my eyes closed.

When I open them, Faith is looking at me with her lips pursed.

'Of course, there is another option,' she says.

'Go and find Harry?'

'And tell him how you feel. Properly, this time. For real.'

'What about him being our agent?'

'I was wrong about that. Plenty of people meet through work. Look at me. Gracie, you should go for it.'

'Shall I go to his flat now?'

'You'll only be a pest if you stay here...'

I hesitate.

Faith smiles. 'I'll take care of your mum. You know what she'd tell you to do.' She plucks the pink carnation from my lapel.

'I'm not sure I'm brave enough to chase him, Faith. What if this is another wrong turn?'

'What if it isn't?'

I look down at my hands. They're shaking.

'Zelda asked me to pass on a message.' Faith bundles me off towards the exit.

'What's that?'

'No rain, no rainbow.'

36

I arrive at Harry's apartment giddy with nerves, to find a broken key jammed in his front door. I knock quietly. Nobody answers. When I knock again, the door swings open.

'Hello,' I call out. 'Anybody home?'

I enter the flat, pulling the door mostly closed behind me.

I walk around inside. The girls aren't here. Harry is outside on the balcony, looking out over the Thames river. The pretty blue and white lights over Tower Bridge are sparkling. The air is warm, a gentle breeze. I sidle to the railing beside him.

'Hi.'

'Hi.' Harry must be surprised to see me, but he smiles.

'You left me?'

'No, the girls...' He trails off. 'Gracie,' he says, gazing into my blue eyes with his pools of dark chocolate. 'Gracie,' he repeats, staring right into me.

'Dance with me, Harry.'

There's no music. Just the faint sounds of the traffic

below, and my heart, pounding in my chest. Dance with me, Harry, I pray to the universe.

Harry steps closer. Wrapping his arms around me, his hands on my waist, I slip mine around his neck. My fingers curl into his thick, blonde hair. We start to sway.

Zelda had warned me of the storm, of the rain I'd have to endure. And now, here I am, in the arms of the man of my dreams.

'I know it's been a bumpy road,' I whisper into his ear. 'I know you're my agent, and things can get complicated.' I pull away to look Harry in the eyes as I finish. 'I also know I've never wanted to be with anyone more in my life. Harry, you're all the good that came out of all the bad, and because of that, I trust you. I trust you to be there for me. To make me laugh and to have fun with, and to take care of me. To see the best in me, when I've forgotten how to do it for myself. You're my rainbow, Harry. You are.'

Whatever comes of it from here, I'm proud of myself for finding the courage to say this.

'A rainbow, hey?' Harry says. He nuzzles my neck with his short stubble and kisses my skin and my body and soul heave with relief. He wants me, too. He does. 'I've been called worse. And I suppose you're my Crazie?' he laughs.

'I suppose. Though it isn't very romantic.'

But I don't want hearts and flowers – well, maybe flowers. I want love. Real love.

Harry pulls me to him fiercely.

'Kitten,' he breathes into my ear. 'Do you like that better?'

'Mmm. Much better.'

My hand slides inside his shirt, against his warm, bare chest. Everything fits between us. Everything feels right. My body tingles, but sex won't be the glue that binds us. It will accent everything else we have. For all my mishaps and missteps at parties and in cubicles, I'm a girl who likes cooking and pottering in the garden and snuggling. For all his cheesy wall of fame and witty asides, Harry is a guy who likes to work hard, take care of others and do the right thing. Being here with him is everything I dared to dream, and all of this is real.

The constant worry I had the entire time I was with Jordan is gone.

Love. You know it when you feel it. To love, and to be loved in return.

I breathe Harry into me. His intoxicating scent. His comfort and charm. And from the way he's kissing me now, he's mine, and I don't ever want him to stop. This man, who stuck by me through thick and thin – he's really mine.

ACKNOWLEDGMENTS

To my agent, David Riley, for his dedication and belief in me and in this book. You made my dream come true. Thank you. (And to your wife.) More fun to come.

To the entire team at Boldwood. I'm beyond excited to debut in your first stable of authors. Thank you for taking the chance on me. Special thanks to my editors. Jade Craddock for the copy edit and extra dollops of humour. Susan Lamprell for the final polish and line edits, ensuring the book is as smooth as it needs to be (and for your kindness in helping me to let this go). To my publisher, Caroline Ridding – how to thank you? Your guidance on the structural edits completely transformed this book. You gave me the insights to give Gracie her rightful journey and happy ending. Life isn't a consolation prize – it should be magical. I hope I have done you proud.

To Dea Parkin, Nick May, Brian Cook and Louise Wareham Leonard for early guidance. So much putting this down and picking it up again, but I got there.

To all of my family and friends for your love and encouragement over many years. Writing is a hard graft and a confidence trick. Not one of you ever told me to stop. For this, and so much more, I thank you all.

Special thanks. For reading early bits and pieces: Alicia, Amber, Angela, Anthea, Elise and Shanny. To my mother, Sue, for reading everything since I was a child, and who writes so beautifully. To Lindsay for help with television stuff and to Asia for intro to David. To Alicia and Phil for photos, the lovely team at Peakon for letting me disappear on edits and to Phil and Adam for the non de plume I didn't go with. RIP Phoebe Reeves. Neil: white shirt uniform is for you.

To my Dad and Annie and Sak and Elise for being there during a very dark time. Never mind the book, your love and your showing up kept me going.

To Emma who read multiple early drafts, squeezing edits and advice into her busy schedule as a writer and another single mother. You're an incredible woman. Every wispy dress and cherry-red lip stain description is in your honour.

To Kirsten, for too many things to mention. Your encouragement, your little notes, your ruthless editing, your cracking wit and for drinking wine with me. From the very first draft to the final copy, you were invested in this story and never once waivered. You're next, darling. You got this!

Last, but not least, to Julie for suggesting, all those years ago, that I write a novel about a chef that gets all spicy over meatballs. Here you go, Bushy Boo. And to my sister Tammy and my daughter Alice, who are least likely to ever read this (or any book) but who will never forgive me if they aren't mentioned. I love you both.

MORE FROM SIMONE GOODMAN

We hope you enjoyed reading *Look At Me Now*. If you did, please leave a review.

If you'd like to gift a copy, this book is also available as a ebook, digital audio download and audiobook CD.

Sign up to Simone Goodman's mailing list for news, competitions and updates on future books:

http://bit.ly/SimoneGoodmanNewsletter

ABOUT THE AUTHOR

Simone Goodman is CFO at one of the fastest growing tech companies in Europe. She is Australian and lives in London with her daughter and her two cats.

facebook.com/simone.goodman.735

twitter.com/simonegoodmanauthor

instagram.com/simonegoodmanauthor

ABOUT BOLDWOOD BOOKS

Boldwood Books is a fiction publishing company seeking out the best stories from around the world.

Find out more at www.boldwoodbooks.com

Sign up to the Book and Tonic newsletter for news, offers and competitions from Boldwood Books!

http://www.bit.ly/bookandtonic

We'd love to hear from you, follow us on social media:

 facebook.com/BookandTonic

 twitter.com/BoldwoodBooks

 instagram.com/BookandTonic

Printed in Great Britain
by Amazon

32990339R00197